NELSON NYE
TREASURE TRAIL
FROM TUCSON/THE FEUD
AT SLEEPY CAT

LEISURE BOOKS  **NEW YORK CITY**

A LEISURE BOOK®

December 1993

Published by

Dorchester Publishing Co., Inc.
276 Fifth Avenue
New York, NY 10001

TREASURE TRAIL FROM TUCSON Copyright © MCMLXIV by Nelson Nye
THE FEUD AT SLEEPY CAT Copyright © MCMLXVII by Nelson Nye

Printed in the United States of America.

TWO ACTION-PACKED NOVELS BY THE OLD WEST'S MOST POPULAR STORYTELLER NELSON NYE

TREASURE TRAIL FROM TUCSON

Walker, waving his arms, cried excitedly, "Bad place! Heap bad!" And the rest of the Papagos, long faced and edgy, looked about ready to dig for the tules.

Meeders said, scowling, "What the hell have I got here, a bunch of damn squaws?"

Walker's look turned darker. His stringy arms were folded across his greasy white man's vest. "Injun go home. Pay now."

Charlie didn't know what had got into their craws but he had put too much sweat and worry into this to sit calmly. Lifting the Sharps off his lap he said with its bore fixed on Walker's chest, "You hired out t' do a piece of work. Now git up an' do it."

THE FEUD AT SLEEPY CAT

Some time today, a group of dark-clad horsemen had come charging from the hilltops and dashed spurring among the buildings. They must have packed baled straw or oil-soaked rags—nothing else could have caused such a conflagration. And when Harp's crew had come staggering from the burning buildings, the raiders had shot them down.

This was Cross-Draw's conclusion. It was drawn from such incontestable facts as tracks, three dead broncs with the brands gouged from their hides, the dead bodies of four Harp riders, and the mangled remains of Shamus O'Reilly himself.

Nauseated, yet with a terrible rage redly gnawing at his shock-dulled consciousness, Cross-Draw commenced probing the smouldering debris for other bodies. He was searching still when the snarl and curse of panting voices wheeled him around to face the curdled shadows of the chaparral.

TREASURE TRAIL
FROM TUCSON

I

SHE WAS a sorry looking sight, no two ways about it.

Teetered back in his swivel Sheriff Andy McFarron continued with increasing irritation to stare. The yarn she'd come up with seemed about as unlikely as playing a harp with a hammer and, while he did not personally care for any part of it, certain aspects of it were going to have to be looked into. Banker Jones, anyway, could be relied on to think so.

Irascibly the sheriff blew the drip off his nose.

The dingy room was thick with trapped heat. This was Tucson in the belly of July and the range lay parched as buzzard picked bones. Hell was the only hotter place a man could picture. The forlorn bawling of gaunted cattle filled the midmorning quiet, monotonous and oppressive as the notions clambering through McFarron's head. "How long you been out there?"

The girl licked at cracked lips. "It was always night," she said, belligerent. She couldn't have looked much worse if she'd been hauled through a knot hole. Yet back of her bangles, the torn, stained tawdry rags of an itinerant gypsy, she was shapely, emotional, cramjammed with passion. But her eyes were too watchful.

There had to be more to this deal than she'd told. The seething resentment boiling out of each gesture had to have more basis than was so far apparent. Not that her yarn wasn't loco enough! Cougar wild it was—you might's well say downright preposterous, and yet. . . .

McFarron, grimacing, pushed a hand through damp hair.

This wasn't like Charlie; but deep inside he could see the fool doing it. They had known each other clean back to the days they had both punched cows for John Slaughter. Even then Charlie Medders had been a "character". Nothing had been too reckless for him, and nothing McFarron had heard about him since held out any hope his temper had changed much.

Man ought to stretch a few points for old times' sake and, had it been anyone else, McFarron probably would have but—politics being what they were around here—he was caught in a bind. Tiberius K. Jones, local arbiter of destiny, was after Medders' scalp and the sheriff, with elections coming on, had to keep his fences up.

He considered the girl again, trying to make her claims fit the man she was accusing, and growled under his breath. All his life Charlie'd shied away from women, and this was the bone McFarron couldn't shake. He said, leaning forward: "You sure it was Medders?"

You could see it put her hackles up.

McFarron saw, but went on to speak anyway. "Mebbe you better describe him," he said but, time she got done, there was' no possibility of it being someone else. She had old Charlie right under the nether millstone.

Though he'd taken her over the story three times McFarron couldn't faze her, couldn't even begin to. She had it down letter perfect, and if she ever got into a court with this yarn cold winters wasn't going to bother Charlie any more.

Beneath those brush clawed tatters she was hard as nails. An alley cat, plainly—a thieving gitana, he thought, sweatily writhing. Some of the language she'd used when she'd come dragging it in here would have taken the bark off a white oak post. But that wouldn't help. There wasn't nothing going to help if she was bent on putting the dang fool away. No jury this side of the pearly gates was going to run counter to her wants in this matter.

If she just hadn't been so God-awful young!

That, and him keeping her there, could weigh powerful bad in a country that venerated unsullied womanhood.

As she watched his face her lips twisted into a gamin grin. She didn't care what he thought; she could always go higher if he wouldn't cooperate. Lie, bite and gouge—she'd do whatever she had to. It was plain in her eyes, so brazenly scornful. Why did men have to be such damn fools? He grumbled, getting up. "Let's take a look at that critter." She followed him out, complacent as a kitten with a mouthful of feathers.

The "critter" referred to was, according to her story, the means by which she had cut loose of Charlie. A flop-eared dun colored mule with black points—brazen as she was, standing there masticating a jawful of wood pulp cribbed from the tie rail. The sheriff, exasperated, threw out a fist but the spavined monster never backed off a step. He didn't even blink.

Only difference between him and something found at a taxidermist's was the phlegmatic motion of those mangy jaws. The stilt-like locust was so dadburned thin you had to look twice to make sure he was standing there; and McFarron had never set eyes on him before. Not that it mattered. He could still be Charlie's property, tying Medders to this girl tight as matted tail hair.

But of course if no one recognized. . . .

It was the only vestige of hope in sight and the sheriff, reluctantly aware he could procrastinate no longer, untied the critter and with a hard, shuddery breath struck off across the street.

When he hit the end of the lead shank he stopped as though he'd come against a stone wall. The mule, stubbornly set in its tracks, wouldn't budge. Nothing the sheriff tried would move him.

The girl said thoughtfully, "He's probably tired," and McFarron glared, fuming.

"You want somethin' done about this business, or don't you?" he said.

She considered him darkly. "I want Medders brought in. I've got some rights," she said grimly.

The sheriff let go of the rope. "So has Medders.

Story like that, it's got to be checked. Only concrete fact in sight is this mule. *You* claim it's Charlie's."

"I see. Yes, of course." If that bothered her any it was not apparent. You want—"

"I want him over to Fritchet's livery. If he belongs to Medders somebody will know about it."

She didn't point out all the holes in that notion, just scooped up the rope with a slanchways look, said, "Come, Eduardo," and stepped into the sunscorched dust of the street, the mule lumbering along like a dog at her heels. McFarron, plodding after them, mouthed a bitter curse.

But, breasting the bank, he pulled the chin off his chest. He had his own career to consider and Jones, if there was anything to this yarn, might decide to postpone Charlie's trip to the pen. The sheriff cleared his throat. "We'll step in here."

The girl looked around, eyed the bank and shrugged. She handed Eduardo over to the curb, dropped his rope across the rail and stood coolly waiting on McFarron's pleasure.

He jerked his chin at the doors. "Straight ahead," he grunted, and closed in behind.

A hard faced man in blue serge and brass buttons after scraping them with a raspy glance passed them on into a lobby designed expressly to impress the unwashed hordes that placed their trust in Tiberius Jones.

The girl took in the floor's deep pile, expensive hangings and wrought iron fixtures. If she was cut down to size she kept it hidden, stood disdainfully waiting for McFarron to make his play.

Beyond the cages and directly in front of the gate

to the inner sanctum a blonde sat behind a desk drawn up by the rail. "Good morning, Sheriff," she exclaimed with a smile. "And what can we do for you?"

Imogene Winters, McFarron thought sourly, was as much a part of the bank's facade as the overwhelming rest of the fixtures and furnishings so painstakingly selected to put all comers in a proper frame of mind. She had the charm of Lillian Russell, the face of a Gibson girl and a figure that would turn a man's tongue dry as chalk. She was as efficient as she was breathtaking, and her job was to smile and refuse.

McFarron had been over the route before. "Is the Commissioner in?"

She continued to smile while her gentian eyes, grown increasingly doubtful, assessed the girl with a bright distrust. "He's terribly busy. I'm afraid—"

"You tell him it's about Charlie Medders," the sheriff said, and it was like he'd rubbed Aladdin's lamp. Taking up her pencil the magnificent creature hastily scribbled several words, tore the slip from her pad and passed it to a boy who took it through the rail. In twenty seconds, head bobbing, he was back, and Miss Winters graciously waved them toward the magic portal.

The great man was alone behind an imposing desk whose polished surface was unblemished by even so little as a solitary paper. He did not rise or waste any time on unprofitable amenities. "What about Medders?"

"Might be we've got just about what you want," McFarron announced, indicating the girl. "Belita

Storn. Figured you'd want to be the first to hear her story—"

"I've no time for stories."

"That's plain enough." McFarron turned on his heel. "Let's go," he growled, shooing the girl ahead of him.

"Now just a dang minute!" the banker expostulated. "What's a fool girl got to do with that robber?"

"Sometime, mebbe, when you're not so busy—"

"You come back here!" the great man barked, turning purple. "That's an order, Sheriff!"

McFarron, shrugging, reluctantly faced around. Sometimes Jones was powerful hard to take.

"Well. . .?" the banker rasped impatiently. "What's this gypsy got to do with Charlie Medders?"

McFarron rubbed the end of his nose. "Claims she just got away from him. Claims he's been holdin' her incommunicado out to his mine."

"Mine!" Jones cried, like the word made him sick. Looking half strangled he surged from his chair. He was shaking all over. "That salted hole in the ground. . . ." Words seemed to fail him, and the sheriff's sour grin didn't help matters any.

It was the bane of Jones' life that some fairly rich ore Charlie'd passed around last winter had led the great man to make a horrible misjudgment. He had got an assayer's report on the stuff, made sure the claim had been filed and, on the strength of these findings, allowed Medders to borrow fifteen thousand at usurious rates to develop what had shown every evidence of becoming an extremely valuable property.

He had, of course, taken the precaution of drawing up papers for the protection of this loan. But when Medders failed to meet these payments he'd gone out with McFarron to take possession of this gilt-edged collateral. All that could be found was a worked-over dump and an empty hole. Medders had plainly picked up and gone and without leaving even the solace of a forwarding address.

Jones refused to believe it, had been desperately determined they had come to the wrong place. He'd sent out a survey gang under Dry Camp Burks, the bank's trouble shooter, but every figure tallied. It was the place, all right. And of course the word got around.

That the wound had not healed was disturbingly evident. "At least," the sheriff said, "he's back in business if you can believe what she says." McFarron tipped a nod at the girl. "Tell him."

She went over it again. She'd set out for Ehrenberg, doing most of her traveling after dark to avoid the heat. The fourth night out they'd been caught up in a sandstorm. They'd been driven off the trail or in any event lost it and that—for this part—was all she could swear to. Medders, and here she was admittedly dependent on the man's version of it, had someway found, rescued, and nursed her back to health.

"How do you know he was Medders?" Jones snapped.

"He told me his name. He'd found me wandering about in the desert, half dead from exposure and thirst. I'd been going around in circles, he said, and the buzzards had led him to me. And barely in time, by his tell of it. All I know is I woke up in this cave, so weak and dizzy I couldn't lift a finger."

She seemed to dig back through a huddle of memories. "Inside it was more like a series of caverns, one leading into another—sometimes two. In the largest of these—it had a queer sort of cabin built into one wall that he always kept padlocked, there was a windlass and some rickety, half rotten ladders that went down into the mine—"

Jones, snorting like a porpoise, waved the rest of it away. That word really irritated him. "You can save your breath," he declared, looking scornful, and reached for his chair as though the interview were over. "I've better things to do than...." Flushing angrily, he snarled: "If that dastard ever dares show his face—"

"If you'd let her tell her story," McFarron said, "it's possible you might find a way to get at him."

The banker stared, testily threw up his hands. "Well ... all right, but make it short." He looked at his watch. "I'm due at a meeting in about five minutes."

Medders, by her tell, had offered her half the rock they got out in exchange for helping him work it. He would not let her down in the stopes; her job was to bring the ore up with the windlass and pack it in sacks while he was loading again.

Jones said disparagingly: "So, actually, you never *saw* any mine!"

"I saw the ore he sent up." She poked around in her bodice and tossed him a sample.

The banker, catching it, stepped over to the window. McFarron saw his jaw drop, watched the banker get out a penknife and scratch at it and presently thoughtfully stow it in his pocket. Com-

ing back the great man said to Belita, "I presume
you know what sort of ore this is?"

She gave him a hard grin. "It's a kind 'of a
keepsake," and put out her hand.

After he'd reluctantly returned the specimen
Tiberius Jones very casually suggested it was likely
the prettiest piece of the lot.

The girl shook her head. "One of the poorest,
really. I swiped this piece because I didn't think
he'd miss it or discover I had it on me. Some of
those chunks must have been pure silver." She
smiled at the greed peering out of Jones' stare.
"That vein, in some places, should be a solid foot
through and at least a yard wide. It would have to
be, judging by what he sent up."

"The point," McFarron said, "is what do we do
about it?"

II

IT WAS EASY to see that Tiberius Jones had clean forgot all about the meeting he had been so anxious to get to. Nor was it hard to imagine the drift of thoughts stimulated by the pictures this girl had set up. But once stung, twice shy, as the old saying went, and cagey suspicions were beginning already to fray the fine edges of the triumph he'd glimpsed. It was just too pat, too good to be true.

The sheriff frowned at him, sighing. "Now what's the matter?"

"Too much hook sticking out of that yarn."

"Hook?" McFarron said, peering around.

"You think it makes sense a hardshell like Medders would let this fluff get out of his sight with a story like that? Smells like sweetening mixed to smear on a trap!" Jones, regarding Belita, snorted. "Five dollars says she's never seen Charlie Medders!"

The girl stiffened. Her chin shot out. Her eyes began to snap. Starting toward him she cried,

"Whose mule do you reckon is chewing up your hitch rail?"

"Mule? Rail?"

"She claims," the sheriff interpreted, "to have got away from Medders on one of his mules. The monstrosity is tied—"

"Recognize it, do you?"

McFarron grimaced, shaking his head. "But if it does belong to Charlie somebody over at Fritchet's oughta—"

"You don't need to go to all that bother," Belita Storn exclaimed. Eyeing them scornfully, she fished again inside the front of her dress and dug out a paper which she contemptuously tossed on that fine polished desk. Jones stared at the grimy folds as though he looked for a snake to come slithering out. McFarron caught it up. "What's this?" he said, bending to smooth the creases.

"It's the partnership agreement I told you about."

The banker stepped closer, peering over the sheriff's shoulder. In the anxious quiet his sudden intake of breath was disagreeable as a curse. McFarron twisted a look at him. "That Charlie's hand?"

Strangely pale the banker yanked at the bell pull. When the boy put his head in the door Jones growled, "Tell Mr. Turpen I want that Medders folder out of the vault."

As the boy departed the girl sent McFarron a twisted grin and put one hip against an edge of the desk, ignoring the affronted look Jones flung her. She was a cool one all right. The nerve of her won McFarron's grudging respect. She was not one of those he would have cared to play poker with.

Someone knocked at the door; they watched it open. A tall weedy type in black sleeve guards and visor stepped tentatively in with a bulge of folded cardboard. "The Medders account, sir," he said, reaching it out.

Opening it on his desk as far from the girl as the wood allowed, the banker commenced scowlingly to thumb through a sheaf of clipped papers. Picking out a couple he set them down alongside the cause of all this commotion. Covering all but the signature on Belita's paper he signed to his clerk to come take a look. The man bent over, engrossed, at last straightening. "Same hand, I'd say."

Jones beckoned McFarron.

The clerk stepped back. The sheriff, squinting, nodded emphatically. "Looks like you got what you asked for. If Charlie signed those, he signed this one, too. Expect we'll have to accept—"

"I," Jones said, "accept nothing till it's proved."

The sheriff shrugged, not fooled in the least. Anyone could see the banker was hooked. A child could sense the greed working in him.

McFarron picked up his hat. Belita Storn, reaching over, snatched up her agreement. "Here—not so fast," Jones growled, looking testy.

Ignoring him, the girl crammed it into her bodice, the look of her eyes pinning McFarron in his tracks. "Where do you think you're off to now?"

"Might's well get an identification on that mule—"

"What good's that? You already know from his signed agreement—"

"Words," McFarron said, directing a sour smile

at Jones. "Marks on a paper don't signify a mine—ain't that so, T.K.?"

The banker, flushing, clenched white fists, looking more than half ready to go up in smoke.

"But he *has!*" the girl cried. "I tell you I *saw* it!"

The sheriff shook his head. "All you saw was the hand picked stuff he sent up for you to look at. How much ore did you see in place? By your own tell, ma'am, you didn't get below that windlass. For all you know that stuff could've been packed in from Tombstone, Tonopah or Ticonderoga."

"It came out of that mine," Belita Storn said doggedly. She whipped the hair back out of her eyes. "Do you think I'm a fool! There was muck on those chunks—the same kind of muck he had on his boots every time he came up!"

McFarron smiled tolerantly. "Have it your way. But if it's that good a deal what'd you want to light out for? You had half comin' just for helpin' him work it. You so wallerin' in wealth you could—"

"I never agreed to be no damn peon!" she yelled, her eyes wild as lightning. "You think I'd stay shut up in that hold with a nut like him? Chained every night like a dog on a wire!" She glared at him, furious. "Lookit my ankles!"

Since she wore no stockings the calloused evidence of shackled was hardly to be denied. The sheriff winced as he looked at the leg she stuck out. It would go hard with Charlie if a jury saw that. Jones, he observed, was trying hard to look shocked, but you could tell by his eyes the kind of thoughts he was hugging.

McFarron asked finally, "Could you dig out the sort of ore she's described fast as ever she could stuff it into sacks? Be reasonable," he grumbled, peering disgustedly at the banker.

But Jones said stubbornly: "You can't talk away those ridges on her legs." Satisfaction glimmered from every cranny of his overfed face. "Just what you'd expect of a scoundrel like Medders—keeping a poor innocent girl penned out there against her will." His jowls shook and joggled like a turkey gobbler's wattles. "Feller ought to be tarred and feathered, by godfreys!"

"Oh, fer cripes sake," McFarron growled, clapping on his hat.

The banker was not distracted. Fatly beaming at the girl he pushed out the overstuffed chair beside his desk, not the visitor's straightback but the one he kept for show. "Miss Storn, you sit right down and be comfortable. You have certainly been through a terrible experience, but now all that's behind—you're not to worry about a thing. We're going to see you get all that's coming to you, believe me. Now . . . where'd you say this place is at?"

She'd allowed herself to be ensconced in the overstuffed, spread the tatters of her skirt about those bare and sunbrowned legs. "Why," she said, smiling back at him, "it's out in the desert."

Jones chewed his lip, grinding down on his impatience. "That desert takes in considerable ground."

Belita Storn inclined her head.

He considered her a moment. "I am going to be blunt. Exactly what are you after?"

She didn't boggle over that. "I want him brought in."

"Ah!" Jones nodded with a crafty smile. "You

wish your grievances redressed by the court." He looked pleased as Punch. "You want an example made of this feller."

The girl's amber eyes surveyed him. "Not really. I would not care to seem . . . vindictive, but. . . ."

"I see," the banker said, rubbing one chubby hand with the palm of the other. "In view of the extreme mental anguish, the confinement and hardships—"

"I'd want only what the court feels is right, Mr. Jones."

The conniving hussy! Butter, McFarron thought, wouldn't have melted in her mouth. Poor Charlie! He felt like shaking her goddam teeth out.

"They're pretty certain to award you damages," Jones said, and stood a moment, thoughtful. "Only trouble is, with this kind of case there'd have to be a jury, and with juries," he sighed, shaking his head, "you never know. If they're all men, you're in, but it could drag on for months with postponements and adjournments—"

He banged one hand sharply into the other. "You don't have to get tied up in this fashion . . . there's another, quicker way!"

"There is?" Belita said, eyes opening wide.

The banker nodded. "You could have the money in your hands inside an hour."

"However in the world—"

"Miss Storn," Jones said, "how much is that piece of paper worth to you?"

"My part interest?"

"Up to now," Jones said with a curl of the lip, "all you've got is a scrap of paper. I don't even know that it's binding."

"But you are offering to purchase whatever part in it I've got?"

"My dear young lady. We're just trying to find out what would be best for you. A court case involving a young defenseless female—no matter how it turns out a lot of loose jawed people . . . Anyway," Jones said, squirming, "if you sold it to me you'd have your money and be out of this thing. Surely—"

"And how much," she asked, "were you thinking to offer?"

"Well . . ." Jones said, "it's by way of being considerably speculative. . . . What would you say to five hundred dollars?"

"You really aren't joking?"

"I know," he nodded, "that's a right smart amount of money, but I'd like to feel you've been looked out for. . . ." He broke off to stare, having discovered she was grinning. The more he considered her the less he liked it. His neck got darker and he began to swell up.

Putting aside her amusement she rose to say briskly, "If what you're talking about is an advance. . . ?"

The banker stared. It must belatedly have occurred to him he might have sold her a trifle short, but he was one who could think pretty quick when it came to matters of finance and was able, if he had to, to set up his sights. Patting the sweat and chagrin off his face he tucked his handkerchief away and hiked up his offer to an even five thousand, magnanimously chuckling as he dug out his wallet.

The girl said, glancing around at McFarron, "I

guess we've taken up enough of his time. If you're ready now, Sheriff—"

"Here . . . hold on!" Jones cried. In a contortion of anguish he came darting forward to catch at her arm. Jaw dropping, he jumped back in ludicrous alarm from the blazing look that banged into his face. "Wh—what's that for?" he spluttered.

"Someone should teach you not to suck eggs." She stood another fierce moment, watching him with a contempt hard to bear. "I suppose that kind of thing is what keeps banks solvent."

Chagrin, the rebellious sting of a man's flustered pride, groped to hold him together above the claws of his fury while he fumblingly attempted to pass it off as a joke. No one joined him in this effort to save face and in the end, McFarron noted, nothing could withstand the livid drive of his cupidity. "Six!" he snarled on the verge of apoplexy.

The girl's knowing eyes were bright with disdain. "And you'd give fifteen thousand for a hole in the ground!" She turned on her heel in a flutter of skirts and sailed through the door without a backward glance.

III

MEANWHILE, OUT IN God's open, the man whose actions had set all this in motion was lazily hazing a pair of fat burros through the noontime heat that crawled and writhed above the blistering dust some hundred rods west of the mission San Xavier del Bac, not a great many miles dead south of the crumbling remains of Tucson's old wall.

The gleaming gypsum white of these ancient buildings raised by Indian sweat to the blackrobes' Cross could be seen a good ways across the swales and hogbacks of the Santa Cruz Valley. Charlie Medders, however, had come down off the granite slopes of the saguaro strewn mountains. Lifting the water bag slung from a shoulder he shook it and, grimacing, reluctantly reckoned he better stop by and fill it.

The Jesuits' community had been laid out along the hump of broad sandy knoll somewhat west of the butte whose gaunt whitened cross from time unremembered had stood lonely vigil over the river's gray wastes and the tops of great cotton-woods greenly trembling where they showed above the bluffs. It was the only place in a parched pile of leagues where the north-flowing *Rio de Santa Maria* had managed to maintain a dependable watering place, for mostly it had long since gone underground except during the blessing of infrequent rains. To be sure, at Tucson there was even a lake, but for the bulk of its length the Santa Cruz, as they were calling it now, was so bone dry you couldn't find a frog without you dug halfway to China.

The Sobaipuri Indians—what was left of them—and the Papagos who made this *rancheria* their refuge, someway pieced together a dreary sort of living from the weaving of baskets and a kind of desultory halfhearted farming.

Medders, twisting his head, scanned several fields of drought dwarfed corn beyond the church's far wall as he came up to the coping of the hand-dug well with its skreaky hoist and copper-bound bucket.

He sent the rope down and uncapped his deflated water bag, in a sweat to get through with this and be on his way. Fact is, he would have bypassed the mission as he generally did, except for the needs of his long-eared charges, so hammered-down under the bulge of heavy packs.

About to fetch up the bucket, his hand was arrested by the swish of cloth and a rasping crunch of oncoming sandals, and he jerked up his chin with a smothered curse. His worst fears were realized: it was Father Eusebio. The portly padre was making straight for the well.

"Peace be with you, my son."

The benediction was free—like the concerned stretch of smile that tiredly tugged the old man's lips, but the sun bleached stare beneath those tufted brows was reaching for Charlie's fiddle-footed conscience with a zeal the Devil himself could not have broken.

Medders began to back off.

"I think," the priest said, "we'll have an accounting. Where have you been since you last passed this way?"

"Prospectin', Father."

The look in those eyes really made a man squirm.

"Is that what they're calling it now? Salting stripped, worthless holes to sell the unwary?"

Medders looked shocked. "Figured *you,* of all people, would think better o' me than that!" He dragged a sweaty hand across his scraggle of whiskers. Dismay, a weary sadness, limped around through his voice. "The things a man's enemies will tell anymore—"

"Charles," the old man said, cutting into it, "how long has it been since you went to confession?"

Medders loosed a great sigh. "As a matter of plain, unvarnished—"

"The truth, boy."

"Too long," Medders muttered, staring down at cracked boots.

Father Eusebio nodded. "Get yourself cleaned up. I'll be—"

"Golly Moses!" Charlie exclaimed, looking sick. He let go of the well rope. "Ain't a thing I'd rather. . . ." He peered around for his burros. "But I just *can't* stop now! Supposed t' be right this minute in T.K.'s office, an' as a man of my word—"

"The road to hell is paved—"

"You straggly-haired numbskulls! Git outa that cornpatch!" Medders yelled in a passion and, tugging a rock from one of his pockets, let fly with it, furious. "Hup thar!" he shouted. "Git up outa that!" And off he went after them, flapping his arms like a ruptured duck.

Shaking his head, Father Eusebio sighed. Poor Charlie, it looked like, was well on the way to becoming incorrigible. Such a waste of God's talents, the good padre mused. Something else crossed his mind that was less understandable and, recalling the glitter of the thing Charlie'd thrown, absently fingering his beads he set off to hunt it down.

When he was far enough away to feel beyond the priest's reach, Medders, giving over, hauled up in the shade of an ancient mesquite to mop his steaming brow. That had been a near thing, he told himself, shuddering. A man wanted to be saved, no getting around that, but—like St. Augustine—not right now. Life was too full of a number of things for a gent with red blood to swear off in his prime all the fun and wild pleasures that put the yeast into it.

Then, chancing to glance back, he went rigidly still.

The priest was in the corn moving jerkily about, head down and bent over like a grazing horse, his face scarcely half a foot above the ground. Even as he watched, Charlie saw the padre pounce and come up with something which he vigorously rubbed against a hiked-up fold of his rusty black soutane.

It didn't take Medders hardly a gulp to get the connection between that rock he'd pitched at Begat and Begetta and the something the old man was so engrossedly studying.

In his sudden perturbation Medders felt half minded to go reclaim the chunk of ore. It was one of his carefully culled jewelry specimens, of about the same weight and worth as the little gleaming beauty that skirted jezebel had made off with after all them fine words about soul mates and marriage and the wonderful tomorrows they could share in double harness. Women!

Charlie snorted.

Worse than the seven years' itch. Back a man into a corner and take the dang fillin's right out of his teeth! He had learned about women before he'd turned twenty—enough to know better than swaller the hogwash this Belita Storn filly had been painting the cave with whilst running sly fingers through his rumpled-up hair!

She was an armful, all right—cuddly as a kitten. But Charlie Medders, though he might not look it, had been around a fortnight and wasn't to be caught up in no kind of net like that. Cheaper to give her a full half interest and stake that Eduardo mule out where she could get hold of him. Worth half the mine to be rid of her, he'd thought. And, proving him right, off she'd gone like a shot.

Well, she'd talk, like enough. Probably yak her fool head off, so it didn't too much matter about that chunk the padre was fisting. Might even tend to confuse things a little. Might even turn out that a few more wouldn't be wasted if left to be found where these school boys could peddle them.

Tramping after his burros, sweating and mumbling, he put out the bait until his pockets were empty, setting up the last bit in the center of the trail where it made the big loop snaking down to the crossing.

Didn't make no never-mind to Charlie who came onto it. As redskins went these was educated hombres. Any Papago would savvy a hunk of rock rich as this could be wink quick swapped for a snootful of firewater. So let 'em, and to hell with it! Give T.K. something to think about, maybe.

Despite that whopper he had told the priest nothing could have been more remote from his intentions than to find himself closeted with T.K. Jones. When he'd set off on this pack trip three days ago Phoenix had been his avowed destination. But, following Eduardo's tracks, more enticing notions had intervened.

What, after all, could that overstuffed hog of a banker do? A man got bored with hiding out; and it wasn't like Medders had done anything a gent could really be jugged for. If Jones hadn't been so stinking anxious to buy, heckling and pestering to get in on what his own grasping mind had built into a bonanza, he would never have got bit. It was T.K.'s own perseverance that had fashioned the coup, suggesting the soft touch by which Charlie Medders had latched onto a cool fifteen thousand with nothing but a gutted hole for collateral.

Of course Jones had squawked. It had impaired

his public image, made him look a bloody fool. So
what? With his plasters and liens and wholesale
foreclosures he had weaseled into everything of
worth inside a hundred and fifty miles, and had no
more compunctions than could be found in a vulture. Hell, he'd been *asking* for it! And everybody
knew it.

Now if a feller could put any dependence in a
female . . . but such preposterous thoughts was
plumb ridiculous. Medders knew from a heap of
sad remembrances you couldn't. Why, that
dangfool critter might end up in Hermosillo! Sure,
he'd slipped into their conversations every landmark she'd need to see her safely into Tucson, but
it was no guarantee she had got there. Second day
out a wind had sprung up; he never had come onto
that mule's tracks again. She could have wound up
in Globe, or Winkelman, or Ajo.

Her guile and excitements might have led some
fellers right up the garden path. She had played it
pretty slick, making out to be lost and half out of
her head—he'd thought for a while she really was.
And then, convalescing, all them blandishments
and calf's eyes. It wasn't that Medders had been
less susceptible that had led him to see through her
artful dodges; he'd been long enough around to
have had most of these enticements worked on him
before. So he'd put out bait, offered her half the
lode in exchange for a little fabricated help, and to
prove that he meant business had put it down in
writing.

She'd eased up some then, not dropping him like
no hot potato but not pushing any more on the
rose-colored wonders of life in double harness.

Then he'd staked out the mule, and off she'd gone.

When he had tucked those mileposts into the evening gab fests he had not, of course, been figuring to pull Jones into this, only trying to make sure that in ridding himself of her she didn't come to grief. But the more he'd got to mulling it over the better the whole thing looked with Jones cast again in the role of big fish. It could be a real lark!

Putting one over on Tiberius Jones had been the kind of thing a man could date time by, and if it happened again the lard-bottomed skinflint might be laughed clean out of the golrammed country. A lot of those who in the past had been so free with their jeers could be glad to shake the hand of a man who accomplished that. Might even be hailed as a public benefactor!

Caught up in so salubrious a prospect it seemed no time at all until Medders found himself and burros churning up the dust of Tucson's *barrio libre,* the old part of town that led past Sol Warner's store off the Plaza de Armas, a saddle maker's shop, assayer's office and three-four saloons before in a jogging hit-or-miss fashion the way opened up to disclose the turreted structure housing T.K.'s abominated bank.

One might suppose he would have used a little more caution in the manner of his approach, but it never occurred to Charlie's day-dreaming mind the girl might have gone to the sheriff about those scars, thinking to grab it all, or that she knew more about this ore he'd found than he did.

IV

FIRST STOP, he reckoned, might as well be Tiny O'Toole's. He wanted to get this ore off his hands before T.K. got out an order restraining him and, while the town had more firms engaged in assaying than the amount of moved ore appeared honestly to warrant, none of the others had O'Toole's unique facilities. With the ore disposed of he could leave Begat and Begetta with Frichet while he sought and enjoyed the ministrations of a barber, got himself some new duds and helped the word get round that Charlie Medders, dang his eyes, had finally made a real winning.

Physically O'Toole was a strapping big six-footer with a black Irish mug, hands like hams, and a mind that was sharper than the proverbial steel trap. Sizing up the burros' packs from behind his stone filled windows, he came out on the street in his stained leather apron to wring Medders' fist like a jovial bear.

"Let's git this stuff under cover," Charlie

grumbled, cutting short the offered pleasantries with a nervous scowl. "This'll have to be fer cash an' I ain't figurin' to do much standing around."

O'Toole, saying nothing, merely jerked his chin.

Charlie threw off the ropes and the big Irishman helped manhandle the packs while the burros, snuffling, began to hunt round for a good place to roll.

Inside, with the first of the sacks opened up and the contents spilled across the top of a counter, Medders stood fidgeting in a squirm of impatience while the misnamed mick considered the ore, once or twice picking up a piece to thoughtfully handle, even lifting one chunk into the garish arc of an overhead Rochester. When, finally, he turned to reach for a hammer, Medders said testily: "Never mind that! Just make me a price!"

O'Toole hung a hip on the counter and stared. He knocked out a brier, scooped it full, tamped and lighted it, still with the blue of his look darkly digging. Through swirls of layering smoke he said thinly, "Twenty-eight hundred."

Medders, livid, commenced stuffing the ore back into his sack.

"Four thousand." O'Toole sighed.

Charlie said, glaring: "This ain't stolen ore—"

"Then why such a tearin' sweat to be shed of it?"

"Because," Medders growled, "I don't want it impounded," and O'Toole showed his teeth.

"Now ye're talkin'. Takes some doin' to get ahead of Jones. His bank got out a restrainin' order right after you took to the brush. Every assayer in town's been warned. Where you think that leaves *me* if he decides to come down on it?"

"But he can't!" Medders snarled.

O'Toole asked, scornful, "Which of the hierarchy did you git that from? You ever hear of a time inside this county when T.K. Jones, the almight Tiberius, could not seize an' gobble anything he put his mind to?"

"But ... Hell," Charlie protested, "once it's outa my hands—"

"You don't know that." The blue-jowled Irishman peered irascibly. "I'll go to fifty-two hundred."

"Jesus H. Christ!" Charlie pawed at his face. "The four of them sacks'll run close t' ten thousand!"

"Well," O'Toole grimaced, dusting off his dukes, "I got to have some kind of margin. Besides, it's peculiar."

"If you mean that muck—"

"I'm talkin' about the color."

Charlie's eyes rolled. "It's practically *pure silver!*"

"You heard me. Fifty-two hundred, an' that's as far as I'll go. If it's in your head some nump will cough up more you better go grab it. But don't," he warned darkly, "come wailin' at me if McFarron tromps in afore ye've pocketed yer money."

Medders swore in a passion, but he knew O'Toole had him. Nobody else with enough ready cash was like to risk crossing up the county's biggest mogul just to stay on trading terms with a bum like Charlie Medders. If he did dig up so wild a gambler there was no guarantee he'd come out any better.

And the longer he took setting up a deal the

greater the peril of the sheriff stepping in on the strength of that paper Jones had got from the court.

It went sore against his grain to give in but he could see, still fuming, it was either give in or chance having the whole dratted haul took away from him. And he would almost sooner *give* it away than see it scooped up by that straggly-haired banker!

"You win," he grumbled. But it just wasn't in him to take a licking with good grace. Stomping around like a sore-footed bull while the Irishman was getting the hard cash from his safe, Charlie went on at some length and then started all over. "What really gets me goin'," he growled, "is to think all this time I been considerin' you a *friend*!"

This seemed a pretty harsh indictment but O'Toole went coolly on with his counting. Stacking up the last bulging handful of twenties the Irishman shut his safe, spun the dial and, arms akimbo, considered Medders sourly.

"Fifty-two hundred, coin of the realm. Now suppose you take it an' git the hell out av here."

"Why, you liver eatin' hound!" Charlie cried, affronted, and stepped back to give himself room to square off. "I'm goin' to—"

"So it's a fight ye're wantin' now then, is it?" O'Toole, nothing loath, began to roll up his sleeves. He was just moving forward when a man tore in off the street, pop eyed and panting. "The sheriff!" he gasped, and seemed to have used all the breath he had left.

Medders spun toward the window, cursed, and white-cheeked lunged for the mound of gleaming coins. As he crammed them frantically into his pockets it became all too apparent he would run out of space before he ran out of dollars.

O'Toole, watching, grinned. If he had any worries about his own part in this, such qualms did not noticeably impair his amusement.

"Fer cripes sake," Medders howled, copiously perspiring, "hurry up, you guys, an' give me a hand!"

Nobody moved.

The bloke who'd run in off the street with the news stood goggling—still heaving and puffing—like Charlie was some kind of two-headed freak. And O'Toole, in his enjoyment, was a hard cross to bear. "Reminds me," he said, "of the half starved mouse that got into the corncrib and stuffed so hearty he couldn't git out."

Medders, looking around wildly, began turning out his pockets, disgorging silver dollars in a desperate attempt to make room for those stacks of gleaming gold eagles—but there just wasn't time. With a last despairing snarl—too hurried even to unload his spleen in the ominous crunch of that approaching tread—Charlie scooped all he could into his up-ended hat and made a staggering bolt for the shop's rear door.

V

THE IRISHMAN, wiping his eyes, looked to be in the final shakes of a belly laugh when Tiberius Jones slammed into the place with a red headed woman practically riding his heels. She had the hard used appearance of a fortune teller put through the brush by a pack of disgruntled housewives.

Blinking, O'Toole, in a kind of double take, astonishedly returned the girl's appraising stare. Besides being almost painfully young she was, he discovered, in some outlandish gypsyish fashion extraordinarily attractive. Thus engaged, he did not at once realize McFarron had not stepped in with them. When this caught at his notice he put the girl out of mind and considered Jones warily.

The banker's protuberant eyes, prowling the shop, wheeled like a pair of hovering vultures to disquietingly fasten O'Toole in his tracks. "You find my presence humorous?" he asked, staring nastily; then said, harsh as Moses about to seize the golden calf: "*Where is he?*"

O'Toole looked puzzled, but Jones was not in any game-playing mood. Impatient, testy, the lash of his glance snaking past the big Irishman's blocking shape spied the glint of spilled coins and stopped, bright as fire, against the ore cluttered counter.

His lips spread thin in a yellow grin. "Where'd *that* come from?"

O'Toole said, surprised, "Them sacks, you mean?" and wheeled back, disgusted. "More of that loco desert rat junk—"

"Don't look like junk to me," Jones growled, brushing past the assayer for a closer stare. Snatching up a piece, cheeks flushed and furious, he thrust it under O'Toole's twitching nose. "You call that 'junk'? It's damn near solid silver!"

The Irishman, snorting, peered at the banker like he thought T.K. had gone off his rocker. "That greenish lookin' crap?" He loosed a dubious cackle. "Pullin' my leg, eh? Look—I'm laughin'."

Jones wasn't laughing. "You ran a test on this stuff?"

"A test, the man says!" O'Toole rolled his eyes. "Chri'sake, T.K., silver's black—it ain't *green*!"

"Sure, sure. You run some of this through the works right away. I'll foot the bill," the banker smiled, standing back.

O'Toole chewed his cheek. "I can't do that."

"Then what would you say if I impounded this ore and had the Court—"

"I don't think you could get away with it," O'Toole said, sweating. "Public opinion—"

"The public," Jones said, "are a bunch of damn sheep, and you know it!"

O'Toole had too much tied up in this to throw in his hand if he could find a way around it. With a show of confidence he said, crisply blunt: "That court order you got hardly gives you a license to grab everything you happen to fancy."

A tide of red crept above the banker's tight fitting collar; his eyes bulged more noticeably. Then a scornful smile nastily twisted his mouth. "I imagine the Court in its continued good judgment, once the facts are exposed, will decide in the bank's favor." He threw up an imperious hand as the Irishman's impatience seemed about to interrupt. "The restraint, it is true, was imposed against Medders, but if you're bursting to point out this ore does not belong to him I would advise you to consider the following circumstances.

"First of all," Jones smiled, "this unprincipled swindler—and I'm speaking of Medders—was observed to enter town with two heavily laden burros known, I believe, as Begat and Begetta. Those animals, stripped of their packs, are presently standing outside this shop. You have a table that is covered with a lot of high-grade specimens and three unopened packs."

He paused to stab a triumphant glance across the shine of dropped coins. "And I would remind you," he said, his satisfaction crammed with malice, "that all assayers, including yourself, were apprised of the Court's order and warned against buying any ore from Charlie Medders. Now," he chuckled, insufferably pleasant, as Andy McFarron sauntered in from out back, "if you want to claim this ore, put yourself on record."

"You all through?" O'Toole asked.

"Just answer the question. Is this your ore or isn't it?"

"I don't quite see—"

"All we want out of you is an answer!"

"I think," said the sheriff as O'Toole's jaw tightened, "you won't do yourself any good bein' stubborn."

A shine of sweat slicked the Irishman's cheeks and his glance clawed around like a wet footed cat while McFarron stood watching for a sign from the banker and the deepening silence grew increasingly uncomfortable.

When he could stand it no longer O'Toole pulled up his head and on a bitter outrush of breath declared the ore didn't belong to Medders.

Jones and the sheriff exchanged unreadable looks. "Then it's yours?" the banker prompted.

"I haven't said so."

"Maybe you won't have to."

"I expect," McFarron drawled, "you know how it happens to be settin' on that bench."

"A desert rat—"

"Sure," Jones grinned. "A rat named Charlie Medders."

When the assayer failed to respond the banker said to McFarron: "Bring in your prisoner, Sheriff."

McFarron said gruffly, "I don't have a prisoner. Wasn't nobody out there."

O'Toole, finding hope, showed a dry lift of lips.

"Well, no matter," Jones said, darkly eyeing his sheriff. "I believe we can show to the court's satisfaction it was Medders, all right, that fetched the stuff in here." He slanched a glance at the girl.

"Show Mr. O'Toole that specimen you fetched from Medders' mine, my dear."

The girl stared back, looking fussed and balky, but finally dug the little chunk from her bodice and dropped it into the banker's outstretched palm. Jones, beckoning the assayer, went back to the bench and placed the sample beside one of the bigger hunks. "What do you think the Court will say to that?"

There was no room for argument. The greenish tinge was evident throughout. Both pieces had obviously come from the same source.

O'Toole fidgeted. "Hell, I don't know where she got it!" he blustered. But his eyes looked sick.

The banker laughed. "She got it from Medders' cave, as we'll prove." He picked up the girl's sample and stood a while, grinning. "You want to change your story while you still got time?"

O'Toole's eyes looked mean, the whole shape of him sullen with the kind of frustration a man could hardly bear. He finally said stubbornly, "All you've got to hook this ore up to Medders is a lot of fool talk!"

"We've got more than that." Jones peered at him smugly. "This girl is Medders' partner with a full half interest in every ounce he sells—what's more, she's got it sewed up in writing, and chain marks on her legs to prove the chiseling son of a bitch has been keeping her penned up out there like a goddam peon! McFarron," he said, "you've got the court's warrant. I want this ore, every piece of it, impounded."

O'Toole, gnashing his teeth, waved his arms like crazy. "God damn it," he cried, "you can't—"

"Before I get through I'll have you *both* behind bars," the banker said with the tone and look one might expect of a man so vindictively self-righteous. He was like a cat having fun with a mouse. "Most silver," he said, "as you yourself pointed out, in its natural state generally tends to seem dark, sometimes almost black as it comes from the ground—which is not to say it can never look green. One source," he declared with considerable satisfaction, "discovered in this vicinity during the Spanish occupation, had this strange peculiarity. It came from the Weeping Widow, one of the fabulous Lost Padre mines."

If the implication had not been so outrageous, if O'Toole had not been so bitterly preoccupied with his own frustrations and probable plight, he might have noticed the pallor, the rigid stance of the girl.

Neither man did, but O'Toole cried, incredulous: "You figure Medders has stumbled onto it?"

"That will be our contention when we take this to court."

VI

AT ABOUT THE point where the sheriff got to wondering if Charlie Medders had any idea what sort of prospect he was fiddling around with, the subject of this not uncharitable speculation was inspecting his reflected splendor in the full-length glass of The Boston Store—R.G. Appopolus, Prop.

Bathed, barbered and freshly outfitted from forty dollar benchmade boots to the finest product of the John B. Stetson (cowman's hat) Company, it might be reasonably assumed the gentleman in question was basking not only in the best of health but enjoying the good fortune of a carefree mind.

As a matter of fact, he looked rather glum. Despite being taken advantage of and suckered into leaving more behind than he could stomach, he was again in funds, had outsmarted T.K. and should have been sitting on top of the world. It was what he'd been telling himself ever since, stumbling out of O'Toole's back door, he'd run smack into the arms of Sheriff Andy McFarron.

To be sure, the dour Scot had preached a pretty stern sermon before stepping aside to let him pass, but this sort of thing—coming in at one ear and leaving by the other—could hardly be charged with upsetting a man. Of course Andy had turned him loose—what *else* could he have done? Hadn't the pair of them been compadres all the way back to Slaughter? Cripes, wasn't that what a man's friends was for?

Only thing McFarron had told him he hadn't already known, or suspected, was that cussed girl running to the law with her unvarnished whoppers and—more disgusting—teaming up with Jones to whipsaw him out of this caveful of silver.

Well, hell, he reflected, what could you expect of a thieving gitana, and a female at that! It was the dang ungratefulness of it that gnawed him—selling half the share he had plain outright *give* her, and to of all people that straggly haired banker!

Though enough to make a polecat cuss this was not, strictly speaking, the rock-bottomed source of Medders' fluttery disquiet. Leastways he did not think it was, but he had a nagging jumpety hunch he wasn't going to feel better till he got out of this burg.

Which was what Sheriff Andy had advised him to do. But a gent that was free, white and old enough to vote was bound to do some toe-dragging before letting any ham-hocked, hog-faced, weasel-eyed grabber of widders' mites and old ladies' homesteads put him on public notice. Folks might reckon the durn cottonmouth had sure enough sent him packing! Danged if he'd give them that much satisfaction.

Confidence thus precariously bolstered, fed up with all those precautionary antics which had so far kept him out of Jones' clutches, Charlie forthwith quit his safe obscurity to sally forth into the lamplit shadows of the town's main drag. This was still a free country. Jones' bank might control its purse strings but the streets belonged to nobody. Not even Belita Storn with her lies could have him picked up without due process.

It was this which had finally decided him. His new wealth was hot as live coals in his pockets, and a gent which had spent six months in the brush craved something more exciting than bare walls to look at.

About to step into the Red Herring for a beer, a bleary eyed galoot floundering out of the place blundered roughly into him. With the stench of a bar rag the fellow pushed free then began, like a bullwhacker, to dress Medders down.

It was Phineas O'Toole, the barrel-chested assayer who had got Charlie's high-grade for half its worth, guffawing like a loony when Medders had been stampeded into leaving part of that.

He wasn't laughing now. The bleary eyes, regarding Charlie's fine clothes, suddenly flared with a savage recognition. Drunk and unmistakably ugly he thrust his glowering face into Charlie's, grabbed a fistful of shirtfront and, wheeling, slammed Medders furiously against a wall. "Ye pussy-footin' crook! I've a moind," he snarled, "t' take it out av yer hide!"

Medders, too breathless and shaken for speech,

had enough red fox curling round through his makeup to know the better part of valor held no brief for broken bones. Going limp and loose in every joint he hung from the assayer's brawny grip looking pitiful and wilted as a yanked-up flower.

Startled, O'Toole peered down at him. Snarling with disgust he pitched the sagging weight aside to stare drop-jawed and ludicrous as Medders, bounding to his feet, struck off into the coagulating shadows with no more ado than a departing mosquito.

With a shout of rage the big Irishman took after him.

Medders, hearing the plunging strike of those boots banging nearer and louder at every heart jolting stride, didn't need any diagrams to guess what would happen if those whopping great fists laid hold of him again. McFarron, he reckoned, must have grabbed all that ore. O'Toole, at the very least, would clean Charlie's pockets. In his present state of mind the man might cripple him for life!

A dozen brash expedients clawed through the churn of Charlie's thoughts, but there was little time for cleverness and none at all for dodges. If the assayer latched onto him about the best a man could hope for was that some passer-by might stop to sweep up the pieces. Medders didn't dare swap words with O'Toole and it began to sink in he wasn't about to outrun him.

The man's lunging breath was hot against his neck—he could picture those hair-matted arms reaching for him. There was one crazy chance and, desperately, Charlie took it.

Gasping and wheezing he dug in his heels and

went down in a convulsive twisting fall. He heard the Irishman curse, but the man couldn't catch himself. Something crashed agonizingly against Charlie's hip as O'Toole, banging into him, went ass over elbows to land spraddled out in a teeth-cracking sprawl.

Charlie wasted no time trying to help the guy up. Hardly pausing to feel himself over he took off and got out by the shortest route.

But Phineas O'Toole was not a man easily shaken.

Medders knew before he'd gone half a block the fellow was after him. He tried to lose the assayer in a maze of dark alleys. Glancing back as he came forth with ragged breath into the lamp-laced traffic of Meyer Street, Charlie cursed. The guy was a regular bloodhound!

Shoving frantically across a pedestrian crammed walk Medders dashed recklessly into the street, wildly diving in front of a twelve-horse hitch. Skirting a hack, barely missed by the wheels, scarcely hearing the angry yells of its driver, he ducked through a rack of tied ponies and, in sheer desperation, flung himself through the batwings of Tony Florido's swank Carleton House bar.

It was the only safe place he could think of. A kind of sanctum sanctorum, the retreat of big business, it had become over the years a sort of unofficial club for the town's top strata citizens, gents like Sol Warner, Digby Rhodes, Hiram Walker, Archie Bell and other big moguls of the mining, cattle and mercantile trades. No bums were allowed, no brawls tolerated; and Charlie Medders, who had never passed through its varnished portal

before, looked around in awe at the plush up-
holstering, panelled woodwork, the whole overwhelming aroma of elegance.

With a sigh of relief Medders headed for the bar,
pleased to discover that, except for hired help and
several well dressed gents with their silk tiled heads
bent over a far table, the place at this early hour
was practically deserted.

Just as he was fixing to plop a hoof on the rail
the baldheaded barkeep, leaning forward confiden-
tially, said *sotto voce* above the glass he had been
polishing: "Ain't you got into the wrong pew,
Jack?"

Suspiciously sniffing Medders peered at him,
puzzled; and just about there someone dug his sore
ribs with a mighty rude elbow. "Outside, Mac, an'
don't give me no sass."

Charlie, twisting his head, beheld a burly shape
in tails and stiff shirt grimly flexing its muscles perhaps a half a step away. With that off-center nose,
battered ears and outthrust jaw the guy was obviously a bouncer.

Instinctively backing off a bit, uncomfortably
aware of the road grime and the gaping torn knee
of one split trouser leg, Medders had a disquieting
vision of O'Toole hunched and waiting just beyond
the varnished doors.

The skin began to darken in irate patches about
his ears. Swelling up, he said affronted, "You're
talkin' to a man which could buy this dump an'
tear it down!" He slapped a handful of double
eagles ringing on the bar. "Set 'em up," he said,
"the drinks are on—"

The bouncer dropped a splayed paw on his arm.

From the corner of a steel-trap mouth he rasped:
"Out!" with a jerk of the jaw in the direction of the
street.

Medders shook off the hand. Peering arrogantly
down the length of his nose he tapped the man's
chest. "Do you know who I am?"

The man, big enough almost to make two of
Medders, seemed taken aback and Charlie, thus
encouraged, swung around to the barkeep. "Come,
come, my good man," he cried, pounding a rock-
scarred fist on the bar. "The drinks are on me, and
there's the cash to—"

"Takes more than cash," the baldhead stated,
"to stand treat in this place. First you've got to
belong. An' you're six hundred short," he sighed,
dribbling the gold like checks through stacked fingers, "of havin' the price."

"What?" Medders goggled. "One thousand
dollars!" He stared, aghast.

"It's a gentleman's club."

Charlie pulled himself together. "Well, all
right," he muttered, and counted another six hundred onto the bar. "There! I guess that does it.
Now set 'em up fer—"

"Man," the barkeep sighed, "don't you hear
good? I told you this here is a *gentleman's* club."

Charlie said, snorting, "It would have to be at
that price! Well, what're you waitin' on? You've
got my money—"

"It ain't a question of money. You gotta be
asked," the baldhead grinned, and gave his
bouncer the nod.

Charlie never had a chance. A fist exploded
against his head. He spun backwards, sagging,

bringing up against the bar. Something slugged him in the stomach with the whack of a mule's hind hoof and the floor rushed up, dissolving like a burst egg.

He felt himself being lifted. He got back enough vision to see the boards blur beneath him, to have a peculiar sense of flying. Then his head cracked the batwings and he went through, still scrabbling with ineffectual hands, to sail hurtling across the rough planks of the walk toward a wild lifting tangle of steel-shod hoofs.

The spooked broncs tore away, dragging the snapped-off rail.

When he collected enough gumption to think of picking himself up, the first thing Charlie's groggy stare fastened onto was the toothy grin of Tiberius Jones.

VII

TOO STUNNED TO cuss, too bushed to run, Medders stood like Chicken Little waiting for the sky to fall, eyes bugged out like knots on a stick. Jones, exuding satisfaction, looked tickled as Delilah peering down at shorn Samson or Salome viewing the head of dead John.

As the first awful grip of his fright began to loosen, Charlie's stare, quickened by hope, anxiously prowled the hemming faces, finding little to reassure him.

Long ago he'd exhausted the last vestige of his credit, sacrificing friendship to a miscellany of pranks, repaying people's patience with a clatter of unkept promises. Now, with a caveful of silver, needing only time to move it, he was flanked by the claws of this grinning Legree and no one, it looked like, would say a stinking word for him.

He burned to tell them what he had—that he could pay every claim, and with a heaped high bonus for those who had waited longest, but it would be wasted breath. He was the unhappy veteran of too many strikes which had failed to pan out. They were glad to see him caught up with.

It was the measure of their remembering contempt that, while they had no love for Tiberius Jones, not one of these hardshells would lift a finger to shield Charlie Medders from this polecat's revenge.

No, not one.

Hauling his chin up he twisted a look about.

"Why, Charles," Jones said, "is that truly you?"

Ignoring the titters, Medders brushed himself off. "I've been throwed out of better places," he growled, counting faces. But he could not find McFarron's and interpreted this to be an ominous sign.

Being jailed was not the worst that could happen. Jones had his big casino with him—Dry Camp Burks, that would no more worry about potting a guy than he would at discovering a worm in his chawing.

Charlie felt his scraped jaw. Didn't no one need to spell out his plight; he was between a rock and a hard place for sure, and if he got loose of this he was not going to be caught again—no matter how it looked—without some kind of a handle he could grab for. Leaving his gun in his room had been a pretty dumb stunt, but he was danged if he would beg!

Jones with a widening grin observed, "Appears you've about reached the end of your tether." When this got no answer he said, nastily chuckling, "I guess you're all squared off to pay back that loan."

It got powerfully quiet, all those counter-jumpers holding their breaths, so glued to their listening they couldn't even swallow. Yet what could he say? What *dared* he say?

A gent was perfectly willing to take care of his obligations, but how could you know after all this while which were real and which drummed up to take advantage of his predicament?

The more he peered the madder Charlie got. Nobody wants to be backed into a corner; and if he paid out one dime the whole push would be after him. Why, half of them slobs was droolin' right now!

He covered his fears with a scowl and stood pat; whereupon, with some unction, the great man suggested they adjourn someplace and have a shareholders' meeting.

"Shareholders!"

Medders came out of his shell with a shout. With a fist shaken furiously under Jones' nose he cried: "You ain't goin' to move in on *me* like that! You think I was born yesterday?"

The banker said with curled lip: "You came into this town with four sacks of ore which the sheriff, by court order, has impounded. In your packratting around you've obviously stumbled onto something." He looked about to say more, but changed his mind when his glance, rather irritably, took note of the gaping faces. He said, motioning curtly, "I think we had better step over to my office."

Medders wanted no part of any bind like that. "You got anythin' to say you can say it right here —in front of witnesses, by grab." He held up his ripped trouser leg. "I ain't trustin' myself alone again with your plug-uglies!"

The implication, though little better than a barefaced lie, served to turn Jones cautious. Enough so that when the hard-faced Burks started toward Medders, glancing back for the high sign, the banker reluctantly shook his head. The rough stuff would keep.

Few knew better than Tiberius Jones how unstably fickle a crowd's whim could be, and right now these galoots, themselves whipsawed by this slickery customer, stood squarely behind him. He did not often have so comforting a feeling.

His intentions toward Medders had not changed in the least but there were other ways than violence of getting at the man. Appearing nettled he said: "I am not here to argue. What these gentlemen want is some sort of installment against the bills you've run up. A little earnest money," he suggested, smiling when the shopkeepers growled. "Is that too much to ask?"

"Well . . . no." Charlie, feeling through his clothes, was not as stupid as he looked. He could bend with the wind if that were the lesser of two hateful courses. "I'd admire to do what's right. You divvy this up the way you reckon is best. Hold out your hat," he grumbled, and emptied his pockets.

The alacrity of his capitulation darkly sharpened the banker's stare but, concealing his annoyance, Jones toted up the coins and currency, saying at last in deeper disgruntlement, "I make it four hundred, seventy-eight dollars and forty-seven cents."

The merchants, looking thunderstruck, regarded the banker with considerable suspicion. Jones colored angrily. "Where's the rest of it? You got more than that!"

Charlie sighing, slung wide both arms. "Well, look for yerself—don't take my word for it."

Jones glared, speechless; and Burks, shifting his chew, said, "I'll git it out of him!"

"Here—wait," Jones cried, and Burks spat disgustedly. But the banker couldn't afford to make a martyr of Charlie; not, anyway, at this stage of the game. "All you boys that have a claim against Medders, if you'll step round to the bank tomorrow with your figures, can have a pro rata share of what he's turned over. Meanwhile—"

"That's right," Charlie grinned, "show up an' git yer dimes an' nickels, because you can bet yer bottom dollar that's all there'll be when his bank gits done with it."

Jones winced, but he had seen this coming and hung onto his temper. "Meanwhile," he said, speaking up strong to put the heat back on Medders, "we'll have a stockholder's meeting at one o'clock sharp and issue shares in this strike—"

"Oh, no you don't!"

Charlie, carried away by the enormity of this proposal, flashed his teeth like a cornered wolf. "You're not slicin' up any find of mine to put yourself in good with these counter-jumpers! You may own the bank an' two-thirds of this town but you ain't puttin' me through that kinda hoop! What's mine is mine an'—"

"You see the kind of crook we're up against," Jones said. "But I assure you, gentlemen, the law will prevail. You shall have your just shares—"

"There *ain't* no shares!" Charlie yelled, beside

himself. "All's I've got. . ."

"We know what you've got," the banker spoke
to the crowd, "and you can't turn your back, now
you've struck it rich, on all these fellows who have
clothed you and fed you and kept you going the
Lord only knows how many weary months when
except for them you would have starved to death."
He considered Charlie with considerable distaste,
suddenly disclaiming in a loud and terrible voice,
"Do you deny that these good people have kept
you afloat?"

Medders found himself boxed. He tried to get off
the hook with the disparaging concession that, "If
you want to call a few sacks of rusty beans, some
castoff jeans an' a old coat or two—" but the
growls this brought on made him falter and stop.

He began to sweat and his skin felt full of
prickles. "All right," he snarled, putting the best
face he could on it, "I'm no ingrate! Some of these
gents has sure-enough helped me an' I'll take care
of 'em—but that don't mean I'll let a whoppyjawed
loan shark carve up my winnin' like I hadn't no
rights! Who the hell found it, that's what *I* wanta
know! Not *him!*" Medders shouted, with a look no
real man could possibly abide.

But the only looks which mattered to Jones was
how this looked—or might be made to look—to
these yokels who made up the consensus of public
opinion.

With these in mind he said, tired but patient,
"All we require is that you satisfy your debts. To
those who've helped little some small token should
be given, each in just measure, while those who
have borne the brunt of your finagling should be

recompensed, obviously, in like proportion. Now, wait—" he cautioned, holding up a hand as Médders appeared about to jump from his pants. "You can treat everyone fairly and still have the lion's share left for yourself. You've only to form a company, float some stock—."

"An' find myself with the widders an' orphans! I ain't fallin' fer that," Charlie said with a sneer.

Jones considered him. "I rather imagine you will." Then he said sharp and clear: "Or do you want to be hailed into court to face that girl?"

"Girl!" Medders cried, staring about wildly. "*What* girl?"

"Is there more than one?" The banker said caustically, "I'm surprised you haven't been tarred and feathered."

Though Charlie waved clenched fists and, snarling, denied in opprobrious language even the faintest idea of what Jones was driving at, it was evident to all that this was nothing but bluster. The mean look of his eyes, the blotched cheeks, told the story.

"The choice," Jones said, "is yours; but if I have to I'll put Belita Storn on the stand and let her tell what happened to her out in those hills and down. . ."

But Medders, cursing, had already fled.

VIII

WITH HIS BURROS Medders spent the shank of that night in the mountains high above the robbers' roost men called Tucson, scowling at the jumble of flittery lights glowing like jewels from the ghostly dark that hid dusty streets and trash littered alleys. He'd been too upset to go back to his room for what was left of the money he had got from O'Toole. So filled with alarm at what the banker had said and by things implied, he had even come away without the supplies he'd gone in for.

He was still in a muddle of confused apprehensions as he watched gray dawn begin to creep up out of the east. Who could guess what kind of rotten deal a skunk slick as Jones might have talked that girl into! Or what lies she had told in the grip of ambitions put into her head by the banker's glib whoppers! According to McFarron she had already been tricked into handing Jones half of the half interest Charlie, in a kind of moon madness, had so impulsively given her.

He was caught in the tug of conflicting desires.

Every instinct honed by danger urged toward flight while the way was still open. Other notions, equally fierce and quite as bitterly compelling, made Medders reluctant to take to the brush while the banker—justified by frustrated creditors—proceeded to cut up Charlie's find and take over.

The bastard could get away with it, too! No one had to tell Charlie. With that girl on his side and the law in his pocket Jones could ride roughshod over Medders' objections, do just about anything he wanted with the property. Who was to stop him? He could marshal control of fifty percent. He could do just what he had said he would—form a company, float stock and, in Charlie's absence, juggle things around to suit himself. He could buy up the notes Charlie'd given those merchants, then sue for a judgment and use Charlie's shares to pay himself off with. There was no damned end to the things he might do.

When it came to skullduggery you had to stay up all night if you hoped to stay even with T.K. Jones!

Medders cursed in a passion and shook both fists.

This was why he'd pulled out of his run to wait here where he could see if the banker meant to have him followed. He couldn't believe Jones would pass up the chance, because without that girl could find her way back he didn't have nothing but a few lumps of ore and a pile of hot air.

Charlie had never filed on this claim, hadn't staked it out or recorded it, either. This was not, on his part, either laziness or ignorance.

He guessed he was pretty ignorant, come right

down to it. But he had known well enough the laws about claims and filing—sufficient anyway to want to keep clean away from them. The whole history of mining was crammed with litigations and the sad sad stories of guys like himself that had been jumped or frozen out.

To record his find—or so Charlie'd reckoned—would have been right down tantamount to handing Jones the means of taking it away from him. So long as the source of this ore stayed a mystery he had figured to be able to laugh at the man. But then that girl had come along half out of her noggin.

He'd had to stumble onto her and, because she'd seemed so young and helpless looking, he had let a natural pity get the upper hand of caution. After fetching her to the caves and getting her on her feet he had woke up one day to the fact that he was stuck with her. This had never had any part in his plans and, in the increasing disquiet of their close proximity, spooked by her transparent attempts to maneuver him into double harness, he'd been led into making the mistake of his life.

He had thought getting rid of her would be worth half his horde; had been glad to give it to her and gladder still when she'd rose to the bait and took off with that paper. Now it looked like he had been a damn fool.

His head was filled with a hodgepodge of things laced through with worries and premonitions of disaster. And behind everything else, buried deep but far from quiet, was the sour and restive knowledge that, in brass tacks fact, he had actually been *afraid* to put this find on record.

He reckoned if anyone ever got wind of it they would count him ready for a string of spools for sure. And sometimes, down in the dumps, he would wonder if maybe this wasn't the horrible truth. In such a frame of mind one time he'd yanked out his six-shooter staring like a ninny for upwards of an hour before, with a snort, he'd come out of it enough to go hunt up his jug.

Just the same, by grab, this whole deal was peculiar—and not just the ore with them palish green streaks that was stacked up like firewood clean across the far wall of that bottommost cavern. Even the caves themselves wasn't like no others he had ever been into. They was enough, by God, to give a man the shakes coming onto them like he had!

That top one had looked natural enough, even with the cabin and its padlocked door—until he'd got inside and discovered that windlass with the rope rotted off it. It wasn't until he'd happened to peer into the hole that he had spotted the hidden ladder and, driven by curiosity, had fashioned a pitchpine torch and gingerly crept down the thing to have himself a look.

Three levels opened off that shaft; he had used up most of a day poking around, going through each one as he came to it. He'd had trouble with the ladders which were in bad shape and crudely made to begin with. The lashings which bound the rungs to the uprights had apparently been fashioned from strips of rawhide and some of these were rotten, letting go under his weight several times to scare him mightily.

The first and second levels beneath the cabin

cave had been mostly given over to a series of chambers remindful of pictures he had seen of old castles, tiny dungeon-like cubicles hardly bigger than monks' cells with rusted chains bolted into the rocks and a stink coming off them that, while not exactly loud, wasn't anything a feller would care to sniff for very long.

As a matter of fact he hadn't been through either level again after his first trip down that bottom ladder. One gut-squeezing look in the light of his torch at the far wall of the cavern which composed the lowest opening, or lateral, had pretty near turned his legs weak as water.

Yellow, it was, like the three nearer walls but, unlike those, queer figures and outlandish designs had in some faroff time been daubed on it in red, possibly to conceal the presence there of plaster, and perhaps for a time it had. But now this was cracked and buckled with a great hole yawning just under the ceiling where the ore he'd fetched O'Toole had toppled to spill across the floor. That whole great wall was nothing but a fooler of plaster, five or six layers deep, layed up to hide the ore stacked like cordwood from floor to roof.

He had no way of guessing how long it had been there, but more was packed in behind the chunks that had fallen—at least two more stackings, and every bit of it jewelry rock!

Thinking back on it now as he watched the day brighten from gray to pink to fast-spreading gold, he felt reasonably sure what he'd got hold of was not, strictly speaking, a mine but hidden booty— buried plunder, and the federal government had laws about that.

Laws, if he could find a way around them, meant no more to Charlie Medders than they did to T.K. Jones. Laws was for other people; but nobody that had all his marbles was like to hand over a haul like this for any bunch of dang bureaucrats in Washington to squabble over. A man would *have* to be a fool to do a crazy thing like that!

Charlie, staring, cursed again. There was no sound of dogs, no sign of trackers. He had looked for Burks to have his Injuns out by this time. It didn't make sense Jones would let him get away without his greedy mind had fastened on something better; and the only thing Medders could think of was that stock-baited meeting the banker had called for one o'clock.

He clapped a hand to his brow, groaning aloud, reluctant to even consider going back, and yet . . . he couldn't stand the thought of being someplace else while the fate of what he had found was decided with no one to stand between himself and the poorhouse. Jones would pick him cleaner than a neck-wrung hen!

IX

Spurred by his apprehensions Medders got back to town well ahead of the meeting to find the streets seething in a froth of excitement. Slipping around to his room he stuffed into his pockets the rest of the cash he had got for his ore, caught up his pistol and then, by back alleys, hustled over to Fritchet's to pick up a sack of grain, just in case.

There was nobody around but the old man himself, half asleep in the shade on a tipped-back chair with his hat pulled over his face against flies.

"Well," he said, with a sour look at Charlie, "reckon you're off to join the stampede."

"What stampede?"

"Mean you ain't heard about them Injuns? Where the hell you been? Three diff'ent Papagos come in this mornin' with pieces of rock that was damn near pure silver. Whole town's gone loco! All the bar flies an' saddle tramps has took out for the mission with just about everything they could steal, beg or borrow. Talk about commotion!"

Medders, grinning, said, "Musta been some of that stuff I pitched away."

"I guess it must've," Fritchet said dryly. Then his swung-about stare became sharply probing. "Didn't I hear you'd made some kinda strike?"

Medders sniffed. "What's the chances of pryin' you loose of a sack of that grain you got stacked yonder?"

"Cash or credit?"

"Didn't figure my credit was good around here."

"It ain't," Fritchet said, not bothering to get up. But he mighty near tipped over his chair when Medders tossed a gold piece into his lap. Eyeing it askance he came onto his feet. "One be enough?"

"One's plenty," Charlie grinned, "an' you kin keep the change."

The old man insisted on helping him load; but the story was different when he got to Sol Warner's adobe-fronted mercantile. The place looked like a cyclone had hit it. "No, you can't!" Warner snapped. "Lookit them shelves—body'd think I been host to a convention of locusts! Picks, shovels, blastin' powder—even cleaned me out of rice an' flour! Hmm ... you're in luck," the merchant grunted, peering into a limp sack. "Seems I've still got a pound or two left. Beans, I mean. You fixed t' tote 'em this way?"

He reached out the sack and Medders, taking it, paid him.

"Wouldn't be surprised if you run into a mite of wind," Warner said, considering him slanchways. "Town dads was lined up outside the bank—"

"*Was!*"

"That's right. Sent Burks around with a change

of time and a fresh proposition. Said he'd buy up
your debts at full ledger value or, if stock was
voted, a man could have it in shares at four cents
on the—"

But Medders, wild of eye, was already half
across the street and moving faster with every leap.

He tore into the bank like a gust of brimstone,
sent Brass Buttons sprawling; but hauled up,
breathing hard, before Miss Winters' anxious
smile.

"Gracious!" she said worriedly, her gentian
glance darting up at the clock. "I think you'd better hurry. Mr. Jones held things up as long as he
could . . . Go right on in, Mr. Medders."

So it was *Mister* Medders now, Charlie noted,
but was not to be softsoaped by titles and smiles.
He went through the gate and flung open Jones'
door. Talk and the smoke of fifty cent cigars
swirled around him like a wave as he strode into
the crowd packed five deep about Jones' desk.

No one straightaway appeared to notice his presence and from the squabble of voices it was quickly
apparent not all of this bunch was wholeheartedly
happy with the way things were going. The
banker's tones cut abruptly through the bickering
gabble. "There you are, Mr. Tooper . . . forty-three
dollars and sixty-four cents. Now," Jones said,
clearing his throat and speaking briskly, "if there's
nobody else who wants to settle for cash, those
who have can depart and the rest of us will get
down to the business in hand."

His glance, sliding through the disgruntled
rumble of those going out, suddenly lit upon Medders and turned narrowly blank. But he was not

easily put out of countenance. "Well, Charles," he said through the clomp of feet and departing mumble, "I see you finally managed to get here," and coldly smiled as he gathered up and began squaring the edges of a considerable batch of papers left on his desk by Medders' paid-off creditors.

"Didn't figure," Charlie said, "you could git very far without me."

Behind this brave front there was a dismal wind blowing through his hopes as he eyed that bunch of bills in Jones' hands.

When Burks had got the leavers all herded from the room you could count the ones left and have fingers to spare. One was Burks himself who was lower, by Medders' reckoning, than the belly of a snake and had no more right to be among those present than a cow had with bloomers. It was plain Jones aimed for him to stay. The others—except the girl—were all persons of some consequence, like Ferris of Ores Amalgamated and old man Rawlins that owned the Boxed Bar T.

Jones got the meeting called to order and they all sat down in the chairs Burks fetched in, Ferris and Rawlins lighting up fresh smokes from the box passed around and then T.K., getting up behind his desk, put on his brightest smile. "All of us here know Charlie Medders, I guess, but you should also nod to Miss Belita Storn who, along with myself, has been one of Charles' partners in a rediscovered property from which these samples are fairly typical specimens. Mr. Burks will pass them around."

Medders didn't much care for a great deal of

that—the "rediscovered" bit particularly—but chewed down on his tongue to listen in stony silence to the astonished exclamations that followed the rocks around. Ferris, as Burks took them back to their keeper, peered sharply at Charlie, but kept his notions to himself. Rawlins, concerned for his range, stared glumly at his boots. It was Heintzleman—a mortician who kept among his boxes a cheap sideline of household furnishings—that demanded to be told where the specimens had come from.

"Glad you brought that up, Abe. This is the ore fetched in by those Indians that sent half the town stampeding for the Santa Cruz." Jones grinned at their startled looks and chuckled. "Our associate, Mr. Medders, is a great hand for jokes. There's nothing around that mission, I assure you, that Charles has not deliberately put there. It will buy us, I think, whatever time we'll need to locate the main ore bodies and have them filed on in the name of the Company."

The grudging looks of respect sent Charlie's way by these words lifted Medders' head and thawed much of his antagonism, being the first of the kind he'd ever got from these wallopers. Then his glance fell on the girl, turning sour as he remembered the purpose of this meeting. It put his back up again, bunched the muscles in his cheeks.

Rawlins, rolling the smoke across his teeth, grumbled, "How much capital will be needed to develop these claims?"

"We'll get to that presently. First thing we've got to do is form a company—we'd better have Miss Winters in," Jones said, pressing a buzzer. "Now, with regard to electing a head, unless someone has a better idea I think, inasmuch as this was Charles' discovery, it is certainly just and eminently proper he should be our first President—all in favor so signify by saying 'aye'."

"Aye!"

"Objection?"

Not a sound could be heard.

Medders, with his jaw hanging ludicrously open, was so completely astounded, so bewilderingly filled with the sanctified importance of so signal an honor being unanimously tendered by the town's mightiest moguls, that he was too choked up to speak.

Several of them grinned, two or three reached over to clap him on the back. Heintzleman, grabbing his fist, solemnly pumped it. By the time Charlie emerged from roseate visions and the enveloping warmth of brotherly love enough to become aware of what was going on, the company was formed and Miss Winters was reading back the names of those elected to hold office. Jones, it appeared, had been installed as Vice President. Heintzleman was Secretary, Rawlins was the Treasurer and Ferris, of Ores Amalgamated, was General Superintendent. An issue of preferred stock had been declared, of which each single share was to have a par value of one hundred dollars and they were ready now to vote as to whether or not common stock should be put on the market to finance development.

Medders, appalled, suddenly jumped to his feet. "Now just a dang minute! I dunno much about this business of stock, but—"

"I'll handle that end of it," Jones said smoothly. "All you have to do, Charles, is sit back and figure out some way to spend your profits. And that," the banker smiled, "should be occupation enough for even a man of your unbounded talent."

"Yeah. Well," Medders said, taking a long hard look at him, "I might not have got to the front row on figures but as President of this outfit I reckon I've got enough say to be heard."

"Certainly," Jones chuckled. "You go right ahead."

"Well, it's not goin' to cost all that much to git the ore out that we've got to come up with a stock sale t' do it."

"I'm surely relieved to hear that," Rawlins said, brightening somewhat.

"But the facts of the matter is," Ferris pointed out, "no big operation in this kind of thing ever figures to spend its own money on development." And Jones vigorously nodded. "It's not a business-like approach, and anyway," he added, mouth tightening around his smile, "it's not among the President's prerogatives to say how the Company's financial affairs—"

Medders said, interrupting: "I don't know much about company jobs, but it seems like a feller hold-in' fifty percent of an outfit's shares would have considerable—"

"Let's not put the cart before the horse," Jones said. "The handling of stock is my department. I'm afraid you're out of order. Perhaps we had better deal with first things first." He looked around for the Board's approval.

Medders, leaning over the table, growled, "I go

fer that. When you've got the stock ready to be passed out, hang your drawers in the winder an' we'll git together. Meetin' adjourned."

"Now see here," Jones cried, "we've had enough of your lip! You served your function when you uncovered this ore. Production—what we want and need now—requires abilities far beyond the scope and savvy of any shirt-tail, single-blanket jackass prospector! You going to argue that?"

Medders, too, was up on his feet, looking nervous and uncertain, half inclined toward bluster. "Just the same," he growled stubbornly, "it seems like to me a guy with fifty percent of a company's holdings—"

"That's exactly the point. When the shares are passed out you won't have but twenty-five, the same as Miss Storn and myself."

Medders stared. "I guess," he said, "I better straighten you out. I might be soft in the head but I ain't that soft. The only part of this find that don't belong t' me is that half interest I—"

"Perhaps you're forgetting something." Jones, grabbing up the sheaf of papers he had clipped together, strode around his desk to shake them under Charlie's nose. "The receipted notes for those debts you run up—remember? The bank took them in to save the Company embarrassment, but you needn't imagine I'm going to absorb them.

"Ferris and Rawlins—and Heintzleman, too— are entitled to stock. When the shares are divided the bank will turn these back to you in exchange for your surplus twenty-five shares, which the bank will then turn over to these gentlemen for cash in the amount paid out on your debts."

While they stood like that, fiercely glaring at

each other, Belita Storn, strangely pale in a wasp-waisted gown and feathered hat of burgundy velvet, sat twisting her hands with her eyes big as buckets.

Rawlins grinned, watching Charlie feel the turn of the screw. Even Ferris, though continuing to hold his face poker sober, must have counted those shares as good as tucked in his pocket.

"Go on," Medders grunted, "git the rest of it spit out."

A vague uneasiness tinged the banker's stare—a creep of puzzlement, too; but a glance at the girl appeared to bolster his faith, and again the sly smile commenced to tighten about his teeth. "That's it," he nodded. "That's all there is to it. Play square with us, turn over those shares, or explain to the court what went on out there between you and a child of Miss Storn's tender years, and how those chain scabs—"

Medders laughed. "Got it all figured out, eh?" He must have seen what a spot he was in, but "Go right ahead," he said, "an' see where it gits you. That jezebel's been dang handsome paid for whatever time she may have put in out there with me!"

"I think," Jones began, "when she tells her side of it—"

But Medders, already backing off, grinned sourly. "Sure, sure . . . be a lot of tears fall. Like to make me powerful hard to find, but don't you worry. When you've got your mine in that 'production' you mentioned just drop me a line an' I'll come right over. Meanwhile, I'm gittin' outa here —see?" and he banged one hand slapping down against his pistol.

Heintzleman cringed. The banker's face turned

livid. Rawlins, under that malevolent stare, looked ready to dive for the protection of Jones' desk.

Medders openly sneered. "Them that stays put won't require lamentations." Waving derisively he ducked through the door.

X

THERE WAS OBVIOUSLY much Charlie Medders
didn't know, but any kid in three-cornered pants
could have sensed this was no time to be lingering
in the environs of Tucson.

Jones would be after his scalp now for sure, and
wouldn't much care how he lifted it, either, so long
as it was probably the work of others and he could
see in the offing any reasonable chance of subse-
quently turning up the source of Charlie's ore.

Swearing at his burros, Medders struck out once
more toward the blue and gray shapes of the
Tucson Mountains, pelting his charges with rocks
to keep them humping. He was nursing no delusions as to how far Jones would go; about the
only thing Charlie could find on his side was the
certainty that, up to this point anyway, the banker
could not know precisely where this horde was hidden.

But there was danger in the fact that Belita Storn
had been there.

It didn't seem likely, by herself, that she could find her way back; but Jones and his cohorts, if they hadn't already, would soon worm out of her everything she could remember and, while in desert country one batch of hills looked pretty much like another, there were differences Apaches would have little trouble deciphering. Burks would have Injuns swarming all over, you could bet your old clay pipe on that.

He hadn't covered more than three-four miles when, scanning his backtrail from the vantage of a rise, he discovered dust and, eyes narrowing against the glare, presently made out the bent-forward shapes of three hard-riding horsebackers. They were hot on his tracks, no doubt about that. Without a glass he couldn't yet be sure of their identity, but the one in the lead had the build and look of Dry Camp Burks.

Medders, hotfooting after his burros, yanked loose his rifle from the ties of Begetta's pack and gave each of the beasts a double handful of grain while keeping one eye on the progress of the trio bent on running him to earth. If this were Burks, as he suspected, it was plain enough by the fact he'd fetched help the bank's removal expert wasn't taking this pasear just to exercise his horse.

They came on methodically, riding a high trot, quite apparently indifferent to Charlie's warlike preparations. About a mile away they broke apart, one cutting around to the north, one canting off into the south, the other—obviously Burks—keeping straight on. But just out of rifle range he stopped and swung down, watching his helpers completing their surround.

Medders, jacking a cartridge into the firing position, rested his rifle across the shelf of a boulder, adjusted his sights and settled back to wait.

Though matters more urgent nagged and scratched for his attention, Belita Storn in her fancy duds came big-eyed into his thinking, almost seeming as he recalled her now to be less than plumb happy with the turn things were taking. Probably regretting having brought such a grasper into this deal. She would not be the first to find Jones' charm wearing thin on closer acquaintance.

The demands of greed were hard to abide and the influence of power, with all its concomitant wants and drives, an abomination no real man could stomach; and the banker, at least by Charlie's lights, was no exception to this deplorable pattern. Every jasper within reach of his voice was expected, even compelled; to do precisely as T.K. ordered. Without you were a Rawlins or Ferris there was no other way to get along with the bugger. He was not the kind to tolerate free thought. You were for him or against him, and those who fell into the latter slot could expect short shrift and some pretty rough going.

Medders, baring his teeth, squeezed off a shot and watched Burks jump. He put his second slug closer, the third right on him. Then he dumped the pack off Begetta, scrambled onto her back and, as Jones' hardcase fled, went larruping after him. Time he got down onto the bottoms, however, Burks was just a departing dust.

Charlie watched that dust tear off east and pulled up, disgusted. There was no point running the hoofs off Begetta. To hell with a man that wouldn't stand and fight!

He peered around for the others, found they'd ducked out of sight like the coyotes they were. It was the way of their kind, hit and run, strike only when terrain and opportunity favored. Like a Injun—and maybe, by godfreys, that's what they were! Now he come to think of it, that one who'd cut south might have been old Pantsless Pete, the Papago tracker.

There was a way to find out, if you could lure him into it.

Turning back, Medders heeled Begetta up the ridge where Begat stood watch over the thrown-down pack. Getting off, Charlie replaced it and then, still toting his rifle, hazed both animals into a little known trail you'd have hardly believed even a goat could climb. These were slippery rocks scoured smooth by sand laden winds off the desert with a cliff to one side and fearful drops off the other. Someway the burros' sharp shod hoofs found purchase and Charlie, hanging on to Begat's stubby tail, was pulled along with them, sweating and cursing, shuddering each time a chunk of loose shale went clattering down out of sight far below.

By hard work Medders looked to rim out before dark. If Burks & Company didn't come sneaking after him Charlie figured to throw a circle and strike off for the cave across a windy stretch that by morning would show no more sign than a fly would leave on a crust of dry bread. Hell, why take chances with this bunch of drygulchers when his ore could be sold just as easy at Yuma or Phoenix!

It was well after six when they came out on a crest of bald rock and Medders, digging the glass

from his pack, squatted down for a long careful
look. He could see from this vantage San Xavier
del Bac and considerable activity between the
gypsum white of its structures and the tree-fringed
gorge of the Santa Cruz where that bunch of
Tucson loafers were busily gophering up the
ground. Off to the north another spread of dust
was inching along the Ajo trail bound straight for
the granite-ribbed slopes of this very peak, and it
was not being raised by any two-three hombres.

Bitterly counting dots, near as Charlie could figure there was upwards of fifteen rannies down
there slicking leather—a heap too many to be anything but a posse. And there was just one answer to
that. Jones had given his sheriff orders to fetch
Medders in.

After another ten minutes of trying to locate
Burks and that pair he had with him, it came over
Charlie suddenly their whole purpose in being out
here could be to effect a surround and drive him
into the arms of McFarron's deputies.

If this were true he had given that black-haired
pair time enough to get through and be waiting to
pick him up when he came out of the rocks, which
he would have to do if he was minded to cross the
Altar Valley, his original intention. The hills he
was bound for were hidden from here, west and
somewhat south, beyond the Baboquivaries, all
Papago country, rough and wild as a javelina.

He could work north from here—if Burks didn't
spot him—and drop down into the Avra Valley,
another arid stretch fifty miles off his course, and
from there, swinging south around the Roskruge
Mountains, reach the cave—if him or the burros

didn't give out first. But there was no water that
way, and the big fly here was the whereabouts of
Burks. It didn't have to follow that because he
couldn't spot Burks the bank's trouble-shooter was
under a like handicap. The ugly son of a bitch
could be watching right now!

It wasn't enough they had stolen his ore,
glommed onto that four hundred and more of
O'Toole stingy cash he'd been forced to pitch into
the banker's hat—they had to whipsaw him out of
the whole shebang and, when that hadn't worked,
drive him into the rocks!

Fury yanked back his lips in the snarl of a
cougar. If it was fight they wanted he would give
them a bellyful!

Reloading his rifle, the sixteen pound Sharps
that could knock a man kicking at a thousand
yards, he sent Begat and Begetta grumbling over
the divide and in a lathering froth of self pity and
outrage started recklessly down the mountain's far
side, muttering and mumbling like a pulque drunk
squaw.

These tumbled west slopes—blood red in the
rays of the near-vanished sun, the top rind of which
still thrust a lighthouse arc across the jagged scarp
of Dobbs Buttes towering above the far sea of the
desert's darkening floor—were but lightly clad
with a gnarled growth's stubble, offering only spo-
radic chances of concealment. But Charlie, in a
mood to welcome violence, pressed on uncaring as
a prodded bull.

The rocks over here were still hot to the touch,
sun glare flittering and flashing from their slants,
the roasted air still as stove lids. If they were over

here they would probably spot him—there was just
this one trail down from where he'd been. There
was no good grousing at what couldn't be helped.
You couldn't hide the clop and clatter. The big
thing now was to get into the sand drifts where he
had some prospect of losing the banker's minions
and where, once night fell, no glass could spy him
out.

The roundabout brush and rocks turned blue-
gray as the sun fell suddenly behind black buttes
and, partway down, Medders stopped long enough
at a cliffside seep pawed from the shale by mountain wildlife to let his burros tank up while he
threw off their packs, afterwards letting them roll
and stretch before, reloading, he again choused
them on.

He kept sharp watch but in the curdle of shadows found nothing to alarm him. That posse, ere
now, had likely got through the pass, but it wasn't
McFarron's crowd that bothered him. They'd be
just average fellers that could be scraped up any-
place, counter jumpers and maybe a merchant or
two, pieced out with whatever ranch hands had
happened to be available. It was the whereabouts
of Burks and his two long-haired partners that was
keeping Charlie's hide filled with prickles and
itchings. Them was the kind a man had to look out
for.

Still raking the gloom with hard stabs of his
glance Medders followed his charges off the last
shelves of detritus and on toward the final outcrops
of rock that, here, toadlike crouched against the
darkening night.

The wind was coming up now, whistling in off

the desert. It would be good to get back and hole-up in his cave; and he was able to let down a little just thinking of it. This being keyed up all the time was no good. Be smarter, probably, to leave the damned ore where it was and keep riding; and if he hadn't been crowded so much maybe he would have, he told Begetta, watching her flop her ears in the dark. But it was too late for that. To ride off now, after the way he'd been treated, was more than a man of spirit could abide, knuckling under to a bunch of paid gunnies, tucking his tail like the rest of these yahoos every time Jones saw fit to stamp a boot. *Somebody* had to take a stand against those buggers!

With Begat in the lead and Charlie tugging the fractious Begetta—knee deep in the tantrum she generally threw whenever she was hungry or worked beyond her quota—they forged into the gale with nothing beyond that last reef of rock but the dark and wind-tossed wastes of the desert.

Begat, abruptly snorting, threw up his head and whistled like an elk. About to whirl he coughed and dropped. Medders, ducking, heard the crack of a rifle. Begetta, tail up, went past like a cat streaking over a tin roof as Charlie, palming his six-shooter, emptied it about him and, yelling like a Comanche, took to his heels.

XI

THAT BLAST OF wild fire he'd flung into the night may well have been all that saved Charlie's bacon. At least it had pinned the bushwhackers down for what time he'd used getting past those rocks and into the wind driven howl of the desert.

A man had to fight just to catch his breath in the swirl of grit whipped up off these drifts, but there was this much about it: in this screaming dark that was thicker than gar soup laced with tadpoles no one was going to match him up with a bullet without he got turned around and went blundering into them. Or into those horsebackers McFarron had hunting him.

He hated losing Begat, but he hadn't much time to get worked up about it, having all he could do to keep hold of Begetta. Now that her recent fright was forgotten the great bulk of her energy was being devoted to displaying her displeasure. She didn't *like* being hauled into the teeth of such a gale, did everything she could to make Charlie's progress as difficult as possible, twisting and jerking, grunting and trying to plant her feet against his intention—even so, finally, practically sitting on her haunches. Which was when, fed to the gills, Medders went for her with the rope's end.

Snorting with surprise the startled burro sprang erect in considerable haste. *Prowww!* she exclaimed in unmistakable outrage. But when her master, with peeled-back lips, shook out his rope she stood not upon the order of her going but, with gritted teeth and tucked-in tail, went stomping ahead with flattened ears.

Bucking the scour of those sandblasting gusts was no joke in all conscience, but it was better than a bullet, Medders figured, wallowing after her. And a hell of a sight better than being forced to choose between surrendering the location of his cache or going to jail on the trumped-up charges of that ungrateful jezebel—her and that banker! There was two of a kind for you!

He found it hard to understand people like that. Ready to do anything, just so it showed a profit!

He pushed along with what speed he could, knowing from much experience of this region the worst of the blow probably wouldn't last much over a couple of hours. The more ground they could cover before beginning to leave tracks the better. In fact, Charlie concluded after much weighing of possible courses, it might turn out to be smarter not to head for the cave.

Crossing this stretch of the Avra was likely to take the best part of the night and no guarantee of being under cover then. Once the sun got up, and with no sand blowing, it might be possible with a glass for someone back there in the mountains to get a line on them—just to catch a flash of movement would be all a guy sharp as Burks would need.

Deciding he'd best not risk it, Medders let Begetta drift a bit to the left, more into the east if there'd been any east to see. This allowed her to feel she was putting something over; it threw the wind on their flank, making for faster and easier travel.

The valley was narrower off in that quarter. In addition to offering a shorter trek to cover, it held the added attraction of dropping any sign they might eventually leave in a region Burks and his redskins could prowl to their hearts' content.

Might even carry them to Sombrero Butte or, beyond, up into the Twin Buttes country, which was all right with Charlie. This was south of the mission, and he knew for a fact there was considerable float all through those hills.

Burks might very well pick up some chunks, wedding him to the natural and erroneous conviction he was hot on the trail of his quarry's hidden lode. While the hue and cry was raging off there Charlie and Begetta, having swung west again, could be following the San Juan, later dropping south to slip through the Baboquivaries and move leisurely north up their western flanks to come at his cache without one chance in a hundred of tipping their hand.

The only risk was water. They'd be cooked sure enough if they couldn't find water. But in mountain country, if you knew what to look for, you nearly always could. He wasn't worried about that; in fact, the prospect was so pleasing he had a couple good belly laughs picturing Burks and those poor damn Injuns.

The wind continued vigorously to pummel, lash and tug at them. He had never known it so belligerent or persistent. Once, slapped out of his thoughts by its fury, he found it nipping at his heels. This time, alarmed, he lit into Begetta with the lead shank as well. "Just like a goddam woman!" he railed. "How many times does a jasper have t' tell you?" He raised his voice in a yell. "You go shyin' off again, by grab, I'll put you straight into it!" He gave her another taste of the rope and climbed onto her then to make sure she remembered.

Perhaps he dozed. Next thing he knew—at least the next time he noticed—she was stone-still stopped and peering back at him reproachful.

Medders jerked up his head.

The damn wind had quit. He guessed it was still short of morning but nowhere near as dark as it had been—nor was this all. He could remember closing his eyes against the grit but he could not recall any slackening of the gale. There was something just ahead, looming up through the murk like . . . well, it *looked* like a wall . . . probably a cliff or a butte. Begetta had apparently pulled into the lee. . . .

He looked again, legs clamping.

It *was* a wall. With a kind of sick horror it came over him he was staring at the rear of Fritchet's stable. He was back in town! Turned around by that storm he had come full circle.

XII

MIGHTY INFREQUENT had the buffetings of fate ever caught Charlie Medders without some kind of comeback; but, honest to John, the crumpling weight of this latest disaster sat so heavily on him he could not even cuss.

He couldn't stay here. And no one but a idjit would think to head back into that desert, crawling like it was with T.K. deputies and gunslingers.

Clutched by panic, held fast by facts, Medders hunkered there gulping like a buzzard too gorged to get off the ground.

There were other ways open—he didn't *have* to head west. Off north were the Santa Catalinas and, beyond, still more mountains. Northeast were the Rincons and Galiuros and, straightout east, the Dragoons, Winchesters and Dos Cabezas. There was no lack of hideouts if a man could reach them.

Stepping back he stood bitterly considering Begetta. Her spraddle-legged stance showed how far he'd get on *her*; and that stack of grain he'd

bought off Fritchet had someway got torn open
and was now plastered to her like a wrung-out rag.
If he could get a horse from Fritchet . . .

He thrust a hand in his pocket and groaned. The
weight of what coins he'd departed this town with
had brought on a hole, and past experience with
the liveryman did not encourage pinning hope on
credit.

A search of his other pockets turned up one
crumpled handkerchief, twenty-five hand-loaded
shells for the Sharps and eight pistol cartridges for
the shot-dry gun tucked into his waistband.

And it was getting light fast.

He stripped his gear off Begetta and turned her
loose. She didn't move from her tracks, just huddled there, head hanging, looking woebegone and
friendless as Charlie felt himself.

They had sure as hell come to a fine pass, he
thought. Glaring about wildly, he wondered if he
could slip back up to his room.

A dog barked somewhere while Charlie, cring-
ing, desperately dredged up the names of his most
likely acquaintances. There wasn't one he could
think of who might cross up Jones to help him.

He edged along the wall as breath-held and fluttery as though at any moment he figured to step on
a cat, hoping the stable's back door had not been
fastened. But, arrived before it in the graying
gloom, envisioning the uproar that would be
loosed if he were discovered, try as he would he
couldn't bring himself to touch it. There were
horses in some of those pens off yonder but
Fritchet was the kind who slept with one eye open
and a sawed-off at his elbow.

It was plain he had to do something, and quick.

Going to be plumb light inside another half hour. If he hadn't squeezed into some hole before then he could wind up dead in the trash of some alley.

It wasn't Burks so much that he was scared of now but the crazy damn talk that would be flying around about him feuding with Jones, and the way McFarron's posse would sure as hell come into this. Be plenty of trigger-happy jaspers around that might think to curry favor by knocking him off. Guys had turned up dead before in this town!

He wasn't at all keen for stepping out into that street. He took a good look first, up one side and down the other, not liking any part of it. Next door there were two vacant lots or maybe three; beyond, however, both sides were packed solid, buildings cheek by jowl and even closer, business establishments all the way clean to Main where the bank's watchtower turret starkly rose above the town's false fronts.

Tucson's climate rarely produced mist but the curdled shadows, like dirty fleece, seemed to crawl in weaving swirls and stringers, almost alive. Every open place was choked with the stuff—thin like smoke writhing away as a man advanced. Like a mirage, Charlie thought, nervously shivering in this pre-dawn gloom.

Shoulders hunched and hat pulled low he struck off obliquely across the vacant lots, aiming behind these marts of trade to come into the back streets given over to homes, hoping among such countrified parts to come onto some empty house or barn. If he could just find somewhere to drop out of sight till night came again to enlarge his chances. . . .

At least these places had more space between

them, but it was graying up faster with each passing moment. He was two streets over from Fritchet's already and no sign of anything a man might crawl into. He didn't dare run. There was a barn up ahead with weeds grown around it and a couple of boards off the side that looked enough abandoned to maybe make do.

He swerved toward it, then stopped. He scrubbed the sweat from his eyes and peered again at the house and fence beyond. A white and green frame, newly painted by the look; something about it tugging fierce but calling up nothing he could put a finger on. Still toting the Sharps he stepped gingerly into the barn's musty dark, thankful he didn't have to hunt for a door.

It was quiet in here as a tubful of grass and Charlie stood, stiff with listening waiting for his eyes to grow adjusted to the gloom. Something moving outside was snuffling around in the weeds. Clamped to his rifle Charlie stood without breathing, expecting any moment to be discovered. But no alarms exploded, no shout went up. It got so still he could hear his goddam heart.

The place was thick with dust and cobwebs. Old lumber lay stacked in one corner, gray and bowed with time and warp. Three box stalls, empty except for tatters of straw, and on the far side a great closed door and a closed smaller one built into one corner. Several scraps of rusty harness hung from pegs against one wall. Two lengths of baled hay lay gray with dust and folds of spider web near the middle of this ramshackle shell. Charlie finally moved over, gingerly perched on one of them, cradling the Sharps across his lap.

"Well!" a female voice said abruptly. "What are *you* doing here?"

Medders, jerked to his feet, peered apprehensively about. Neither door had been opened. Not a soul was in sight, but through the hole in the siding he could see gray sand and the green of weeds; by this he knew another morning had begun. But all remained so quiet he began presently to wonder if he had really heard the words or, dozing, only imagined them.

He was not long in doubt. "Come on, now . . . I'm not going to hurt you," she coaxed.

Charlie's glance stabbed wildly at the barn's four corners, from their obscurity skittering panicky to the place in the wall where the boards had fallen off. Begetta, ears cocked, stood peering in and back of her, coolly considering him across the burro's tawny shoulders, was the inscrutably handsome face of Miss Winters.

Medders loosed a shaky sigh. He understood now what had gripped him outside when he'd spotted that house with its white picket fence—the old Winters place that her father had left before he'd shuffled off and Imogene, to feed herself, had gone to work in Jones' bank as private scribe and sweet-talking watchdog to the man's inner sanctum.

While they stared at each other through the stickery stillness Charlie reckoned he could hardly have gotten deeper into the fat had he camped on the doorstep of T.K. himself. With Jones, at least, he could have put up a scrap, but faced with the elegant Imogene Winters a guy was tied to the mast, left not even the solace of swearing.

"I rather imagined you were in there," she said. "What really eludes me is what you thought . . . Well! The whole town knows Begetta. If you were hoping to hide—"

"How'd I know the dang fool was out there! I expect," Charlie growled, "you're goin' to have to turn me in?"

"All those men . . . it *is* a bit expensive. What would you suggest?"

Medders' jaw fell open. Miss Winters smiled and, when his look turned suspicious, loosed a tinkle of silvery laughter. "I suppose you are feeling pretty sorry for yourself. You mustn't judge everyone in the light of T.K. You did make him look pretty silly, you know."

"You mean . . ." Charlie swallowed like he doubted his hearing.

"He is pretty worked up over you, I'll admit." She stood silent then, lips slightly parted, tip of pink tongue thoughtfully crossing the lower one. "Actually, you've no need to hide out—"

"No need!" Charlie gasped. "What about Burks an' them Injuns! An' that dadburned posse!"

She said, "Perhaps I'd better get under cover," and stepped out of his sight. Before he could gather enough spit to swear, the smaller door opened and she came into the barn, Begetta rather gingerly stepping in after her. "Burks and those deputies were just to keep you hopping around until he has this business fully organized and rolling."

Charlie couldn't peg that, was so mixed up by this time he couldn't have recognized dung from wild honey. He stood there goggling like he was short on his marbles count. "You mind trampin' that trail again?"

"The new venture," she said. "The company they've organized to exploit your find. I'd no idea there was so much to do ... machinery to be bought and transported, drills, blasting powder—such a miscellany of equipment. We were all there working till almost one o'clock last night. I would never have guessed a mine required—"

"But there *ain't* no mine!" Medders cried, exasperated. "Alls I've got ..."

Her smile cut him off. "You can't keep a thing big as this off the street—T.K. said so himself. The whole town was in an uproar, especially after Father Eusebio told us those pieces of ore his Papagos brought in were chunks you'd thrown trying to scare your burros out of his corn." She said as though it were a pity: "T.K., of course, had to give it to the papers. I suppose by now they've put the story on the wire—"

"*What* story?"

She peered at him, astonished. "Why ... about you uncovering the old Weeping Widow that's been lost all these years. Well, he had to tell them *something*," she declared with a flash of defiance for what she saw in his face.

Her look changed, though, when Medders, flinging down his hat, began to guffaw like a loony. "Is that what he told 'em? That I found the Weepin' Widder?"

Mis Winters' eyes seemed a little uneasy. "You *did* find it, didn't you?"

"Hell, no! Alls I've got is a cache of stacked ore

some bunch of highgraders went an' buried in a cave!"

Miss Winters cringed as though she'd been struck; but whether this was caused by his language or its import was not apparent. With shock still in her stare she said, rising determinedly above it: "T.K. had your number, all right. He said you would try to upset everything. But they've allowed for your spleen—this dog in the manger attitude. Once the operation is down on the books it will be money in the bank no matter how loud you shout."

"Got it all figured, hey?"

She considered him belligerently. "T.K. believes in the fact accomplished. You're not the first desert rat he's been involved with; he knows how obstinate and unreasonable prospectors can be, always stirring up trouble, haggling over every move."

She seemed to catch herself, drew a long shaky breath. "I shouldn't be talking like this . . . I can't think what has come over me." She caught a lip between white teeth, eyes nearly hidden behind the cover of dark lashes. "Practically *trading* with the enemy."

Medders got the message. "Ever think of swappin' sides?"

"But wouldn't that be disloyal?" Her eyes seemed suddenly big as buckets. "I mean, a girl does have to look out for herself, but . . ."

"Shucks," Charlie said, "there ain't no buts about it. *You* ought t' know how these big moguls operate. In business today it's every wolf fer himself." He let her digest that, then said quick and easy: "Be worth a little somethin' fer me t' know what's in them minutes. After all, I guess you could say I *founded* the Company. I got a right t'know, ain't I?"

"Well, but . . ."

She was plainly wavering. "Miss Winters—" he broke off.

A timid, half scared bit of smile was on her lips. "W-wouldn't you rather call me 'Ginnie'?"

Medders noticeably gulped. But a man had to strike while the iron was hot. Clambering over his alarm he grumbled, "You bet . . . Ginnie. Now, look . . . as the duly elected boss of this outfit I oughta know what was decided after I walked out —I wanta see them minutes."

"They're locked in the safe."

"You took notes, didn't you?"

She said, shaking her head: "T.K. wouldn't like it."

"How's he goin' t' find out?"

She searched his face, dubious. Charlie patted her shoulder. For a clincher he said, "If there was somethin' you liked an' I could manage t' git it . . ." and grinned at her, waiting.

She stood twisting her fingers and, not looking at him, blurted: "A s-share in the C-Company?"

Charlie's grin got a little brittle.

What the hell! he told himself. If it came to a vote he was up the crick anyway if Jones went ahead and split this up like he'd threatened. A feller needed to know what that scissorbill was up to, somebody on the inside to *keep* him in the know. These shares didn't mean a goddam thing without that bunch found out where the ore was. And he sure wasn't about to tell anyone that!

He gave her the nod. While she scooted to the house to fetch her squiggles he cast up in his head the percentages Jones had pushed as a basis for dividing up the Company shares. Belita, Jones and Charlie, it appeared, would account in equal amounts for 75% of the Company's control, the remaining 25 to be distributed between Ferris, Rawlins and that bootlicking Heintzleman.

If that was the way it was going to be sliced, another share more or less wouldn't make any difference. A blind mule could see he was already staring down the throat of the gun, his equity whittled to a measly quarter interest, and no say at all when it came to setting up policy. As general superintendent Ferris would be in charge of production which, in actual practice, would mean the whole works—cave, ore, and all the rest of the tangible assets, with Jones in control and Medders, who had made it all possible, nothing but a name at the top of the sheet.

It was enough to cramp rats; but, wild as it was, Charlie still held the joker—the hugged-closed knowledge of the source of the ore on which this whole deal was predicated. He didn't see how they were going to get around that and, bad debts or no, it was a pretty big stick—the club he figured would get back his fifty percent.

So when Miss Winters returned with her book of notes, rather than admit his backwardness at reading, he found a blank page, handed the book back, and told her to dash off an order on the Company instructing Jones to turn over one share of Medders' interest in said Company to her, after which he took the pencil and laboriously scrawled his name.

"Now," he said, sleeving the sweat off his cheeks, "you flip through them laundry marks an' say what's been done. Just the facts—never mind the whereases an' wherefores."

It took them ten minutes to get through the orders for miscellaneous equipment, the gangs to handle it and put down a road, the drilling and mucking, timbering, hauling, and the staggering maze of detailed other services projected by the quorum of Board members Charlie had walked out on. Then the shares were brought up and passed out to those present, and right about there Medders lunged to his feet.

"Passed out!" he shouted, grabbing off his hat. "Hell's fire—how *could* they? Ain't been enough time even to hev any *printed!*" And he glared so fierce Imogene shrank back, eyes like scorched holes in the bedsheet pallor of her pulled-tight cheeks.

Yet it was not fright which made her peer at him so—or perhaps it was, a little. Mostly, however, this was caused by distaste, a patrician repugnance for the crudity of him, his offensive language, the reckless ever-churning tendency she felt in him toward violence.

To all of these she was bitterly opposed, by rearing and environment as well as natural inclination; and, despite the willowy, sweet-smelling daintiness of figure and presence for which the bank had hired her, she had that hard core of stubbornness which comes of handling facts.

Looking down her nose she said clearly and sharply: "You are wrong about that. T.K.'s been way ahead of you. The share certificates, needing only the signature of the Secretary Treasurer, were already printed and in the drawer of his desk when you left in such a dudgeon. Anticipating your reaction, knowing the Board would almost certainly approve the floating of a stock issue to be sold the general public, it may astonish you to know he had those ready, too; they'll be offered through the Exchange as soon as the wire service stories have encouraged a proper demand."

Like the kiss of death her smile curled around him; and then, still hugging her notebook with the page he had stupidly signed, she was gone.

XIII

IT TOOK SEVERAL moments for Medders to realize
the implications wrapped up in her disclosures.
What he grasped straightaway was that once again
the banker had got the best of him. It wasn't until
he'd gone over her remarks the third or fourth time
that he began to glimpse the full scope of T.K.'s
triumph. It came over Charlie then how neat he'd
been set up to catch the whole blame and direst
penalties of the law if this swindle they were
launching ever happened to get caught up with.

That it *was* a swindle he could no longer doubt.
Jones had been so anxious to get that stock on the
market he'd had the certificates printed before the
Company was organized. He hadn't cared a snap
of the fingers whether what Charlie'd found was a
mine or just another damn hole in the ground. All
he'd actually needed was those four sacks of ore
Charlie'd sold O'Toole, and that court order he'd
had McFarron serve, impounding them, had given
him ready access. By now they were probably being

shipped in dribbles and dabs all over the goddam country, specimens to tie in with those rushed-to-press stories crediting Medders with rediscovering the fabulous Weeping Widow all the featherbrains had been hunting for upwards of who knew how long! Then Jones had made him head of the Company so his name, as president, could be plastered on all the come-ons and letterheads!

Jones sure enough had him by the short hairs this time. It was the worst damn bind he had ever stumbled into; and when his assessment of the situation reached this conclusion he took the route of panic, jumped aboard his burro and, before the hour was out, was flogging Begetta deep into the raging winds of the desert.

This was wild rough country with nobody in it but coyotes and jackrabbits, tarantulas, scorpions and suchlike, but he still had his Sharps tight-clenched in his hand and was of a mind now to use it on the first two-legged varmint that showed.

He was through with towns. A honest man didn't have no more chance than a snowball in hell trying to abide by Christian principles among the scribes and Pharisees you found in control of the marts of trade. Out here a man had a halfway chance, and a gun made everyone equal.

Medders lost himself in the heart of the storm and when it blew itself out his mind was made up. Jones and his stooges had rigged the deck. With his name and his ore they had everything stacked to make a big killing. All that machinery and other equipment so brazenly detailed in the Company minutes didn't mean that they had it or ever would

—except on paper. It would make a prospectus look awfully good to the widows and orphans and the rest of the suckers.

Hell! nobody had appointed Charlie their keeper. He was through batting *his* head against a stone wall! He peered around, got his bearings, and struck off north, hauling Begetta drag-footed after him. He had two big cans of water buried close and, soon as the moon got properly up, he reckoned to find them. It was all right to talk, but deep in his bones Medders knew mighty well he had not yet heard the last of that banker.

No matter how much they grossed with their fraudulent stock, Jones and his cohorts would never be satisfied. They would always be wondering if he *did* have a mine, and sooner or later they'd take steps to find out.

Well, a man had no recourse against such vultures in town, but out here things were different. A good man with a rifle could get a run for his money.

Let 'em bring on their Injuns! Nobody knew this wild country like he did. He could live off land where them town sports would starve, and one of these times—soon's he got around to it—he'd take off a few days and put in some more of these tin-can springs . . . just in case.

As for that swivel-hipped Ginnie, she could have her share and welcome. The more he saw of women, by grab, the better he liked their four-legged sisters. With a burro a man knew where he was at, but a woman was just another name for trouble.

And he went grumbling on, swearing and snarling at the way he'd been taken, telling himself that if he had it to do over he'd have emptied some hats before he lit out. And he would sure as hell do it if any of that bunch ever got up the nerve to come snooping around!

He spent a cold night with nothing to put over him or inside his belly. Begetta wasn't partial to it, either, and was not averse to letting him know it. He finally had to tear a couple strips from his shirt tail and stuff them in his ears before he could get any sleep.

It was well after six when the dadburned critter, egged on no doubt by her empty gut, nuzzled him out of his uneasy dreams. Sore eyed and tousled from his bout with the winds Charlie, aching and miserable, pushed up with a curse.

He took a long look around. Then, hawking and spitting, he sluiced out his throat from the can they'd dug up, took a grimacing swig for the good of his tapeworm, gurgled some into his hat for Begetta, reburied the rest and caught up his rifle. Squinting again over the far swell of drifts he gave Begetta the nod and, with a scowl for the scoured-clean brightness of the day, morosely struck out after her.

Inside two hours it was uncomfortably hot. Before mid-morning they were out of the wind belt and into a region of sparse vegetation, none of it tall enough to throw any shade—greasewood and yucca, patches of prickly pear, Spanish dagger spikes. He peeled a few purple pears that were bitter enough to pucker a pig's mouth. He offered some to Begetta, watched her lip them suspiciously, make a horrible face and go snorting away. He managed to get down the rest of them himself after knocking out the seeds, but as a breakfast he found them pretty puny for a fact.

Distant hills began to shimmer and writhe in the furnace-dry heat, the mountains behind them turning gray as smoke through the interlacing film. The glare became ferocious; but three hours past noon wolf's candle appeared with its thorny gray wands and occasional vermillion blossom, and sparse clumps of grass began to fringe the climbing swells. Soon they were in better country, following a draw up into higher ground; the yucca fell behind and stunted mesquites began to rear their gnarled trunks. Begetta, with quickening steps, was already crossing a spur up ahead before Medders spotted the outcrop he'd been hunting.

Now he could hear the burro scrambling up his private trail. The way rose slowly and with deceptive ease, but after the first bench it struck a steeper pitch, and from there on up it became one sharper slant piled on top of another. And there was wind up here among these treacherous rocks, sharp sudden gusts that could slam a man straight out into space. He gained another bench, somewhat better than halfway up and, tottering into the lee of a house-sized boulder, flopped down to rest, too goddam beat to go another foot.

But presently, after his muscles quit jumping and he got back some of his breath, he pulled himself up and took another long glower out over the country they'd just crawled out of. And again he cursed Jones, thinking bitterly of Begat and the loss of his glass, and of three or four things he would like to see happen to Dry Camp Burks.

So far as he could see there was no sign of

pursuit. Now that T.K. had things going his way he had probably called off his gun thrower and ordered McFarron's posse home.

Still muttering and mumbling Medders resumed the climb to his cave. He'd take another look there, but he guessed—for a while at least—he could let down a little and not expect every moment to have to cut and run or be ducking a blue whistler. Nothing wore a man down quicker than that kind of thing, and except for the way it would have made him look he might have seriously considered packing up and pulling out. No damned ore, not even silver rich as this, was worth getting killed for!

But next morning things looked different. Food and a good night's sleep had driven most of the daunsiness out of him. Whistling cheerfully, he fried up a breakfast of sow belly liberally seasoned with frijoles and chili peppers which he afterwards washed down with java hot from the can in which he had boiled it, strong enough to float a he-kangaroo.

He further relaxed in the fragrance of Durham and, when this was finished, climbed up to the cave mouth where, concealed by a tangle of manzanita, he considered again the dun miles spread below. His perch looked over some real desolation, a vast panorama of sunlit sand, here and there dappled by the dark thrust of mountains. But, pick and pry as he would and did, his hawklike stare could not raise one dust that was not stirred by some vagary of wind. It was a peaceful scene, quiet as two six-shooters in the same belt.

He got up presently, climbed around some more rocks and peered down into the wild hay trap. Hav-

ing satisfied himself he need have no worries about
Begetta, who was dozing hipshot in the shade of a
beanless mesquite, he went back in the cave, dug
up a spare candle, put on his miner's cap and began
a cautious descent of the reinforced ladders which
brought him, after some seven or eight minutes,
into the chamber where he'd found that cache of
what he still considered to be stolen highgrade.

He got a hammer from his pocket and walked
around tapping walls. Every blow rang solid. He
found no evidence at all that might indicate even
the remotest possibility of blocked-up passages or
other hidden hoards. He would have liked to believe this *was* an old Spanish mine, but it seemed
pretty obvious it was nothing of the sort.

He knocked loose more ore from the place he'd
got the rest of it, digging back of what was already
exposed to uncover another layer of equally rich
specimens. But when, excited, he lifted several of
these out in the hope there might be more, all he
found for the bother was a wall of solid granite.
Though he widened the hole to a full yard across,
each chunk removed uncovered nothing but more
granite. The ore had not been extracted from that.
It wasn't even the same color.

Medders, however, being human, was disap-
pointed. That talk Jones had started kept gnawing
at his thinking like a pack of hungry rats. Common
sense told him the talk was nothing but sucker bait,
part of that bunk T.K. had fed to the papers to
stimulate demand for the worthless stock they pro-
posed to foist on the public. Just the same he
reckoned, peering cynically around, another pasear
along those echoing corridors in the number 2 and

3 levels should settle the matter one way or the other.

He took another hard look at that torn-open wall. Three layers of this kind of stuff from floor to ceiling—even at the prices you had to take from a fence—wasn't nothing to be sneezed at. Well over a hundred thousand dollars' worth for certain.

Returning to the well shaft he started up the ladder. Peering into the blackness of that number 3 level he stood a while, scowling, remembering that series of tiny dungeon-like cubicles with the rusted chains bolted into the rock and the stink swirling round that made a man want to puke. He wasn't at all sure he cared to prowl the length of them again. Yet he hated to think of settling for the ore already stacked if there was any chance of this being a mine.

He left the shaft, reluctantly advancing into the black horror of this noisome passage whose shadows gave way like cornered beasts before the sizzling carbide arc of his lamp. Pistol gripped in sweaty palm, ears stretched, mouth breathlessly open, Charlie shuddered to a stop beside the first cell he came to. He knew from memory they were all alike, open faced and bare, yet forced his jumpety nerves to go on and so arrived, as he had that other time at gallery's end, against the same rough surface of cinnamon rock.

Crouched there, peering, he did a sudden double take.

This wasn't granite! Reaching out he touched the wall's raspy feel, backing hastily off to swap the pistol into his other hand while directing the lamp on his twisting head into the nearest of those dingy crypts.

It looked like the rest, rusty chain and all. He hardly glanced at the chain. It was the rock that held his bugged-out stare, the dull ginger rock from which these cubicles had been hewn.

He had previously imagined these caves to have been the habitat or ceremonial chambers of some prehistoric tribe long gone and forgotten. But now, with Jones' talk banging through his mind, he was vibrantly aware of pale greenish veins he had not noticed before in the stone which had been left to form the cell partitions. The same greenish tinge O'Toole had marked in that ore!

His daunsy fears abruptly lost in the rush of this new excitement, Medders put the gun away and got the miner's hammer out of his pants and struck the partition a ringing blow. Then, head bent to get the lamp up close, he considered the place with burning eyes; and with pounding heart spun around, breathing hard, to crash his hammer against the ungiving rock that formed the passage's end. Again, and furiously again, he struck that cinnamon wall, finally stepping back to peer exultantly at the flaked-off lines which now disclosed a hidden door.

A rock slab it was, smoothly fitted without handle or knob, adamant as steel against the maul of his hammer, counterbalanced probably to swing on some concealed pivot could a man but find the release that triggered it.

Soaked with sweat, breathing hard, Charlie traced the cracks with trembling fingers, finding no give to the thing at all. Without he could locate the mechanical impulse—the something to be pushed or pulled or whatever—he might have to use dynamite. He could not believe this snug fit had been managed and then caulked with caliche and brushed with mud just to hide a few pots.

"More to it than that," he was telling himself when the lamp on his cap began to splutter.

He grabbed it off and furiously shook it. The light, brightening briefly, commenced despite his best efforts to grow steadily dimmer. Swearing, he dug out his candle, breaking three matches before the wick fired. His sweat turned cold as the monstrous black like some fungoid fog, edging balefully nearer, reduced his vision to the lonely isolation of the candle's feeble flame.

Drawing back uneasily into the angle of the wall, Charlie nervously considered going up for more carbide and maybe bringing down a couple of sticks of Number 1. But as his dubious glance swung once more to assess the stubborn look of this rock the short hairs rose on his neck like hackles. The two vertical cracks exposed by his hammer seemed . . . *Yes!*

The slab was moving!

Every muscle congealed in the nightmare grip of horrid fascination immobilizing him, Medders breathlessly watched the great stone slowly, ponderously, revolve on its axis with no more sound than tumblers dropping behind the gray iron of Jones' Tucson safe. Though his eyes felt about to roll off his cheekbones, Charlie could not have lifted so much as one finger had the Devil himself suddenly stepped from the hole.

Nothing squeezed past the stopped slab of that door; but some things you don't *have* to see to be scared of. Sometimes the things a man knows least about tend to frighten him most.

Nothing came out but a rush of bad air smelling strongly of death—strong enough to move Medders. He was in such a hurry to get out of its touch he went ten flying strides through ththat boot-banging clamor in his dash for the ladders before discovering his candle had got blown out. He couldn't see a thing. He couldn't stop, either. Terror closed in and, in that suffocating black, he lost all sense of direction, crashing headlong into unyielding rock.

It must have shaken a little sense into him. At least, when he got back enough strength to move, he stayed where he was, ears stretched, heart pounding, for what seemed an eternity. He didn't know what might come out of this murk, but when nothing did he twisted onto all fours and eventually got up. Even then he waited, scarcely daring to draw breath, until his jittery stare found a vague area of grayness which he reckoned to be the shaft.

And it was.

Weak with relief his hands found the ladder. Rung by rung he pulled himself up, wondering if each new hold might not be his last. But when he stepped off at the number 2 level, with nothing untoward having provided further alarm, he was inclined somewhat testily to believe he had let his imagination run away with him, that he'd probably someway triggered that slab himself. He decided, just the same, to stay topside a while until the stink in that passage had had a chance to air out.

Dragging his weight up the final climb it came over him this would be as good a time as any to go bury a few more tins of good water. He was still thinking about it when his head came above the well shaft coping and saw, in the refracted light from the cave's concealed entrance, the closed door to the cabin which he himself had left open.

Still clamped to the ladder in the shock of this discovery, something cold and round came hard against the back of his neck.

XIV

STUDENTS OF MEDICINE might be surprised to learn how many separate and individual notions—mostly irrelevant—pass through a man's head in moments of crisis while the mind is first staggered by premonitions of disaster.

There was nothing really complicated about Charlie Medders; as a product of his environment he was a pretty average guy. Out of his element, beyond his depth, he had—down below—been up against dreads he could not understand, allowing primitive fears to stampede and make a fool of him.

But a gun dug into the back of his neck was within the realm of familiar experience. He stayed "put" as the saying goes, his strongest emotion one of bitter disgust. "You don't hev to shoot," he growled. "I know when I'm beat."

"All who believe that can stand on their heads! Now, be careful. I'm jumpety as a pocketful of crickets," the voice of Belita Storn remarked dryly, "and you know what they say about excitable women."

Medders, beneath his breath, cursed. It burnt a feller up enough having *anyone* get the drop on him, but to discover he'd let a woman and of all women this one, was a cross no man had ought to have to bear. Still, he wasn't too astonished. With his kind of luck it had been about time for her to throw some more wrenches. He'd been suspecting for some while she might find her way back. "You come by yourself?"

Behind the resentful bitterness of it this sounded like a chump about to pitch in his hand.

But she hadn't come out here to sympathize with him. "Burks and his red brothers are out there someplace—I got a look at them yesterday, off west of Gu Chuapo. You don't have to worry," she advised with a sniff, "they won't show up here through any carelessness of mine. You can climb out and turn around. But watch yourself, hombre."

Medders looked as disgruntled and fed up as he'd sounded.

This could go either way. She was aware of it and worried, not knowing quite how to say what she had in mind. These burro men were a stiff-necked lot, touchy as teased snakes, and prone to get their backs up over things less notionable persons might not waste a second thought on.

Not finding any better way, she said straight-out: "You ought to have a keeper!"

Medders, beginning to bridle, broke off to peer more carefully at her. "What's that supposed t' mean?"

"You've really fixed yourself up fine, prancing around with that Imogene Winters! You think she'd look twice at a nump like you?"

"Now, just a dang minute—"

"You listen to me! When they were talking it up, didn't you claim any common stock put out for this mine would be nothing but bait to fleece widows and orphans? Yes or no?"

"Sure, but—"

"Then it's not only Jones that's made you look like a panhandling bum! Another meeting was called just before I left town and your prissy friend Winters, all smiles and dimples, sat in with those shares and voted, with T.K. and Heintzleman, to okay that stock." Belita's eyes flashed with scorn. "What will those widows and orphans think now with your picture, big as life, printed right on the face of it!"

Charlie peered at her, stunned. "B-B-But—"

Glaring, she said angrily: "You had Rawlins convinced; even Ferris was worried. When Jones handed around the shares and gave Winters ten signed over by you, I naturally assumed. . . ." She looked at him sharply. "It was Winters' votes—"

"But I only give her *one!*" Medders wailed. Then his cheeks turned hot as he realized how the curvaceous Ginnie had tricked him, substituting ten for the one he had granted her.

"Well," Belita said, having read his face and added a few notions of her own to the total, "I suppose you agreed to trade her a share in return for . . . umm . . . value received. You mean are such—"

"It wasn't . . . I was tryin' t' find out," Charlie

growled, red to the ears, "what went on after I left. She offered t' show me her notes of the minutes if. . . ."

Belita Storn sniffed. "I'll bet!" The way she snapped out the words made it pretty apparent she reckoned this was not all Ginnie had offered.

Made Charlie feel like a lyin' hound, a dang egg-suckin' skunk, until he happened to remember it was *her* that had brought Jones into this deal. This didn't much help because he knew he looked guilty with his face feeling hotter than a two-dollar pistol; and he began to swell up, too riled to think straight, about ready, by grab, to let her have both barrels. But she abruptly took the wind from his sails, coming right out with what he was fixing to get said.

"You'll be thinking," she smiled, "I haven't much room to talk, turning half of those shares you gave *me* over to Jones—and you're probably right. It was a breach of trust, although I thought at the time. . . ." She shook her head. "No matter. It was a poor thing to do. I can see that, now. With the shares *she* dug out of you, the ones Jones has and the block he grabbed for those bad debts, you're just about back to where you were before—"

"Not quite," Medders growled. "I'm still squattin' on this ore an'—without you've told me—they don't even know where t' start lookin'."

Belita shook her head again. "I haven't told," she said, "but it looks like I'm responsible for most of your hard luck." She reached into her blouse. "Would it help if I gave back—"

"I'm not *that* hard up," Charlie said like he was

affronted. "You own half of everything that comes outa here. When I give a person somethin' I *give* it to him—see? An' I don't recognize no company set up by Jones t' milk no bunch of suckers outa what it's taken 'em a lifetime t' save!"

"But that company is legal. You can't—"

"The hell I can't!" Medders said, skinning the lips off his teeth like a sure enough wolf. He peered at her fiercely. "Long's I've got ol' Betsy an' shells t' cram into her there better not nobody come monkeyin' round here!"

In the glitter of that stare Belita kind of shivered. She said dubiously, "I'm not sure. . . ." and appeared to have tied into some stubborn notions of her own. "It's all so mixed up! This *is* the Weeping Widow, you know." She sighed. "You've done a lot for me and it's been hard to live with, knowing how ungrateful I must seem, selling half of what you gave me to that awful banker—and what you just now said about us still being partners, it . . . it shames me even more."

She dropped her eyes and Medders shuffled his feet. "Well, hell," he gruffed, uncomfortably embarrassed, "you had your reasons, I reckon."

"I—*yes!* I resented you terribly. It was a horrible jolt to find someone here, to have come all the way from Durango only to discover some ignorant desert rat had beaten me to it. I . . . I saw your burros," she said as though this cleared up everything. But Medders still had his mouth open. She said, color piling into her cheeks: "It was a pretty sneaky thing I did, pretending to be lost and letting you find me . . . acting like I was out of my head."

Charlie shrugged. She looked so tore up and

humble he told her magnanimously, "No skin lost. Comin' right down t' cases I ain't so lily white myself if it comes t' that."

She stared at him oddly. Perhaps she found it hard to believe a grown man could be such a chump. Recall of other things he had done apparently relieved whatever fleeting disquiet had given her pause. She plunged into her story.

Her mother had been a great Spanish beauty, daughter of an old and socially prominent family which had been living for years on inherited wealth. Belita's father, a transplanted American of considerable dash and charm, one gathered was believed to have been in the Santa Fe trade, though she was frank to admit certain jealous competitors had spread unproved rumors connecting his wagons with the transport of contraband.

After the death of her mother in a hunting accident, Belita, aged five, had been taken by the Spanish grandparents to raise. She had seen her father but infrequently after this. He had been killed two years later in a quarrel over cards. Fate's bony hand, when she was twelve, had struck again. Cholera swept the city, taking both grandparents. When the courts and the lawyers had finished with their bickerings, and gotten rid of the creditors, the estate had been reduced to a few hundred dollars and a folio of musty time-yellowed papers.

Belita, at fourteen, had been forced to find work. "And what could I do?" she demanded graphically of Medders. "I had been trained in graces befitting a station I could no longer claim." There'd been no other relatives she could go to. When the money ran out there had seemed but two choices, the

streets or the convent. Desperate, she had finally
persuaded Gregorio Guttierez, a tavern keeper, to
let her sing in his bar for room and board. "It was
terrible!" she cried, regarding Medders slanchways
through the curl of sorrel lashes. "You've no idea
what that place was like," she said with a visible
shudder.

Charlie's face should have been a great comfort.
He looked as though he had lived every minute of
it.

And then one night about two months ago, unable to put up with any more of it, she said, she had
fled the place in the gypsy clothes she'd had to don
for her "appearances" and a handful of pesos she
had taken from the till.

Among the musty papers she'd received from the
grandparents' estate was a map she had cherished,
and this had given her the strength to break away
from Guttierez. She'd made up her mind to come
to Arizona and find the wonderful mine her great-
grandfather had been forced to abandon during the
Indian revolt of 1751.

She hadn't had too much trouble getting out of
Durango, but had been turned back at the border
by the immigration authorities. With sixteen sum-
mers she had become a desirable woman able to
pass herself off as a gitana of the Bear Folki and so
found work as a flamenco dancer among the dives
of Juarez and Agua Prieta where one night she had
crossed the border with smugglers.

Medders was regarding her with something close
to awe. As she paused for breath, he said, shaking
his head: "I can't see how you ever done it—all
them miles! Just a chit of a girl—"

"A girl, when she has to, can do many things. I was desperate, you understand. Something in here"—she clapped a hand to her breast—"something deep inside was driving me. Where there is a will God will show the way. Without His help, and the intercession of the Saints, I would never have got here."

"An' the map," Medders said. "Hows about my havin' a squint at it?"

"Of course," Belita smiled and, reaching inside the neck of her mannish new shield-fronted shirt, passed over a square of folded paper.

Charlie's face was a study. But as he smoothed it against the shaft coping, disbelief and astonishment were swiftly replaced by a lively interest. This was a map, all right, replete with a set of hand lettered directions. He bent over it, mumbling as he spelled out the words.

Belita, having meanwhile put away her derringer, smiled more widely as he looked up from the paper to meet the challenge of her stare. "Now do you believe?"

But Medders' eyes were narrowed. A frown was twisting the whisker-scraggled cheeks. "If, like you say, this was your great-gran'pappy's mine, how come this stuff—all them directions an' such—ain't written in Spanish? An' if it was that long ago when he skipped out how come this paper ain't fell plumb apart?"

The girl laughed. "Because it's new paper, silly; a copy I made myself."

Charlie tapped the map with a knobby finger. "It don't say Weepin' Widder, it says Esmeralda."

"My grandmother had a bracelet set with pieces

of ore taken out of this mine. Many times I have seen it. The ore is the same. This is the place or I could not have come here. The mountains, the buttes, every landmark is here. My people named it Esmeralda for the color of the ore. How must one have to convince you, hombre? Look—" she said, and touched the map. "C-A-V-E spells *cave*, does it not?"

Medders grudgingly nodded. Then he said like it hurt him: "I reckon it's yours."

XV

"OURS," SHE CORRECTED, pumping his hand. "We're partners—remember? Full partners," she grinned, nodding with approval as Charlie's look perked up. "It was the gringos, new people coming in after your General Kearny took New Mexico away from us, that gave this Weeping Widow tag to it. Perhaps we should call it Esmeralda like great-grand-father—"

"Changing the name won't stand in Jones' way."

"Back in Durango I have the original Perez map. . . ."

"The courts wouldn't recognize a claim based on that. It's been a lost mine for more'n a hundred years, an' the law around here eats right outa that polecat's paw. Nope," Medders scowled, "we'll have t' keep her hid an' sell off the ore in dribbles an' drabs."

She looked at him doubtfully.

"There ain't no other way," he growled. "That highbinder's got his foot in now an' with them

shares an' that company. . . ." He threw up his
hands. "You oughta know by now how that
bustard operates. He'd skin a flea fer its hide an'
taller!"

She looked a little let down. "I guess there's not
much chance of selling ore in Tucson. What did
you get for that load you brought in?"

"Under five thousan', time I got done with it,"
Medders growled, remembering. "An' then got
beat outa most of that! But there's other places."
His face wrinkled up as he thought about some.
"Be a heap longer haul," he told her at last, "an'
we'd hev t' watch out fer Burks an' them Injuns,
but if we could git it to a stampmill we'd be paid
what it's worth."

He passed back her map, braced a hip against
the coping. "First I'll have t' set up some more
springs—it can git pretty dry chasin' around in that
desert." He recollected something else but before
he could get it shaped into words she cut in to ask:
"If we had more burros couldn't we take out
more?"

"You got someone in mind wants t' give away a
dozen?"

"No, but—"

"I been thinkin'," he said, gruffer still with his
tone. "Jones threatened t' hev me in court over you
—somethin' about chain marks an' keepin' you
pris'ner. You tell him that?"

It was her eyes that dropped. Looking pretty uncomfortable, she faced him straightly. "I said you
kept me chained like a peon—I had to tell him
something! I thought, being a banker, he would
have enough money to open this mine. . . ."

Medders stared at her, scowling. She saw his fists clench. She backed off a little, eyes widening, wary. "An' the marks?" Medders said.

She gnawed at her lip. Finally, sighing, she slipped off a boot and shyly poked the foot toward him. "They're about gone now."

They were, for a fact. But the scars could be seen, pale ridges of tissue, suggestive and ugly. Charlie wasn't looking too pleasant himself. "What made 'em?"

"Well . . . if you must know, I did." Rather plaintively she added, "I had to have something to back up my story. . . ."

"Yeah. Like that bracelet," Medders said, "an' the map you fixed up. What did T.K. think of it?"

She drew back with a gasp. Color rushed into stiffened cheeks through which her stare burned like fanned coals. Slowly brightness faded. "I guess I had that coming," she said, but stood her ground, almost pleading now. "You can't really think I'd do a thing like that?"

Looking bitterly again at the signs of her duplicity Medders blew through his teeth but grudgingly shook his head. Jones, if he'd ever got a squint at that map, would have had his understrappers around here thicker than cloves on a Christmas ham. But she'd have seen that, too! Eyes sharp as hers wasn't like to. . . . "Ahr," he said, "t' hell with it!"

But she caught his arm as he was about to stride off. "Can't you see I'm trying to be *honest* with you?"

"While you're bein' so honest why'd you come back? Afraid I'd make off with what was left of this stuff?"

"That's a brutal thing to say to a friend who threw up a sure thing to come out here and help you—"

"All who believe that can go stand on their heads," Medders mimicked, disgusted. Face darkening, he said, "It's friends like you a guy had better watch out fer!" and, flinging off her hand, went stomping into the cabin.

When he came out with the Sharps she was just where he'd quit her, an arrested shape against the shaft coping. "You're . . . going?" There was no hope left in that voice.

"That's right—put the blame on *me!*" Charlie growled, but she didn't lash back as he'd expected her to. She seemed someway sort of lost and defenseless and, though he wouldn't have put it that way, more appealing. Her sorrel mane, pulled back in the Spanish fashion, gave her the look of a skinned rabbit. "I'm not in a position to blame anyone," she said in a very small voice.

This was certainly news. He stared at her, puzzled.

Her eyes looked oddly soft and swimmy. "If you would only change your mind. . . ." She said abruptly: "Here—you keep the map, hostage to my continued good faith. It may help you believe I've been telling the truth . . . I really *did* come back to make amends if I could."

He would sooner have looked to find a bull in bloomers than to hear her talking like the meek were about to do their inheriting and there could still be hope she'd find her name in the pot. She had something up her sleeve and you could lay to that!

"All right," she said with a shaky little laugh. "I

suppose in your eyes I'm a first class Judas goat, a
conniving Jezebel, a Delilah of the wastelands. I
guess, in your place, I might be suspicious too. But
I'd never walk off without giving you a chance."

Medders, who hadn't the least intention of stepping out of this, grunted. He'd picked up the rifle,
thinking to have a look around. "Where-at was
they working' when them Injuns run·'em off?"

She said reluctantly, "I don't know."

"Didn't figure you did. Well," he said, tearing
up her map until it looked like something the rats
had been at, "we got mebbe a week—ten days if
we're lucky, before your Tucson banker friend gits
around t' really bearin' down.

She was watching as though she couldn't quite
believe it the tiny bits of paper fluttering away from
his fists. He said, grinning sourly, "So we'll hev to'
move fast." And, when her stare came up, he
handed her his cap. "You'll find carbide fer this
inside the shack. I'll be away fer a bit. If you're
minded t' do somethin' helpful, see if you can uncover that ore face—an' keep outa sight.
Bushwhacker bullets don't care who they smack."

It took the best part of two nights and a tagalong
day to get his water buried where, should this deal
turn sticky, it might make the precious difference
between what would suit Jones and what he'd settle
for himself.

Watching the sun drop over the hump and begin
its long slide toward the darker side of things,
Charlie was reminded that his petticoat partner
might be having to make do on some pretty slim
pickings back there at the mine with that horror
he'd uncovered.

He was anxious to get back, but Begetta was tough and with a bit of pushing could probably raise Tubac inside three-four hours. Tubac, oldest town founded by white men in the territory and seat of the first newspaper—the *Weekly Arizonian* —was now, owing to the spasmodic attentions of hostile Apaches, in a pretty advanced state of decay. But a handful of families, most of them Mexican, still eked out a living from peaches, pomegranates and a few hills of maize, and a general store had managed to keep open in the interest of roundabout ranches.

The girl and himself would need more grub, and those twenty-five loaded shells for the Sharps might go pretty fast if Jones decided to really clamp down. Food and cartridges were prime necessities; he still had what cash he'd picked up from that Tucson hotel room. He decided to risk it.

Lavender shadows lay long across the range and, by the look and smells, Tubac was sitting down to supper when Charlie and Begetta trudged wearily past the white-plastered adobe Roman Catholic church. He left Begetta at the livery happily munching oats, and walked around to the store where the first thing he purchased was four boxes of cartridges, one for his pistol and the rest for the Sharps. Then he ordered up two sacks of flour, salt, sow belly and fifty pounds of beans, reluctantly deciding not to weight himself down with tinned stuffs. Then he made a quick supper on a can of tomatoes, a slab of cheese and some crackers, paid his bill, ran a hand through his whiskers and said he'd be back.

There was a guy in the chair when he stepped through the barber's door, and another gent reading the hair tonic labels from a bench by the door while he waited. "Just getting my ears freed," this one said with a grin as Medders started to back off. "Say!" The man's eyes suddenly sharpened. "Aren't you Charlie Medders, the feller that opened—"

But Medders was already out in the street. Heating his axles he took off round a corner, ducked into a passage between empty store fronts, came out breathing hard and made a bee line for the livery, blessedly in sight less than half a block away.

Short of reaching it, really puffing now, a rabbity look twisted over his shoulder having glimpsed no commotion, he dropped into a walk. He couldn't recollect ever seeing the guy before, but he'd been given a fright and wasn't over it yet. Jones had a mighty long arm in this country, and plenty of jaspers not on his paysheet was sure not above trying to curry his favor.

Still panting and glowering, Charlie, all nerves, swung into the runway, discovering the proprietor, perched on a crate, leisurely shaving a stick.

"Didn't take you long t' go through our town."

Medders peered at him suspiciously but let the thought go. "You got three mules in that corral out there. What's the rock bottom price on them?"

The stableman scrinched up his eyes for a look. "Hundred apiece on them two browns. That there sand-colored jigger ort t' bring about fifty." He considered Charlie cagily. "Make it three twenty-five fer the lot and they're yours."

Charlie scowled toward the backs of those two empty buildings. "Throw in a saddle," he grumbled, "an' it's a deal."

The proprietor, briefly hesitating, decided not to push his luck. "Done!" he declared; and was getting up to go find a kak for this gullible pilgrim when Charlie, bent under the pull of a leadshank, came dragging Begetta away from the feed rack. "Git 'em ready t' travel, an' lash on a couple sacks of cracked oats," he called. "I'll be back directly."

With Begetta snubbed to a porch post he went into the store and hurried out with his provisions, including as an afterthought a gray flannel shirt and a pair of Texas pants for Belita. It was while he was tieing these purchases in place that a voice spoke up so close to his elbow he pretty near jumped clean over Begetta.

Full dark had by this time closed down the view, but in the light shafting out of the storekeeper's windows Charlie found himself confronted by the one man in town he had hoped to avoid, the derby-hatted jasper who had accosted him at the barber's.

"Name is Jennison Jelks," the guy said, boring in, "local correspondent for the Arizona *Republic* —all I want is to get something authentic on this whopping development your company's issuing stock for." He was talking fast with his ingratiating grin, trying to keep Medders pinned till he could get enough out of him to send to his paper. "Hell, you're a hero! A single-blanket jackass prospector who, with nothing but persistence and his own ingenuity, has apparently uncovered the biggest find of the century. Is it really as big as—Here, wait! Have a heart. . . ."

Medders, who had been fidgeting to get away, relaxed enough from his fright to grumble, scowling suspiciously: "What do you want me to say?"

"Just give us the truth. Something I can tell fifty-four hundred readers bustin' to get their teeth into notions that haven't stemmed mainly from a desire to sell stock."

"All right," Charlie said, beginning to take a grim pleasure from this. "I don't know what's comin' out Company headquarters, but I can state for a fact there ain't been a lick of development done in that mine since I opened it up."

The reporter stared skeptically. "According to the prospectus—"

"That come straight outa the mouth of T.K. Jones!"

"I can't print that," Jelks said, disgusted.

"Why not? You asked fer the truth an', by grab, you're gittin' it. The whole thing's a fraud. All that's back of that stock is a bunch of hot air, an' you can say I said so."

Jelks, with a notebook propped against his belly, was writing like mad. "I can quote you on that?"

"Word fer word," Charlie growled. "An' you can furthermore say I told you flat out the whole deal smells so bad I give up my seat on the Board, refused any share in the Company an' washed my hands of the whole swindlin' works. You can tell your readers I'm thinkin' of suing them buggers for defamation of character in the unauthorized use of my picture on them certificates."

Jelks scribbled this down, then looked up to peer at Medders rather queerly for a moment. "But it was my understanding you fetched in several sacks of this ore . . . Mr. Jones—"

"Yeah! He says a heap of things besides his prayers! He's the topdog crook of the whole shebang!"

The reporter, shifting his stance, eyed Medders uneasily. "That's a pretty wild accusation, you know, against a man as big as Tiberius Jones." He chewed on his pencil, torn between doubt and the burning desire to make the most of what this fool had been giving him. Caution finally got the best of him.

Medders could see that. "Listen!" he growled, and proceeded to blurt out the whole story of Jones' connection with the Weeping Widow, including a description of the various squeeze plays put on by the banker to take over the company and load the market with stock that was strictly pie in the sky. "Them certificates ain't worth a quarter of what you'd git fer a trunkful of Confederate shinplasters! Don't take my word fer it," he said; "ask the girl!"

Jelks looked dubious. He seemed sympathetic but distrustful when he said, "You might be telling me the gospel truth but I'm afraid it's no go. The only way my paper would go to press with that story would be over your name. Too bad, but there it is."

Charlie, with one of his twisted grins, took the stub of pencil and blackly wrote his name across the bottom of Jelks' notes. "An' while you're at it," he said, "it might pay off fer you to spend a mite of time in the recorder's office. Then ask that great hypothecator just where this wonderful mine is at."

Having said which, he untied Begetta from her mooring at the porch and went off through the dark to pick up his three mules.

XVI

DURING THE HOURS he spent getting back to the mine Charlie not infrequently astonished his mules with the guffaws and belly laughs that came jouncing out of him from picturing Jones' face when that story got around. The tycoon of Tucson would sure have his hands full keeping up his front bombarded by the questions and letters pouring in with demands for an accounting!

Not all of those miles were covered in such glee. He had some conscience stricken intervals when he thought about Belita coming onto that chamberful of dried-up wretches left to starve to death behind the rock door. At the time he had figured it would serve her right and that she'd sure had it coming, but there was moments when he felt pretty meaching about her, stuck off there alone with such ghastly reminders of her family's shame.

More often, however, and with increasing disquiet, he got to worrying about himself and the hereafter looming larger every time he poked a squint at it. It came over him maybe he had been a mite hasty pricking the bubble of this stock fraud, and all, the way he had. Jones, when he got enough over that punch to catch a fresh breath, would be several shades closer to full-scale explosion than a case of thawed dynamite left to dry by an open fire.

Humiliated, publicly embarrassed and denied the loot his machinations had been aimed at, he would be not only cram-jammed with fury but brought to realize his only chance of recapturing his former high place in the community was to prove possession of a mine he didn't have—and not even this would be really sufficient. He would certainly have to produce a bonanza or, skewered by Medders' exposure, get out of the country. And it did not take much figuring to understand which he was most likely to try for.

Clutched with the nag of these nerve-frazzling glimpses Charlie lost several hours profanely endeavoring to louse up his trail. He plowed through sand he might otherwise have skirted; at one stretch he spent upwards of ninety minutes working his animals through a maze of broken rock ledges and then, still pursued by visions of his come-uppance, cut over into Papago country west of the Baboquivaris where he frittered away another half day trying to buy additional mules and engage a crew with nothing more substantial to put into the deal than promises.

These heroic efforts resulted in seven sorry-looking long-eared specimens blown up in the bargaining to three times their worth and five teen-age boys—obvious malcontents—whose worth was untried and so plainly debatable no one less desperate than Medders would have even looked twice at them.

What he had wanted were several case-hardened bucks who would do what he told them and not cloud the issue with a lot of fool questions. But time was running out on him; he took what he could get and hung onto his temper.

He now had quite a caravan to string out over these empty miles, and the size of it did not noticeably lighten the burden of his thoughts. On the contrary, he grew steadily more concerned about the diminished chances of eluding discovery. So much so that he put two of his schoolboys behind the last mule with branches of mesquite and vigorous orders to wipe out all signs of their passage.

The self elected segundo of this bunch was a pock-faced delinquent with an oversized nose and two mismatched eyes who went, he said, by the name of Heap Walker, and who apparently found very little in life which could approach the satisfaction he got from his own voice. He carried an old and beat-up Henry repeater and was, he told Medders, the world's greatest marksman.

It was the middle of the following day, and hotter than the hinges of hell's hip pocket, when Charlie finally sighted the hills that hid the Weeping Widow. Impatient as he was, he did not swing directly toward them but antigodled around to come up from the south behind an outlying spur which concealed the secret trail he had worked out through the rocks. He had no more than put the dun mule into an apparent slant for this than the pock-nosed Walker, breaking into a torrent of hard sounding Papago, came whittle-whanging up with a look black as thunder.

"No go there! Bad place, them hill!"

Charlie hooked a knee around his hull's cracked horn. "Yeah? What's the matter with it?"

Walker, waving his arms, cried excitedly: "Bad place! Heap bad!" and the rest of the Papagos, long faced and edgy, looked about ready to dig for the tules.

Medders said, scowling, "What the hell have I got here, a bunch of damn squaws?"

Walker's look turned darker. His stringy arms were folded across his greasy white man's vest. When he failed to stare Medders down the Papago stuck out a dirty claw. "Injun go home. Pay now."

Charlie didn't know what had got into their craws but he had put too much sweat and worry into this to sit calmly by while an ignorant savage kicked the props out from under him. Lifting the Sharps off his lap he said with its bore fixed on Walker's chest: "You hired out t' do a piece of work. Now git up there an' do it."

The fellow skinned back his lips in a horrible grimace and showed the whites of his eyes but in the end, very ugly, jerked his mount's head around and kicked it on up the trail, the rest of the crew sullenly filing past to fall in behind.

Sleeving sweat off his cheeks and apprehensively wondering what Belita would be making of this, he gave the burro a nod and, rounding up the loose mules, went nervously clattering after them. From up there she'd not be able to see who they were, not anyways to pick out faces. About all he needed right now was to have her open up with that pocket gun!

But nothing untoward occurred. His schoolboys were waiting in a shivery huddle when he rounded the last rock and came in sight of the cave. He motioned them off toward the hay trap. "Turn these critters in there. When you git back we'll stir up some grub."

He was a lot more worried than he saw fit to let on. Considering what was down below he'd expected the girl to be camped up here, and finding no sign of her scared the bejazus out of him.

Of course she may have skedaddled, he reminded himself with a queer, unexpected feeling of emptiness, but even as the notion tramped through his head it seemed a lot less than likely. She had shown too much grit, too much brass bound gall, to let any bunch of dead Injuns run her off. *But what if that trick door had shut on her?*

His stomach turned over and crawled at the thought. Cold sweat cracked through the pores of his skin and his knees got to shaking before common sense caught a strong enough grip to shove back this horror and show it up for sheer nonsense. No girl would walk into a hole filled with mummies.

Someway he was not much comforted. Saying so didn't make it so. Not many girls would, but Belita might. She had enough guts to charge hell with a bucket, and the last thing he'd told her. . . . The shakes came back as he remembered his words. *If you're minded t' do somethin' helpful, see if you can uncover that ore face.*

Of course she'd gone in! He could see her standing there, realizing her debt to him, squaring her jaw. She'd have conquered her revulsion, the things that had driven Charlie back himself—this was the test, the chance she had pleaded for . . . her opportunity to prove herself a pardner he could depend on. *She was in there now.* He could see that rock door, like some carnivorous plant, slowly, stealthily closing behind her.

With a snarling curse Medders tore through the curtain of breaking brush, scrambled into the cave and—in that moment of blindness while his vision adjusted—strode headlong into something roundly rigid that sent the breath whistling through his teeth.

There is something about the snout of a firearm that is seldom mistaken for anything else. Stopped cold in his tracks there wasn't much Medders could do but goggle and try to suck in his gut. Even the return of his sight was no great advantage in the glare of those eyes blazing into his own.

"I—"

"Don't open your mouth!" Belita Storn said in a voice that would have broke off a white oak post. For moments they stood like things backed out of wood in a stillness rasped only by the jerk of her breathing. In a flutter of sound leaching in from outside he could feel the shake of her hand through the gun steel.

Then, abruptly, she pulled the pistol away and stepped back.

Charlie stayed where he was. She said, "I can't do it!" and whirled in a swirl of skirts and stalked off.

Not till then did Medders draw a full-grown breath, and mighty near came apart with it. Only the barefooted slap of hurrying feet going past galvanized him enough to take him stumbling through brush to fling a tremulous shout at his departing hired hands.

XVII

CHARLIE SIGHED like he had the whole world on his back.

He did have some problems. They were beginning to close in like the Sioux on Custer, but one thing stood out too plain to miss. Let these boys get away from him and he could sure wave goodbye to any chance of getting out the rest of that ore.

He could see that creepy Heap Walker's black stare and the magpie looks of at least a couple others twisting round to take his measure. To get respect from their kind you had to show you could command it.

He raised the Sharps. This could prove kind of tricky what with all them rocks, the drop and desperate energy put into their flight by the lift of that rifle. He pushed the aperture of the sight vane up to the 200-yard mark, squinted carefully, picked a finger of rock that leaned out over the trail, found a crotch to rest the barrel on and waited for his quarry to come into the target area.

The loudmouthed Walker, going hellity larrup, was the first to come bounding into the lens. Medders opened his mouth, quit breathing, and squeezed off. The recoil belted his shoulder. The deep-throated boom of exploded powder went whamming out over the canyon's rock faces with the ground shaking racket of a battery of howitzers. Through the rolling white stench the stone finger flew apart in a burst of shattered fragments not three jumps ahead of that high-bounding Walker.

The insurrection was over.

They came dragging themselves back, meaneyed, sullen but cowed—at least for the moment. Past the white cheeked Belita, Charlie, poker eyed and ready, motioned them into the cave one by one until it came Walker's turn, the last of the lot. He was the only one packing a firearm and Medders curtly told him to give it to Belita.

He broke into a gabble that Charlie cut short. "You won't have any use fer it down below. When it's needed we'll see. Now git out to that hay trap an' fetch them supplies."

"Send boy—"

"I'm sendin' *you!*"

The pock-nosed Papago was not a reassuring sight. Snake-eyed with rage and humiliation, cut up like he was from flying rock, he looked positively poisonous. But that buffalo gun was powerful medicine. With a final snarl he slammed down his rifle and struck off up the trail like a wetfooted cat.

Charlie picked up the Henry, held it out to Belita. Face expressionless as pounded clay, she considered him a moment before taking the repeater; it was Medders' look that twisted free. He said, turning red, "I, ah—fetched you a present."

Something passed through her eyes, gone as quick as smoke. Her mouth tightened up. "It's no good," she said, pushing the hair off her cheek. "You were right all the time . . . this deal is played out."

Charlie's face had the look of a new-hatched nestling, a little bit puzzled but confidently waiting for mama to drop the worm. His bewilderment grew when all she did was stand there. "If you mean you're fed up—"

This brought an impatient snort. She said irritably: "Can't you understand! We've *got* all there is! I found what you were looking for—it was behind that door." She shuddered. "They quit in borrasca. There's nothing left to mine."

"Oh. . . ." Medders said, and perceptibly brightened. "Then all we got t' worry about—"

"You sound," she cried sharply, "like you couldn't care less!"

He peered at her, baffled. "Well, it's simpler this way. Takes a load off my mind if you want the plain truth. Alls we got t' do now is pack out what's showin'. One trip an' we're clear." He told about his talk with Jennison Jelks, the Tubac correspondent for the big Phoenix paper. "One's about all we're goin' t' have time fer, an' we better git at it."

She looked at him slanchways, like maybe he'd grown an extra head in the course of this conversation. Her expression was so peculiar Charlie twisted around, half expecting to find Heap Walker sneaking up on him, but nobody was in sight.

"Soon as that bugger fetches in the stuff I brought," he said, "mebbe you better stir up a batch of grub. We'll be at this all night an'—"

"I believe you really *enjoy* chasing rainbows!"

When he stared at her blankly she said, "How long have you been stumbling around after burros?"

"Prospectin'? Seven-eight years, give or take a couple months."

"That's what I mean!" She sounded exasperated. "All that time! Living from hand to mouth, spending your life at the tag end of noplace, talking up a storm to some waggle-eared jack—is *that* what you want?"

Medders, hiking his hat to where it fell precariously across one eye, scratched the back of his head while he studied her, baffled, from beneath the flopped brim. "I never was much fer towns. . . ."

She looked even more put out than she had sounded. It was kind of hard to figure with her raking him over like he hadn't the gumption to pound sand down a rat hole. Then he got it, too late. She'd pushed through the manzanita, leaving him with the jumbled whirl of his thoughts, incredulously staring at her disappearing back.

It always had been enough but now—in spite of his distrust—he wasn't sure about anything. When the pock-faced Walker came staggering down from the hay trap with the stuff he'd got off Begetta, Medders waved him on into the cave, scarcely seeing him. He was, by then, neck deep in the engulfing flood her remarks had let loose, kicking out in all directions in the half-strangled hope of somewhere finding a piece of bottom solid enough to let him come to grips with himself.

It just didn't work out. He fell back on habit as he nearly always did when discovering himself out of step with events. It was easier to drift and kind of bend with the pressure of things that looked too fierce to be coped with. Most knotty problems, he had found, would get impatient like that girl and take themselves off if a man had the wit to sit tight and let them.

The cave, when he finally squirmed his way into it, was filled with light coming out of the shack along with the sounds and stomach-stirring smells whipped up by things Belita had on the stove. The irate Walker and his surly schoolboys had their heads together in a huddle by the shaft; he wasn't bothered by that. He didn't give a whack how mutinous they looked long as none of them got their mitts on a gun. They probably all had knives, but there wasn't enough spunk in the whole kit and caboodle to go up against the Sharps if he could just stay awake and keep his eyes skinned.

What did get under his hide was the *feel* of things around here. He could always tell when a storm was building up by the misery of aches that got to pulling on his bones. It had nothing to do with them Injuns. The pressure was coming right out of that shack along with the heat kicked up by the stove.

When he couldn't tolerate this discomfort any longer he took himself over to lounge a while in the open door. Chicken pox and measles was things a waddy couldn't fight, and any guy what valued his peace of mind was bound sooner or later to put

women right along with 'em. Like them or not,
there was things in this world a feller had to go
along with, and red headed women was at the top
of the list.

And it got mighty quick plain if there was to be
any meeting of minds in this matter Medders was
going to have to take the first step. This graveled
him, too, for he could tell she figured she had
right on her side. "You find that shirt an' them
pants—"

She skewered him with a bitter glance, and only
then did he notice she had the duds on. It made
him feel like a fool. He didn't know what to say,
hardly, and put it down in his mind as another
mark against her. But he presently scraped up
voice enough to say, apropos of the truths that lay
festering in him: "I make out well enough, if that
was what you meant. I look after my own. 'Tain't
so much what I find as the lookin' that pleasures
me."

She loosed a kind of sniff, never glancing
around. She shoved one pot back, jabbed a spoon
in another and stirred with such a clatter even the
Papagoes out by the shaft looked up. "Just a flat-
footed bum," she remarked with disdain. "I will
never marry a man who won't work."

Medders gawped, but the gall of her got the best
of him. "I'm not the marryin' kind!" he snarled,
and glowered fierce as any bot-bit bull. "No pants-
wearin' female will ever git *me* up in front of no
preacher!"

She tossed the spoon in the pot. "Come an' get
it," she yelled, "before I throw it away."

XVIII

CHARLIE FUMED and fretted his way through the meal, hardly knowing what he put into him, scarcely peering any higher than the freckled and florid perfection of Belita's sleeve-rolled arms. He could have eaten fried curbstone with about as much pleasure.

He had no thought for the chomp and clatter of the voracious schoolboys. Two goals kept top priority through the churn and lash of his seething visions—getting through and getting out. Yet here, once more, he was faced with the girl.

Had it not been so bitterly impossible he'd have played off the rest of this deal plumb solo. But it just wasn't in the cards, and he knew it. Squirm and wriggle as he could and did he was turned back from every strategy by the graveling realization that without Belita's help he was not going to get this ore out in time.

It wasn't in Medders to pull out empty-handed; he wouldn't even consider such a weaselly solution.

This was *his* ore; he wasn't about to walk out on it. And yet it wasn't the prospect of gain that held him; he'd gotten by before and could do it again. It was the *principle,* that's what it was . . . the unpalatable notion of being beat out of it!

He might lack a few jumps of understanding females, but bankers and the ways of the desert he savvied. Even so, this would be no trip for weak hearts; it could be touch and go every step of the way. He saw this, accepted it. Every facet of the plan had got to mesh and mesh right and it could be no better than what was put into it.

He had to put in what lay ready to hand, the mules he'd picked up, these Papago packers . . . his own life and . . . maybe even Belita's. He didn't waste time wondering what he would do if it didn't work out.

He got up and said bluntly: "We're goin' t' move ore, try to pack it t' Charleston, over beyond the Santa Ritas. It ain't goin' t' be easy. We'll probably run into gunfire. But if we git this stuff through, every galoot that's on tap when we deliver it at the T.M. & M. will have a equal share of whatever we git fer it."

He watched them a moment, put up a hand to quell the gabble of voices. "I know. I promised t' pay fer them mules, promised you boys wages, but this way you'd stand t' make a heap more. Them in favor of the original deal put your paws up."

The Papagos looked at each other. Medders could see they weren't happy, but no hands came up. "All right," he said, "it'll be share an' share alike. Now the longer this takes the bigger the chance we'll run into trouble, so let's git at it. You

an' you"—he pointed out Walker and the youngest
of the bunch, a dark burly hombre who called himself Flores—"will work down below. With me," he
smiled grimly. "You," he said, singling out another, "will go fetch in the stock, an' then do whatever
the girl here says. There's the winch to be worked,
the ore t' be sacked and packed on them critters.
Figure t' be movin' afore first light."

He passed a long stare about, watching them
through the cracks of his eyes. "One more thing."
He let the stillness pile up. "I taken you into this
deal as full brothers. I see anythin' don't fit that
picture this buff'ler gun won't be waitin' around fer
no *re*peat performance. It won't be knockin' no
rocks down neither!"

When the sun peered over the rimrocks, slanting
its bright fire across the cold sands, Operation
Mulepack was well under way.

Belita, on the flop-eared dun colored Eduardo
who had fetched her lovely lies into Tucson and
more recently brought her penitently back, was
well out in front riding point. After her, strung out
like a Mexican smuggler caravan over most of a
quarter mile, came the heavy-laden mules plodding
briskly along to the barks and jabs of the prod-
carrying strawhatted Papagos, Charlie Medders
on Begetta watchfully bringing up the rear.

Every animal carried a full waterskin in addition
to its pack, and Medders carried his big Sharps rifle prominently displayed, but there were no tin-
kling bells—so beloved by the runners of contraband
—to herald their progress. And there was very little
talking.

They nooned at a dry lake some ten or twelve

miles southwest of the Cerro Colorados and, after
resting the mules for an hour, re-packed and
pushed on, cutting north of Arivaca across the
flanks of the San Louis Mountains where the
going, not too bad, offered a little more protection
than could be found on the yucca studded flats
they'd left behind.

Charlie wasn't too keen about having Belita
away off there at the front after that talk he had
thrown at the schoolboys. Cutting the pie in seven
pieces he didn't reckon would be sitting too well
with her—not that he figured it would come to
that; but if it did she'd have less than she might
have got from Jones. He couldn't help being uneasy about her, but Walker he didn't trust out of
his sight.

He'd told her at noon, when he was setting up
the route, they'd stop again about five and pull the
packs off the mules for a couple hours' rest. He
wanted to keep all the strength he could in them
against the time when they might have to run.
Tomorrow they'd be climbing through some pretty
rough country.

At about four-thirty, by the look of his shadow,
Charlie rode Begetta into the gut of a draw and
found Belita, above a fire of dead mesquite fronds,
already working with the food for their supper
while the Papagos were still hauling packs off the
mules. Looking the animals over he came back and
told Walker to hang onto the oats and put the critters out on hobbles. "We'll be layin' over here till
the moon comes up."

Which was about two hours longer than he'd figured to be here, but on what they could forage they

would need that much rest. Belita, too, seemed kind of gray in the face.

He could have used some shuteye himself if it wasn't for feeling he had to keep his eyes peeled. So far everything had gone like clockwork, but Walker's good behavior wasn't fooling him at all.

Soon as the grub was cooked Medders stomped out the fire, and after they had eaten he climbed a rocky point and stared out over the darkening landscape, finding nothing to alarm him though he watched for half an hour. Restless and edgy he came lugging his worries back into camp to find Flores industriously sharpening a knife, the rest lolling around like they was too full to poop. Then Charlie, counting noses, came up one short. Pock faced big-nosed Walker was missing!

With a curse Medders whirled to look for Belita. Already afoot and moving toward him, she called: "What's wrong?"

The night had thickened to where you couldn't much more than make out faces, but he could tell by her voice she was edgy as he was. Sight of Walker's rifle in her hands took some of the teeth from the sharpest of his worries. He spun away without answering, running toward the mules, slowing as he saw their heads come up, stopping when one of them snorted.

He heard the girl stop behind him while his eyes combed the shadows, heard the mule grunt again. "Walker!"

The guttural bark of a laugh fell out of the murk. A deeper blackness took shape and moving nearer became unmistakably the man he was seeking. "W'at you want?"

"Thought you might be gittin' ready to slope."

"You nervous, Boss? Me check mule." The Papago grinned.

"Back up," Medders growled, "I want a look at that critter."

It was wasted breath. There was nothing to see when Walker pointed him out. Medders felt the mule over, could find nothing wrong beyond the obvious fact the pockmarked segundo had got back his cockiness. Charlie, grinding his teeth, waved the man back to camp. "What is it?" Belita whispered as they fell in behind.

"I dunno," Medders grunted, stare fixed on that shuffling shape. "He never come out here t' scratch his butt. You watch out fer that jigger. He's slipperier'n slobbers."

The ugly Papago was tickled over something, and such high spirits were plumb unlikely in a buck who had lost as much face as Heap Walker. If he'd lamed any of the mules. . . .

Back in camp, still fuming, Charlie peered around suspiciously. The rest of the redskins were sprawled like dropped logs, hats over faces, a couple of them filling the night with raucous snores. Medders, suddenly stiffening, loosed a furious shout. "All right, you possum-playin' coyotes! Git me some light!" he snarled at Belita.

Another boy was missing—he'd looked twice, recounting heads, to make sure. As the fire blazed up he discovered it was the youngest, the burly youth called Flores.

He looked minded to take Heap Walker by the throat. "Where is he?"

Black eyes stared sullenly. "Boy 'fraid, I guess," Walker said. "Go home."

Charlie struggled with his rage, knowing he could not afford any more mistakes. "What'd he have t' be scairt of?"

"No like go down that hole. Heap bad," Walker grumbled. "Cave of dead. Mebbeso spirit—"

"Don't pigeon-talk me, you sorghum faced reprobate—you can do better'n that!"

The pock-nosed Walker with an elaborate shrug mumbled something in Papago about "lost spirits" and "Ancient Ones" and, folding his arms, relapsed into silence.

Medders knew enough about those Ancient Ones—the people who had been on this land before the Papagos—to know this educated schoolboy was giving him the runaround. But, short of working him over Apache-style, and he didn't for a minute reckon the girl would stand for that, there wasn't no way he could dig the truth out of them. He had an uneasy feeling juning around through his system that Flores' departure was hooked up to this ore.

"Mistake I made," he said, eyeing them bitterly, "was tryin' t' treat Injuns like they was halfway human, but don't count on me makin' the same mistake twice." He got four shells for the Sharps out of a pocket and held them up where the light could strike across them. "I'm goin' t' read you what it says on the noses of these buggers: Ramon, Jacinto, Ricardo, Walker—one of 'em fer each of you. Next boy that wanders off is goin' t' git lost an' *stay* lost. Now pack them mules, we're gittin' outa here pronto!"

They made three brief stops during the night to rest the animals, some ninety minutes all told,

Charlie stomping around with his Sharps and his cursing, begrudging every instant they were not upon the trail. And there was more to his desire to cover ground than baseless fright. Two discoveries had been made which increased the florid complexion of Flores' disappearance. Belita's pocket pistol had sprouted wings and her faithful steed, the angular flop-eared Eduardo, had turned up missing while the mules were being packed. This was all Medders needed to clinch his conviction the Papagos were plotting to make off with his ore.

He had the girl on Begetta, armed with Walker's repeater—six shells in the magazine and one in the barrel, and cautioned to fire at the first hint of trouble.

Each time they'd stopped he'd gone around checking packs, checking the lashings, counting noses. He was over a barrel—too damned vulnerable on too many counts! That kid, if he was off on Walker's orders, might do any one of a number of things. He could be out there ahead of them setting up an ambush. He could right this minute be pacing alongside, waiting for a chance at Charlie with that pistol. He could be going for reinforcements or trying to make contact with some of Jones' scouts.

These were educated Indians with a patina of Christian doctrine priested onto them for upwards of two hundred years, which might have stuck no better than it had with some whites exposed even longer to its gentling influence.

Point was, these Papagos understood better than most what money could do for them. They would see in this ore not only the possibility of escape from a lifetime of drudgery but a chance to strike back for all the abuses of white supremacy. And the dead called up by Walker—the "lost spirits" trapped behind rock in that mine, whose unquiet blood through all these years would have been crying for revenge—could put real fire into whatever means Walker was taking to separate these packs from their rightful owners. After all, why share when, with a pinch of risk and a dab of ingenuity, they could grab the whole works and avenge their ancient dead?

What it all amounted to from where Medders stood was that now, on top of everything else, he was faced with the very real threat of mutiny, committed to constant viligance with death the price of that first careless move.

XIX

TROUBLE WAS he couldn't divide himself up, couldn't be in more than one place at one time. And there was a choice to be made.

They were moving now through a low range of foothills, rolling and thinly stubbled with drought stunted mesquites, the greater mass of the Diablitos behind them.

Ahead lay Tubac with not much between but open flats and, beyond the river, more of the same on an upward slant to the towering slabs of the Santa Rita Mountains, reputed to shelter bands of hostile Apaches led by a local medicine man operating under the name of Geronimo. From the train's present placement to the steeps of these mountains was pretty close, Charlie judged, to being a full twenty miles, and with hardly enough cover to hide a big dog.

He passed the word for another halt to give all hands whatever rest they might snatch while he reconsidered, in the light of suspicions roused by

Flores' defection, whether to make a bee line for
Tubac and try to bull through by the shortest
route, or drop south at once and, regardless of time
and the added miles, attempt to get through the
mountains by way of Sonoita Creek which, from
what he recalled, looked to be both easier and considerably safer.

He was aiming, of course, for the new stamps at
Charleston, recently installed by the Tombstone
Mining & Milling Company. Once he had the
mill's receipt they could jog over to Tombstone,
pick up and cash the Company's check, get rid of
the extra mules and break up. With the Weeping
Widow gutted of ore, Belita, like enough, would be
off to mañana land; he thought he might perhaps
ride along, as far anyways as Naco. In that border
town a man could thumb his nose at Jones with
impunity because, if things became too uproarious,
he had only to step across the line to be safe.

There was a considerable attraction to this picture of Naco, but first they would have to get the
ore to Charleston and, while a dash straight
through the mountains would be quickest, in the
hope of cutting out a few of the risks he'd about
decided to drop south and take the Sonoita Creek
route when, chancing to brush against one of the
waterskins, he went as suddenly still as though a
diamondback rattler had reared up in his path. He
stood, damp with sweat, finally reaching back a
hand. That skin had scarcely ten swallows left in it!

Although, like the Papagos, he'd spent the
whole night on his feet, he had not been conscious
of thirst until now. His own canteen, strapped over
his shoulder, was practically full, but the next wa-

terskin he felt of was empty—and the next. With
the schoolboys watching he ran to another. It was
still a little clammy where the water had leaked
away. The slit it had leaked from told the whole
story. Too scared to curse, he was aware of time
running out on him. The skins on the other mules
would be empty, too, and a dehydrated mule was
mighty close to being a dead one. He was minded
to shoot Heap Walker out of hand.

He looked around for him and someone, a couple hundred yards nearer the front, ducked between two mules. But the girl kicked Begetta into a
run and cut him off. "What is it?" she called, and
Medders bitterly told her.

"Empty!" she cried. "But they can't—"

"Every last one of 'em's been slashed with a
knife!" Charlie growled, hurrying up. There was
no telling how many of the Papagos had been in on
it, but it was near enough light that he could see
Walker's sneer. "Fer two cents," Medders snarled,
"I'd slit his goddam throat!"

He was riled enough to, anyway. Sonoita Creek
could be dry; most of the creeks had dried up in
this drought. He was so filled with fury his legs
were shaking.

The first flush of day was creeping over the
sandy flats off ahead. Charlie knuckled the red
rims of his sunken eyes. If he tried to go through
those mountains with Walker they could all wind
up at the bottom of some gulch. "Give him his
head," he told the girl; and, to Walker: *"Git!"*

The Papago eyed Charlie's Sharps like a cornered coyote, then took off at a lope, disappearing
behind a brush fringed ridge. The other three boys

peered at Medders uneasily, but none felt bold
enough to open his mouth. "The deal," Charlie
said, "still stands, but the next whippoorwill t' lift
s'much as a finger will be took care of, an' plumb
permanent."

The loss of that water could turn out to be serious, no use kidding himself. Between here and
Tubac, maybe three miles ahead, there was a tin-
can spring, the last of his hidden water, two big
cans that were going to have to be dug up and carried; and he was angrily thinking of the ore they'd
have to jettison when something about the tightening silence wore through his absorption to spin
him, Sharps lifting, in the direction of his crew.

Against the brightening east all three stood mo-
tionless, rigid as gophers. And Charlie, twisting to
follow those gray faced stares, felt his own eyes
swell. He blinked, peered again, and savagely
swore.

In the still morning air, back the way they had
come but farther north, a spiral of smoke blackly
climbed, like a finger, above the sun splashed crest
of Colorado Peak.

Even as he anxiously watched, clutched by dismay, Belita's bleak cry pulled his face around to
see, toward Tucson, an answering signal swirling
up in quick puffs. This was coming from Twin
Buttes, south and west of San Xavier, the stamping
ground of Burks, hatchet man for banker Jones.

Medders blew out his cheeks in a violent fury,
but could no longer doubt. Burks' scouts had a line
on him and were alerting Jones' lieutenants wher-
ever they might be, calling his understrappers into
the field. The dangers were doubled. Burks' spies in

the rimrocks would pick him up in two shakes if he moved onto those flats, and he was sure as hell going to have to. He had to cross the Santa Ritas or go around them, one—and there was nothing but desert between him and the mountains.

"Git goin'!" he yelled, and cursed the mules into motion.

There was no help for it, and no hiding their tracks. The Sonoita Creek route was out—they couldn't risk it now. They had to have that buried water or chance the loss of every mule!

As the ore-laden mules were being rushed toward the flats Medders, shaking and swearing as though out of his mind, was trying frantically to determine what chance they had of getting into those mountains. They were twenty miles off. Whoever had sent up the first gout of smoke had to someway eat fifteen miles of back country just to come up to Charlie's present position and—since he had no intention of standing around—could be forgotten; and Twin Buttes was better than forty miles to the north, while Medders' own party would be driving straight east.

But that bunch at Twin Buttes would be well mounted, traveling light. No pack animals to slow them and the promise of cash bonuses if they ran him to earth; once they made out he was bound for those mountains they'd move diagonally to cut him off. These were obvious facts, and Burks' reputation would be spurring them hard.

And the law of this land was in Jones' pocket.

Still, Charlie thought, they just might squeak through. It was the meanest kind of country up there, much of it hidden in timber, all standing on end, cut up with gulches, sheer slabs of rock towering hundreds of feet, drops that would make a man's stomach turn over. A gamble, sure—but what had they to lose that was not lost already?

What T.K. told his sheriff would have little relation to the orders given his pet exterminator. This had gone beyond silver. Dry Camp Burks would be out for the kill. But if Medders could get his mules into those mountains they'd at least have a chance to save their lives. There was places back there where one determined man could stand off an army, so long as his shells and the grub held out.

Such plans as he could shape were filled with ifs and maybes, but inside the first hour they had reached, unearthed and sampled the hidden water, stripped one mule of its silver, dropped the packs in the pit, tramped sand over them, strapped the dug-up cans to the unpacked mule, fed each animal its bait of oats and got far enough along in their dash for the mountains to bring Tubac town near enough without glasses to be apprehensively distrustful of its abandoned appearance. Even his Papago packers looked dubious; and Belita, twisting around, called nervously: "Hadn't we better pass this place up?"

"Looks like they've had some kind of a scare," Medders growled, waving her on. "There's a well in the square—like t' be the last water we'll see this side of Charleston."

He had his eyes peeled sharp for tricks but the air of utter desertion that hung over the place, the desolate stillness of the empty square, the boarded-up windows of the store—and its open door—all spoke in silent shouts of panic flight.

Whatever it was, Charlie thought, it hadn't hit; and he was still peering around with the hairs standing stiff along the back of his neck when a Papago's shout jerked a look across his shoulder.

South of the town, and not far south at that, a new boil of smoke was raggedly rising in a churn of leaden clouds that had nothing to do with signals. That spreading, billowing, black bottomed pall, increasingly tinted with edgings of pink, spilled its screaming answer through Medders' mind. Two miles down the road the tiny Mexican hamlet of Carmen was damn well being put to the torch, and the only thing a man could get out of that was Geronimo and his Cherrycow Apaches!

He dived for the store, coming out on the run with several boxes of cartridges and three of Mr. Henry's .44-40 repeaters taking the same black-power loads as most of the hand guns generally in use, and which he passed to his packers along with instructions to water the stock—but *lightly,* for this was no time or place to be stuck with foundered animals.

While this was being taken care of and he was trying to decide if they should hole up here where at least they would have some walls to get behind, he was scouring the town in the anxious hope of coming onto some kind of overlooked transportation ... like a good stout mule forgotten when these people had so hastily departed.

The livery was bare of everything but feed and harness. He ran limping around through a few more yards of tumbledown sheds, a faint but plaintive nicker brought him up with an old, nearly toothless mare. Any other time he would not have looked twice at her, but he was not right then in any mind to be choosey.

Dragging her back to the livery, anxiously scanning that pall of black smoke, he flung an ear-stall over her roman-nosed head and, about to grab up a saddle, instead heaved a sack of oats up across her withers, and climbed aboard with a heartfelt sigh. She might not be much but she sure beat walking.

They were all waiting for him when he got back to the square, impatiently staring with scared looks at the smoke. "All right," he called, "let's git outa here." No one argued.

In less than ten minutes they were at the river, pushing through cottonwoods and spraggly willows and on across its rock and sandchoked bottom, bone dry for weeks by the look of it.

For a while, except for scattered patches of brush, the way was fairly open, as he had figured it would be; and since the rise or pitch was not as sharp as it had seemed, they were doing pretty well. But along about midmorning, with two-thirds of the jump behind, one of the boys, pointing northeast, fastened all eyes on a new outbreak of smoke. This was obviously rising from some hidden peak and was just as certainly some kind of signal. Even worse, it was rising from the very mountains they were now committed to. Still, it was a long way north, up around Greaterville someplace, and Charlie, up to his ears in more urgent worries, put it out of mind.

It was Belita, long silent, who brought into sharp focus the crux of their danger, discovering a problem in tactics which could not be got around.

The terrain had considerably changed. They were now in a region of dwarf mesquite which, practically useless as cover, was becoming increasingly hard to get through. And the ground itself was more ruggedly rising, cut up and gouged by barrancas and cutbanks channeled through the centuries by storm-water runoffs. Progress had been reduced to a snail's pace; the mules were taking ten steps to get ahead scarcely one. And it was while they were cursing their way through this that the girl, leading Begetta, discovered the horsemen barreling up on their flank.

Charlie's first thought, when she cried out, was Apaches, and he whirled to peer south across a prickling shoulder. "The other way!" Belita called.

He saw them then, perhaps five miles off but coming up at a tangent and moving at the speed of a wind-pushed cloud shadow. There looked to be about a dozen in the bunch. He couldn't be sure without a glass, but it seemed not unreasonable to assume, since they were coming from the general direction of Tucson, that this was the go-gettem outfit intrusted to Burk's—the cure-or-kill unit of the banker's organization.

He hung fire a moment, trying to estimate whether Burks could wring more out of them and, if he could, would the increase be likely to put them into the eroding detritus and blocks of fallen granite he could see poking up below the base of yonder bastions before his boys could arrive with the mules. And he could not find either for or against. Jones' understrappers, while unquestionably moving a great deal faster, had at least five extra miles to make up. Coldly, Medders knew he hadn't much choice. To try to hold them off here was plainly out of the question.

Kicking the mare into some semblance of a run, pushing past the frightened scowls of his Papagos, he grumbled at Belita, "We're gonna have t' run fer it!" and put the mare, on her haunches, down a slope of sliding shale.

This wasn't what he wanted, but it was going to have to do. He was going to have to trust the girl to keep the animals bunched and moving. This arroyo he'd dropped into was cluttered with brush and boulders that would slow them further and, because of its tangent, would fetch them to the base of those towering cliffs a good ways off from the spot he had chosen, but at least it would keep them hidden from Burks.

There was no predicting what his Papagos would do, now he'd armed them; he could only hope Belita and their fright would keep them in line.

The arroyo petered out a hundred yards from cliffs that looked, when he came out of it, to be not only unbroken but too sheer even for a goat to find a foot hold. In this exposed position he twisted around to look for Burks and his hardcases, churning up quite a splatter of electrifying hope when they were not at once apparent. But this relief was short lived; they were out there, all right. They came surging abruptly from a gully scarce a rifleshot away, and the whistling *whang-g-g* of a ricochet screaming Charlie's name as it tore off past his elbow very amply described the pitch of their temper.

He flung himself from the mare like a ruptured

duck and, as the first of the mules came panting into the open, went scuttling with his Sharps for the nearest rock—seeing, even as he did so, the sun skittering off the wicked drive of raked spurs.

From the corners of his stare he got an impression of more mules bounding white-eyed past in snorting flight toward the cliffs. *"Keep 'em goin'!"* he yelled at the girl's frightened face, and brought the buffalo gun to his shoulder, feeling the recoil in every muscle of his body.

Through the blackpowder smoke he saw two outflung arms and a man reeling off the back of his horse. With no time for adjusting the sight he fired again, holding lower to compensate, seeing a second man pitch from the saddle as the rest sheered off to hunt cover like rabbits. And he was up and running himself on the instant, putting into it every ounce of drive he could summon, to fall wheezing behind the rotten rock of an outcrop some good forty yards nearer the base of the cliffs.

Blood pounding in his ears, he couldn't hear for the bedlam of enraged shouts and gunfire as Burks' dismounted scalp hunters tried to blast him off the face of the earth. Rock chips struck like hail around him as he lay squeezed flat against the stony ground.

XX

WE ARE TOLD uncounted times how a man, faced
with death, knows regret for past mistakes as in
those last fleeting moments forgotten faces in
flying sequence flash across the stricken mind.

It was not that way with Medders.

Though between a rock and the devil's own
doorstep, crammed with the bitterness of frustrated hate—scared to move and even more afraid
not to—the only thing he was regretting right then
was that he could not take a lot more of them with
him. Particularly Burks.

Behind him the mules had all passed out of sight;
the only things to be seen back there was cliffs,
fallen rock and sunbaked shale. He had never felt
so alone in his life.

He could twist his head but dared move nothing
else. Most of the noise had dropped away till there
was just enough firing to keep him pinned down
while his thoughts cringed and snarled at imagined
activities given cold credence by sundry scrapings

and scufflings, the occasional clatter of disturbed stones.

To lift his head up to where he might see was almost certain to summon that last blue whistler, and if he didn't look soon that bunch would be all over him. He had cut his twine too short for this play; and just as he was snapping the lever on another 525-grain bullet, gathering his muscles to come up shooting, the sudden slam of two rifles barking viciously back of him changed the whole look of everything.

Convinced he'd run his string plumb out, relief rushing through him almost turned him dizzy when one of Burks' scalp hunters let out a cry and several booted pairs of nearby feet broke simultaneously into a frantically departing dash for cover.

Charlie, lunging erect, knocked one of them sprawling, and was fumbling to thumb a fresh load into the breech when the girl's jumpety voice cried: "Back here—*hurry!*"

Still crammed with the spleen of unappeared anger, belligerent and reckless with strain and resentment, he would have stayed to shoot more except that all who were able had ducked out of sight.

Disgusted, he finally limped toward Belita who, with one of the boys, was still banging away. "Put some whack in it," she snapped. "We can't hold them forever!"

In the nest of rocks they had his caught mare waiting and from there he could see the narrow slot in the cinnamon cliffs through which the mules had been driven. The girl, pointing toward it as he climbed onto the mare, said, "It opens into a canyon about a quarter mile back."

"We better hope," Medders grunted, "it don't turn out t' be a *box*."

They caught up with the mules and the other two schoolboys about a mile farther on and Medders knew inside the next quarter hour that if this gulch dead-ended they would have no recourse but to fight their way out, which—considering the odds if Burks' bunch forted up—was no salubrious prospect.

And, sure enough, the damned walls darkly towering above them commenced with alarming suddenness to close up, pinching in until Eddie Two-Cow, up at the front, had a hard time keeping them off his elbows. The girl kept peering anxiously at Medders and Charlie, bull stubborn, kept waving them on. To go back, in his opinion, was no better than plain suicide and, anyway, this crevice had grown so narrow there wasn't room to turn around. His two-legged animals could probably manage and maybe even the burro, but not those mules.

The cant of the ground grew rougher and steeper, and more and more often became all but closed off with rock chunks dropped from the rotten rims which had to be scrambled over. If one of the animals broke a leg in the process. . . .

He refused to follow so repugnant a thought; the things he *had* to look at held all the grief one man could stomach.

The rock strewn bed of this twisting crevice led the clatter of hoofs and these mute, stumbling humans ever higher and deeper into the stone ribbed flank of the mountain, the walls climbing with

them toward a blue crack of sky which seemed
presently as remote as the likelihood of getting the
ore through to Charleston.

Though he frequently looked back, expecting
each time to find Burks plunging after them, he
was more fiercely concerned lest this tortuous passage either pinch out completely or become im-
passably choked. If it narrowed another five inches
they would have no choice but to abandon the ore
—at least the bigger part of it, and he was not even
sure they would be *able* to.

Where, for instance, could they put it?

Not in their pockets. And if they dumped it onto
this ribbon of ground how—cramped as they were,
traveling head to tail—would any but the first be
able to get past? Sure, Medders thought bitterly,
the girl, the Papagos and himself could manage to
scramble over it no doubt—but never those mules!

Though he had not yet caught a glimpse of
Burks or any sign Jones' kill crew was back of
them, he could not believe a pistolero of Dry
Camp's vanity and grudge-ridden pertinacity
would ever willingly give over with the end so close
to his hate-bared choppers. The guy was simply
playing it cautious, waiting for Charlie to trap himself for them or get into some bind where it would
be just the same as shooting fish in a barrel. That
was Burks every time—he got paid for scalps, not
for taking crazy chances!

And there was another wicked hunch breathing
down Charlie's neck, a nasty premonition that he
may have been outfigured. When you counted the
resources at Jones' disposal, all the bonus hunting
men he'd put into the field, you couldn't hardly feel

it likely the banker any longer would have much doubt of their destination.

And then, abruptly, the worst of Charlie's fears came home to roost. Unable to gauge how far or high they had come—except that the walls hanging over him seemed lower—Medders rounded another of the crack's sharp twists and found the whole train stopped.

It wasn't the end of the road, but it might just as well have been, he guessed in the bitterness of consternation. Ahead of them the passage stretched out, ironically, straight as an arrow and, within five hundred yards, climbed into the sunswept windy open—just five hundred goddam yards, Medders thought.

To be licked, that near, by forty feet of fallen rock!

But there it was, jammed tight, forty feet of piled-up rubble, jagged chunks sticking out that nothing short of dynamite could move in a month of Sundays! There was no possibility of taking the mules over this—they couldn't even be turned around. There was nothing, by God, he could do but shoot them. Mare and mules! It damn near made him cry.

He put Belita with Walker's rifle around the bend to watch for Burks. The rest of them, sweating like pigs, went to work. He gave the last of their water in his hat to Begetta and then, the boys helping, manhandled her bodily over the worst spots while the mules stood patiently waiting their turn. Charlie groaned, as in fever, but they were too big to handle.

It took an hour and twenty minutes to get the

burro past that jumble of wedged-in broken sections of rimrock, to retrieve a pack saddle and as much of the ore as he dared risk putting on her. Long before they were finished Belita's rifle cracked twice, filling the gorge with a bedlam of echoes. Charlie sent one of the Papagos back to help her keep Burks pinned down, glad that the bend concealed their reason for having stopped. Had Burks known their predicament he might have talked his toughs into making an all-out effort. As it was—faced as it seemed with determined resistance—he could tell himself there was nothing to be gained that could not be taken care of easier and cheaper in the dark of the moon. At least Medders hoped that was how Dry Camp would see it.

When they were ready he slipped back and with a hand-sign called in the girl and Papago. Just as they were about to squeeze past the mules he said, keeping his voice down: "Any ore you wanta take along in yer clothes you can keep without dividin', but it'll sure git heavier with every mile you lug it."

"Thanks for nothing," Belita said, grimacing, and squirmed on by without so much as a look. Medders stepped aside to let the schoolboy through, but education got the best of Eddie. He stopped by the last split-open pack, fastened his pantslegs tight at the ankles, unloosened his belt and filled both sides to bulging. He put several of the smaller chunks inside his shirt and finally jammed three more up under his hat.

Medders got the Sharps, slung his canteen over a shoulder, and followed. The boy was making rough work of the rockpile. Belita was just scrambling down the far side when Medders, re-

lieving Eddie Two-Cow of his Henry repeater, let
go a deep sigh and started shooting mules.

It made a hellish racket, and when he was done
he smashed the wooden stock and bent the barrel
out of shape before flinging it away from him. This
didn't make him feel any better but it was something he could do. He caught up with Eddie, helped
him down off the rocks and then, still looking like
hell warmed over, struck off after the others. He
glanced back once, halfway to the crest, and discovered Eddie Two-Cow throwing away some of
the ore he had stuffed in his pantslegs.

The others, with Begetta, stood waiting at the
summit, and he was just coming up with them
when a rattle of rifleshots jerked him around, to
find Eddie staggering into a run, to see him
knocked off his feet with his mouth stretched wide
in a yell that never came, and Burks' bunch back of
him swarming onto the rock jam. He pulled the
Sharps' sight up as far as it would go, clapped the
stock to his shoulder and hauled back on the trigger.

The solid boom of that buffalo gun cut through
lesser sounds like the crash of a cannon. One of
Burks' rannies went down as though swept from
his knees by a scythe. Crazily Medders stood pouring lead into them, firing as fast as he could cram
in the shells. One fellow spun, taking another guy
with him. One, almost clear, fell with both arms
flopping.

When Charlie, still fuming, came up with Belita,
the girl said: "Is that it?"

The whole world, it seemed like, was spread out
below them. Following her look Charlie, glower-

ing, nodded. It was not so terrible far as the crow flew but the way they would have to go, hoofing each mile with their loss and anxieties, Charleston seemed almost at the ends of the earth.

Notwithstanding the bitter thoughts they kept chewing, parched throats, burning feet, empty bellies and the constant worry of running into Apaches, at just a fraction past nine of the following morning Medders, sourly waving his paper to dry off the ink, stepped from the office of the T.M. & M. full into the smash of the climbing sun to suddenly stop as though hit by a mallet.

Equally stunned, the others stopped back of him to stand anxiously peering into the fat shaved-hog face of Tiberius Jones and his gaunt-shouldered sheriff.

Bad enough it had been to get scarcely more for the ore on Begetta than half what he'd got from O'Toole back in Tucson. Break this into four shares, he'd disgustedly thought, and it would just about manage to take care of his chewing. And now to be caught flat-footed, check still in hand, put such a strain on the clutch of his temper that if he'd been packing a pistol he'd probably have grabbed it. He hadn't even a pocket knife and his Sharps, belatedly remembered, was still in the office, uselessly leaning where he'd set it against the damned counter.

McFarron, recalling perhaps better days when they'd been cronies, shifted and, scowling, started to open his mouth. But Jones, staring hard at the check, waved back his sheriff.

Breaking through the tight fit of his Judas smile

the great man said like an elder brother: "All right —you win. I'm a big enough sport to own up when I'm beat. Put a reasonable price on that mine and I'll buy it."

Charlie almost choked. But the banker, misreading him and quick to seize any sign of an advantage, declared like Moses handing down the great stones: "I'll give you one hundred thousand, sight unseen—that's fair enough, isn't it?"

"It ain't a question of fair—"

"Make it a hundred and fifty," Belita said, "and you've got it."

Charlie glared at her; Jones, peering at both of them, switched his attention to the girl. Caught between caution and greed he said carefully, "I'd have to go out there, you know . . . I've got to be able to find it again."

"These boys here can show you," Belita smiled, watching Charlie. "They know where it is—they helped us pack in that ore. Put a cashier's check in my hand and it's yours."

Charlie looked apoplectic. "Here, wait—"

Jones said: "It's a deal!"

THE FEUD AT SLEEPY CAT

For
George Fitzpatrick

1

Ordered Out

CROSS-DRAW BOB BOYD backed stiffly from the cabin with both arms held above his head and a gun's hard muzzle grimly prodding at his belly.

It was in no sense an enviable plight for the hero of Agua Prieta to be finding himself in. But held-up hombres are seldom choosers. He continued his careful backing till his shoulder-blades rubbed up against the rump of his ground-hitched horse.

"Jest keep right on a goin'," advised the scowling holder of the drop. "Goldfield lies off yonder; Medicine Bend over that way. Both trails is plumb open an' easy found. If there's ary a wheel in your think-box, you won't be doin' any stopping till you're clear on out of the country."

"Like I been tryin'," Cross-Draw said, "to tell you, I—"

"Git aboard that bronc an' drift!"

There could be no doubting the earnest and ominous timbre of the gun-wielder's instructive words. Ready gun and watchful stare were a team to command obedience.

Cross-Draw got on his horse. But once aboard, he twisted 'round in his saddle and put a glittering glare upon the fellow. "You needn't think, just—"

"Git!"

And, still muttering under his breath, Cross-Draw *got*.

But he didn't go very far—not nearly so far as the other man must have imagined. Only around the shoulder of the mountain. And there he stopped.

And cursed.

Vigorously and in words of Anglo-Saxon vintage he described the dictatorial gentleman's ancestry, condition, clothes and future. A canny portrait—a spitting likeness. The fellow's friends would have been amazed.

No terrific accomplishment, but it was a whistle for Cross-Draw's feelings; a little one. After that he rolled himself up some Durham and began taking stock of the situation.

It was not that Cross-Draw had in mind any particular destination. He just didn't like to be shoved. He'd just been wandering 'round the country with an eye to seeing the other side of some hills—any old hills would have done.

But now all that was changed. Gents didn't try running fellows out of the country just to limber up an appetite. There was more in this than met the eye, and he had a powerful hankering to know what it was. A craving he meant to satisfy. By cripes, he'd show a few jaspers five or six things!

It had all got started when, half an hour ago, hot and dusty and hungry to boot, he had ridden up to that cabin. He had, to be sure, considered the cabin's situation a rather secluded one. But after all, these Superstition Mountains were full of boobs with gold colic, and some of these goddam prospectors were crazy enough to throw up a cabin any place. The shack had appeared deserted; he'd seen no sign of horses. Hungry, and packing divers aches from too-long hours in the saddle, he'd made up his mind to move in for a bit and do a spot of resting.

8

The decision had been short-lived.

Climbing down from the saddle he'd trailed the reins and, humming a snatch from *Suzanna*, had gone unsuspectingly up to the door. Even after stepping inside he'd felt no qualms, although he'd found the place occupied. No misgiving or thought of gunplay had been in his mind. The hospitality of this mountain country was a thing too well established; the feeding and lodging of strangers traditional.

"Hello!" he'd said with a friendly grin.

There'd been two men inside the cabin. One—apparently sick or asleep—had been under blankets on a bunk with his head bent toward the wall. His companion—an older jasper—had been sitting near by employing a knife on the sole of a boot. The fellow's eyes had jumped at the sound of his voice.

Right then Bob had got his first warning.

It had sharpened his glance and slammed vivid emphasis upon certain details of the layout: the man's startled look, the blade in his hand, the cocked and loaded rifle standing ready against a wall. Most particularly it had focused his interest on the man in the bunk. He had twisted a haggard face with fresh-rocketing hope driving some of the scared look out of his eyes.

Barely had Cross-Draw grabbed these impressions when the seated guy's curse yanked his gaze around sharply. His breathing slowed and his eyes had sprung wide. Knife forgotten, the fellow was on his feet and with a pistol grimly staring from a brown and rigid fist.

Cross-Draw had taken one look and gulped. "What's the big idea?"

"The idear is this hotel's full up—*see?* Either you

9

pack your carcass some place else or you'll be parkin' it right here permanent! Go on!" he gritted. "Git goin' before I change my mind!"

So he had gone. There'd been nothing else he *could* do.

And now, concealed from view by the shoulder of the mountain, he was trying to make up his mind.

There were two or three courses open to him. He could take the knife-sharpener's advice at face value and cut his stick for other parts. He could paw around and from some point of vantage eventually learn the wind-up of this business. Or he could circle 'round, approach the cabin from another direction and perhaps—with a bit of luck—manage to set free the guy in the bunk.

It was toward the latter course that Cross-Draw's adventurous nature was most strongly inclined. He could not tolerate injustice of any sort. And that the fellow in the bunk was getting a raw deal he'd have bet his last thin dime.

It was of course none of his damned never-mind. And he usually kept his nose where it belonged. But this affair was a little different. He'd been ordered out at gun-point.

His spirit chafed just to think of it.

He was not compatible to being frozen out of anything. And his sympathies could wax amazing warm toward anyone who had the look of being an underdog. And if any gent ever *had* had that look—

Hell! That guy in the bunk was a prisoner! No two ways about it! And if Cross-Draw was any judge of character, he was not expecting to be a prisoner long—nor would he, judging by the loving care with which the snake-eyed gent had been whetting up that knife!

10

Dirty work was afoot in that cabin and no mistake!

Cross-Draw had seen enough dirty work in his time to know the smell of it ten miles off.

There was considerable contrast between the shack's two occupants, he reflected. *Quite* a contrast. And it did not reflect any credit on the guy with the Arkansas toothpick! A surly-looking devil, he; gloomy-cheeked and bitter-eyed—the kind that must have sailed with Morgan, Cross-Draw thought.

On the other hand, the fellow in the bunk was young. He had a wholesome face and good clean teeth—a fine looking kid. The kind Cross-Draw's brother might have been, had Cross-Draw had one.

Something would have to be done; a bit of action was indicated. If that fellow on the bunk were to be extricated from his predicament in time for said extrication to do him any good, he would have to be snaked out of there quick. And Cross-Draw would have to do it. And anyway it would be a real pleasure, he decided, to show that knife-sharpening jasper there were other catfish in the sea!

So thinking, Cross-Draw urged his flea-bitten buckskin down the mountain's flank. After putting an angling drop of several hundred feet between himself and the cabin's level, he turned the animal left and began retracing his way about the mountain's shoulder.

When he figured he'd about reached the logical spot, he swung down from the saddle and left his mount on grounded reins. Giving him a few final admonitions anent keeping his "damned trap shut," Cross-Draw began a cautious inching forward, gradually working upward toward the shack.

11

It was a long and wearisome business, but it didn't weary Cross-Draw—he reveled in it. By George, he'd put a spoke in that knife-sharpener's wheel that wouldn't get yanked out in no damn hurry!

Half an hour later he had the cabin well in sight; the rearmost part of its anatomy. And—glory to glory and four hands around—a sack-hung window stared him blankly in the eye!

That was luck!

Of course, it was just possible old squinch-face had an eye to a crack there some place. But Cross-Draw didn't think so. Squinch-face, if he were expecting any encore at all, was bound to have his cannon pointed trailward.

Probably there was a cog missing some place in his reasoning. But he was in no mood to notice. Having decided Squinch-face wasn't looking, he lost no time in discarding caution. Brave as a painted lion he went catfooting up to the window.

Tow-sack, he found, wasn't the best of materials to see through. But as most of the light inside was coming from the front, he managed in a hazy sort of way to make things out. Squinch-face, he saw, was back in his chair again honing up his knife; but now the chair stood by the door. And the door was open a crack. And the rifle—which had been standing against the wall—was cached quite handy in Squinch-face's lap.

Cross-Draw grinned.

This was going to be duck soup!

After a little hunting he found a rock about twice the size of a hen's egg. Stepping back a pace he heaved it high above the roof, then glued his eye to the window. The rock came down with a clatter.

Cross-Draw had no way of knowing what it struck, but it landed on the cabin's far side and the result was all he could have hoped for.

Squinch-face stiffened like putty in his chair. His head cocked to one side abruptly in an attitude of listening. Then, with the quiet stealth of a cougar he got out of the chair, putting his knife down on the floor and crouching, rifle ready, at the door-crack.

In a blur of motion Cross-Draw yanked both pistols, crashed their muzzles through the glass and yelled: "Hands up!"

Squinch-face jumped like a pin had pierced his tintype. But he was a man of fast reactions. He flung his torso half around and like a wink lammed two shots through the window.

They both put holes through Cross-Draw's hat!

But Cross-Draw hadn't been taking chances. His hat was on a stick, and as it fell he drummed the rifle from Squinch-face's hands with five quick shots.

Squinch-face reared back cursing.

"Never mind the compliments," said Cross-Draw, stepping through the window. "Just get them mitts up over your head unless you're hankerin' for a boothill epitaph. By George, one yip outa you an' I'll blast you flatter than a monkey's ankle!"

Snarling his rage, Squinch-face thrust his hands up.

Cross-Draw strode across the room, kicked the knife and rifle into a corner, jerked the pistol from the fellow's holster and threw it out the window.

"Now," he said, "we'll get down to business. Go loose that fellow of his shackles—"

"Go to hell!"

"That place has been reserved for you," grinned

13

Cross-Draw. "Go get that fellow untied now," he added, scowling, "before I get mad an' work you over."

It looked like Squinch-face was about to loose another burst of profanity. But something he must have read in Cross-Draw's stare seemed to change his mind. He strode sullenly to the bunk and hurled the blanket on the floor. Fifty-three seconds later the prisoner, with a malignant smile, swung his booted feet to the floor and began scrubbing the circulation back into his arms.

Squinch-face leaned against the wall and glowered.

"How you feelin', son?" Cross-Draw asked the man he'd rescued.

The young fellow flung him a funny look. "I'll get along," he said, and kept on rubbing his arms. Cross-Draw grinned. "Sure you will," he chuckled. "We'll both get along soon's you're ready. I got no more hankerin' to linger round this polecat specimen than you have."

He eyed the erstwhile captive curiously. "What was he up to, anyhow?"

"It'll keep," said the youngster grimly. He went to a curtained soapbox nailed in a corner and got his belt and gun; strapped them about his clean-limbed body with evident satisfaction.

"There'll be another day," growled Squinch-face.

The youth didn't even look at him.

"You been expectin' company?" Cross-Draw asked.

Both men looked at him. Neither one spoke.

Cross-Draw shrugged. "Just thinkin' we'd ought to tie this pelican up, mebbe. Kind of hate to do it though if there won't be anyone 'round. He—"

"Don't worry about him," the released man cut in smoothly. "Be a waste of time to tie him up—just leave him loose. We'll take the horses. He won't get very far afoot."

Squinch-face cursed with abandon.

"Sure has got a talent," Cross-Draw murmured admiringly. "Musta had a mighty fine education in his day—"

"Come on," said the young fellow, sloshing on his hat. "Time we were cuttin' stick. Got a long way to go before dark—"

"You better tie me up an' leave them horses—"

"Perhaps we'd better at that," said the young man very quiet. "But we're takin' the horses anyhow." He drew his pistol with a quick smooth motion. "Get onto that bunk. Face down. . . . I haven't much time to argue," he said clearly.

It was kind of amazing in a way, the promptitude with which old Squinch-face got himself onto that bunk. The look he gave the young fellow was enough to have soured new milk. But he did as directed just the same, and he didn't lose any time about it either, Cross-Draw noticed. Nor was much time lost in the young man's manipulation of the rope. An expert job in practically nothing flat.

Leaving the cabin, true to the youngster's predictions, they found a trio of excellent cowponies cached in a cleverly hidden dugout back from the trail a piece some thirty yards farther on.

Kind of looked, Cross-Draw thought, like maybe that young fellow might have something on the ball.

He had more definite information on the subject when, still driving the extra horses, an hour later they came to a place where someone had thrown a gate and cattle guard across the road.

"May be padlocked," the young gent said. "Blow the damn thing off if it is."

Cross-Draw wasn't too certain of the propriety of blowing some other man's lock to bits. He chucked his companion a questioning look. But the young fellow nodded earnestly. A bit impatient, too, Bob thought. He seemed to know what he was doing.

So he got down and going forward found that the erstwhile captive had been right. There *was* a padlock. With a shrug Cross-Draw did as he'd been bidden. He held the gate open while the young man drove the horses through; then, being a thorough-going cowhand, he swung it shut.

He reached for his horn and brought a foot up for the stirrup.

He was like that, set to swing up, when the young fellow's voice pulled his head around.

His eyes bugged out and his jaw went slack.

He was staring into the bore of the young gent's pistol.

The young gent's face was very grave. "No need you climbin' into that saddle," he said. "Here's where we're partin' company. Just hang your gun belts on the horn—an' careful, buddy, *careful*."

"I'll Make You Holler Caff Rope!"

WHEN CROSS-DRAW got his breath, he took the top from his can of cusswords in no uncertain manner. He swore high and wide and handsome. And was unreeling some of his choicest epithets a second time when the young fellow's slanchways grin hauled him up with a disgruntled snort. "Just put that gun away," he snarled, "an' I'll bat your ears down t' where they'll do fer wings!" He glared in baffled fury. "Of all the unmitigated, swivel-eyed—"

"When you're all done, just hang them gun belts on the saddle horn," said the young gent coolly. His yellow eyes gleamed with a kind of quiet amusement, but the muzzle of his pistol didn't waver by a fraction. "An' you better get a wiggle on. Unless you want to stay here permanent."

Tight-lipped with anger, Cross-Draw unbuckled his belts and, glaring, hung them as directed. Then he stepped back. He said: "If I ever cross your tracks again, you better dive down a hole an' pull the damn thing after you!"

"If you're smart," said the young gent blandly, "you'll do what that pelican back at the cabin told you. Get out of this country by the quickest trail. Case you ain't honin' to go back past that cabin, there's another—"

17

"Save your breath," growled Cross-Draw. "I ain't leavin'."

"That's too bad. Course, I can see what your game was, gettin' me away from Torrence—it was a pretty slick move an' might of worked if I wasn't dry behind the ears. But just the same, as it turned out, you got me out of a jackpot. So I'll remind you again, you'll live a heap longer if you jerk up your picket pin an' drift."

"Yeah—that's rightdown thoughty of you!" Cross-Draw blared.

"Not at all. You did me a favor, gettin' me loose of that cabin, so—"

"With true Christian charity you're takin' my guns an' puttin' me afoot! By George, I'll make you holler caff rope or my name ain't Cross-Draw Boyd!"

The glint in the young gent's eyes had changed. He was staring at Cross-Draw intently now, a little queerly.

"Boyd, eh?" he said. And then: "No matter. This climate ain't healthy for strangers an'—"

"By George, I'm goin' to *make* it healthy!" Cross-Draw snapped.

"In that case..." Smiling apologetically, the wholesome, good-looking young fellow squeezed the trigger of his leveled pistol.

Cross-Draw, a look a stupefaction on his face and with both hands clawing at his chest, staggered three half-hearted paces and went down.

HE CAME TO with a terrible aching in his chest. The left side of his chest. It was like all hell's helpers were banging him with blunted brass sledge hammers. It was like nothing he had known before or wanted to know again. A deep sigh welled from him and he

18

closed his eyes.

But not for long.

It struck him suddenly that he was still alive—nothing could hurt so bad if he were dead. Keeping his eyes still closed, he reached a hand up to the spot where pain was greatest. Dull and throbbing, kind of, like the time that damfool dentist over at Yuma had yanked the wrong molar.

He jerked his eyes open suddenly with an astounded curse. That was funny! He got to an elbow and stared amazedly at his chest.

Where in hell was the blood!

First time he'd ever been shot that he hadn't bled profusely!

The bullet hole was there, right enough.

He thrust an alarmed hand inside his shirt; grimaced, and brought it out. No sign of blood! Of all the cockeyed things—

Then suddenly he knew.

He pulled the big stem-winding silver watch from his vest pocket. And sure enough. Its timekeeping days were forever over. There was a big deep dent dead-center. Damned thing looked like a doughnut with the hole not quite punched out.

And doggone lucky it wasn't, or St. Pete would sure be getting him measured for a harp and halo!

Then, suddenly, he made another discovery; or rather, a series of them. His gun belts, with full cargo, were strapped about his waist. His horse stood over yonder, anchored by trailing reins. The tall young gent with the wholesome face was gone. And there was a note pinned to his shirt.

He grabbed it off with an oath.

Squinting up his eyes he read:

We got plenty more where this lead came from!

.3.

Worse, and More Of It

MAYBE SO.

But that guy had tried to kill him; had ridden off leaving him for dead. It was enough to make any man mad. If these fools thought a gent like Cross-Draw Bob could be scared into quitting before he got to the bottom of this screwy business, they were crazy as a bunch of woodpeckers—crazier, in fact!

Half an hour's riding brought him within sight of Sleepy Cat, an old rail and cow town hardly more than a David's stone-throw from the oftmentioned Continental Divide. High country, this, and with an atmosphere that dried one's sweat before it started. A place that periodically saw the gathering of cattle clans from the northern ranges, wool-raisers from the Spider River, and occasionally a swaggering dark-hued gun fighter from the Spanish Flats.

But mostly, like just now, the town was practically deserted. A drab collection of rickety, false-fronted buildings whipsawed from the adjacent hills, and looming gaunt and gray as the forgotten relics of a ghost town.

Which, indeed, it nearly was.

It had been many a year since gold in any quantity had been taken from the Superstitions. Even the cattle and sheep interests used the town but twice a year, and only upon those brief occasions did the puffing snort of the iron horse disturb its slumberous hush.

Glancing about with frank curiosity, and with a weather eye peeled for further hostile actions toward his person, Cross-Draw rode his walking buckskin down its straggly main street. Over yonder was the once-pretentious depot, its red paint faded and dust-darkened to a rusty brown, doors padlocked and windows boarded up. There was the railroad hash-house with its old Fred Harvey sign, and off a bit to one side the abandoned division-headquarters buildings of the absent railroad bosses. There was a great long yard of sidings, bumpers, switches; two shops and a round-house, also boarded up. Nine saloons and honkey-tonks. A livery stable and corral. A blacksmith shop, still open, if one could judge from the thin wisp of smoke curling grayly from its decrepit chimney. A down-at-the-heels hotel whose rambling size still hinted at former splendor, though its windows now peered rheumily through a coating of dust and cobwebs. A number of boarded-up stores. A general store, still open, and with one ancient lounger snoring wheezily in the cracked and wire-bound rocker on its porch. And off to the south there, among a welter of vines and creepers, the gaunt old wreck of what looked like a one-time dance hall.

Then Cross-Draw came to a saloon that had three cowponies racked at the rail before it.

"Must be open," he mused thirstily, and parked his buckskin beside those dozing others.

A glance at his shadow showed the time to be nearing five o'clock. No wonder he felt in need of nourishment. He hadn't partaken of a bite since early morning.

21

He shoved his way through the batwings with a hand draped carelessly over a Colt, half suspecting he might find that wholesome young vinegarroon loitering at the bar.

But the young gent wasn't there.

A paunchy gray-haired barkeep leaned with folded arms among his bottles. Over in a corner at a scrubbed-white table a stocky man was eating supper, and not caring much who heard him. A man in the habitual rig of a gambler was dealing a hand of Klondyke at a table across the room. Against the old scarred bar stood a guy with a short beer in front of him and hands plying steadily between the free lunch platter and his mouth.

Cross-Draw took a place beside him. "Large beer," he grunted, and rested an elbow on the bar. The paunchy man in the white apron drew a glass and with a dexterous flip spun it the length of the mahogany where it stopped directly in front of Cross-Draw without having spilled a drop.

Cross-Draw eyed the fellow admiringly, pulled a two-bit piece from his pocket and imitated the barman's spin. The coin, unlike the glass, forgot to stop. It left the bar, spun through the air and went clattering to the floor in some obscure corner. The barman looked a mite reproachful, but made no effort to retrieve the coin.

"Say! Don't I get any change?" Cross-Draw demanded.

"Not unless you get down and hunt fer that quarter."

Cross-Draw scowled; decided if the bartender wasn't going to hunt, he wasn't either. The hell with it.

He reached for a sandwich and started munching.

The beer was good, but a little warm. Sandwich was first rate.

Cross-Draw reached for another. His hand closed on the fellow's at the side of him. They looked at each other scowling. "Wot's the idear? Tyke yer blinkin' 'and awy!"

Cross-Draw removed the offending hand. This funny talker was a solemn, horse-faced chap; not so tall, but lean and wiry as a keg of nails. He was dressed as a range hand and packed a gun. But he sure talked like a foreigner and his sunburned mug looked foreign, too. He had, Cross-Draw noticed, appropriated the sandwich Cross-Draw had been reaching for.

With a muttered grunt Cross-Draw looked over the diminishing platter and decided on another. Again his reaching hand came down to close upon the foreign hombre's quicker-reaching mitt.

Cross-Draw looked at the guy and scowled. "Blimey!" the guy said, "cawn't yer leave me 'and alone?"

Cross-Draw swore. "Get your damn paw outa the way then! Think you're the only mug in these parts wants to eat?"

"Does them sandwitches belong ter *you?*"

"They don't belong to *you,* do they?"

"'Oo said they did?"

"Well, for Crissakes," Cross-Draw growled, and reached once more.

But again the other got a hand there first.

"'Ere! Wotcher up ter?"

"Listen here, you Mormon-eyed sidewinder, I want some of them sandwiches myself!"

"Whyn't yer tike 'em then?"

"Are you aimin' to stop me?" Cross-Draw

23

snarled. He dropped a hand to gun belt.

"None o' that, now!" exclaimed the foreign hombre fiercely. "Wot yer tryin' on? Tryin' ter start a fight?"

Cross-Draw swore indignantly. "Of all the goddam hogs—"

"'Oo's a 'og?" snarled the stranger, screwing up his eyes. "You tike that back or I'll tie you up in a knot it'll tike yer a week ter untangle."

The others were watching now. Cross-Draw could feel their interested gaze upon him speculatively; could see their staring faces in the backbar mirror. All but the barkeep. He was eying the pair of them disapprovingly. "'F you birds are aimin' to swap lead," he said resentfully, "go on outside to do it."

"'Oo's goin' ter swap lead?" the skinny guy demanded. "Me an' '*im?* Don't yer believe it. 'F 'e tries gettin' gay with me I'll put 'im in a corffin—"

"You an' who else?" snarled Cross-Draw, getting red.

"Jest me—that's 'oo. Go a'ead. Try it on, guv'nor!"

Cross-Draw started a jolting right toward the bounder's face, but cut it short with a startled oath when, quick as a wink, the fellow whisked a gun from some place and jabbed it in his belly.

"W'y don'tcher, guv'nor?" The skinny man grinned malignantly.

But Cross-Draw wasn't having any—not against those odds. "What the hell kind of country is this, anyway?" he demanded, glowering. He flung a resentful look at the barkeep. "You goin' to let him get away with this?"

"Hell, I give up all claim to that lunch twenty

24

minutes ago! You're the only guy that's got anything to eat off that platter since he came in here."

Cross-Draw swung back to the fellow. "Put that gun away an' let's start even—"

"Wot fer? I'm satisfied the wy it is. Tike yer own gun orf if yer wanter bury the 'atchet."

Cross-Draw was hungry. He was broke, to boot. But it sure went against the grain to let that wrinkle-faced little shrimp get away with this. He was of half a mind to yank his guns out anyway. He was debating the probable outcome when the stranger, with a disgusted snort, put his hogleg up. He did it in a way that showed premeditated insult.

While Cross-Draw was trying to make up his mind what ought to be done about it, the fellow pivoted on a bootheel and, with a smothered exclamation, went catfooting to the window.

Puzzled, Cross-Draw slammed a look of his own in that direction. "Holy cow!" he gasped, and went hurrying to the cockney's side.

He was not alone. Apparently others were susceptible to the excitement. The gambler, the noisy eater—even the gray-haired barkeep, forgot their occupations and came crowding precipitately forward.

The whole works stood there, like sparrows on a telegraph wire, scarcely breathing, intently staring at the person coming down the steps of the yonder general store.

She was quite an eyeful.

Chestnut-haired—"teeshun" was the word in Cross-Draw's mind. Tall, she was, and willowy; albeit with plenty of curves in the right places. Irish, too, with long slim silk-clad legs, scarlet lips and eyes like a pair of shamrocks.

25

"By Gawd!" Cross-Draw said. "Bee trees is gall beside her!"

The girl's arms were filled with bundles. One of them, at that particular moment, wedged free of its companions and went bopping down the steps. Split-seconds later the remainder of her purchases were doing their best to give realistic presentation of a landslide.

Cross-Draw and the stranger made identical decisions. The cockney spun men off his elbows and sprinted for the door. Cross-Draw waded through the shambles half a step behind him. They got to the batwings simultaneously and damned near tore them from the hinges. Winning clear of them with spluttered curses, they built twin dustclouds across the road.

Both bent down together. Together they reached for the very same package.

It was like a while ago all over again.

"Lumme! Wot yer up ter?" snarled the red-faced cockney. "Tyke yer bloody 'and orf that parcel!"

Cross-Draw was getting mad. "*I'll* pick 'em up for the lady!"

"Oh! will yer? 'Oo said so?"

"*I* did!" Cross-Draw snapped belligerently. "I've had enough of your yap! Leggo that now an'—"

"Leggo yerself or I'll plarster yer teeth orl over the lan'scape!"

"Who the hell do you think you are?"

"Comes ter that, 'oo the 'ell do yer think *you* are? The President?"

"Gentlemen," the girl said firmly. "After all, it'll soon be dark and I've quite a ways to go. Couldn't you manage to hurry it a little?"

Her friendly smile was bright, impartial. As public as the sun.

The two belligerents straightened. The cockney dragged his hat from his head, grinned and made a leg. Cross-Draw wasted no time with his headgear but, drawing himself up stiffly, said: "Madam, permit me," and stooped to gather up the recalcitrant bundles.

But the cockney put a hearty boot in the back of his lap and Cross-Draw skidded through the packages on his chin.

With a furious oath he came up out of the dust and sprang. A malicious right took the sunburned man on the side of the jaw and sent him spinning like a dervish, strewing gathered bundles at every whirl.

"Please!" cried the girl imploringly. "*Please!* You're stepping all over them!"

They looked at her shamefacedly.

"Lumme! if this 'ere blighter— Hit's orl 'is fault!" declared the cockney bitterly.

"If this pie-billed grief would keep out of the way," exploded Cross-Draw, "I'd have 'em all picked up by now." He glowered at the cockney furiously. "Thank Gawd I don't have t' live in England!"

"Aw, close yer face—they wouldn't 'ave yer fer a chimley-sweep! They wouldn't let yer parst the light! They—"

"Now, look. I'm sure I'm more than in the debt of both you boys," declared Shamrock-Eyes placatingly. "But since it's evidently impossible for you to get together on this thing—"

"That's orl right, Miss. '*E* can pick 'em up 'f 'e wants ter," the cockney said magnanimously. He whistled the dust from his hat and clapped it on his head. Rasped rough hands across his chaps. Brought one hand up and thoughtfully scrubbed it across his low and wrinkled forehead. He said brightly:

"W'ereat's yer equipage, Miss—yer tally-'o?"

She laughed. "That's our wagon over there by the Chandler House." She pointed toward the hotel with the cobwebbed windows.

"Yer ain't stayin' there, are yer?"

"Gracious, no! My father owns a ranch up the valley. The Harp."

"Come on, then," said the cockney, taking her by the arm. "I'll guide yer to it—ter the waggin. Algernon can bring the blinkin' parcels."

"Algernon! Who you talkin' at?" snarled Cross-Draw. "I'll have you know my name is Boyd—Cross-Draw Boyd."

"Wot abaht it? Eh?"

"Nothin' about it—only don't try callin' me Algernon!"

"'Oo is?"

Cross-Draw glared. He said: "On second thought, I'll conduct Miss—Miss—?"

"O'Reilly," she said smiling.

"Yer a thort too late! I'll tike the I—" The cockney stopped as the beautiful O'Reilly heaved a definite sigh.

She said ruefully: "This seems to be quite a problem. But we must get it solved in a hurry because I'm late getting back already. Suppose this gentleman—"

"Loving's me nyme, Miss—and loving's me nyture. Halbert Loving."

Her eyes showed a mischievous twinkle. She said hastily, to cover Cross-Draw's vulgar snort: "All right, then; Mr. Loving will se me to the wagon and Mr. Boyd will carry my parcels. I wonder if you boys would like to come out to the ranch. Dad—"

"I'll be glad to come," said Cross-Draw promptly.

28

"'Oo ast yer? I'll come meself, hif it comes ter that. I'm a hard-working bloke—if I do say it meself. As 'ard a bloke as ever set a saddle. Be a valu'ble asset ter *any* spread. I—"

He pulled up abruptly, screwing up his bright little eyes and staring at her intently. He said suspiciously: "Hit ain't a dude ranch, is it?"

"Good Lord, no—it's a working cow spread."

"Good! No need tykin' Algernon, then. There won't be any plyce for ornments—"

"Hell's hinges!" shouted Cross-Draw. "Who you callin' a ornament? Why, you slab-sided, shriveled-up wart—"

"Boys—*please!* Dad can find a place for both of you. So let's get going. Albert can escort me to the wagon, and you, Cross-Draw, can drive."

Cross-Draw muttered bitter curses under his breath and started gathering up the packages. A fine time he'd have driving, while back of him that blasted British blighter sat with the O'Reilly holding hands!

A Pretty Kettle of Fish

IT WAS quite dark when they reached the ranch.

No lights showed.

The buildings shoved up gaunt and dim-seen outlines against the deeper gloom of the yonder hills.

The girl broke into the *Rocky Road to Dublin,* whistling it clear and sweet as any man.

Cross-Draw flung a look across his shoulder. "Stable?"

"To the right."

Cross-Draw swung the team in that direction.

A challenge ripped the murk and flattened. Shamrock-Eyes shouted: "Eileen—with company."

The cockney chuckled.

Cross-Draw scowled. Powerful strange, he thought, when a fellow had to go romping through a rigmarole like that just to get into his own headquarters.

But the girl offered no explanation.

Cross-Draw kept his questions to himself. Seemed like this whole damn country was somewhat off its axle. But he'd been round enough to savvy this was time to keep his mouth shut.

A hand met them at the stable and Cross-Draw tossed him the lines. He would have helped Shamrock-Eyes to alight, but "Halbert" beat him to it. No one spoke as the girl led the way toward the house.

The girl pulled open a door. "Be careful, now," she warned. "Don't fall over the furniture—"

"Holy cow!" gasped Cross-Draw, reaching for a shin. "What's the damn stuff made of—*iron?*"

The soft laugh that came from Shamrock-Eyes was like the sound of muted temple bells. Then she was pulling open another door. A gush of light spilled across the threshold, and the acrid smell of pipe smoke made a stench in Cross-Draw's nostrils.

Then they were inside and Cross-Draw's glance went immediately to the man getting out of the rocker. He had big rolling shoulders and massive hands, and the way smoke boiled and gurgled from the fellow's old dudeen reminded him of a bad chimney he'd once fixed for a Polack back in Texas.

"My dad, Shamus O'Reilly," the girl was saying.

He had a shaved-hog face with fat, smooth cheeks and wide unwrinkled forehead. But Cross-Draw wasn't noticing at the moment.

"Company, bejasus!" Shamus flung a black scowl at the girl and rubbed a hand against a holster. "An' 'tis a hell av a toim to be brangin' company here!"

"This isn't company—I've brought you some gunslammers, Dad."

"Whoa!" thought Cross-Draw, and was starting for the door as Shamus said with a completely changed manner: "Oh! gunslammers, is it? Well, sure they're welcome as holy water to a soul in Purgatory. Come right in, bhoys—'tis glad I am t' see yez."

Yeah! Cross-Draw could understand that, all right. A dark ranch headquarters, countersigns, challenges—not to mention that artful invitation to be gun bait. *Gunslammers!* Yes, indeed, this fat-faced Shamus had something to be glad about, if

31

he and Loving were fools enough to get their names in his tally book!

Well, Loving could, if he wanted to. It was a great opportunity. But not for Cross-Draw Boyd.

He started through the door.

"Here—where are you going?" cried Shamrock-Eyes reproachfully.

That was where Cross-Draw pulled a boner. He should, he afterwards reflected, have been firm and kept on going. But that temple-bells voice and faintly reproachful look must have undermined his willpower. He stopped and turned.

"I'm goin' back to town...."

The last of it sort of trailed off, like hair from a shedding dog. He found he couldn't meet the look in her eye, and stood there twisting his hat like a damfool country bumpkin.

It was no way for the hero of Agua Prieta to be acting. But he couldn't help it. And when she said: "Going back to town!" like that, his determination had kind of wilted. "Well, er—you see—I—"

She shook her head. "That's all right. You don't need to stutter," she said coldly. "We quite understand. You needn't work for us if you think it might be too dangerous. We—"

"It ain't that," Cross-Draw blurted. "It's just that— Well, I'd kind of like to know what's up before I get my oar mixed into this."

Shamus looked at him thoughtfully and nodded. "Ye're dead right, sor, to be lookin' that far ahead," he declared approvingly. "'Tis many the time I've told me own son if he'd looked ahead a bit he'd not have bought so many dom pigs in a poke! Ye're a sharp lad—jist the kind the Harp's been needin'."

Cross-Draw started to stick his chest out, then

32

thought better of the notion. It sounded like he was about to get roped in on a range war, and he didn't want any part in it. He was going to have his hands full putting the skids under that bright young whippoorwill who'd plunked a bullet in his watch and ridden off leaving him for the buzzards. He wasn't going to have any time for—

And right there that blasted Albert butted in with: "Give us the story, guv'nor."

Old Shamus scowled, and smoked his villainous pipe in a dark reflective silence. At last he said: "Tell 'em, Eileen."

"I suppose I should have told you before I got you out here," she began; "but it's hard work getting hold of hands these days and I was afraid you might not come if I told you there in town. The truth is, we've been having trouble with the Flying V. It got started over some water that we own. They claimed it was on their range and that we'd no right to it. Of course it wasn't on their land at all; but it was close to the boundary between their ranch and ours, and the Pools thought they could bully us out of it—"

"Whoa up a second," Cross-Draw muttered. "Who're the Pools?"

"Owners of the Flyin' V," said Shamus grimly. "An' a blacker-hearted lot ye'll niver find!"

It was going to be a range war, Cross-Draw saw. It had all the earmarks. "I can see you ain't give the water up," he said. "What happened then?"

She looked a little flustered. "Well, one thing led to another," she told him hurriedly. "That water quarrel developed other quarrels, until right now we daren't show a light in the house for fear of getting killed."

"Lumme!" Albert gasped.

"It's got to the shootin' stage then, has it?" Cross-Draw asked.

"Sure, an' it's after bein' way past that," growled Shamus vehemently. "Bejasus yes! 'Tis scared I am ivery time Eileen goes into Sleepy Cat for groceries. I set here in fear an' tremblin' that she'll be comin' home in a sheet! Why, didn't the black-hearted vipers murther me own poor Tim who was hardly turned twinty last grass? Shot him down like a dorg as he stepped from the cabin door!"

Albert made clucking sounds with his tongue. "Blimey! The bloody blighters!" he exclaimed.

Cross-Draw saw that Eileen's face, during the recounting of the tale, had grown white as a rag. But he said: "It seems to me, with all due politeness, that if things have got that bad Eileen shouldn't be allowed to go to town. If your supplies got low, why didn't you send one of your hands or go yourself?"

"He can't ride," cried Shamrock-Eyes reproachfully.

"Me dom spine is out av whack," explained O'Reilly with what looked to be regret. "As for thim bawstard hands—bejasus ye can't git a one av thim to go within gunshot av the place! It's Eileen or starve."

Cross-Draw mulled this over for a bit.

Albert said: "Wotcher need is starin' yer spang in the eyes, guv'nor. *Me*—as sta'nch a bloke as hever thumbed a 'ammer."

Shamus beamed approvingly. Eileen caught her hands together. "Oh, Albert!" she cried softly, and the look in her blue-green eyes made Cross-Draw curse.

"Shucks," said Albert with a sudden grin. "That ain't nothink—not a blinkin' candle ter wot I'd do fer

34

you." And his surly eyes got bold and glimmery as she let him hold her hand. But suddenly he seemed to remember something, and grunted. "Better be sendin' Algernon back ter town—" he began, when Cross-Draw snarled:

"Algernon—if you're referrin' to me—ain't goin' back; he's stayin' right here! An' if you call me Algernon again," he said, gritting his teeth like he could chew the sights off a six-gun, "I'll smack you s'far it'll take a bloodhound a week t' find you! *Savvy?*"

Eileen moved back a pace in quick alarm. But Albert sneered. "Ain't no more 'arm in 'im than in a chambermaid," he assured her; "han' if 'e don't pipe dahn, I'll kick 'is pants up rahnd 'is neck s' tight they'll choke 'im to death."

Cross-Draw ignored him, feeling it beneath his dignity to bandy words with a specimen of Albert's caliber. "You can put my name on your pay-chart, too," he said to Shamus. "Let nobody get the idea Cross-Draw Boyd is afraid of any two-bit fracas—"

"Bah!" grunted Albert inelegantly. "I wouldn't 'ire yer t' keep a windmill goin'!"

But Shamus told Cross-Draw hastily, "Sure an' I was hopin' ye'd see the light, bhoy. 'Tis glad I am to have yez. Jist take your roll to the bunkhouse—"

"But they came off without their horses, Dad," cried Shamrock-Eyes contritely. "We left in such a hurry—"

"Think nothing of it," Cross-Draw told her. "You'll have a night-horse caught up, I reckon," he said to Shamus. "I'll just ride it in to town an' get our nags."

But Shamus shook his head. "Albert can go for the horses. You stay here with me, bhoy. There's that

35

on me mind I'm wantin' an answer to, an' I'm thinkin' yez are the wan to give it. Jist set ye down on the couch over there an'—"

He paused as the door was flung open and swiftly closed again. The man who stood with his back against it was tall, lithe and muscular. He had high cheekbones like an Indian's, and a vulture's beak of a nose that had been broken in some forgotten brawl and badly set. But a ready grin quirked the corners of his mouth and Cross-Draw took to him instantly.

Shamus said: "Sure an' ye're back already, Tam? Did ye—ah, git the work done nicely?"

"Done to a turn," Tam chuckled; and Shamus told the new hands proudly: "This is Tam, me youngest—an' a crazy spalpeen if there iver was wan." He looked Tam over fondly. "Tam," he said, "I've jist hired on these bhoys. Two fire-eaters, Eileen says. They go by Albert Loving an' Cross-Draw Bhoyd. I want ye to be after showing Misther Loving where the night-horses are kept up. He's a little errand to do before mornin'."

"He's going to Sleepy Cat," Eileen said quickly.

"Sure, I'll go with him then," Tam said, pulling on his gloves. "Come along, Misther Loving; 'tis not over-safe for any Harp hand to go riding this range alone."

AFTER ALBERT AND Tam had left, and Shamus had sent Eileen to bed, the old man hitched his chair around and ran his bright little eyes over Cross-Draw appraisingly. " 'Tis a foin figure of a man ye are, Misther Bhoyd," was his considered verdict. "Full desarvin' of ye Irish name. Did yer folks come from the auld sod, now?"

"Yeah—from County Cork. Just after they got

married," Cross-Draw added. He relapsed into silence then, leaving it up to O'Reilly to shape the talk, and wishing the hell the fellow would put his damned pipe away. It was the vilest hod Cross-Draw had ever smelled.

But it seemed Shamus used the pipe to clarify his thoughts. He knocked the dottle from its bowl and packed it with fresh fodder—a kind of green tobacco like none Cross-Draw had ever seen before. He tamped a fistful tightly in the bowl and struck a match on the seat of his rocker.

"'Tis wonderin' that ye are no doubt jist what I've kep' ye back for," O'Reilly said, and puffed great gusts of smoke about with evident satisfaction. "Can ye use thim cutters ye've got strapped to your pants?"

Cross-Draw hesitated and Shamus said: "What I mean is, can ye *really* use thim? How good are ye? Have ye iver killed a man?"

"None that wasn't needin' killin'," Cross-Draw muttered grimly. "I'm a man of peace if I'm let alone. An' them that's got any sense so lets me," he added darkly.

"I see," said Shamus thoughtfully, and nodded. After which he puffed awhile in silence.

"If you're wantin' t' have some of them Pools salivated," Cross-Draw pointed out, "you better talk to Albert. That guy would as soon salt down a gent as look at him. Me—I got some qualms."

"I got a few meself," admitted Shamus; "but there's a sneakin' pot-shootin' bawstard in this country that has got to be rubbed out—an' the quicker he's got rid of the better I'm goin' to like it."

He smoked reflectively a moment. "The hell av it is," he said, "I can't put any handle to the bawstard. He's killed three of me hands I know of, an' he's the

37

murtherin' blatherskite that shot me poor Tim down outside the door."

"How do you know if you got no notion who he is?"

"I know all right. You can kiss the Book on that!" muttered Shamus grimly. "He puts his mark on ivery job—a .45-90 rifle shell between ivery dead man's teeth!"

Cross-Draw stared for long-drawn moments. Then he said: "I don't see how he could have done that with your son. You say—"

"He was shot comin' out the door? He was! We found the shell where the bawstard had been layin'," Shamus explained. "An' 'tis the same man who shot the others. Thim caliber rifles ain't yet common round this country."

He puffed furiously for several minutes till Cross-Draw felt like he was going to choke.

But just as suffocation seemed most certain, Shamus took the pipe from his mouth and tapped his chair-arm savagely. "That man has got to be stopped—an' he can't be stopped by ordinary means. Nor by the O'Reillys, for the O'Reillys," he added bitterly, "have already tried. It's got to be some stranger he ain't watchin' for—some man that's slick as bear grease, brave as a lion, an' can throw a gun with the best av thim."

He paused to eye Cross-Draw searchingly.

"If ye can qualify for the part—an' can git the murtherin' hound—bejasus I'll pay ye foive hundred dollars—*cash!* An' no questions asked, bejabbers. Will ye try yer hand?"

"Why not put it up to Albert?"

Cross-Draw hesitated. "You Think it's a Pool?"

38

"A Pool or wan of their gun-slamming hands. Who else would it be?"

"You got no other enemies then?"

"None that's afoot an' frothin'," Shamus growled. "It's the Flyin' V that's behind it, an' ye can kiss the Book on that!"

"You seem pretty sure—"

"I am! Why, thim Pools will—But niver mind!" He looked at Cross-Draw sharply. "Will ye take the job or not?"

"Well I'll have to think it over," Cross-Draw muttered. "It's a little out of my line. Like I said, I'm a man of peace. I try to live by the Golden Rule, an'—"

"Sure, an' I wouldn't have asked ye otherwise. Ye've the look av a man to be trusted—which is more'n I can say fer that Albert." He looked at Cross-Draw shrewdly. "Your pay fer a hand will go on all the same, but—"

Feet pounded across the outer room. The connecting door banged open and a tall, lank man with depressing gloom-filled eyes stood on the threshold breathing heavily. His patched and faded clothes were covered with dust and the slant of his cheeks was bitter.

He said savagely: "The goddam bastard got a—" and choked off short as his glance blundered into Cross-Draw.

Cross-Draw groaned.

It was Squinch-Face of the cabin!

.5.

Neck Meat or Nothing

CROSS-DRAW WASN'T waiting around for any explanations, for there weren't any he could give that would get that look off of Squinch-Face's mug—and he knew it!

With no preliminaries he slammed his body forward in a flying tackle that caught the newcomer squarely in the abdomen with a force that knocked him sprawling.

Squinch-Face went down in the wreck of the table and Cross-Draw went through the door.

He ploughed across that darkened outer room like a whirlwind, ignoring Shamus' shouted blasphemies, and cursing raucously on his own hook every time he bumped a piece of furniture. What he did to that room was a caution; but he had graver things in mind than the hurried destruction of unseen furnishings, and lost no time in hunting a place where he could do his thinking in more leisureliness and comfort.

That place was going to be the back of a pounding bronc—if he could find one.

A challenge bit across the yard as he burst through the outside door. But challenges were nothing in his young life, and he kept right on. Even the bullet that abruptly kicked dust from his tracks only spurred him on to greater effort.

Dimly he could see the slatted shadows of a pole

corral. He headed that way in a zigzag sprint, dragging out his guns as he did so. Next time flame blossomed from the murk of the stable doorway he flung three quick shots in that direction and had the pleasure of hearing whoever'd been doing the firing beat a hurried retreat.

Then Cross-Draw was at the corral.

He snatched a rope from the saddle-hung kakpole and clambered inside. He followed the snorting horses, shaking out a loop. Then quick as light his rope shot out and snagged a squealing gelding.

There wasn't going to be any time to get a saddle on. He was going to have to do a Lady Godiva and do it quick if he aimed to get out of this place with a whole hide. Already Shamus and Squinch-Face were piling out of the house, and hands were bulging from the bunkhouse. It was like he'd kicked a red ants' nest.

There were a lot of shouts and curses and every once in a while somebody let a gun off. But they hadn't located him yet—and even when they did, he thought, there wouldn't be any lead thrown his way until he got away from that corral. On the other hand, he'd have to be cutting loose of the corral right pronto or they'd get him surrounded.

There was no telling what might happen in that event; but Cross-Draw felt pretty sure it wouldn't be especially pleasant. Be a lot more reminiscent, he thought grimly, of Old Home Week in Hell!

He scanned his chances and found them bad. If he pulled open that gate good time would be lost—to say nothing of the telltale groans and creaks any touching of it would be most likely to produce. And he had no way of knowing whether the bronc he'd got his rope on was any kind of a jumper; mostly range horses weren't.

One thing was certain: In their present mood this crazy bunch of Irishmen would just as soon throw down on him as shave—and a whole heap *sooner,* probably! Not until he'd had a chance to spiel some kind of an explanation was it going to be safe to get in gunshot of them; and the way things looked right now no kind of explanation was going to be satisfactory.

There was just one thing to do, and without stopping for more than a glance at possible consequences, Cross-Draw did it. Throwing a leg across the gelding's back and using his lasso for a hackamore, Cross-Draw put the bronc straight at the fence and prayed the fool critter could jump!

.6.

A Startling Disclosure

STRAIGHT AT THE fence the gelding drove like a ram.

When it seemed that nothing but oblivion could lie ahead and Cross-Draw was entertaining a belated regret for some of the more obstreperous things he'd done in this life, the big cowpony rose like a bird. They cleared the corral's top bar with fetlocks flying.

But somebody saw them. The cry went up. Six-guns beat an ominous chatter and lead screamed shrilly all about them. Cross-Draw could hear it smacking the peeled pine poles; could hear the shouts and furious curses of the sprinting Harp hands.

"There goes that damn spy!" shrilled Squinch-Face. "Quick—he's cuttin' left!"

"Git the bawstard!" Shamus roared. "A fifty-dollar bonus for the man thet brings him down!"

"The chiseling shanty Irish!" Cross-Draw muttered. Fifty dollars for the hero of Agua Prieta! Why, he ought to burn the place down!

They were almost clear of the yard now. Another twenty feet would see them into the hemming chaparral. He flung a look across his shoulder.

Damned night looked like a fireflies' reunion!

"Just you wait!" Cross-Draw howled vindictively. "When I get a little leisure I'm comin' back an' empty some hats, by Gawd!"

It was at that precise moment that Fate stepped in.

The gelding gave a sudden lurch, screamed, and went pinwheeling end over end. Cross-Draw emulated a bullet and kept on going. Straight ahead, like the celebrated trapeze fellow.

He lit in the chaparral and it was no damned bed of roses!

He rolled over twice and came up with a pistol. The bucking throb of its recoil against his palm was a charming feeling—definitely.

Before that blast the whooping minions of Shamus O'Reilly faltered, turned tail and fled. Shamus' hoarse threats and Squinch-Face's curses were powerless to stop the rout.

There was only one thing wrong with the picture:
Cross-Draw was irrevocably afoot.

THE SUN WAS two hours high when he came dragging into Sleepy Cat. Weary and bedraggled, he was sore as a snake-bit squaw. A sole desire burned incense in his mind—the same desire that put the strained white look about his mouth corners, slanted his cheeks to a wicked purpose and gave to his lean gray eyes the look of polished flint. A furnace-hot yen for vengeance.

He went directly to the Sheriff's office; hammered on its door.

When repeated hammering got no answer, he parked a portion of his anatomy on the step and gingerly pried off his boots. God, but those feet hurt! There was a separate ache in every joint and a blister on every toe.

It was a hell of a shape in which for the hero of Agua Prieta to be finding himself.

"But just you wait," he muttered. "*I'll* fix 'em! I'll take this country plumb apart! I'll break it up for

44

vest buttons! Fool around with Cross-Draw Boyd, eh? I'll make these butcher-birds wish they'd never stepped out of the shell!"

He pulled off his socks to give his feet more air, and when that didn't seem to help much, began fanning them with his hat. He was still taking turns with his hat and his oaths when the clank of spurs drew his glance up suddenly.

A fellow in a pinto vest was approaching. A taciturn-looking hombre, with pale blue eyes and a stubborn jaw. The eyes looked Cross-Draw over from a tangle of bushy brows.

"Athlete's foot?" he asked concernedly.

"Naw—chilblains from walkin' down hell's highway!" Cross-Draw snorted. "When does the slab-sided squirt that's sheriffin' this county hold office hours? I been waitin' here long enough t' grow more hair than the Smith Brothers got! I—"

"Well, usually," the pinto-vested gentleman remarked ruminatively, "he manages to gi' aroun' sometime i' the day. What did ye want to see him aboot?"

"I'll be takin' that up with him personal," Cross-Draw muttered, gingerly feeling of his toes. "What the hell's good for blisters?"

"We-el—" the man in the vest said reflectively, "ha' ye ever tried axle grease? Myself, I always use liniment, but there's those that think it a wee brash."

Cross-Draw stared. And then: "Tread gently, brother," he growled, "'cause I've got my bristles up an' I'm in a sure-enough horn-tossin' mood. I ain't t' be trifled with—savvy?"

"I noted yer lum was nae reekin', lad," murmured the gent in the pinto vest, and went sautering off down the street.

45

"If you see that so-an'-so Sheriff," called Cross-Draw after him, "send the damn fool down here. 'F he don't come pretty soon, I'm goin' to tear this place apart!"

It was enough to make a preacher curse.

Seemed like even Fate was conspiring against him. There was a moment when he almost wished he'd taken Squinch-Face's advice and ridden on out of the country. Only the lack of a horse and a natural reluctance toward displaying what might have been taken for a white feather kept him from doing it right now.

Abrupt contact, however, between his big left toe and a splinter from the step brought his mind to a sharper focus on his grievances. "Leave *hell!*" he snarled, picking up his socks. "*I'll* show 'em! No durn whippoorwill can play ring-around-the-rosie with Cross-Draw Bob an' get away with it! I'll give this country the dangdest overhaulin' it's had since Noah!"

With extreme caution he pulled the socks on over his swollen feet. Slipping a couple fingers through his bootstraps and with the arm left free thrust out for balance, he got up and picked a crane-like passage across the empty street. Up yonder was the one saloon still open in this town. And slowly, laboriously, with much display of acquaintance with profanity, he beat his way in that direction.

It took him ten minutes to make the haven and he was sweating like the devil's first assistant when he got there.

He pushed his shoulders through the batwings and staggered to the bar. Several other customers were already resting their elbows on it, but he paid them no attention. Not even when he felt their

46

curious gaze. For he knew damn well that if he did, and one of them smiled, there was going to be a funeral; and he was too durn exhausted to officiate.

That is, he thought he was.

But he was evidently wrong, for the barkeep had parted his face to say something and at Cross-Draw's look had promptly frozen with his mouth still open.

"My Gawd! No wonder!" he thought, catching sight of himself in the backbar mirror. The reflected specimen showed a wild-eyed ranny in dark scuffed chaps and with crossed gun belts sagging tied-down holsters at either hip. A bronzed-faced ruffian whose tough-hombre look was made more vivid by a razorline black mustache that was stretched to the corners of as grim and forbidding a pair of lips as had ever been packed into the Superstition Mountains. Nor was this quite all. The cleft chin had been raked by a wicked wound at some past date and in its wake had left a livid scar.

Cross-Draw grimaced and set his boots down on the bar.

"Whisky," he said bleakly, and the barkeep made haste to get it.

Holding the bottle in his left hand, Cross-Draw sloshed his glass full; set the bottle down with a solid thump. "Can you tell me where," he growled, "I can find that swivel-eyed Sheriff?"

A flicker of surprise briefly lighted the barman's gaze. He jerked a thumb toward the end of the bar. "That's Sheriff MacIllwraith, there."

Cross-Draw downed his whisky and turned a slanchways glance into the mirror. He gasped, made pale by what he saw.

Then anger had its way with him. Fury rioted in

his veins and he whirled with a bitter oath. "What the hell!" he snarled, and striding up to the sheriff shook a doubled fist beneath his long Scots nose. "Listen, you old buzzard-beaked so-an'-so! What was the big idea?"

The stubbled roan cheeks of the man in the pinto vest showed no resentment. "I dinna get yer meanin', lad. Better ride the trail again. Chew it a wee bit finer," he said with a dour Scots smile.

Cross-Draw planted both brown fists on his hips and glowered. "Hell's backlog!" he exploded. "Whyn't you *say* you was the sheriff when I asked you what time he opened up? What'd you think I was talkin' for—to hear m' head rattle?"

The sheriff appeared to be weighing the problem seriously. When finally he spoke, his long Scots face was solemn and his voice was brau as his northland moors. He said: "There was some doot in m' mind aboot the technicalities o' the matter. Ye had a badness in yer eye an' ye'd just returned the noo from O'Reilly's. 'Tis nae you I was avoidin', lad; 'twas ma conscience an' ma dooty. Shamus O'Reilly and the eldest Pool, ye'll ken, are commissioners o' the county."

"Oh—you're figurin' to be a fence-sitter, are you?" Cross-Draw scoffed. His lips curled back in a cold contempt. "You're a hell of a—"

MacIllwraith's roan cheeks darkened, and there was a stubborn forward throw to his scraggly Scots jaw that made the Texan hesitate. MacIllwraith said: "'Tis nae what you think, lad. I hae no love for feuds an' I canna hold wi' murder. Shamus O'Reilly is a hard man, ye'll ken, and the eldest Pool is nae sa weak."

Cross-Draw looked at the sober faces of these

48

other men consideringly. He did not pretend to understand this situation. It was patent that the sheriff wanted no part in what he appeared firmly to believe was a budding range war. He wished to remain strictly neutral and so was being careful to do nothing that would seem to favor either party.

"Why not pull out of the limelight then? Whyn't you resign an' hand 'em back their dad-burned star?"

Slowly Angus shook his head. "Ye dinna ken, lad. The MacIllwraiths are a doughty clan," he said with his dour Scots smile.

Cross-Draw was about to make a pertinent remark. But just then he noticed the avid curiosity in the eyes of the watching loungers. He picked up his boots and, moving like he was walking on crushed toads, started for the door. "C'mon," he growled. "Let's go someplace where there ain't so many ear-stretchers. I got a coupla things t' tell you. We better talk it over private."

MacIllwraith followed reluctantly. The resentful stares of the "ear-stretchers" followed both of them.

In the Sheriff's office Cross-Draw helped himself to the comfortablest chair, cocked his feet up on the desk and thrust his thumbs up under his galluses. "It looks to me like the country's done gone haywire."

MacIllwraith nodded slowly. "She's nae sa gude."

Cross-Draw growled: "She's dynamite with a fuse attached an' burnin'," and told him of his experiences at the cabin, at the cattle guard, and at O'Reilly's. He said nothing, however, about Shamus' proposition that he catch the mysterious killer.

The sheriff nodded, scanning something in his mind, but saying little. "Ay, lad; it all fits into the pattern." He rasped a reflective hand across a bristled cheek. "'Tis nae sa gude. The brave bricht

49

mon ye rescued from yon cabin was Zeneas Pool—"

"An' who was the pleasant scorpion that was whettin' up that knife?"

"That," MacIllwraith told him dourly, "was Torrence O'Reilly. A black Irishman who can nurse hate like an Apache. Ye did yerself no gude when ye crossed Black Torrence, laddie." He shook his head and with the gloomy prediction lapsed into silence.

Cross-Draw jerked him from it with an oath. "The hell with him," he snarled. "His hate ain't no skin off *my* nose! No hombre," he gritted, shaking an emphatic finger under MacIllwraith's long Scots nose, "can go round proddin' his hogleg in *my* belly an' get away with it. I'm—"

He broke off suddenly to stare intent and earnest at the sheriff's unrevealing countenance. "By George, I've got it! You make me chief deputy for this here county an' we'll show them birds a few!"

MacIllwraith rubbed his chin. He frowned.

"That's the ticket," Cross-Draw said enthusiastically. "Me, I'm a man of peace when I'm let alone. But when sawed-off squirts like this Zeneas Pool an' that snake-eyed O'Reilly sidewinder start—"

"Nae," the sheriff grunted, with the frown spreading up to his pale blue eyes. "That wouldna be sae gude, lad." He shook his head more vigorously. "Ye'd be only fermentin' more devil's work. It wouldna do at all, mon."

"What you fixin' to do?" scowled Cross-Draw. "Sit around on the back of your pants till that feud wipes out your voters? Hell's hinges! I thought the MacIllwraiths had bones in their spinal columns!"

"Ye dinna—"

"Ahr-r, don't tell *me*—what you got's a goddam wishbone!" snorted Cross-Draw, and with gusty oaths stamped his feet down into his boots. "Jest keep your seat! *I'll* tend to these back-country brush-poppers! Feuders, eh? I'll show 'em which end of a gun the *smoke* curls outa!"

MacIllwraith caught him by the arm. "Hoot, mon! Slow down a wee bit, laddie. If I make ye a deppity—"

"No!" blared Cross-Draw. "I've changed my mind—don't wanta be no deputy! It'd cramp my style. I got to have a free hand in this thing. I—"

MacIllwraith spluttered like a leaky bagpipe. He hopped about like a Highlander back from a three days' toot. "Ye canna do it, lad! I canna hae ye tearin' roon this country like a wild mon! Put y'r hand up an' I'll swear ye in—"

So Cross-Draw Robert Boyd became chief deputy of Pinal County.

He grinned a little grin and winked at Angus. "Dooty is dooty," he said blithely. "An' may the devil's pitchfork jab the laggards."

"Nae—ye mustna take that sperit, lad. Remember ye are under orders! Our wor-rk is to maintain peace—"

"Sure! That's me all over," Cross-Draw grinned. "I'll maintain it if I have t' kill haff the county doin' it. Just watch my smoke!"

MacIllwraith gave him a fishy stare. He shook his grizzled head, muttering displeasedly as he took a badge from the drawer and pushed it across the desk.

Cross-Draw picked it up and blew on it. He shined it on an elbow and pinned it to his vest. "Ye'll have to mend y'r ways, mon," the sheriff admonished. "Peace is what this country wants—not bloodshed."

Cross-Draw showed a chastened spirit. "Post me on the feud," he said.

He was soon posted. MacIllwraith had little to

51

add beyond what Cross-Draw had learned at the Harp. He mentioned one point, though, that Eileen had skipped. The most significant point in the whole affair. The feud had actually started over water rights, as so many other Western fracases had started. But what the girl had not seen fit to mention was that Tam O'Reilly had run off with Kate—a girl betrothed to Zeneas Pool.

"Ay," old Angus nodded. "A sorry thing." He shook his head regretfully. "'Twas the stealin' o' that bonny lass that started all these shootin's."

"Oho!" grunted Cross-Draw, grinning. "No wonder them Pools want action!" He slapped his leg with great delight. "That Tam is quite a corker!" He put his head back and laughed till the tears rolled down his cheeks. "God, but I'd give somethin' to have seen Zeneas' face! Practically snatched her right out of his blanket, eh?"

"Three days before the wedding," MacIllwraith nodded, and muttered gloomily to himself.

"Where is she now?" asked Cross-Draw. "At O'Reilly's?" And at the sheriff's nod, "Why ain't the Pools gone out there after her?"

"Ye dinna ken Zeneas Pool. He is a verra proud man with all his chimneys reekin'. He'll hae nothin' more t' do wi' her, an' has swore a terrible oath. He'll not rest till the last O'Reilly is a-lyin' in his casket." The sheriff sighed.

Cross-Draw heaved a sigh himself. He said reflectively, "I could feel that way about Shamus' daughter—"

He broke off abruptly to stare at the curious expression on the sheriff's wrinkled countenance.

"Daughter?" Angus pricked up his ears and eyed

Cross-Draw intently. "O'Reilly has no daughter," he said grimly. "Y'r thinkin' o' Kate Eileen—the promised bride of Pool."

A Word to the Wise

INTO THE STARTLED silence broke the beat of a horse's hoofs. It was coming fast and its rataplan of sound drummed loudly on the Arizona stillness, jerking Sleepy Cat's few citizens from their mid-morning somnolence, and ceasing before MacIllwraith's door.

A rider's boots hit dirt; thudded across the warped plank walk and hammered up the steps.

The door burst open and a swarthy wild-eyed Mexican came puffing in as though it were he and not the horse who'd made that hurried dash.

"Señor! Señor!" he cried, dragging off his hat and twisting it in feverish hands. "He ees muerto—muchas muerto!"

"Dead? Who's dead?" the sheriff demanded with his roan cheeks going dark.

"Señor Torrence! He ees muerto weeth a rifle shell between hees teet'!" the Mexican said, and crossed himself.

It was a pregnant moment.

Cross-Draw, recovering first, swore furiously. "It's that damn catclaw killer again!" he snarled, and flung his torso 'round to glare accusingly at the sheriff. "I told you this thing wasn't goin' t' get settled by warmin' the seat of your pants!"

MacIllwraith paid him no attention. He said to the Mexican: "When did it happen?" and at the

54

latter's Latin shrug: "Who found him, an' when?"

"Not t'ree hours ago, señor. The *patron* was go for find eef—"

And suddenly he stopped, staring wide-eyed at Cross-Draw Bob, and with his swarthy cheeks going pale as ashes. He backed three lurching backward paces and put a trembling hand before him as though to ward off something evil.

Cross-Draw and the sheriff stared at him amazedly. "What the hell!" growled Cross-Draw; and MacIllwraith said: "Are ye sick, mon?"

The Mexican shook his head mechanically, his glassy eyes never leaving Cross-Draw's face. Like a man coming out of a trance, he brushed a hand across his eyes, seemed to pull himself together and, making the sign of the cross, suddenly whirled and dashed precipitately from the office.

An instant later there was a babble of excited voices, shouts, curses and the pound of rapidly receding hoofbeats.

Cross-Draw and the sheriff eyed each other incredulously. MacIllwraith said: "The mon is daft!" And Cross-Draw swore.

The sheriff rasped a hand across his roan and bristly cheek. He regarded gloomily the palms of his calloused hands.

"Well, that's torn it," Cross-Draw muttered. "Ain't nothin' you *can* do now but give 'em action. You got a range war on your hands whether you want one on 'em or not."

The sheriff heaved a doleful sigh. "I ken it, mon; I ken it."

"How many been killed so far?"

"On the Pool side, only one," MacIllwraith muttered. "Old mon Pool himself. Shamus O'Reilly

55

has lost three hands an' two sons—Tim an' Torrence. The oldest and the youngest."

"Don't anything in that business strike you funny?"

MacIllwraith eyed him dourly. "I ne'er was one for humor, lad—"

"I don't mean funny that way," Cross-Draw grunted. "I mean uncommon odd . . ." He scowled, and looked up suddenly. "All them O'Reilly deaths have been the work of one man—or meant to look that way. This mysterious killer," he mused thoughtfully, "with his goddam trademark of a rifle shell between each victim's teeth. You know, Angus, we got to stop that fella."

The sheriff nodded. "Ay. But why did ye call him the catclaw killer awhile ago, lad? An' what makes ye so sure he's the one that's thinnin' the O'Reillys out?"

"Because Shamus told me that that trademark shell was between the three punchers' teeth, an' that he'd found a brass shell just like the others where this killer had been layin' after Tim was dropped. I called him the catclaw killer," Cross-Draw added, "because so far as they know, none of the O'Reillys have ever got a look at him. None, that is, that's still alive to talk about it."

"'Tis one of the Pool's gun throwers," muttered MacIllwraith, nodding thoughtfully.

"Or one of the Pools themselves," added Cross-Draw darkly. "That young squirt, now—that Zeneas! That hombre's colder than a well-chain in February!" He added grimly: "I ain't forgot how he put a bullet through my watch an' rode off leavin' me for dead!"

"Didn't leave no cartridge shell between your teeth, though," Angus grunted. "No, lad; I'm thinkin' ye'll ha' to look—"

56

"You goin' out to the Harp to look into this Torrence killin'?" Cross-Draw broke in suddenly.

"I suppose I'll ha' to," the sheriff grimaced. "You didna want to be going oot, did ye?"

Cross-Draw scowled, as though in bitter remembrance of his discovery of Shamrock-Eyes' identity. "No!" he answered coldly. "But I was thinkin'... While you're busy out there, I believe I'll scout around a bit. No tellin' what I might turn up—"

"Watch out ye don't turn up missing!"

.8.

The Proof of the Murder...

Sheriff Angus MacIllwraith, for all his hardy Scots exterior, was a mighty uneasy man as he put his horse to a jog trot in the direction of O'Reilly's Harp. And to his dour way of thinking there was more than plenty to make him so.

Who, for instance, was this stranger, Cross-Draw Boyd? A carefree, hellbent spirit, a man would say, to judge by appearance—but Angus was never one to judge that way. A canny man, he was a firm believer in the old saw regarding the deceptiveness of appearances. So it was he pondered on the man's identity; and the more he pondered, the more uneasy he became.

He liked the stranger and believed him honest, else he'd not have made him deputy. But now he'd sworn the fellow in, Angus was becoming prey to lots of doubts. Of course he could always get rid of the gentleman—that is, he could take his star away. But thinking back over what little he knew of the man, Angus was not at all sure that would be so easy as it sounded. There was, he recalled, upon certain occasions a distinctly grim and forbidding look about the fellow's mouth. A kind of flinty look to the depths of his eyes was not conducive, either, to any feeling of equanimity on Angus' part. And there was, too, the dark and smoothly ominous appearance of his gun butts.

Taken in conjunction with the fact of Torrence O'Reilly's murder these things were cause for perturbation.

It was, therefore, in a more than usually gloomy frame of mind that Pinal's sheriff arrived some two hours later at O'Reilly's Harp. And though his sharp Scots eyes had observed the hands with rifles casually lounging in stable, blacksmith shop and saddle shed, he kept the fact to himself.

Racking his horse before the veranda, he mounted the steps and knocked upon the front door's rickety screen.

Shamrock-Eyes herself came forward to greet him. She appeared subdued this noon and there were dark circles beneath her blue-green eyes. The wan smile she showed him pinched his heart. Must be tough, he thought, to feel oneself responsible for all this bloodshed.

"A bonny mornin', lass," he greeted in a voice as rough as a pallbearer's glove. "I would like to speak wi' Shamus."

She nodded briefly and led him into the parlor. "I will tell him," she said tiredly.

Moments later Shamus came clumping in with a bitter twist to his Irish mouth; blue eyes ablaze with wrath. "What's this," he growled, "I been hearin' av yez huggin' an' kissin' 'round with Cross-Draw Boyd? Sure birds av a feather flock together; but bejasus I'd not have thought a MacIllwraith would be havin' truck with any lowdown murtherin' hound!"

"What's this, mon?" cried MacIllwraith, taken aback. "Are ye callin' Cross-Draw Boyd a murderin' hound?"

"I am," said Shamus flatly. "And Concho tells me

59

ye've pinned a star to the black'ard's vest!" His blue eyes flamed accusingly. "An' the shell still warm that he put betwain me Torrence's teeth!"

MacIllwraith rubbed his bristled jowls to conceal anxiety. His worst fears appeared well on the way to being realized. He should never, he thought bitterly, have deputized that hard-bitten stranger in the first place. But repentance of the fact would not be stopping the two-gun man in whatever he was up to now. Nor was the sheriff one quickly to admit himself in the wrong.

He said: "This Boyd was seen then wi' a smoking gun i' hand?"

"Not seen with the gun," growled Shamus bitterly, "but—"

"He was seen then slipping the shell between the lad's teeth?"

"No," muttered Shamus reluctantly. "He—"

"Then tell me, mon, who found your son an' when?"

"I found him," Shamus said. "By the big corral before daylight—"

"An' why did ye wait sa long before sendin' y'r mon tae tell me?"

"Bejasus, an' d'ye think I had nothing t' do but think of *you?*" blared Shamus, cursing. "With me own son layin' there dead! An'—"

"What proof ye got, mon, that my deputy killed him?" Angus interrupted, getting back to basic matters. "What—"

"Proof! *Proof!*" howled Shamus excitedly. "I've got the blawsted shell the divel put in me poor bhoy's mouth, ain't I?" And he jerked it from a pocket and slammed it into Angus' hand.

"Ay—it's the shell, like enough," MacIllwraith

said; "but ye didna see him put it there, an' ye didna see him shoot—"

"Listen to me, MacIllwraith. If y'r intendin' t' kape y'r bony shanks warm the winter, ye'll be after usin' y'r ears an' kapin' y'r questions to yerself! I tell you that this blatherskite Cross-Draw Bob is the bawstard killer of me bhoy. Now niver mind askin' questions—go ketch him!"

"It may ha' slipped ye mind, mon," said MacIllwraith dourly, "but I'll be remindin' ye I'm still the Sheriff of Pinal County. An' I'll arrest no mon wi'out strong proof o' his guilt! I've heard all aboot the doin's oot here las' evenin' an' I'll not see the Law's long arm used t' pay off any grudges! Hae ye got the proof or ain't ye?"

For bitter moments the two men stared across three feet of crackling silence. Shamus' breath grew labored, wheezy, and his look was like a thunder-cloud.

But Angus looked not the least perturbed. He stood with gnarled hands at his sides, his stubborn Scots jaw thrust forward and his pale blue eyes expressionless as the snow on his native heather.

"Hae ye got it noo, or ain't ye?"

Rage flushed Shamus' features and, clenching his big fists furiously, he started a forward, threatening stride. "'Tis a hell av a toime t' be standin' here wranglin', with me poor bhoy's body hardly cold! But if ye want it that way—"

"Noo just a minute, mon," said Angus, standing his ground. "I'm nae wantin' to quarrel wi' ye, an' I've no consarn i' y'r feud wi' the Pools. But I'm arrestin' no mon wi'out plenty o' proof. Ye should ken by noo, O'Reilly, that I'm no' the mon to bully."

Shamus' shaved-hog cheeks went as bitter-bleak

61

and tight as those of MacIllwraith. He wheeled abruptly without reply and strode to the hall door, rudely yanking it open. "Eileen! Be tellin' yon Albert to come into the house."

He came back and dropped himself into a chair and crossed his fat legs savagely.

"Smoke y'r pipe, mon," the sheriff advised. "It will put ye in a better mood. Has the lass set the day for y'r son's wedding yet?"

O'Reilly glowered but made no answer, the lips of him seeming locked even tighter than his fists.

Then Albert came clanking in through the open hall door, and looking from one to the other of them growled suspiciously:

"'Ere—wotcher up ter?"

"I want ye to be after tellin' the sheriff what yez were tellin' me. About that killer," he said, with a triumphant leer at MacIllwraith.

"Wot killer?"

"Why," said Shamus scowling, "bejasus there ain't but one! The killer of me poor bhoy Torrence—"

"Wotcher torkin' abaht?"

A twinkle gleamed remotely behind the blue of Angus' eyes.

But there was no sign of a twinkle in O'Reilly's. He looked like Carrie Nation—all he needed was the axe and the saloon. He snarled, surging to his feet: "Didn't you tell me Cross-Draw Boyd—"

"If I told yer I've fergot it," declared Albert flatly. "Anyway, I ain't tellin' no bloody sheriff!"

Angus decided to take a hand. He said friendly enough: "On what did ye base y'r opinions, lad?"

Albert regarded him suspiciously. "Ain't got no blarsted opinions."

62

Swearing, Shamus started for him, both fists clenched and swinging.

"None o' that, now! Tyke it easy, guv'nor! H'I'm a bad man in a corner!"

"Come, mon," said Angus hurriedly. "If ye've got evidence, there can be nae harm in partin' wi' it."

"Orl right," muttered Albert, squaring off. "I'll tell yer. We found the dead bloke over by the big corral. I quartered round the brush till I came to where they sy this Cross-Draw blighter went spinnin' from 'is 'orse. I could see w'ere 'e picked 'imself up an' w'ere 'e beat it. I could see w'ere 'e came back, too— I can show yer. Right there I found this!" and from a pocket he pulled a cartridge and dropped it in the sheriff's hand.

Angus took one look, and pulled the shell Shamus had given him from his vest. The exploded shell and the fresh cartridge lay there side by side in the shrieval palm. The shrieval countenance, Scotch and dour though it was, began giving off signs of perturbation. There could be no slip-up: Both exhibits had been manufactured to fit a .45-90 rifle!

.9.

"Here's Your Goddam Badge!"

"Did ye discover anything whilst I was gone, lad?"

"No," muttered Cross-Draw disgustedly. "I went over an' poked about that cabin where Torrence was holdin' Pool. But there wasn't nothin' there. If there was I didn't find it—the place was clean as a monkey's elbow."

"'Tis a shame," Angus said, "the Harp wasna likewise," and laid his two exhibits on the table.

"Forty-five nineties, eh?" said Cross-Draw, indifferently eying them. Then abruptly his indifference vanished, replaced by a look of cold intentness. "Where'd you get 'em?"

Angus told him. He said: "Albert claims he picked the cartridge up close by y'r dead horse—"

"Mebbe he did," Cross-Draw said, and thoughtfully rolled him up a smoke. "That don't necessarily mean much, though..."

"This Albert seemed to think it did. O'Reilly thinks so, too. He's comin' in today an' swear out a warrant for y'r arrest."

"Oh, he is, is he!" Cross-Draw blared. "The damn' shanty Irish! What's he up to anyway? 'S he tryin' t' frame me for that killin'?"

"We-el, it looks unco' like it," Angus admitted. And shook his head. "Y'r in a fierce predicament, laddie. Y'r known t' ha' been oot there—"

"Was I the only fella out there? Applefeathers!

64

What about that swivel-eyed Albert?"

"The mon supports the case ag'in' ye—"

"Hell's hinges!" Cross-Draw shouted. "They can't frame me for that killin'! I didn't even have a rifle!"

"'Twill make nae difference, lad. This Albert mon found the place where ye went back, where ye lay behint ye'r dead bronc waitin' fer y'r chance to drop poor Torrence. Behint the horse is where he found the cartridge where it must ha' rolled from ye'r pocket. They've a case ag'in' ye, mon—an' comin' back like ye did after the excitement was all over has the look o' plain premeditation. Not tae mention how yon Torrence was shot i' the back!"

Cross-Draw stared, his cheeks slowly going white. "Did you see the body?"

"Ay, that I did. That lad was shot i' the back, all richt."

"But I didn't *have* a rifle, man! He *was* killed with a rifle, wasn't he?", demanded Cross-Draw desperately. "From a long shot? I recall that bronc dropped quite a piece from the corral—"

"Ay. A long shot, and wi' a rifle. But ye canna git aroon the evidence, lad." MacIllwraith stared at him gloomily. "The tracks show ye left the place after drivin' them back wi' y'r pistols. An' the tracks show ye come back later wi' y'r rifle—"

Cross-Draw's narrowed eyes showed a fiercening gleam. "Think back," he muttered. "My rifle was on my horse. I'd left the horse in town when I rode with Albert and the girl to the ranch last night. Albert an' Tam O'Reilly went back to town for the horses." He paused to collect his reflections. "It was after they'd left that Shamus told me about the killer an' put up his proposition. I wasn't crazy about any scalp-hunting—anyway, he was tryin' to get me to take on

65

the job when Squinch-Face, or Torrence or whatever his damn name was, came in the door. After that things happened fast. I lit out an' cut for the corral. Some guy in the yard—he was over by the stable—slung a few slugs at me an' I slammed a couple back, drivin' him to shelter. I got a rope an' jumped in the corral. Soon as I caught a bronc I put it to the fence hopin' to make a getaway. By that time the whole damn spread was on the prod. Shamus an' Squinch-Face was hotfootin' it from the house. The crew was boilin' from the bunk shack. Lead was smackin' all around me."

He paused to scrub a hand across his eyes.

"I was almost to the chaparral when somebody rammed the bronc. He went head over heels, throwin' me clear on into the brush. I'd grabbed out my guns soon as I felt myself goin'. When I got my wind I started unravelin' lead—purposely keepin' my shots a little high; just close enough to put the fear of God into them Harps. Soon's they started scatterin', I hit out for town."

"We-el, p'raps ye did, lad; but ye went back— there's tracks t' proov it," Angus sighed.

"Hell's hinges!" Cross-Draw snarled. "I didn't *go* back! How many times I got t' tell you? An' even if I *had* gone back, what the hell difference could it make. I didn't have a rifle. The rifle was on my horse an'—"

"I ken," said Angus wearily. "The rifle was on y'r horse, an' Albert an' the O'Reilly lad were on their way to get it. But there was nothin' to prevent ye gettin' another—"

"*Where?*" snarled Cross-Draw furiously? "Off a sagebrush? For God's sake, man—use what brains you have! Where could I get hold of a rifle that time of night? An' a .45-90, that even Shamus claims is practically unknown around—"

"But ye canna get away from the tracks," grunted Angus stubbornly. "I'll ha' to ask ye for that badge."

Cross-Draw swore in a passion. But when he looked up the sheriff was covering him with a pistol. Angus' face showed a reluctance. But the glint of his eye was determined and the muzzle of his pistol grim and steady. "I'll be askin' fer ye guns, too, lad."

Cross-Draw, when he could control his voice enough to speak, looked at MacIllwraith scornfully. "So you're joinin' the gang against me, are you?"

"I'm joinin' nothing, lad. But I've got t' do ma dooty, an' wi' the evidence at hand, I must arrest ye for the—"

That far he got when the door banged open and Shamus O'Reilly, followed by his trusty gunslammer, Albert, came striding in. Albert shut the door with satisfaction.

Shamus slapped a stiff-paper document down upon the sheriff's desk. "There's a warrant, MacIllwraith—" he began, then stopped as he caught sight of the leveled pistol. "Oh! An' so ye've changed yer moind at last. 'Tis glad I am t' see that ye've come to yer senses." And he glared maliciously at Boyd.

"Look," said Cross-Draw earnestly. "You don't really think I killed that fella, do you? I—"

"Sure ye killed him—an' bejasus I'll see that yez hang fer it, too!" snarled Shamus fiercely. "Two av me bhoys ye've cut down in their youth—not t' mention me three hired hands! Sure, Saint Peter himself could have no more mercy than I've got. I'll see that yez git a fair trial, an' I'll see that they hang yez higher than a kite!"

67

Cross-Draw ground the butt of his smoke beneath a bootheel and stared down grimly at his hands. "Dammit," he said, "my rifle's a .30-30! An' I didn't have it, anyway! You said yourself—"

"Niver moind what I said!" growled Shamus loudly. "I'll not be listenin' to yer lies!"

"But—"

"Save it fer the judge! Y' coulda had the gun hid out someplace—"

"In the pocket with my watch, I guess," sneered Boyd derisively.

"Inside 'is pants," suggested Albert.

Cross-Draw's brows went up three inches. "My Gawd—what you birds don't think of! A rifle in my pantsleg!" He looked at Albert wickedly. "How much is pig-face payin' you for this lyin'—"

"Well, it's been done," said Angus dourly. "I call to mind the time the Dalton boys.... Anyway, a strap aroon the leg—"

But Cross-Draw had had enough.

This crowd was out to frame him like a picture. If the facts didn't fit they ignored them. They were after his hide and aimed to get it.

"Here's your goddam badge!" he snarled, and drove it straight at the sheriff's face.

MacIllwraith's gun went off. Shamus' shout drowned Albert's gasp. A bit of chinking fell from the roof poles. But even *that* did not touch Cross-Draw. He was gone through the window with one quick lunge.

.10.

Out of the Frying Pan—

HE LIT on his feet and reached for a pistol. But he didn't stop moving for a moment. Too many waddies back there were aiming to make a sieve of him.

Over a shoulder he saw O'Reilly leveling a pistol through the window and he smashed a slug above the frame in hopes of disconcerting the swearing Harp owner from a hit.

Then Albert and the sheriff came bulging out the door and he scurried like a bee-stung dog for the protection of a building corner, ducking, dodging, cursing.

Then he was behind its protection and sprinting down an alley, reloading his six-gun as he ran.

It was mighty galling for the hero of Agua Prieta to be running from a fight. These birds didn't give a whoop in hell if they punctured his mortal tintype! But the trouble was, unless he wanted to be an outlaw and live forever on the dodge, he couldn't very well return their fire with like intent.

But there was, he assured himself grimly, a definite limit to his patience. He could be shoved just so far. After that things were like to happen in a way to make the undertakers grin!

And that limit wasn't far from being reached!

He ducked into a doorway just as Shamus rammed around the corner directly ahead. Shamus' shout could have been heard all over town—and probably was. But Cross-Draw wasn't waiting for the town to join this manhunt. He was seeking some way in which he could get his pursuers away from the broncs hitched before the sheriff's office.

And it looked like he had found it.

He could hear Shamus fumbling at the door he'd slammed behind him.

He sprang through two rooms, slamming the first door and jamming a rickety chair beneath the knob of the second. Lucky for him the place was uninhabited, and he wasted no time thinking about what the owner might say when he returned.

This second room looked out upon the alley, and just as O'Reilly could be heard breaking through the outside door, Cross-Draw hurled a chair straight at the window and in the crash of glass that followed he left the room, lunging into another that looked out on the street.

The sheriff and Albert were not in sight, no doubt drawn to the alley by the racket. Cross-Draw eased up a window and slipped through, sprinting desperately for the horses racked before the office.

Wonder of wonders, he saw his own flea-bitten buckskin—as fast a horse as ever peeked through a bridle. Albert must have ridden the animal in. But whether he did or not, Cross-Draw was not the one to worry how it had got there.

He sprang into the saddle, jerked the slipknot loose, and sank his spurs. The buckskin reared with a snort and a squeal, then shot forward with hip-jolting violence and bolted for the open range.

Shouts and oaths slammed up behind, and a spatter of pistol shots beat dust about the buckskin's feet.

Cross-Draw turned in the saddle to thumb his nose, then leaning well forward along the game bronc's neck applied both quirt and spurs. Moments later a bend in the trail shut off the whistling bullets and the uproar left behind.

But Cross-Draw labored under no delusions. That crowd would be swarming after him just as soon as they could back their broncs. If Saint Pete had no more mercy than Shamus O'Reilly, it was time he looked for another job.

Cross-Draw hadn't the faintest idea where he was heading and was in no mood to care. Right now distance was all that concerned him—the distance he could put between himself and that larruping posse.

He risked a glance across his shoulder. The pursuit was not a half mile back. Well up in the van rode O'Reilly and that Albert, with Angus Mac-Illwraith not half a length behind. All three were gouging their horses for all they were worth and the townsmen were being left in the dust.

This was certainly the damndest country!

Seemed like ever since he'd hit it hot water had been his natural element. Out of the frying pan into the fire! And all that stuff.

It was enough to make a parson boil!

And Cross-Draw was far from being any parson. For the next quarter hour, while posse lead knocked splinters from the growth about him, he gave himself over to thoughts of vengeance. Just wait till he got a breathing spell! He'd show these mangy whip-poorwills that he was no dang man to fool with!

But right now the most important thing was to get away and he put his energies into the task with a will. Time enough for vengeance later.

Several times some break in the scenery put

thoughts of ambush in his mind. But he had never been one to take unfair advantage of an adversary; and unless the going got considerably rougher he did not intend to do so now.

But if they pushed him far enough—*look out!*

He could deal out misery with the best of them.

But it had him fighting his hat to figure what the hell it was all about. Of course it was plain as paint that the Pools would be plenty peeved about Tam's swiping of Zeneas' girl. And that water-rights business had been a basis for contention on better ranges than this one. But just the same, why was everyone so set to make a goat of *him?*

Must be a lot more to this than met the eye—must be some kind of underhand skullduggery going on, to make both sides so golrammed leary of strangers!

One thing was certain. In *his* mind, anyway. Both the Pools and O'Reillys were not the kind to waste any time on scruples. What they wanted they went after, and the devil take the hindermost—which right about now looked like being Cross-Draw Boyd himself!

Well, every dog had its day, and Cross-Draw—when his time came round—sure aimed to make it a memorable one.

He got to thinking about that business of the rifle.

He was being framed all right; a little thought would prove that fact to anyone. It wasn't as if this squinch-faced Torrence were the only dead man in the cactus. There had been this Tim, and the Pools' old man—not to mention the hired Harp hands that had met Saint Pete with a bit of brass between their teeth. Hell's bells and twenty-three catfishes! He couldn't have killed them *all*!

72

Why, he'd only just got into the country, and this killer had been at work for weeks!

The more he thought about it, the madder Cross-Draw got. Frame him for a Boothill residence, would they? By cripes, he'd show 'em! Cross-Draw Boyd was no safe man to monkey with, and the quicker these polecats found it out, the better for all concerned!

It was about that time that he looked up—and got the shock of his life.

Thirty short yards ahead of him loomed the buildings of the Harp; and on the Harp veranda stood Shamrock-Eyes with a rifle!

.11.

—Into the Fire!

HE WAS within ten yards of the porch before Cross-Draw came out of his daze.

He sawed back on the reins and was swinging the buckskin 'round, when the girl's quick call reached out to stop him. "Cross-Draw— Wait!" she cried; and so thoroughly was she Helen of Troy, Delilah and all the other great dames of history wrapped into one, that Cross-Draw stopped his bronc and waited.

She was at his side in a twinkling.

"What is it?" she cried. "What's all that shouting and shooting back there on the trail?"

"Angus an' his golrammed posse!" Cross-Draw snarled with an oath.

"They're after you?"

"They ain't huntin' no Queen of Sheba!"

She caught a hand to her breast with a cry of despair. "But *why*?" she moaned. "But why?"

"Say! don't ask me!" snapped Cross-Draw bitterly. "I'm jest the innercent bystander—the one that always gets hurt!"

"It's all my fault," she cried, and her self-reproach shook Cross-Draw strangely; purged him of his anger. "Tam has made up his mind you're a rival and he's sworn to run you out of the country—it's Tam has turned Shamus against you!"

"*Tam*—" Cross-Draw eyed her incredulously. "But Tam hardly knows me! Why—"

"Nonetheless it is Tam that you've got to look out for," she warned. She came closer, still dragging the rifle, and laid her free hand on his knee. "He is a crazy one to think there could ever be anything between you and me! I have heard of you and know that in your own country you are regarded as a fierce caballero, a man who never rests till wrong has been righted; a champion of the underprivileged, a reliever of the oppressed, a chastiser of the wicked. One who would have scant time to waste on women."

She looked at him shyly from beneath half-lowered lashes.

"And is it not the truth for sure?"

Cross-Draw scrubbed a hand across his chin and sat his saddle tongue-tied. Her lips were like crushed cherries and the sun ran sparkles of burnished copper through the chestnut masses of her hair.

But then he remembered and he said coldly: "I guess you're right; I ain't got much time for women—not that it'd matter in this case whether I had or not. After all, you're engaged to Tam an'—"

"As if that could make any difference!" she said indignantly. "Does he let that stop him when he sees desirable calico? He should have been a Mormon—he treats me like a piece of baggage!"

Cross-Draw stared at her amazed. He was astounded by the depth of feeling she put into the words; by the stormy bitterness of her eyes.

"It is true," she cried with curling lips. "He treats me like a horse or steer he's run his brand on. No one else must look at me—"

She broke off sharply as the approaching pound of horses' hoofs beat round the trail and echoed against the hemming cliffs, intermingled with shouts and curses.

"Quick!" she cried. "Come into the house and I will hide you—"

"No," said Cross-Draw shaking his head. "They'll see my horse and—"

"Put it behind the house. After I hide you I will drive it off—there is a little box-canyon I know of close. Please! You must not let them catch you. . . ."

"Well—"

"Quick! They'll round the bend any moment! They would kill you like a snake!"

Tight-lipped Cross-Draw nodded. "O.K.," he said, and kneed his horse around the house while she ran inside and opened the back door for him.

A HELL OF a place in which for the hero of Agua Prieta to be finding himself, thought Cross-Draw with a smothered curse. If this was not a lady's boudoir he'd be a pop-eyed Chinaman!

Hot color crept up his neck and blossomed on his cheeks as he peered through the maze of feminine apparel behind which she'd hidden him in a closet. The door was a little ajar—for air, she'd said—and through the crack he could see a gay little room bedecked in frills and flounces.

The thought of being found in here spread gooseflesh along his back and put his teeth on edge.

He just had to get out of that closet!

Parting a smear of hung-up garments and with their fragrance playing havoc with his senses, he pushed the closet door wide open and crept out into the room.

The sound of arriving riders drew him cautiously to a window and, crouching to one side, he peered through a crack in the curtain.

It was the posse. And there was Tam O'Reilly

questioning Eileen. He could not hear what they were saying, but there was a patent suspicion in young O'Reilly's attitude that could not be missed. Cross-Draw saw him pointing toward the ground; saw Eileen fling a hand in the direction leading behind the house. He could see the mingled emotions crossing the tense-sitting riders' faces.

He wished the hell he were out of here. He could not quite understand how he'd been foolish enough to come into the house in the first place—least of all what had ever prompted him to let her stow him in here. Oh, she was a good-looking girl all right—none better. But she seemed too dang anxious to get strapped in double harness! And Cross-Draw felt not the faintest inclination toward—

Damn!

They were dismounting. Shamus, Tam, the sheriff and Albert were, at any rate. And—yes! They were coming into the house!

Cross-Draw left off his thinking in a hurry and went scuttling back inside the closet.

Sweat broke out all over him as the sound of approaching feet banged down the hall. This was awful! If they ever caught him in this place— He dismissed the thought with a shudder as Angus said: "The lass is probably richt, though, Shamus. It seems a crazy way to go, but I'll be sendin' yon posse after them tracks—"

"An' the rest of us'll wait right here," Tam broke in nastily, "just in case he doubled back."

MacIllwraith clanked out to give his orders to the posse and Shamus said: "Will ye be after repeatin' the tale again?" presumably to Eileen, for she promptly said: "I was just putting lunch upon the table when I heard the crash of a running horse. I ran to the window. A big buckskin was coming round the bend. I watched him plunge across the yard, trying to make out the rider. But I couldn't. It was impossible. He was crouched along his horse's neck, jamming his spurs and swinging his quirt with every jump. He was gone behind the angle of the living room almost as soon as I'd seen him."

"And ye dinna think the mon was Cross-Draw Boyd?" questioned MacIllwraith coming back.

"I didn't get that impression," the girl said thoughtfully. "But it might have been. As I say, I couldn't tell. His head was down behind the neck of his horse—"

"An' he didna stop at all, eh?"

"No—why should he?"

"There's somethin' mighty funny about them tracks then," Tam growled suspiciously. "The sign shows that bronc was stopped. An' there's the marks of bootheels reaching out to meet it. Like the bronc's, they're pretty plain. Like the rider and the walker stood awhile an' did some talkin'."

The following stillness was pretty grim. Cross-Draw's heart began thumping like a giant base viol, and his breath seemed to stick in his throat.

But the girl said angrily: "Are you hinting that I've been lying?"

"No, lass," MacIllwraith cut in smoothly. "We wouldna be doing that. 'Tis only that it's a bit queer, ye ken. The sign—"

"C'mon," Tam interrupted curtly. "I think we better search the house."

"Sure, an' Eileen wouldn't be deceivin' us," Shamus muttered.

But the girl laughed, clear and scornful. "Let him search. I'm going to pack my things. When you're

78

ready to go back to town, Sheriff, please call me—"

"Bejasus an' what is this?" demanded Shamus. "Ye'll not be after leavin' the O'Reillys—"

But the girl's scornful tones bit through his words like acid. "Do you think I'm going to stay any longer where the least lift of my littlest finger becomes the focus of such suspicion?" Her laugh was like the sound of breaking icicles. "I've stood enough around this place. You've been fine to me, Shamus O'Reilly, but your son doesn't want a wife—he needs a harem."

"Sure, the bhoy's a little wild," muttered Shamus, breaking the silence, "but a bit av age'll cure him. Just ye—"

"I've gray hair enough, right now," purred Eileen sweetly. "I'm going to pack my things," and Cross-Draw could hear the pound of her shoes coming toward him.

"Let her pack 'em," snapped Tam gruffly. "I can take care of her! C'mon—let's get that searchin' started. I got a hunch..." And the rest trailed off as Shamus, Angus and Albert tramped after him to begin the hunt.

CROSS-DRAW CAME OUT of the closet as the girl came into the room.

"Quick!" she cried. "Climb out of this window! The coast is clear and all the possemen are up in that canyon chasing the tracks of your horse." With a jerk she flung up the window.

"You shouldn't be gettin' yourself in trouble like this," growled Cross-Draw, eyes roving her willowy shape.

"For you I'd do more that that," she said, coming close and resting a disquieting hand on his shoulder.

She gazed at him daringly, and the light in her eyes whipped Cross-Draw's pulse to a tumult.

He forgot about Pool and he forgot about Tam. Pulling her to him he clasped her slim form in his arms.

"What a bear!" she said when she caught her breath. "But I love you. Quick—kiss me again!"

But suddenly Cross-Draw shoved her aside. The hallway was filled with the scuffle of boots and a wrangle of voices. The searchers were coming and it behooved him to be on his way.

"Just a moment," she whispered, and caught at his arm. She drew him back toward the closet where a bureau sat snug by the wall. Snatching up scissors she sheared a lock from her hair and, smiling, thrust it into his hand. "A token," she murmured. "Wear it next to your heart for protection."

Their eyes met and locked.

Cross-Draw shivered, for the look of her lips was red as ripe berries. Forgetting the dire need for haste, he pulled her to him again and covered the lips with fierce kisses.

A rap on the door roughly jerked them apart.

Cross-Draw whirled toward the window. He checked in mid-flight, froze stiff as a statue—and sneezed.

.12.

Eileen Gets Them Told

THERE WAS an instant of startled silence.

Then Albert's E-string voice could be heard in a quick-gasped, "Lumme!" swiftly followed by a snarling oath from Tam. A fist grabbed heavily at the doorknob and Cross-Draw sprang into the closet.

And just in time!

The in-flung door banged back against the wall beneath the charging rush of Shamus, Angus, Tam and Albert. They swept into the room, pulling up just past the threshold. Their eyes stabbed round amazedly till Albert, whirling, cried: "'E's gorn out the perishin' winder!"

Gritting blasphemies Tam went through it with Albert right at his heels.

Angus' questioning gaze went to the girl who, taking a dainty wisp of kerchief from her mouth, was eying them with a very evident astonishment. "What in the *world* is all the excitement?" She turned to Shamus, slipping the kerchief neatly up her sleeve.

O'Reilly scratched his near-bald head. "Bejabbers, sure an' I'd be likin' t' know meself!" he said, exasperated, and looked her over curiously.

"Was it you jest did that sneezin', lass?" MacIllwraith queried hesitantly.

"And who did you think it was?" she asked, then stopped to stare at them closely while her blue-green

81

eyes went stormy and vividly wigwagged danger. "Never mind!" she cried with her chin up. "*I* know! You think that crazy Cross-Draw Bob was in here!"

She glared at them indignantly and her red lips curled with scorn.

Shamus said: "Sure ye'r always grabbin' at conclusions, darlint—jist like me own bhoy Tam."

She ignored him. "Please saddle my horse, MacIllwraith. I'm going to leave this place at once!" And she flounced 'round, striding bitterly toward the closet.

She yanked open its door and began pulling dresses from their hooks and flinging them on the bed while the silence became more and more uncomfortable and the sheriff stood fiddling with his hat.

"Now look," muttered Shamus worriedly. "Don't be after takin' on like this, Eileen. Sure we were all a bit upset-like, an'—"

"It's no use, Shamus," she said, leaving off her denuding of the closet and getting her suitcase from under the bed. "I'm going! I'll not stay in this place any longer. It's a madhouse! I wouldn't dream of marrying Tam after this if he were the last available man in Arizona! Why, if my father knew—"

She broke off as Tam came clambering through the window with Albert, like a shadow, still dogging his steps.

"Well," Tam growled, "he got away—the bustard! But—"

"Ye found no sign o' the lad?" asked Angus.

"Not 'arf," grunted Albert, dragging a sleeve across his sweating forehead. "Blimey! the blighter got clear away!"

Eileen tossed her head scornfully. "He was never

out there in the first place." She turned her back disdainfully and began throwing her clothes in the suitcase.

Tam looked her way and glowered. "What do you think you're doin'?"

"Does it look like I'm mowing the lawn?"

His cheeks went dark at her sarcasm and he took a half step toward her. Then he seemed to remember something and changed his manner completely. "Sure, Eileen,"—he lowered his voice to soft pleading, "you wouldn't be walking out on poor Tam, now?" And when without looking at him she stepped to the closet as though for more dresses he cried: "Perhaps I said a few things in the heat of the moment I oughtn't. But sure an' you'll not be holdin' a few hard words against me? 'Tis me crazy Irish nature—"

She whirled to face him. "Sure, it's your crazy Irish nature that I'd never be getting along with. Nor with your crazy Irish feud," she added with a scathing flash of her eyes. "The saints be praised that I've found you out in time!"

He stood there abashed a moment.

"Think of the fine plans we've made," he blurted. "About the—"

"You should have thought of them a bit sooner!"

"But—"

"Save your wind. I've made up my mind and it's too late to change it now." And she went on with her packing.

Tam stood with arms akimbo, glaring. Ignoring Shamus' covert warnings and the dour regard of MacIllwraith, he snarled: "*I* know what's come over you! You got a crush on that fourflushin', gun-packin' Cross-Draw!"

83

"And what if I have?" She stared up from her packing. "He's a *man!* He don't need any gang at his back every time he goes hunting a fight! And he knows how to act with a lady!

"Oh!" Tam's fighting mouth hung open. "An' does he, now?" he muttered. And shutting his face hard enough to bust his nut-crackers, he went stamping from the room.

O'Reilly and the sheriff exchanged glances.

With Albert plowing in their wake they started for the door. But just as they were passing through, a crash from the room behind them stopped them rigid in their tracks.

.13.

"Geev Eet to Heem!"

THE TABLEAU HELD but a second.

Then they all slammed round with a curse.

Cross-Draw was emerging in a tangle of gowns from the closet. But ludicrous as the picture was, nobody thought of laughing. Two guns were gripped in Cross-Draw's hands and his glance was like a judgment.

"Just get them grub-hooks up," he snarled, "if you hope to go on breathin'. That's right, Sheriff—you, too! Never mind the clothes, Eileen; slip out an' fetch a pair of horses round to this window. An' don't stop t' pick any posies."

When the girl had departed in a flash of silk-clad legs across the sill, Angus growled: "Ye canna git away wi' this. Ye—"

"No?" Cross-Draw's grin was thin and sudden. He surveyed them coldly. "You're goin' to find, before you're through with me, there's a hell of a lot I can get away with! Crawl out of them gun belts, gents—artillery won't be needed where you're goin'."

Shamus paled, and Albert croaked: "Gawd bless us!" while the sheriff scowled.

MacIllwraith said: "Y'r layin' up a lot of grief—"

"I wasn't expectin' t' lay up treasures in heaven," Cross-Draw derided. "Get out of them gun belts an' be quick about it. My patience is gettin' a little bald."

85

Reluctantly the sheriff unbuckled his belt, let its weight slide down to the floor. As the others were following suit Cross-Draw catfooted three steps slanchways and flicked a glance up the hall. He would have given something to have known just where that swivel-eyed Tam had got to. But he wasn't in sight and Cross-Draw was aware that this was one of those times when discretion had it over valor like a tent.

He catfooted back. "Out of the window, gents," he rasped, and prodded them with his pistols.

The three got over the sill without argument, though with divers murderous glances—particularly from Albert, whose pants had caught on a nail.

"Never mind about that," advised Cross-Draw, grinning. "After you've hoofed it to town—"

"Town!" cried Shamus, aghast. "Sure you wouldn't be after makin' us—"

"Oh, wouldn't I? Live an' let live is my motto—but when a guy gets shoved around as much as I been since I hit this hell's half-acre, he gets t' the point where he'd just as soon return a few favors. I didn't see no one worryin' about how *I* got t' town this mornin'. The walk's goin' to do you good."

If the three had been mad before, they were definitely more so now. Albert looked like he could chew railroad spikes with ease, and even Angus' dour Scots face reflected little pleasure in the prospect. To put a man afoot in cow country was as hefty an insult as could be devised.

And Cross-Draw drew a deal of satisfaction from the knowledge.

He'd show these whippoorwills who was who around this landscape!

But he wished to hell he knew where Tam had got

to; and what was holding up the girl. Surely she'd had plenty of time to get around here with those horses. If she didn't hurry up that dad-burned posse would be coming back.

Cross-Draw felt no urge to be here when that happened!

But just as he was debating the advisability of making his prisoners tie each other up and cutting loose of the place by his lonesome, he saw her. She came around the house with a pair of high, fast-stepping broncs.

"Hurry up," he directed. "Hop in an' get your bag. It's time we was layin' tracks."

She was back with her suitcase in a moment.

"All right," said Cross-Draw. "On your way, *muchachos*," and boosted her into the saddle. "*Andale!*" he cried. "Let's go!"

It was a rough country that hemmed O'Reilly's Harp; a broken land of upthrust crags and sharp-dropping crater-like basins through which the trail wound its tortuous way with towering rock walls along one side and, often as not, quick eighty-foot drops on the other.

Rough country—and when they rounded the bend it got rougher.

Cross-Draw gaped in amazement as his three sweating walkers abruptly hurled themselves flat on the ground.

It was Eileen's scream that cut him loose of astonishment—but the scream was a little bit late.

A rifle's sharp cracking was spattering lead like a ladle.

"Geev eet to heem! Geev eet to heem!" howled Concho. And Tam was sure doing his best!

.14.

Gone North

THE NEXT THING Cross-Draw knew, he was uncomfortably tangled in the branches of a cedar. There was a dead horse piled in a grotesque heap on a tiny ledge beneath him.

Wondering how in hell he'd got like this, he started to hunch his body round a bit to ease a jabbing pain in his side.

It was not the wisest move he'd made and his stomach turned over three times in the process. When the movement stopped he was ten feet lower and sweating like a nigger, with both hands clawed about a groaning branch and blue sky flapping round his dangling feet.

A hell of a situation in which for the hero of Agua Prieta to be finding himself!

His glance jerked round in desperate stabs as the sound of voices reached him from some place high above.

Rearing his head back cautiously he peered upward through a tangle of branches and beheld a row of staring faces half a rope's throw above him.

Memory returned with a vengeance as he recognized the watchers; the grins of Concho, Shamus and Tam O'Reilly, the worried scowl of MacIllwraith, and the scared white face of Eileen. Albert's mug was up there, too; it held a curiously strained expression.

But Cross-Draw was in no mood for analyzing emotions. Nor for philosophic reflections. The Harps were staring downward from that trail he'd left behind.

Yet, though he realized full well its further possibilities, not even the rifle barrel gleaming alongside Tam's grinning features was bothering him just now. The only question in *his* mind was which would be letting go quickest—his grip or the groaning branch!

It was a parlous situation.

But just when Cross-Draw was reluctantly bidding hope goodbye, Tam said with a nasty satisfaction: "I reckon he's dead an' done for. Let's be gettin' back to the ranch."

The faces withdrew beyond the trail's rough edge.

And just in time.

With the receding clack of Angus' dour Scots voice still ringing in his ears, Cross-Draw's branch parted company with its mother and Cross-Draw dropped the remaining fourteen feet like a plane with both wings gone.

He lit on his feet but sat down suddenly and remained there a good five minutes.

He was not really hurt; just bruised, shaken and skinned up considerable, and with one rib feeling like a mule had kicked it—which was probably the result of his landing in the tree. But he had come of a hardy family back there in West Texas, and pretty soon he got to his feet and began taking stock of the situation.

Looked like there wasn't much chance getting back up the cliff; nor for that matter, did there appear to be any great likelihood of his being able to get down. He was stranded on a tiny ledge that was hardly fifteen feet across; it was situated roughly midway from the trail above and the rockstrewn floor of the gulch below.

Cross-Draw sat down to think.

His brows creased grimly in his efforts at concentration. But for a long time results were meagre. Seemed like all he could get his mind on were his numerous aches and bruises.

Which didn't help matters any.

After a bit his thoughts stole out to Eileen. She certainly was an armful! Made Cross-Draw twitch all over just to think of her. What shock, despair and grief must be hers back there at the Harp as she paced her room or lay face down across her bed envisioning him crushed and mangled among the gully's hogbacked rocks.

It was quite a picture, and it made Cross-Draw feel better—like that time when he'd been down with diphtheria and the parson next door had spent the evening rehearsing his funeral oration.

But thoughts of Eileen got his mind to working finally. Maybe, he reflected, she'd slip out of the ranch tonight sometime and come scouting around to make sure he was beyond her helping. Yes, that's what she would do; and he would call to her guardedly and she would go back for a rope. And then he'd get off this damn ledge.

He glanced upward. Already evening was unfolding its somber shades across this great vast country. Within the space of minutes it would be dark. He wished he had his guns, because when she came there was always the chance that somebody'd follow her.

And then he went tense, struck by a bitter recollection: She'd declared her intention of leaving the Harp—had, indeed, been on her way when disaster had overtaken them. And after Cross-Draw'd gone over the cliff Tam had shooed them all back to the ranch.

It didn't take a heap of imagination on Cross-Draw's part to picture a sneering Tam standing guard with his rifle to make sure she stayed where he'd put her!

"Hell's Hinges!" he swore, and began savagely pacing the ledge.

One thing was certain: He had to get off this ledge, and get off in a hurry. Eileen would be a prisoner; but someone else might any minute get the notion it would be a good idea to scout a bit and make sure of Cross-Draw's demise!

It would be just like that confounded Albert!

Then his eye fell upon the huddled heap of the horse Tam had killed with his rifle. Holy cow—what a sap he'd been! There was a good stout rope on that saddle.

Six seconds later he had it in his hand.

No sense trying to win back to the trail above; nothing up there he could cast a loop on. But this tree—

In no time he had his rope lashed fast. With a slow wind roughing his hair, he bent above the lip of his covert and dropped the rest into the gully. It lacked ten feet of reaching the rocky floor—but what was ten feet to a fellow who'd dropped fourteen?

He was over the edge in a twinkling and going down hand under hand.

From time to time his swaying body caromed against the cliff. But he hung on and kept right on descending.

Halfway down a sudden thought broke cold sweat across his forehead. That ledge above was ragged and sharp—what if this weight-strained rope should be parted? Should be sawed in two by friction against the sharp edge?

He put more speed in his progress and breathed a prayer to his God.

But he held. And soon he reached its dangling end and dropped the ten feet to the rocks.

"Whew!" he muttered, dragging a sleeve across his face. He looked around about him in the deepening dusk and wondered which way he should go.

The gully ran north and south.

One thing was certain. In his present condition—sans guns and sans bronc—he'd better stay clear of the Harp.

Still debating he stiffened to a sudden sound. A tiny sound, such as might be made by the scrape of a pebble. But to Cross-Draw just then it rang out like a trumpet—the stealthy scuff of a footfall!

He wasted no more time on which was the better way to go, but went at once. Due north and in a hurry.

.15.

"You Keep Away From Her—Hear?"

"WELL," THE MAN said bluntly, "it's about time you put in an appearance! Where in Jerusalem you been? What in Tophet's *happened* to you?"

And well he might ask.

Cross-Draw had the veteran look of one who'd been through the wars—through, at any rate, some battle more recent than that affair at Agua Prieta. To be sure, a deal of this battered appearance came doubtless from his experience with the tree. There were in addition, however, other divers and sundry marks; abrasions, scratches, cuts and contusions which very likely had been gathered during his unconsidered flight from the prowler of the gully.

He was a sight, all right; and had provoked considerable interest when several minutes previous he'd come lurching into this spread. He was sans guns and sans bronc, his hat was gone and hair was smeared across his forehead in a wanton tangle.

He said, cuffing some of the hair from his eyes: "Mind ridin' that trail again? Reckon I wasn't payin' extra close attention. Did I hear you say you were expectin' me?"

"You sure did. You're a week overdue right now, an' I don't mind sayin' I was gettin' worried. I'd about concluded that bunch of skunks had got you."

Without having the least idea what the fellow was talking about, Cross-Draw sensed that here was something that might well prove important—something he could get his teeth into if he played this business right. He looked at the rancher curiously. "That's funny," he said suspiciously.

"I don't see nothin' funny about it," growled the other. "I put the whole thing up to the Association two-three weeks ago; then I got a wire in code sayin' they were sendin' a man down. That's what we're payin' for, ain't it? Protection?"

The rancher scowled. "Suppose you tell me what's been keepin' you an' what's happened to your horse and guns, and how you got tore up like that."

Cross-Draw stared at his brown scratched hands. Looked like once again he'd planked both feet in the middle of something. This bird was taking him for somebody else—and *expected* somebody whom he didn't know and who had somehow failed to put in an appearance. There was a chance here for a guy that was willing to play his luck. Cross-Draw realized that one self-conscious action would betray him. But he was deeply intrigued by the other's mention of an 'association' and was debating if he could successfully shove his dogs in this expected hombre's boots.

He looked up suddenly, his gray eyes cold and hard. "That was a damfool play, them notifyin' you that way."

The other stared; then he kind of nodded. "You may be right. But I can't see—"

"It's plain to me, though," Cross-Draw grinned at him mirthlessly. "Just look at me. . . . Somebody's tipped them damned skunks off—they probably got their mitts on that wire before you did."

"But the thing was in code," the other protested.

"Code!" Cross-Draw scoffed. "That's kid stuff! What the hell good's a code when—"

"Jerusalem!" The rancher nodded while his lips gave vent to a whistle. "You're right. With every member of the Association knowin' it—"

"Exactly," Cross-Draw said. "Now mebbe you better give me an outline of this business. They didn't tell me much; just said to come down here an' look around. That any information I'd be needin' had better come from you."

The rancher rubbed a reflective hand across his chin. "S'pose you tell me what's happened to you, first," he said, examining Cross-Draw with a vaguely altered gaze.

Cross-Draw didn't like that look a lot. He knew he was skating on damned thin ice. If he made a misplay in this business— Well, he just couldn't afford to. Yet he'd passed the point where safety lay in backing out; he'd already given the impression he was the man this bird was waiting for.

He had to go on with it, come what might.

He gave an appearance of reflection, then said grimly: "They've found out who I am, or this is the craziest mess I ever stepped into," and went on and told about the business of that lonely cabin where Zeneas Pool had been held a prisoner by Torrence O'Reilly, about that business at the Harp and Shamus' proposition, the fight and flight, his brief hours as Pinal County's first deputy, the return to the Harp and Tam's ambush on the trail.

When he'd finished the rancher nodded tautly. "I guess you hit it; they've discovered who you are, all right." He studied Cross-Draw thoughtfully. "I must say you ain't done half bad goin' it blind. Damn

95

lucky for you you stumbled in here, though; if you'd gone back to the Harp they'd probably had you planted now."

"Suppose you sketch me the layout now," suggested Cross-Draw; "I'm gettin' a little tired of playin' this blind. What's goin' on 'round here besides that crazy feud?"

"That feud's a blind—a smoke screen," the rancher said, "to cover up what's really goin' on. Oh, I don't mean," he added, "the O'Reillys and the Pools ain't really on the outs—they'd as soon shoot each other up as eat, I reckon. But their wrangle's bein' used by somebody else—somebody that's out to gobble up this whole damn country."

Cross-Draw had said nothing about the girl in his account; nor did he mention her now. He said: "It seems to me that you better elaborate on that a little—my think-box is sort of gummed this mornin', kinda. F'r instance, where does MacIllwraith come into this? Do you know that bleedin' cockney?"

The rancher shook his head. "First I've heard of this Loving. The sheriff's all right in his rimfire, daily fashion. But he'll get no place with this—it's way beyond his depth. Hell, there's been wholesale rustlin' goin' on for months an' he's got no more notion now than he had when it started who's responsible."

"Have you?"

"I ain't sayin'. I want you to figure this out your own way. 'F I told you who I got in mind—an' I've not a mite of proof—it would only prejudice you an' gum things up. An' God knows they're gummed aplenty now!"

"But you think some guy is out to grab this whole damn country, do you?"

"Think—hell! I know cursed well he is!" the ranchman grumbled. "I've seen this thing comin'. Trouble was, I didn't think it'd go so far. I thought he'd be content with the biggest part of things. But I see now he's after the whole damn works—that's why I wrote the Association. I told 'em about the rustlin', figurin' once they got a man down here he'd soon get wise to what was up."

Oho! A great light broke over Cross-Draw's vision. This guy was referring to the Cattlemen's Association. He was taking Cross-Draw for a range dick.

Cross-Draw suddenly went stiff. *Wasn't it altogether possible the Pools and the O'Reillys were doing likewise?* Suppose they'd got wind this bird had written the Association? A bunch of things would look a whole lot different in that light!

But he said nothing of this notion to the rancher. He asked instead: "Know a gal round here called Kate Eileen?"

The rancher stared at him; strangely, intently, appraisingly. "Guess I ought to," he said curtly. "I'm her father. Didn't you know her name was Collins?"

It was Cross-Draw's turn to stare. "Your daughter?" His wide lips tightened grimly. "No, I didn't ever hear her last name." He looked Collins over peculiarly. "Don't you like her any more?"

"Course I like her! What the hell you gettin' at?"

"Did you know she was engaged to Zeneas Pool?"

"Oh, that!" Collins shrugged contemptuously. "Don't waste your time on a thing like that."

"I guess you know she broke it off, eh?—that she got herself engaged to Tam O'Reilly an' has been stayin' at the Harp?"

"Course I know it—what do you take me for?

She's stayin' there with my consent."

Cross-Draw eyed the rancher coldly. "Not any more she ain't."

"What do you mean?"

"She told Tam where to head in at yesterday an' packed her bag."

Collins scowled. "Now what in Tophet did she want to do that for? Damn the unreliability of women! I told her—"

"You mean," said Cross-Draw gruffly, "you egged her into gettin' hitched up with—"

"I ain't egged her into nothing," Collins snapped. "I told her to get engaged to that young fool an' play the hand till further orders. I—"

"What kind of a hombre are you?"

Collins met Cross-Draw's glaring regard with an impatient shrug of the shoulders. He said in a tone reserved for children: "I wanted somebody in that house so I could know what was goin' on there. No use puttin' a man on the Harp—he wouldn't hear much in the bunkhouse; the O'Reillys ain't exactly *fools*. Her bein' engaged to Tam would let her in without suspicion."

"You mean she's over there as a spy?"

Collins ignored Cross-Draw's very unfavorable regard. "Yes—if you want to call it that. She's there to keep tabs on—"

"Then you better get her out of there! They're keepin' her there by force!"

"Nonsense!" Collins scoffed. "You been smokin' rattleweed! Even if they'd any reason—"

"I'm tellin' you," Cross-Draw blared. "She tried to leave with me last evenin'. When Tam knocked me over the cliff he made her go back to the ranch with 'em—"

"No matter," cut in Collins. "She'll be all right; they wouldn't dare to harm her—Shamus'll see to that."

"Mebbe so," growled Cross-Draw; "but that ain't the point. You said yourself the Pools an' O'Reillys would just as soon shoot each other as eat! What's goin' to happen to Kate Eileen if the Pools get it in their heads to raid that place one of these nights? Mebbe burn it down—mebbe even burn it a-purpose so's they can plug the Harps as they come runnin' out?"

Collins' cheeks showed an edge of pallor. But he stuck by his guns. He said: "We'll have to chance that. I can't pull her out now without tippin' our hand. I—"

"Chrissakes!" swore Cross-Draw hotly. "The hand's tipped anyhow, ain't it? Both those outfits think I'm here from the Association—an' if that don't prove they know you wrote 'em, I'm a stringhalted bug-eyed Mormon!"

"They may know someone wrote the Association—they may even know *I* wrote 'em, but—enough! It's none of *your* worry anyhow—"

"The hell it ain't! I'm figurin' t' marry Kate," said Cross-Draw wrathily.

Collins surged to his feet with an oath. "You get that notion outa your damn head pronto! No slat-sided, saddle-poundin' range dick's goin' to marry *my* daughter—an' you can stick your kak on that! You keep away from her—hear? You tend to your goddam knittin' or I'll send you back in a coffin!"

.16.

No Mistake!

AND THAT was that.

But if this crusty Collins thought he was going to keep Cross-Draw away from Kate Eileen after the fine start Cross-Draw had got, he was crazy as a chipmunk!

All the Alberts, Pools and O'Reillys in Arizona couldn't do *that!*

Just the same, Cross-Draw was glad he'd wound up at this Window-Sash spread. He had a pretty good idea what all this ruckus was about, now. Somebody Collins suspected, but would not name, was out to grab this whole great smear of country—and by hook, crook or bullets, aimed to get it. He saw plainly now the game being played by that catclaw killer with his .45-90 rifle and bushwhacking tactics. He was out to spread a reign of terror that would scare the biggest outfits into pulling out or selling cheap as the two-bit spreads, apparently, had already done.

It was a pretty slick program—if he could cut it.

Cross-Draw felt pretty good about how he'd put it over on Old Man Collins. Here he was an accredited—to Collins' notion—agent of the Cattlemen's Association. All he had to do now was get the deadwood on the scorpion behind the gunsmoke that was brewing up to cloud this range. Not that it would be an easy job! If it had been, Collins would never have sent out that call for help. But this was just the kind of chore Cross-Draw liked to tackle—and in this case he'd plenty of incentive, for they'd treated him like a dog ever since he'd hit the country.

Sure, he could see the reason why they had, all right. The Pools and the O'Reillys in their own little rumpus were likely not above dabbin' their loop on someone else's critters if the critters came easy to hand. Likely enough they rode the range with extra cinch rings in their pockets and a ready eye for whatever came their way.

Somehow they'd found out about Collins' wire to the Association, and when Cross-Draw had ridden up they'd jumped to the natural conclusion—just as Collins had—that Cross Draw was the Association's man. Whether they'd been helping themselves to other folks' cattle or not, they must have been running things pretty fine to be so anxious to get the supposed range dick out of the country.

Whatever their reason, it didn't interest Cross-Draw—all that interested him was getting even for the indignities heaped so lavishly upon him. And he intended *getting* even, too!

And while he was at it, seemed like it might be just as well to stick a spoke in the ambition-wheel of this unknown range hog—the catclaw killer who left exploded rifle shells between the teeth of his victims.

Of course he realized that the killer and the range hog might not actually be one and the same. The killer might even be—as the sheriff appeared to think—someone connected with the Pool outfit.

But that made little difference as far as Cross-Draw was concerned. He was in a sod-pawing mood and more than willing to take on the whole blame country!

"I'll make these whoppy-jawed bedbugs set up an' pull their chins in!" he muttered fiercely. "I'm plumb fed up with bein' shoved around. From now on it's every gent for himself—an' t' hell with rules an' scruples!"

FROM COLLINS Cross-Draw had learned a number of facts which might prove worth knowing. There were three fair-sized spreads within a radius of sixty miles, not counting the Pools' Flying V or the O'Reillys' Harp; these were besides Collins' own Window-Sash, the Crazy L of Tobias Waters, the Quarter-Circle 76, and the Boxed Heart of Chalmers Rey. "I'll put you on as stray man," Collins said; "that'll give you a reasonable excuse for pokin' 'round the range. If you can pin the deadwood on the bird behind all this, there's five hundred dollars in it for you."

Cross-Draw had looked at him keenly, then had gone out and saddled up a bronc. From the back of the bronc he was now regarding the neat headquarters buildings of Rey's Boxed Heart. Chalmers Rey, he decided approvingly, was a cattleman of the first order; his spread looked sleek and shiny as a housekeeper's pin.

He'd dropped by the Quarter-Circle 76 and found it to be a pretty good layout; but its foreman, judging by appearances, was a man with several irons stuck in the fire. Tobias Waters, of the Crazy L, was an easy-going ex-squatter whose cows must have hatched a lot of twins to put him where he was today.

Kneeing his horse toward the veranda of Rey's yonder ranch house, Cross-Draw reflected that as soon's he got this call off his chest he had better be larruping over to the Harp and seeing could he find out anything concerning Kate Eileen. And, if possible, he aimed to cut her loose from there in a hurry—Collins' orders to the contrary notwithstanding. Collins might be Somebody in the cow biz, but when it came to handling Kate Eileen, he was a washout from who laid the chunk!

Cross-Draw had meant what he'd said about the possibility of the Pool bunch raiding O'Reilly's Harp. These Pools were being too quiet by far. It was like the calm that precedes the storm, and Cross-Draw had not forgotten his embarrassing experience at Zeneas' hands.

Zeneas Pool, in his considered opinion, would bear a heap of watching.

Cross-Draw climbed from his horse before the Rey veranda and tossed his reins across the rail. His spurs clanked loudly as he clumped forward and knocked upon the door.

It was far from routine procedure for a strayman to go pounding on an owner's door; the bunkhouse was considered the place for visitors. But Cross-Draw had his line ready, and when a tall, gaunt hombre with loose-shackled eyes came to the door and looked him over, he said briskly: "You're Chalmers Rey?"

"I always have been."

"Uh—yeah. Ha-ha! I guess that's so." He peeled off his gloves, flexed his fingers and, shoving back his hat, scratched his head consideringly. "Been wonderin' if mebbe you mighn't be needin' a first-class range boss, Mister Rey. I—"

"Got any special reason for thinkin' I might?"

"Well, no-o. But—"

"Who sent you over here?"

Cross-Draw took the leap. He said: "Nobody sent me. I'm a stranger round these parts—I come from

Texas. I heard in town you run the biggest iron, so—"

"You any shucks with those pistols?" Rey inquired, his hard eyes cold an' bright.

Cross-Draw shrugged. "I ain't one t' brag. But like I said, I come from Texas where they raise 'em tough. I know which end the smoke curls out of an' I still got both my index fingers. But I'm no gut-shootin' smokeroo. Unless you got a top-screw job floatin' loose-like—"

"Sorry. I got a range boss now," Rey said. Then his ,loose-shackled eyes played over Cross-Draw searchingly. "Tell you what I'll do. I could use an extra hand, I guess, an' if you want to take on as strayman, I'll see you get Ballard's job when he quits."

"Ballard's the top screw, eh? When's he figurin' on quittin'?"

"He ain't," Rey said; "but accidents is liable to happen. It's here today an' gone tomorrow."

Cross-Draw looked at him.

"Well, what do you say?" Rey asked impatiently.

"How much is this stray job payin'?"

"Sixty a month an' found."

"Well." Cross-Draw gave an appearance of talking it over with himself. "The pay's O.K. But I guess I'll shove on over the hump. I'm too used to bossin' to start takin' orders now." And he wheeled back toward his horse.

"Hold on," Rey called, and followed him out. "Would seventy-five a month put a different complexion on it?" He eyed Boyd's guns.

"'Fraid not." Cross-Draw pulled on his gloves. "I'm kinda funny some ways. Was I to be takin' a foreman's pay, I'd expect to give the orders."

He reached for the horn and was thrusting a foot in stirrup when Rey said quietly: "Take a tip from me, young fellow, and get clear out of these mountains. Your horoscope's goin' to read a whole heap different if you go rampin' back to Collins."

CROSS-DRAW SWORE.

It was nothing new; he'd been doing it steady ever since he'd left the Boxed Heart. Of all the damfool plays! If he'd had the brains of a knock-kneed sparrow he'd have kept plumb away from Rey and confined his activities to the Boxed Heart bunkhouse.

And yet that play had looked so good at the time. He'd thought about it all the way from the window-Sash and, while suspecting that Collins wouldn't have shared his enthusiasm, had himself been certain of its feasibility.

From Collins' talk he had got the notion Rey was the rancher the Window-Sash boss suspected. It wasn't anything Collins said; but rather the way he'd said it—the tone of his voice, he shade of his eye, the slant of his cheek.

It had struck Cross-Draw that the logical way to get a line on Rey was to strike the fellow for a job. Obviously he'd get no place asking Rey for any regular job—a range boss always had the say on these. But he'd never heard of a range boss hiring his successor; that was the province of the owner.

It had seemed a pretty slick notion hitting Rey for the top-screw's job. Seemed like he'd been bound to learn something to his advantage.

And so he had—but hardly that which had been hoped for!

One thing was certain; or rather, a couple of

things. Rey was hiring gunslammers and he was on to Collins' game.

It looked like Collins was right in his suspicions. No outfit took on leather-slappers, and the consequent accompanying expense, unless there was some kind of monkey business getting itself afoot.

It looked very much to Cross-Draw as though the Boxed Heart was getting ready to expand.

DUSK'S SHADOWS were lengthening across the range when Cross-Draw, rounding the bend in the trail, came at last in sight of his objective.

Looking down upon O'Reilly's holdings, his jaw went suddenly slack and he pulled his bronc up sharply with a jerk. He swore and scrubbed a disbelieving hand across his eyes.

But there was no mistake.

The Harp was a smouldering ruin with no two rocks remaining one atop the other and with the timbers of the buildings burned to char!

.17.

"The Pools' Is Where We'll Find Her!"

DOWN IN THE VALLEY, Cross-Draw sat his saddle numbly and stared at the gutted ranch. It was a scene of bitter havoc; a desolate and final picture of what could be expected in this country from now until the end.

His first coherent thought was of the Pools—they'd struck as he had warned they would. Suddenly, viciously, and irreparably. The Harp cattle would be gone as surely as was this Harp headquarters. The Harp was finished whether the O'Reillys liked it or not.

Where were the O'Reillys now? Where were their hands?

And where was Kate Eileen?

His mind breaking free of horror, Cross-Draw swung from the saddle. First he quartered back and forth across the clearing, many times circling the site of Shamus' former ranch house. He was like a bloodhound with his nose to a trail, and when he quit he'd a pretty fair idea of what had happened.

Some time today—probably early in the darkness of pre-dawn—a group of dark-clad horsemen had come charging from the hilltops and dashed spurring among the buildings. They must have packed baled straw or oil-soaked rags—nothing less could have caused such a conflagration. And when Harp's crew had come staggering from the burning buildings, the raiders had shot them down.

This was Cross-Draw's conclusion. It was drawn from such incontestable facts as tracks, three dead broncs with the brands gouged from their hides, the dead bodies of four Harp riders, and the mangled remains of Shamus O'Reilly himself.

Nauseated, yet with a terrible rage redly gnawing at his shock-dulled consciousness, Cross-Draw commenced probing the smouldering debris for other bodies.

Doggedly, though afraid and dreading to find it, he bent his wearied energies toward discovering a body with chestnut hair.

He was searching still when the snarl and curse of panting voices wheeled him round to face the curdled shadows of the chaparral.

At the edge of brush, thrity feet away, two bodies were locked in snarling embrace. Back and forth they swayed, grunting, panting, struggling for possession and the chance to use the pistol that flashed aloft in one man's hand. One man had it, but the other man's fist was clamped about his wrist, straining, jerking, striving to shake it free.

The man with the gun was the taller. But the shorter fellow was giving a good account of himself. The bigger man had got his gun, but the smaller man was clinging like a terrier, refusing to let him use it.

There was a sudden shift, a speed-blurred movement; a cry, a gasp—and the shorter man stepped back with the gun.

"Bash 'im on the head with it!" growled Cross-Draw, striding up.

But the man with the gun paid him no attention.

108

"'E couldn't 'ad no and in it!" he bellowed at the cursing taller man. "Use yer ruddy 'ead! 'E's alone, ain't 'e? Then w'ere did 'e git the men? Eh—w'ere'd 'e git 'em? *Noplace!* 'Cors 'e wasn't in it!"

"Don't try to hand me that stuff! He pulled—"

"Shurrup! Close yer fice!" the man with the gun said fiercely. "I'll 'andle this!" And he whirled so quickly, his gun was cocked and leveled before Cross-Draw realized what was up.

He realized then, all right. For the man with the gun was Albert and the bigger man was Tam. And despite Albert's reassuring words, he seemed, himself, to only half believe them. There was an edgy sharpness to his half-closed gaze as he swung the gun on Cross-Draw. It warned that he'd stand little foolishness—that he'd shoot on the slightest provocation.

"W'ere's she at?"

There was no doubt in Cross-Draw's mind whom Albert meant. Far as they were concerned, there was just one 'she' in the country. And it whipped him into a fiercer temper that these men didn't know where she was. For just a second, recognizing them, he'd dared to hope.

"W'ere is she, eh? Yer better tork fast!"

"Don't be a fool!" snarled Cross-Draw. "I haven't got her! I don't know any more about this than you do—if as much. I ain't been here more'n ten minutes. I was searchin'—"

"Yus. We c'ld see yer was! Wot fer?"

"For the other bodies, naturally. Shamus is over there slashed to ribbons. Four of the hands is scattered round, all dead an' sieved with bullets. There's three killed broncs with their brands slashed off. I figured the rest of you was—"

109

"Oh, shut off the goddam gas!" snarled Tam. "An' give me back that gun," he growled at Albert. "If I wasn't half crazy with this thing, I'd have known from the start you wasn't in it—*you* wouldn't be after killin' her!"

"No," gritted Albert, switching round, "but 'e might 'ave run 'er orf someplice—"

"Don't talk like an addlebrained nitwit!" Cross-Draw cursed. "If I knew where whe was, I'd say so. You don't think I'm scared of the likes of you two?"

"Ahr—"

"Watch out where you point that gun. Unless you're figurin' to use it, better put it up—I'm gettin' a little bit nervous myself."

"Where've you been?" demanded Tam; and Albert said: "Yus! Wotcher been up ter?"

"I ain't been up to anything. I struck old Collins for a job an' got it—if it's any of your never-mind. Where've *you* been?"

"It's a cinch we wasn't here," rasped Tam.

"The hell with you," snapped Cross-Draw, and went back to search the wreckage.

Still muttering, Tam and Albert followed.

But though they searched until the last dim light had vanished nothing further was discovered. Cross-Draw leaned against a still-hot chimney and dragged a sleeve across his face. "Might's well quit. She isn't here," he grunted wearily.

"No—I never thought she was," rasped Tam "It's them goddam Pools that's pulled this, an' the Pools' is where we'll find her!"

.18.

Handwriting on the Wall

CROSS-DRAW WAS inclined to agree.

After all, wasn't this what he'd warned would happen?

And now it had. With one fell swoop, the O'Reillys had been dealt what could only be described as a major catastrophe. So far as Cross-Draw could learn, Tam and Albert were the only members of the outfit who'd escaped. They'd been off some place when the raiders had struck.

Maybe, Cross-Draw reflected, it was Zeneas Pool who was out to grab this range. Cross-Draw, who had come from Texas, saw with a sudden clarity what was going on here. This country, hemmed by the rockribbed Superstitions, was a natural cattle empire; it had all any cattleman could want. But crisscrossed and cut up as it now was by more than half a dozen outfits, its resources had been wasted until a bare subsistence could hardly be hacked out of it.

Some man with vision, Cross-Draw thought, had seen this; had glimpsed the ruin being wrought by these short-sighted, overgrazing shoestring ranchers. He had seen his chance, grabbed Time by the forelock and laid his grim campaign.

To Cross-Draw this was an old, old story; back in Texas many times he had watched it played to the bitter end. He understood its moves and strategies, its gun-law and its shambles.

There was but one sure way for a man to take this country over; a tide of fence-cutting, cattle-killing, arson, murder, terrorism, deadlines and stampedes.

The smaller outfits would sell out—indeed, from his talks with Collins, he understood that most of the two-bit spreads had already done so. But no man knew to whom they'd sold, for there'd been no deeds recorded—no sales or quit-claims added to the records.

The smaller outfits were eliminated.

The next grim move must be directed at a larger outfit; one the instigator of this plot was sure would crack. There must be no set-backs, no breathing spell permitted during which the rest might band together.

Here, then, was the explanation to the wind-up of the Harp.

Drygulchings had been inaugurated; fear and terror had tramped their wake. Distrust and suspicion had been sown, and the Harp had turned its energies and attention toward its traditional enemy, the Flying V. And while thus engaged, its strength had been whittled down, its morale cracked. And now—sometime this morning—the final blow had fallen; a quick raid and devastation of the Harp.

These things were part and parcel of the pattern—a pattern which had been old when Abraham was young. A plot that seldom failed.

The next move in this thing—

And right there warning smashed at Cross-Draw like a blow between the eyes.

He hauled his bronc up sharply with a quick, hard

shout at the others. "Hold on a sec—let's talk this business over."

Tam swung 'round with an oath. "What the hell could there be to talk about? Kate's gone, ain't she? Who the hell would have the guts to pack her off but Pool?"

"Depends," said Cross-Draw grimly. "I'm not right sure, but—"

"By God," snarled Tam, "you swingin' 'round to them Pools again?"

"I ain't swingin' 'round to no one. But unless I miss my guess, we'll not find her at the Flyin' V, so why go foggin' over there?"

"You mean an ambush?"

"Like enough. But, anyway, I'll bet—"

"Ahr—you an' your bets!" scoffed Albert.

But Tam growled softly: "You mean we won't be findin' her at Flyin' V?"

"Well, look; let's put it this way," Cross-Draw said uncertainly. "If you were Pool an' you'd grabbed the girl—"

"Where is she then?" Dark suspicion rode Tam's tones and his eyes turned bright and ugly.

"Well, I'm not real sure, but—"

"You're damn' well right you ain't!" Tam shouted. "I got a mind to finish what I started yesterday! You'll go to the Pools with us or—" And he let the rest trail off while he slapped a hand to his gun butt.

"No you don't!" growled Cross-Draw, and jerked both pistols smoothly. "I owe you one for tryin' to get me killed on that cliff. By rights I'd ought to blast your mortal tintype! Get your hand away from there quick or, by George, I will!"

He was thankful now he'd borrowed these pistols from Collins to replace the ones he'd lost when

113

yesterday Tam had knocked him off the trail. All his old animosity against the Harp crowd rushed back to darken his cheeks as Tam stood crouched with his hand whitely wrapped about that gun butt.

"Shake loose of it," Cross-Draw warned, "or I'll let you have it!"

Reluctantly Tam dropped the hand away and straightened in his saddle.

"You better cut your stick an' get out of this country quick," he threatened. "Get out or you'll get planted," he snarled, and with a sign to Albert, he whirled his bronc and went larruping off toward Pools'.

CROSS-DRAW SAT for some time looking thoughtfully after them. With a shrug, he turned his pony finally and rode through the gloom of the backtrail.

Overhead the stars came out as sweet as sleepy mockers. But Cross-Draw had no eyes for abstract beauty; his mind was too filled with the perplexities of this problem. Someone was out to gobble this range and he had to find out who it was.

But he could not concentrate on the business. Kate Eileen's plight weighed him down with sick fear and he rode with a slack rein, looking neither to left nor to right.

Had she been packed off by the raiders after the fight at Harp? Or had she somehow gotten clear?

These were the questions that tramped Boyd's mind. He could not get them out of it. If she'd gotten clear she must be wandering now in the badlands, cold and scared, disheveled; a prey to nameless fears. But if the raiders had got her—

It was an alternative that did not bear thinking on; but the likeliest possibility and a thing that had to be faced.

Had he believed for an instant she was being held prisoner at Pools', he'd have gone pelting over there fast as the rest—ambush or no damned ambush.

But that was the trouble; he didn't.

Seeing in memory the vision of Zeneas Pool's sly, fox-like features had convinced him that if the Flying V was behind that raid and Zeneas Pool had grabbed her, the man's home ranch would be the very last place he'd have taken her.

Pool might be reckless, but he wasn't no fool. He would have seen with a razor-sharp clarity that the Flying V would be the first place searched by avengers.

If Pool had whisked the girl off, he had hidden her some place else.

There could be no damned mistake about that part!

Cross-Draw rode through the night with no thought in his head as to where Kate Eileen could be hidden. Bitter rage was a-churn in his chest and he cursed Pool and all the man's works. He wished mightily now he had left the fellow to whatever fate Squinch-Face had been holding in store.

But regrets, as he knew, oiled no six-guns.

His first impulse had been to comb the range till he found her. But he was certain now she had not gotten clear; that she'd been grabbed by the raiders and hidden.

Had he known the range like this Tam, he'd have scoured all the likeliest places. But he was an outlander in a strange and rough country that might easily defy his best efforts for weeks.

He could be sure of one thing, he reminded himself grimly. If she'd fallen prey to the raiders, she'd be guarded.

That opened a number of possibilities and he set

about to explore them.

The most obvious place to hide the girl would be out in the badlands somewhere. And there were plenty of them in this region. But the drawback to such a hideout was the extreme likelihood that those who sought the girl would search the badlands first. Collins' men would rake these badlands from end to end just as quick as they learned what had happened.

Cross-Draw stiffened.

Had Kate Eileen's abductors figured on this? Had they planned with an eye to just such a search being likely? Had they taken her with the deliberate purpose of draining the man-power from the Window-Sash?

By God! It was a startling thought!

The man behind this business, if Cross-Draw's suspicions held water, was out to grab this whole vast strip of country. What more natural then, than that Collins' spread was the next planned for smashing! It was not so big as Rey's Boxed Heart, but it was big enough to insure the fear of ruin being planted in the others' minds. It was plenty big to serve as warning.

Cross-Draw could almost see the scrawled placards that would be nailed to other doors: "Get out or you'll be next!"

It was like handwriting on the wall. The raiders had grabbed the girl for the deliberate purpose of dragging Collins' riders into the badlands. And while they were gone, Window-Sash would be wrecked as surely and completely as the O'Reillys' Harp!

With an oath, Cross-Draw put spurs to his horse.

.19.

"You Crazy Fool!"

THE LIGHTS of the Window-Sash drove yellow bars across the blackness of the yard.

Straight to the broad veranda Cross-Draw rode and flung from the saddle. His spurs raked jangling sound through the night as he sprang across the floorboards. His fist smashed the door with the noise and rhythm of drumbeats.

Lifting his voice to the bald-knobbed hills he shouted.

"Collins!"

He could hear oaths and sudden footfalls from the bunkhouse. The hands were piling out to see what had got afoot.

But Cross-Draw paid them no attention. "Collins!" he shouted again. Losing patience, he yanked the door open and went clanking down the dark hall. A door ahead opened suddenly, spilling light across the floor; and there was Collins staring at him, his face sharpened to anger and a cold oath falling from his lips.

"Hell's hinges, are you *deaf?*" blared Cross-Draw, snarling.

"What in hell d'you mean by—"

"Listen, you fool! Kate Eileen has gone—do you get it? Abducted, kidnaped, *stolen* by the shootin' hellions that raided Harp an' burned it to the ground!"

117

Collins stood there with his eyes like glass.

"Come alive!" growled Cross-Draw, shaking him. "Wake up! I tell you Kate Eileen's been run off! I warned you last night what would happen—but you wouldn't listen. Now, damn you, she's gone an'—"

Collins caught him by the throat. "God damn you! If you're lyin'—"

But Cross-Draw threw him off.

"Wait'll you see the Harp if you think I'm lyin'. Shamus O'Reilly's lyin' ripped to ribbons in his blood, an' the whole Harp crew but Tam an' Albert sprawled where the bullets dropped 'em in the yard! *Lyin'!* Don't talk to me about lyin'! If you'd listened to me last night, you'd have Kate here, alive an' safe!"

Collins stood there, white and shaken.

"Tell me," he said hoarsely. "What's happened? Where do you think she's gone?"

Cross-Draw told him hurriedly what he'd found at the Harp. "Tam an' that pin-headed Albert've gone larrupin' over to Pools'—"

"Why in hell ain't you over there with 'em?" snarled Collins with eyes blazing. "It's plain enough what happened—"

"Plain as your foot! D'you think if Pool was crazy enough to pull a stunt like this, he'd put his head in a noose by takin' her to his *ranch*? Hell's backlog!" Cross-Draw shouted. "Try usin' your head for somethin' besides a hatrack! You'll not find Kate at the Flyin' V!"

Collins pulled himself together, but his eyes said he wasn't forgetting this, and his look said he wasn't forgetting Cross-Draw had gone to the Harp against his orders.

But all he said right then was, "Then where *is* she?"

118

"Whoever's grabbed her," Cross-Draw said, "is hidin' her out some place where—case she's found—responsibility won't be traced back to 'em. She might be cached out in the badlands—"

"By God, that's where she is!" snapped Collins bitterly, and went slamming for the door.

"Hold on," growled Cross-Draw grabbing him. "Pull up a bit an' think! The badlands are the first place bound to be searched—Well, *ain't they?* All right; if they've cached her out there somewhere, they've done it for a purpose. Because they don't give a damn if you find her—because all they're wantin' is to pull your outfit away from this spread!"

"What the hell for?" blared Collins.

"So they can wreck it like they've done the Harp!"

Collins stopped like he'd been shot. For a second he stood utterly moveless, and Cross-Draw said: "This business has been carefully planned. It's part of this scheme some polecat's got for making this range plumb private. By hook, crook or powder-burnin' he aims to drive you fellas out! Last night—"

"No matter!" Collins growled. "If they got Kate Eileen I'll not rest till—"

"Don't be a fool! Can't you see that's what they want? Can't you see if you go rampin' 'round them badlands you'll be playin' right into their hands? Look here! If—"

"Get out of the way!" snarled Collins, swinging at him.

"You crazy fool!" rasped Cross-Draw. "Do you want to see this spread go up in smoke?"

"By God, you're stayin' here!" Collins said ominously. "You better see it don't!"

.20.

A Ride Through the Night

FOR QUITE a while after Collins and his crew had gone—those of the crew, that is, who were not out guarding cattle—Cross-Draw tramped the bunkhouse floor.

Not that that seemed as if it would do him any good. But he was in a savage mood and too pent up with the things he felt to be still even for a second. Restlessness stirred him like a mighty tide; a wickedly reckless tide. It was in his mind that what he needed was a chance to rip and batter; to take his fists and smash somebody's face in. Zeneas Pool's, or Tam's, or even this damfool Collins'!

The man was nuts! Anyone with a gram of sense—after the warning Cross-Draw had given him—if he had to go off, would at least have left a part of his crew to guard the spread, just in case Cross-Draw was right. But not this goddam Collins!

Serve him right, thought Cross-Draw bitterly, if the raiders *did* wreck Window-Sash!

Thought of the raiders brought Rey into his mind. Rey was the fellow Collins had in mind as best candidate for the role of unknown range hog. Rey, in Collins' estimation, was the man behind all the troubles of this country. Probably, Cross-Draw thought, Collins was not above even suspecting Rey of getting the Pool-O'Reilly feud a-rolling!

But thinking more closely over what he knew of

Chalmers Rey, Cross-Draw was almost inclined despite himself, to believe that in this instance Collins actually *had* something.

This Rey was a taciturn type of hombre. Hard, and tough as a buzzard's uncle—the sort who'd not be apt to let any scruples stand in the way.

He recalled the fellow's tall and gangling figure, his bony, suave yet cold-tooled features; his hard, loose-shackled eyes. Not the kind of jasper—having crossed—you'd care to meet in a dark alley.

One thing he knew from contact with the man: Chalmers Rey was taking on gunslammers, and he knew of Collins' suspicions.

What was the follow up to? Was he hiring guns for protection, or to help him take over the range?

Spurred by impulse, Cross-Draw decided to drift on over to Rey's place and take a look around.

If raiders came during his absence, why that was just tough luck for Collins. He'd warned the man in ample time and owed the fellow nothing. Had Cross-Draw been the Association man Collins believed him, he would not have acted differently.

Collins, against all sense and reason, had abandoned the spread. Why should Cross-Draw play the goat?

Far as that went, though, the raid on Harp must have been just prior to dawn. So that part was all jake and dandy. Cross-Draw aimed to be back here again long before dawn rolled around.

He snuffed the lamp and pulled on his gloves. He was reaching for his hat when the sound of a rider stopping just outside came thinly through the walls.

Softly Cross-Draw catfooted to the door, a leveled pistol gripped firm and eager in a ready hand. Softer still he drew the door ajar. Through the crack

121

he saw the horseman peering at the darkened buildings.

"Scratch a light," purred Cross-Draw wickedly, "or I'll blast your earthly envelope!"

He saw a start and the following rigidity that gripped the unknown rider. There was no moon showing and the yard was dark. But the man on the bronc was close enough for Cross-Draw to observe it if he made out to try any funny business.

"I'm countin' three. You better scratch."

The rider's hand went to his hatbrim. Lowered. A rasp and splutter announced the drag of the match-head across a thumbnail. Then light sprang up cupped guardedly in the fellow's hand.

Cross-Draw stepped outside with an oath.

The rider was Albert Loving.

BACK INSIDE the cabin, and with the lamp turned up once more, Cross-Draw surveyed his unwelcome guest with a scowl.

"What's the big idea comin' over here?"

The cockney cowhand chuckled. "W'y not? Eh?" Albert regarded him slanchways. "Not much to 'old a man to the 'Arp these days—not 'arf. Thought yer might be able ter get me orn with Collins."

"Oh, you did, did you?" Cross-Draw blared. "Since when did I owe *you* anything?"

"Well, wot I s'y," mumbled Albert, "is let bygones stay bygones. The 'Arp is gorn an' I could use a job o' work. Yer wouldn't keep a bloke from makin' 'is livin', would yer?"

"Some blokes," said Cross-Draw unfeelingly, "is a heap better off dead an' planted." He looked Albert over suspiciously. "Where's that crazy O'Reilly? Thought you birds was goin' to spring Kate free of the Pools."

122

"We was fer a fack," Albert nodded. "But we 'ad 'ard luck. We run smack inter a ambush."

Cross-Draw grinned with pleasure. "What'd I tell you! Serves you right, by George—did O'Reilly get shucked of his toughness?"

"I dunno, an' I'm tellin' yer strite. Them Pools opened up like 'twas Christmas. I cut my stick fer the open an' I reckon that Tam did the sime. Any'ow, I ain't seen 'im."

"What about the girl? Have the Pools got her?"

Wrinkles seemed to be holding a reunion on Albert's forehead. He said at last with a scowl: "Blimey, guv'nor, yer got me there. I didn't see any sign of 'er. The Pools 'as got guards posted. We didn't get in stone's throw of the 'ouse."

Cross-Draw thought a bit, debating with himself whether to leave Albert here or to make the fellow go with him. Lack of knowledge concerning Albert's true status in this business finally proved the deciding factor.

Cross-Draw said: "I'm figurin' to take a little pasear over east a bit. You come along with me an' when we get back you can hit old Collins for a job."

"W'ere is 'e now? In bed?"

"Never you mind where he is," growled Cross-Draw. "Button your lip an' get into your saddle."

THE BUILDINGS of the Boxed Heart were ablaze with light when the two men came in sight of Rey's headquarters. They stopped their horses on a little knoll and Cross-Draw studied the place intently.

"'Oo's spread is this?"

"Fella named Rey—the Boxed Heart," Cross-Draw answered. "Keep your voice down. This outfit's ringtailed. They'd just as lief shoot you as snore."

"Yer know 'em?"

"I hit Rey for a job. He's lookin' for gunslammers."

"Oh, ah?" Albert looked at the layout more keenly. "'E the bloke that's 'erdin' idears?"

Cross-Draw didn't answer. It had come to him that things looked mighty quiet down yonder despite the display of lights. No sign of activity in or out was anywhere apparent. No movement of any kind had caught his eye since they'd got the place in sight.

Something queer about that.

Albert evidently thought so, too. "Plice looks deserted," he muttered. "They gorn off with Collins, yer reckon?"

Cross-Draw gave him a scowl. After all, though, he thought, Albert would find out pretty soon anyway. "Collins," he said, "is out searchin' the badlands for Kate."

"In the dark? Blimey! 'E must 'ave eyes like a cat!"

"Where there's a will there's a way," Cross-Draw quoted. "He's sure hell for action, that's certain."

"Mebbe," said Albert tentatively after a little silence; "mebbe the girl was 'ooked jest ter get 'im aw'y from 'is ranch."

"That's what I told Collins."

"'E wouldn't listen, eh?"

"Well, he's out there searchin' the gullies."

"Mebbe we ort to go dahn there," muttered Albert after another interval of silent scrutiny.

"Nope," growled Cross-Draw flatly. "We're headin' back for the ranch. With all this raidin' an' night-ridin' goin' on, no tellin' *what* might happen. After all," he added, beginning to have qualms now about the summary way he'd abandoned the spread, "there may be somethin' in what I been figurin'— about those raiders ridin' off with Kate to pull old

Collins' outfit loose an' give 'em a chance at another bonfire."

Albert looked at him peculiarly. "Lumme!" he said finally. "'As Collins given yer stock in the plice?"

"It ain't that. But after all, he did kinda leave me in charge of things an'—"

"Oh, ah? And is the Hassociation payin' yer fer bein' custodian—"

"Who the hell said the Association's payin' me, anyway? An' what the hell association are you talkin' about?" growled Cross-Draw, sort of taken at a disadvantage.

"Ah!" said Albert, and screwed his red face into a smirk. "Abaht this Rey bloke, now. If yer ain't fer 'im, yer ag'in' 'im, eh? Don't yer kind of reckon, mebbe, 'e's the one that's out to grab this country?"

"You talk too much," growled Cross-Draw, and turned his horse upon the backtrail. He did plenty of thinking though as they rode through the Arizona silence.

Presently the moon came up. Its aid disclosed nearby objects a bit more clearly, and presently the gaunt outlines of what looked to be a line-rider's shack shoved up from the clustered shadows.

Both men eyed it covertly, though neither one commented.

Abruptly Albert swung his horse in that direction.

"Here—where you goin'?"

Albert made no answer, but beckoned Cross-Draw to follow.

Pulling up beside him, Cross-Draw growled suspiciously: "Just who the hell are you, anyway?"

Albert eyed him slanchways. "Come ter that," he grunted, "'oo are you?"

It was at that precise moment that something

whistled between them shrilly. From the direction of the shack a rifle's sharp, flat challenge crashed a hole through the hush.

21

No Need for Rose-Colored Glasses

IT WAS a high-powered rifle. Probably, Cross-Draw thought, a .45-90. And the fellow behind it sure knew how to make it talk.

The air was filled with the sound of hornets. Three more slugs ripped snarling past. One laid a burn across Albert's pony; another jerked at Cross-Draw's hat. Cross-Draw's bronc took fright from Albert's and went into the air with a snorting squeal. Cross-Draw hammered him down to the ground, but he refused to hold still. He bolted.

Albert's mount was ten jumps ahead, nor could all the cockney's swearing slow him.

It was a good three minutes before they got the broncs pulled up. "Hell!" snarled Cross-Draw, glaring at Albert. "A fine mess we made of that! Whyn't you tell me there was somebody at that shack?"

"Did *I* know it?" snapped back Albert.

"What'd you start over there for then?"

"Saw a glint of metal."

"A rusty horseshoe nail, I guess!"

But the sarcasm was wasted on Albert. He was paying no attention, being busy tying his bronc's reins to a mesquite. When he'd got the knots the way he wanted them, he slipped his rifle from its scabbard and with a careful method quickly examined its mechanism. Then he looked up.

"Somethin' tells me," he grunted softly, "they've got the girl in yonder cabing—"

"I was thinkin' that, too," muttered Cross-Draw, and pulled his own carbine from leather. "You wait with the horses—"

"Wite with 'em yerself!" snapped Albert, and started forward, keeping to the thickest shadows. Suddenly he stopped. "Look," he said in a cautious whisper. "We better play this sure; cover both sides. We don't want 'im ter slip us. You tike the back. I'll tike the front. An' be gorldahn careful what yer lam at."

Cross-Draw thought Albert seemed to be taking a deal on himself, and in more leisurely circumstances would have told him where to head in at. But if the guy in that shack was holding Kate prisoner, this was no time to argue trivialities.

Taking a squint for deepest shadow, he started forward in a wide half-circle. Albert already was swinging an arc in the opposite direction. It would take a bit longer this way. But they stood in this manner far better chance of slipping up unobserved. Not—Cross-Draw told himself—that *he* gave a damn whether the vinegarroon saw them or not. But after all, if Kate was in there with the fellow...

It made Cross-Draw boil just to hink of it!

He quit his circling movement, gripped by a furious passion, and went plowing headlong through the chaparral, taking the shortest line between two points and making plenty of noise about it. Sounded a deal more like an army than just one guy from Texas.

Then, suddenly through the racket, came a

high-pitched yip from Albert, a beller of hoarse-voiced oaths, the sharp, slashing crash of the rifle, and a splatter of hoofbeats drumming off swiftly.

When Cross-Draw reached the scene it was to find Albert shamefacedly picking himself from the buckbrush.

"What the hell happened?" snarled Cross-Draw. There was blood on Albert's shirt.

"Don't blime me!" scowled Albert. "If yer'd done wot we agreed on 'e wouldn't 'ave got aw'y."

"Who was it?"

"'E looked like that bloke Concho. But I ain't sure—see? Orl I know fer sure is that the girl was with 'im—an' still is! W'en yer started poundin' through the brush, they lit out o' there like a couple of rabbits—"

"You mean to say," blared Cross-Draw, "Kate Eileen went off with that fish-bellied shorthorn of her own free will?"

"Blimey! I didn't see any ropes!"

Cross-Draw cursed in a passion.

But Albert stopped working with the bit of shirt-tail he was using for a bandage and looked up at Cross-Draw oddly. "Mebbe," he said, "she's with Concho from choice." He ignored Cross-Draw's black frown and went on with his work. The wound was little more than a scratch across his ribs, but it bled profusely until Cross-Draw lent a hand and got the thing wrapped up.

"I'm goin' to take a look inside the shack," he muttered. "She'd never be with that son of a mangy appelative from choice!"

Albert shook his head. "She might. Yer cahn't never tell abaht a woman. I remember the Duchess of Ditchwater; 'er that run orf with 'er coachman—"

129

"Are you tryin' to cast—?"

"Lumme! I ain't tryin' ter do nothink, guv'nor. I was jest pointin' out that 'e might 'ave got 'er loose from the 'Arp durin' that raid, an' be 'idin' 'er out—"

But Cross-Draw snorted. "Don't never think it! If he was aimin' to protect her, first thing he'd do would be to take her home. He ain't, has he? An' the Window-Sash ain't hardly five miles off!"

"They might 'ave seen somethink that scared 'em—"

But Cross-Draw had pulled the shack's door open and now he stepped inside. He snapped a match to flame and swore. "Here's the goddam rope," he snarled. "She was tied, all right—an' plenty!"

He dashed from the place in a lather. "Which way'd they go?"

"'Ow could I tell? That slug in me side spun me rahnd like a ruddy torp! W'en I got me 'ands on me senses—"

He broke off suddenly, staring.

Cross-Draw smashed a glance in that direction. The hurrying clouds were red with reflected radiance over there to the west.

"The Winder-Sash!" cried Albert. "Hit's afire!"

With a string of gusty oaths, Cross-Draw went streaking for his horse.

22

Albert Gives Cross-Draw a Shock

"'ERE WOTCHER up ter?"

"What d'you think?" snarled Cross-Draw, still lamming for his horse. "We gotta git over there—shouldn't have left the golrammed spread in the first place!"

"Oh, ah? Yer goin' ter put that fire out with yer 'ands?"

Cross-Draw floundered to a stop. Indisputable logic rode the cockney's words. "We got to do *something!*" he grunted desperately.

"Sure. But 'arf a mo' now. We ain't goin ter 'elp none by gettin' ouselves kilt! Yer go bargin' over there an' yer'll git weighted down with lead enough ter sink a ship!"

"They won't be there now—"

"Then wot's the rush ter git there?"

Cross-Draw stared at him blankly.

"Look," said Albert quietly. "I think they *are* there. Yer forgettin' the 'Arp. Them flames'll be lightin' up that yard like day. I got a hunch them raiders will be stickin' rahnd. That fire'll be drawin' Winder-Sash 'ands like molasses draws flies in August—them raiders'll be stickin' rahnd to bush 'em w'en they come."

With his anger cooling, Cross-Draw looked at Albert closely. "Just who the hell *are* you, anyway?"

"Never mind that now," said Albert hastily. "The

important thing right now is to consider wot's best done. There was nobody 'ome at the Boxed 'Eart an' 'ere's the Winder-Sash in flames."

"By God!" swore Cross-Draw bitterly. "That—"

"'Old on! Might be nothin' to it. Some trick might've taken the Boxed 'Eart crowd aw'y jest like Collins' bunch got taken. Yer don't want ter go jumpin' ter conclusions."

"You got a head on your shoulders," Cross-Draw said reluctantly. Then he scowled. "What you reckon we ought to do?"

"Way I figure it's like this," said Albert softly. "Orl this is part o' the pattern. This range 'og's nobody's fool—we're up against a slick one. Look—we find the girl cached out on Boxed 'Eart range; the Boxed 'Earters ain't at 'ome an' there's a big fire at the Winder-Sash, w'ich ain't ten miles aw'y."

"Yeah," said Cross-Draw, nodding. "It *does* look kinda fishy. But—"

"Wite." Albert raised a hand. "We been over-lookin' the Pools. Corse w'y? Corse orl the signs been pointin' at Boxed 'Eart."

"But you an' Tam," Cross-Draw objected, "went out there. An' run into an ambush. You can't have an ambush without some guys with rifles. I can't see—"

"Yer ain't considerin' orl the facks. We went out there earlier. *I* got to the Winder-Sash before any fire got started. *I* was at the Pools Flyin' V. Wot was to prevent the Pools from hittin' the Winder-Sash— from gettin' out there jest as quick as I did?"

Cross-Draw's narrowing eyes showed a bright fierce gleam. Albert was right. There was nothing to have stopped the Pools from pulling this. Across his mind flashed the sneering, handsome face of Zeneas

Pool as he had seen it by the cattle guard just before Pool fired his pistol—just before he'd fired the shot that put a permanent stop to Cross-Draw's watch.

"By George," he growled, "I believe you've doped it right. That whoppyjawed Pool's got more damn crust than the Arctic Circle—he's colder'n a monkey's bottom! He—"

And then he stopped to stare suspiciously at Albert. His hands flashed down to his guns. One swift motion and they were out and focused on Albert's middle. "By God, for a minute you almost fooled me! Get up them mitts!"

Albert raised his hands to his shoulders. Irritation stamped his horsey face, but there was no sign of fear on it any place. He did not look like the trapped wolf that he should have.

It worried Cross-Draw. But he said coldly: "You put the thing pretty cute; but you told the truth. You *were* at the Flyin' V an' you *did* get to Collins' place before that fire was started. I don't see how you managed it, but you was last to leave the bunkhouse. *You set that fire yourself!*"

Albert scowled. Then suddenly he smiled. "Reach in my right shirt pocket, will yer, guv'nor? Or—I'll drop my gun first if yer nervous."

Cross-Draw studied him frowningly. "If you're up to any tricks—"

"Blimey! Do yer think—"

"All right," grunted Cross-Draw grimly. "Drop your gun. An' remember, I can see like a cat at night....O.K. Now reach in that pocket yourself, an' whatever's in there bring it out easy or you'll find yourself with a harp an' halo before you can say Jack Robinson!"

"Wotcher mean, a 'arp an' 'alo? Do yer think I'm

133

crazy? There's nothink in that pocket that'll bite yer—"

"You said it. I ain't aimin' to give it a chance. I can see myself gettin' that close to you. I wasn't born yesterday, brother. You reach in that pocket yourself."

Without more ado Albert thrust a hand in the pocket and brought out something that gleamed in the moonlight. He held it out in the palm of his hand, extending the hand toward Cross-Draw.

But Cross-Draw backed off. "Strike a match an' cup it above that jigger."

With his free hand Albert did so, and Cross-Draw swore in amazement.

"I'm the feller," said Albert, "they're orl takin' you fer."

The thing in his hand was a badge!

23

Rey Drops a Warning

"I'LL BE DAMNED!" swore Cross-Draw, a heap disgusted. "You're the Association's man—the range dick!"

"Yus," said Albert, chuckling. "Surprised yer didn't tumble to it sooner. Jest as well, though. Most these cow-wallopers rahnd 'ere figure you're the feller. Better let 'em go on thinkin' so—it'll give me more of a charnce ter get things done. Now wot abaht this sheriff?"

"Well, what about him?"

"Is 'e stright?"

"How would I know?" Cross-Draw blared. "He's been spendin' most of his time tryin' to slap me in his jail! Now for cripes sake cut out the jawin'. All the time we're gassin' here, that guy's gettin' farther off with Kate Eileen, an'—"

"Keep yer pahnts on, pal. She's safe enough—"

"That," snarled Cross-Draw, "is what *you* think! Me, I got different notions! I aim to marry that gal an'—"

"I still s'y keep yer pahnts on. She couldn't be safer on the Rock o' Gibraltar. Corse why? Corse I'm goin' ter be keepin' those blokes so busy, they'll not 'ave time to mess with her! By termorrer night, pal, I'm goin' ter 'ave the big pot wot's behind this business on 'is ruddy w'y ter Yuma! Blarst me buttons hif I ain't!"

Cross-Draw gave him a sour look. "Your talk is big, but I've heard the wind blow before. By tomorrow night the bird behind this stuff may have her clear over the line into Mexico!"

"Don't yer believe it! Kate Eileen was kidnaped fer the prime purpose of pullin' Collins' outfit aw'y from 'is spread so's the raiders could proper wreck it," Albert said emphatically. "Yer jest lettin' this business get in yer 'air. Keep calm, pal. Leave all the worries ter me."

"Start worryin' then," growled Cross-Draw. "What's first?"

"First we're goin' to visit Rey—"

"Rey! Hell's backlog! We been over there once tonight!"

"Yeah. But 'e wasn't 'ome then. Any'ow, a lot o' water's gorn under the bridge since then. Shake it up a bit an' lets git over there."

REY WAS HOME this time.

So were his punchers—and a harder case bunch Cross-Draw had never seen. Three were lolling before the bunkhouse, a couple more were loitering by the stable, one sat on the steps of the ranch house, and he saw another guy's hat in the harness shed.

And Cross-Draw saw with a curse that each man was nursing a rifle.

He nudged Albert. "Figured out what you're goin' to say?"

"Yer goin' ter do the torkin'—yer the Association man, 'cordin' ter their way o'figurin'. Arsk 'im where the 'ell 'e's been."

"All right. Don't give a damn if I do," Cross-Draw muttered. He would ask that spavined horse's south end a-plenty! He sure owed that jigger a few for the threats he'd unloaded yesterday; and if the whoppy-jawed monkey opened his trap, he'd kick every last one of his teeth out!

Cross-Draw was getting tired of being shoved around. It had got his bristles up for sure.

He hammered the door with a six-gun, and when Rey brought his scowl to the porch, Cross-Draw asked where the hell he had been.

"Who wants to know?" asked Rey, looking 'round.

"By God, I do! You talk an' talk quick or I'll part your hair with a pistol!"

Rey gave him a look no fellow would ordinarily take—without it come from his wife. "I don't recognize your authority to go 'round slammin' out questions."

"Oh, you don't, eh?" snarled Cross-Draw, and jabbed his gun deep in Rey's belly. "Mebbe this'll convince you?"

"Well," Rey admitted with a twisted grin, "it's a little bit stronger'n I'd expected. Don't you set any store by your health, Mister Boyd?" And his glance flashed to his paid rifle-packers who were wriggling their ears in quick interest.

"Never mind my health," sneered Cross-Draw, prodding Rey's rotundity roughly. "Get your spiel started an' stick to the truth."

"What is it you're so lathered up to know?"

"We wanta know where you been?"

"Tonight?" And at Cross-Draw's grim nod: "Who's this fella with you?"

"Never you mind about him. Get talkin'—quick!"

"It's a short story an' swift told," said Rey with an air of candor. "We been to a dance."

"A *dance*!"

"Yeah—you know, a leg-shaker. Over at the X Bar B."

"A kind of strangulation jig, I reckon—"

"No, you got it all wrong," Rey corrected him hastily. "This was a perfectly innocent affair. They was a mite stingy on the hog-wash, but—Hell! You can ask around; you'll find we was there all right! Old Quenter was throwin' the shindig for his girl; she's gettin' married next week—going' to hitch up with Tobias Waters. My bunch was there an' a crowd from Quarter-Circle 76, some of the Bar S boys, six or eight fellas from Flyin' V, the Box Underbit crew, an' Crazy L. If you don't want to take my word for it, ask some of them others."

Cross-Draw came out of his daze to growl: "What's the idea of all these waddies packin' rifles, then? Expectin' a revolution?"

"No," said Rey; "but I'll tell you somethin'. On the way home we noticed the Window-Sash was givin' out more than ordinary light. Not knowin' what was up, but puttin' two an' two together from what happened to the Harp, I figured Collins might be entertainin' visitors. Not bein' over-partial to that kind of game myself, I—"

"Yeah—it's too bad about you!" snarled Cross-Draw. "I got a notion I'm bein' loaded to the guards! 'F I find out I am, I'm comin' back an' make you hard to find—savvy?"

Rey showed an insolent grin. "Fair enough, Mister Cattlemen's Association Boyd. Now I'll give *you* a little advice: If you want to keep a whole hide an' go on breathin', you better bend them boots to other pastures. I'm a reasonable man, myself, an' I can understand your feelin's an' how come you to be so brash as to go pokin' your nose in where it plumb ain't wanted. But there's others 'round here that might not be as reasonable an' patient—"

"Is that a threat?"

Rey smiled, very bland, very suave. "Do I look the fool that would waste breath on threats? Consider it, rather, a friendly warning, Mister Boyd. A friendly tip as from one gent to another."

"By George! D'you realize who I *am?*" demanded Cross-Draw, clenching his fists with a scowl.

But Rey shrugged.

"A man's just a man to a bullet," he said, and Cross-Draw's fists dropped with an oath.

.24.

Prophecy Fulfilled

HALF AN HOUR had drummed by to the lope of their broncs when Cross-Draw pulled up with a curse.

"Wot's up?" growled Albert, pulling in beside him.

"D'you suppose," muttered Cross-Draw wickedly, "we've made a big mistake? I'm a little slow sortin' out my thoughts about this business, but somethin' just struck me, an'—"

"Wotcher mean?" scowled Albert, screwing up his eyes.

"Well, look—What if the guy behind this is Collins?"

"*Collins!* Lumme!" Albert gasped. "Yer ain't 'ot, are yer?" Don't feel queer at yer belly? Ain't got no blind staggers now, 'ave yet?"

Cross-Draw snorted. "Ever oil the wheels in your think-box? Might be a good idea, some time. It *could* be Collins," he grunted softly. "Stranger things have happened. Now—"

"Ahr—yer orf yer blinkin' trolley!" growled Albert. "Collins ain't no more the nigger in this woodpile than *you* are. Do yer think e'd be such a perishin' mug as ter burn 'is own spread?"

"Be a pretty slick play if he's guilty. A damn slick play! An' the fella's got plenty ambition—didn't he tell me no damn range dick was goin' to marry *his* daughter? Sure he did! When Kate gets hitched up, they'll have gold harness studded with emeralds if the Ol' Man gets *his* way!"

Albert shook his head. "That's different. Kate ain't in this. This is a clear-cut issue—a simple problem of survival o' the fittest. Somebody wants to hog this whole country, so—"

"Sure—Collins!"

"Don't play dumber than Gawd has mide yer! I tell yer Collins—"

"Look!" snapped Cross-Draw. "If Collins ain't in this, why would he be fool enough to abandon his spread after my warnin', an' go larrupin' off to the badlands to hunt his girl when it's too damn dark to see a black cat on a bedspread? I tell you," he growled, warming up to the subject, "Rey's hiring gunslammers an' he's on to Collins' game. He knew about that wire to the Association. He—"

"Sure! An' I tell you," growled Albert, "that Rey's the guy back o' this business himself! He's hirin' gunslammers—yer said it! He knew abaht Collins' wire! He knew Collins would to 'og-wild w'en someone made orf with 'is daughter! That dahnce at the X Bar B—"

"I guess you're goin' to say there wasn't one!"

Albert glowered. "Sure there was—it's 'is alibi. 'E was there, an' I bet yer 'e was seen by plenty! So 'e thinks that lets 'im out. But hit don't—nort by a jugful! 'E coulda been there, an' still lit the bonfire at Winder-Sash. Or one of 'is men coulda lit it! 'E knew damn well Collins wouldn't be there—"

"The devil!" growled Cross-Draw. "To hell with the business. You know so much, you better unravel your mystery yourself!"

"Oh! Quittin', are yer? Gettin' cold feet, eh? Lettin' Rey scare yer out with 'is 'ighbindin' tork!"

Albert screwed up his face. He spat in the dust. "'Ell of a tough hombre, *you* are!"

Boyd kneed his bronc closer and swung back a fist. "What's that? Say that again an' I'll flatten your head like a shovel!" He flared ferociously. "You hear? Jest say that again if you're wantin' some stars for your crown!"

Albert sniffed. "Tork! Tork!" he muttered. "Orl yer do is tork!"

"Oh, it is, is it? Well, look you here—I'm goin' to find Kate Eileen! An' I'm goin' to marry her, too! Roll that with your Gold Flakes an' smoke it! We'll see about this talkin'!" And he spurred his bronc off in a fury.

What the hell did *he* care about this squabble over range? It was none of *his* affair, and if Albert thought he knew how to run his job why that was his loss—not Cross-Draw's. He'd helped that British blighter every bit he aimed to! From now on he could stew in his own juice!

But one thing Cross-Draw would do—he would find Kate Eileen and he'd marry her!

He'd never thought much about getting hitched in double harness in the past. Had always considered that a sure-fire way to cramp one's style. "To hell," he'd said, "with petticoats an' flounces!" No dang woman was going to wrap her apronstrings round *him!*

But now all that was changed. He'd been wrong—that first look into Kate's green eyes had showed him. Marriage was the ideal state and no two ways about it.

So thinking, he was somewhat amazed to find that his horse had stopped. "What the hell?" he growled, and drove in the spurs.

As they dashed through a break in the mesquite, a rifle went off and something sharp bit his shoulder with the sting of a thousand riled hornets. Fire flashed in his eyes, and he went rolling from the saddle in a wild and headlong fall. There were shouts and oaths and a whirl of dark horsemen went whamming past his prostrate body. As though by muzzle-light he saw the twisted grinning features of Zeneas Pool and heard the man's soft, mocking laughter.

But he could not move. He lay there numbly while the black of night crept thick and close like the feel of a sheep's wool blanket.

The Scalp Hunters

ONE MIGHT THINK, reflected Cross-Draw, turning his bronc toward Sleepy Cat, that folks round here were taking him pretty serious trying to get him killed like that. On the other hand, though, and in point of sober fact, the truth of the matter was that they weren't taking him half serious enough.

One thing was sure. Folks round this country had gone murder-minded. They didn't give a whoop in the hot place *who* they killed, and from now on he wasn't going to give a whoop, either!

He looked like being a red flag to the white-faces on this range; but enough was enough, and by gee this was going to far! He had learned his lesson. The Golden Rule was no good here, and now they had better look out.

Twelve days cached out in the chaparral with a slow-healing shoulder had showed him the error of his ways. It was quite evident that kindness was not worth the bother it cost a guy. The squirts around here understood just one thing—and from here out they'd sure get a bellyful!

He was loaded for bull moose and the first chuckawalla that poked his cabeza above the brush was sure going to get his come-uppance!

It was dang lucky for him he'd had the presence of mind to keep hold of the reins when they'd dropped him. Otherwise he'd be hoofing it now like the night he'd walked home from the Harp.

He guessed he'd been wrong about Collins. Leastways, it hadn't been Collins who'd ambushed him. That dry-gulching had been the work of another. He hadn't got that vision of Pool out of his mind yet; though whether he'd actually seen the man before the blackness had engulfed him, or whether the sight of that sneering face had been sheer imagination was something he'd not been able to make out. He inclined toward the belief that Pool had really been there—that Pool had shot him just like he had at the cattle guard.

Pool had the nerve—he was colder than a frog's hind pocket.

But what Cross-Draw couldn't get was Pool's reason. Why go to such bother to rub out a total stranger? Jealousy over Kate? But no—he hadn't killed Tam; so far as Cross-Draw knew, he hadn't even tried to.

There was just one answer that he could see to account for Pool's animosity. It might be Pool who was after this valley....

Against this thought, however, was a remark dropped by Albert the night of the Window-Sash fire. Something he'd said when he'd first hit the ranch, before they had gone to Boxed Heart.

Well, one thing he could do; he could visit MacIllwraith. He might get to learn something there. During the interval that Cross-Draw'd hid out with that shoulder much might have happened. A talk with Mac was sure on the cards, and he headed for town to obtain it.

CROSS-DRAW STEPPED through the batwings of Sleepy Cat's one still-functioning saloon and found the place deserted save for the man behind the bar. *He* looked up indifferently with a perfunctory swipe of the bar rag at an imaginary circle. On the instant his lazy manner underwent a change. He took another look and pursed his lips in a soundless whistle while he hoisted both hands above his head and a fish-belly pallor spread across his cheeks.

Cross-Draw scowled. "Get them paws down an' quit actin' like a loco-eater. Where the hell's everybody at? Where's Angus? Don't he ever keep no office hours? Got his place shut tighter than a road-agent's tonsils—What's the matter with 'im? Ain't he sheriffin' no more?"

The bartender swallowed uneasily. "No," he muttered, moistening his lips. "No, I don't reckon he is—leastways, not around here."

"How come? That golrammed Zeneas Pool didn't peel his star off, did he?"

The greyhaired barkeep took a look around and stealthily shook his head.

"Well, hell's hinges!" Cross-Draw blared, exasperated. "Where is he? Is it a *secret?*"

The barkeep swallowed, apparently with more than a little effort. He wet his lips again and shot his hands up higher. "He—he's out to the cemetery."

"Oh. Out to Campo Santo, eh? That where the rest of this tumbleweed town has gone?"

The barkeep, whiter than ever, nodded.

Cross-Draw looked at him curiously. "Well, what the hell is goin' on here, anyway? Who's gettin' buried?"

The bartender twitched his shoulders in a philosophical shrug. In a voice hardly louder than a skreaky whisper, he breathed: "MacIllwraith—ex-Sheriff Angus MacIllwraith, killed in line o' duty."

Cross-Draw stared while a quick man might have

146

counted twelve and the feel of ice got in this room. "Mac," he muttered disbelievingly. "Old Mac dead.... Hell's unvarnished hinges!" He bawled suddenly, scowling at the barman's jump. "Who killed him?"

The man in the dirty white apron seemed embarrassed. At least he displayed a highly uneasy reticence. He opened his mouth a number of times reluctantly, but each time appeared to think better of the notion and jerked it shut. "Well—er...ah—" he floundered, and Cross-Draw swore.

"C'mon—open up. I'll see he don't get a chance to blast you. Put a name to the pussy-faced hole in the ground! I'll fix the whoppyjawed polecat! Who is the little coward—*Pool?*"

The barman looked more scared than ever and his eyes kept darting slanchways toward the door. But Cross-Draw, via the backbar mirror, could see there was no one there. "Well," he snarled. "Am I goin' to have to bend a pistol across your scalp to get any information? Speak up—I got other things to do than stand here chinnin'. They got a new man packin' the star yet?"

The barkeep nodded numbly. With great apparent effort he said hoarsely: "Zeneas Pool's the actin' sheriff—"

Cross-Draw whipped the intense silence with a splutter of gusty oaths. "That fish-bellied shorthorn! That swivel-eyed Mormon sidewinder! That cross between a steer an' a she-coyote! Who the hell went an' made *him* sheriff?"

"Well," said the barkeep weakly, "he was one of the county commissioners, you know—"

"Oh! So he made himself a sheriff, did he?" Cross-Draw burst out furiously. "Well, well! And who the hell killed Angus?"

147

The barman gulped. "Pool says *you* did!" he blurted, shaking.

"Oh, he does, does, he?" Cross-Draw shouted. "Now isn't that too bad! I suppose everyone believes him?"

"Well, you see," the barman stammered, "he was killed in the sheriff's office. They found one of your conchos—anyways one like what's on your vest—on the floor beneath him. They found one of your gloves beside the desk an' a rowel," he said, his glance swooping down and up, "Pool swears came off of your spurs—"

"Hell's fire!" swore Cross-Draw viciously, for a downard glance disclosed that sure enough the rowel was missing from his right boot's spur. "Talk about gildin' the lily! That *all* they found?" he demanded.

"Not quite—there was a .45-90 cartridge clamped between his teeth—"

Cross-Draw swore in a passion.

But when he paused for breath, the barkeep said, "Was I you, I'd cut stick an' clear out of here. The town's sure wild for your scalp."

"I'll make 'em wild for a different reason! I'll give 'em somthin' to yowl about! I'll blast this place into kindlin'!" His glance snapped around in quick vicious stabs. "No whoppyjawed Mormon can frame *me* like that! I'll—"

He broke off with a curse as a rattle of hoofbeats pulled up outside. He darted a glance through a window. Riders were swarming the tie rack. Collins, Rey, and Ballard, his foreman. Tobias Waters and two-three others Cross-Draw had seen but whose names he could not remember.

And square in the lead was Zeneas Pool. He was just swinging down from his saddle.

.26.

"It's Not Strictly Legal, But—"

CROSS-DRAW GLARED like a rat in a trap when, *"Hell!"* Collins yelled. "Here, Sheriff—look! Here's my horse that that scoundrel rode off on!"

Cross-Draw whirled with a passion-choked curse.

The grayhaired barkeep had come to life and looked like being the hero of the hour. Still behind his bar, he had a sawed-off shotgun's muzzle trained unwaveringly on Cross-Draw's middle and both hammers drawn to full cock. "Come a-runnin', fellas!" his cracking E-string yell whooped out. "I got the bustard inside here! Got him covered like a tent!"

"The hell you have!" snarled Cross-Draw and whipped out his pistols like magic. WHAM-WHAM! both roared at once.

Bottles went crashing down the shelf behind the bar. Ducking, the barkeep let go with both barrels, creating pandemonium among the shouting gun-wavers just bulging the batwings.

Cross-Draw laughed and went out through a window.

When he came to his feet, both his six-guns were working. The saloon was a place of wild uproar.

Cross-Draw did not stand upon his going, but went at once, reloading as he ran. So they wanted fight, did they? Well, he aimed to oblige; he'd give them a fight to date time by!

He ducked around a corner, zigzagged down an alley and went weaving toward the back door of the abandoned Chandler House, lead zipping dust from his boots at every jounce.

But he made it, and with a curse he slammed the back door shut and barred it. Then he sprang to a window giving out upon the alley and smashed the cobwebbed glass with a pistol. He thrust the muzzle through and worked the weapon fast as he could slip the hammer.

Boots thumped out retreat in a gust of wild shouting.

"C'mon, you flop-eared hounds!" yelled Cross-Draw. "I ain't hardly got my barrels warmed yet! What're you runnin' for? C'mon back an' let me show you how we done at Agua Prieta!"

But the posse wasn't having any. They'd got enough of his crack shooting, and the alley cleared like magic.

But Cross-Draw was not so feeble in the head as to think he had them buffaloed. They might duck back out of this alley, but they'd soon come sneaking in from some other way.

Even as he whirled to see what kind of situation might lie at the building's opposite side, he heard the thump! thump! of some heavy object battering the front door.

Three quick strides took him catfooting into the hall. A flight of rickety stairs led upward to the second floor and he took the steps three at a time. Whirling 'round the banister, he charged for the front room opening off the hall.

And made it just in time!

Kicking the glass from a window he thrust out his head and found that he was directly above the door leading in off the street—the door being attacked, as he now could plainly see, by six or eight men with a twelve-foot log. Thum! Thump! it crashed against the splintering barrier.

"Hell's hinges!" shouted Cross-Draw. "Git away from that before I loose my temper an' do somethin' you'll be regrettin'!" And just for luck he dropped three-four shots among them.

He didn't wait to see what would happen. But even as he jerked his head inside, he heard the men let go their log and scuttle for cover. He heard an oath from somebody who hadn't let go quick enough. But he'd other fish to fry and didn't do any lingering.

Out the door he went and into a room on the side across from the alley. A crash of glass came up from below telling of forced entry. Grunts of satisfaction came up, too. But Cross-Draw swiftly silenced these.

Kicking his foot through the window he grabbed a chair and dropped it out; spun round and caught up a pitcher and basin from the washstand and sent them dashing after.

Shouts, oaths and a couple of groans attested to his aim. Then he ducked back into the room as a rattle of lead beat the side of the house and peppered the place he'd been crouching.

It was time he got out of this. Such luck couldn't last forever. In two-three minutes at most that bunch down there would get in despite him and then the feathers would fly.

He ducked back into the hall, grabbed for the banister, flung a leg over the railing and went sailing down like the man on the flying trapeze.

When his boots smacked the floor, a cold voice said: "Get 'em up, pilgrim, 'fore I—"

Cross-Draw let go with his right-hand gun and didn't stop to sum up the casualties. He bolted toward the back of the house, stuffing fresh cartridges into his guns as he did so.

He got one look into the kitchen and slammed his body backward with bone-jolting violence. Even then his hat was cuffed back by the blast that rocked the room. Five men had been crouched in that kitchen and the whole crowd had let go at once.

Through the rain of splinters clipped from the ceiling, Cross-Draw sprang through a door to the right, banging the barrier shut behind him, and without stopping went right on out through a window.

He lit on his feet and, driving three shots through the wrecked window behind him, went dashing for the street. Before he could make it, three-four loud-voiced shouters jumped into the alley from the hotel's back yard and began beating up the echoes with a vengeance.

A slug jerked Cross-Draw's hat. Another tugged his vest. A third knocked the heel from his lefthand boot—spur and all—and then he had rounded the corner and caromed spang into as neat a deadfall as he'd ever sprung.

Three men stood there with shotguns leveled at his chest. Rey, Collins and Pool—and Pool's was the only expression that had anything pleasant in it. The Flying V boss's handsome face wore a look of extreme satisfaction—a sort of cat-and-canary look that warned Cross-Draw where to get off at.

"Nice, seeing you again," Pool purred. "You won't be needin' them guns—better drop 'em, 'less you're huntin' a grave.... Ah, thank you. The jail's just up the street a bit, Boyd—"

"Never mind that," exploded Collins. "We won't be needin' any jail for no damn, woman-stealin' sheriff-killer! There's a fair-sized cottonwood south of town—"

"That's the ticket," Rey applauded. "Just turn the bastard that way, Pool. No sense wastin' the taxpayers' money."

"We-el..." Pool shrugged abruptly. "It's not strictly legal, but—" He smiled apologetically at Cross-Draw. "Look's like the matter is out of my hands, gentlemen. Er—the prisoner is reluctantly surrendered."

Many a Slip—

CROSS-DRAW jerked his gaze from the cottonwood's sleek branch and ran its bitter judgment across the scowling faces of the gun-gripping men ringed around him. Not one face showed a vestige of sympathy—not one face but held malicious satisfaction and a morbid kind of eagerness to get the last act started. They were here to watch him kick and squirm when the grass-rope necktie 'round his neck should haul him from the saddle.

He scanned his chances and found them bad—never had they seemed so hopeless. The crowd was twelve men strong and every jasper present would be glad to blast him if he so much as wriggled a finger. Collins held the horse's head. Rey stood poised with a quirt by the critter's rump. Tobias Waters spit on his hands and took a good firm grip on the rope; gripping it behind him were four-five others—plenty for the purpose. The rest stood grouped about with itchy fingers on the triggers of leveled weapons.

It was one hell of a situation in which for the hero of Agua Prieta to be finding himself—and no mistake!

It was so damn bad, he was getting ready to cast up his account when he suddenly thought of something. What, he wondered grimly, had caused Albert so abruptly to switch his views the way he had? When the range dick first had joined Cross-

Draw at Collins' ranch, he appeared definitely to have made up his mind that Zeneas Pool was the man behind these moves to hog the range. A bit later, when Cross-Draw after argument had parted company with him, Albert seemed to have his dinero placed on Rey as the Machiavellian schemer behind the troubles of this country.

Cross-Draw found it very confusing. One thing was obvious to him with the clarity of a man's last moments. Something, *or some person,* had changed or influenced Albert's view during that bit of riding they'd done that night.

Cross-Draw recalled how after leaving Albert he had run smack-dab into that ambush in the mesquites; and the fragmentary recollection of that vision he'd had of Pool's sneering face came back to him also. But he could not be sure to save his life if that sight of Pool had been something from fact or only wildest fancy.

He tried a shot in the dark. "Pool," he called, "where'd you go that night after your crowd ambushed me? Were you coming from the burning buildings of the Window-Sash or were you goin'—"

"What," growled Pool, "are you talking about?" And he glared at Cross-Draw wrathfully. "You tryin' to make out—"

"Ain't trying to make out a thing. Was just wonderin' where the hell your crowd came from that night an' where they were goin'."

"I don't know what night you're talking about. And anyway," Pool snapped, "as far as that goes, this is the first time I've laid eyes on you since the day you had that—ah, accident at the cattle guard."

And he looked Boyd straight in the eye.

But Cross-Draw was not to be taken in by any

such tricks as that. He'd met straight-faced liars before; and if Pool was guilty he'd be a cockeyed fool to admit it. But Pool's mention of that business at the cattle guard put a dull dark stain across his cheeks. He owed Pool a few for that, and if he ever skinned clear of this noose, he sure aimed to even the score on that outrage.

But just now it didn't much look like he was going to be in a position to even anything a few moments hence. The light of deadly purpose gleamed maliciously from the avid eyes that ringed him.

Cross-Draw spat with a curse when asked if he'd any last words to utter. "If it was like to do me any good," he scowled, "I'd talk from now till Doomsday. But it's plain you scorpions have already made your minds up. If you've pen an' ink I'd like to write a comfort to my mother—the poor old lady was forever warnin' I'd end up like this."

Pool frowned and looked him over suspiciously. But Cross-Draw seemed quite serious, and finally with an oath the sheriff sent a man to round up the necessary articles. In the interim he gave an impromptu lecture on the evil of men's ways.

"Pity you ain't dried up like the waterholes in this country," Cross-Draw broke in harshly. "You shoulda been a preacher—with all the hellfire an' damnation stored up in your carcass you'd a' been a big success. But since you ain't, kindly choke off the blatt an' let me die in peace."

"You're goin' to die, all right," grinned Zeneas. "Make no mistake about that. Soon's you've writ that letter, up you go. Get busy, now; here's your truck—an' make it short. Some of these gents has other work to do."

"Yeah—it's too dang bad about them," snarled

Cross-Draw bitterly. "What'm I supposed t' write this on—the saddle horn?"

Pool looked around and picked up an empty cartridge box. "Set your paper on here," he said. "An' get a wiggle on. We'll give you five minutes exactly—not a second more."

Four and a half of the promised five minutes went by in a tight-stretched silence. No sound marred the hush but the sound of his scratching pen—and that only at infrequent intervals.

He had been playing a game to stall for time; but since Pool had set a definite limit, there seemed little point in writing. The little old lady Cross-Draw had mentioned was only a bit of fiction; he'd been a lone orphan as long as he could remember.

"Oh, hell!" he said, and threw pen, ink, paper and cartridge box down into the dust with a curse. "Get on with your hog-killin', damn you!"

"You still got half a minute," Collins growled.

Then out of the south rushed the pound of wild hoofbeats. Heads jerked around and Cross-Draw gathered his muscles. But Sheriff Pool's grin slacked his nerves in a hurry, and Cross-Draw turned round with an oath.

Nearer and nearer rose the hoof-pound swift-drumming.

Out from Sleepy Cat's street swept a big-hatted horseman. Up and down fell his quirt and his spurs flashed like knife-blades in the afternoon sun. He pulled up by the group in a slather of dust, jerking his bronc back on its haunches.

"Geev eet to heem!" he cried enthusiastically. "Geev eet to heem!"

It was Concho, the half-breed Mex from the Harp.

Pool eyed him suspiciously. "What the hell was the hurry?"

"'Urry, señor? Oh, yes!" Concho said, and flashed his big grin. "Señor Tam send me een weeth word thees hombre she wan you look for. The *patron* 'ave found the señorita—she say eet was thees man, Two-Gons, w'at 'ave taken her off!"

"You're a low-down lyin' hound!" snarled Cross-Draw in a fury. "I—"

"Many thanks—*muchas gracias,* son," smiled Sheriff Pool urbanely, patting Concho on the shoulder, and the Mexican swelled up like a toad. "'Course, we knew he was guilty anyhow, but we're glad of the verification. I wouldn't," he said, enlarging his grin for Cross-Draw, "want the wheels of justice to grind the wrong gent up.

"Well, you're bossin' this, Collins. Are you ready?"

"Goddam right," snarled Collins. "C'mon, boys! One...Two—"

"HOLD IT!" yelled a voice, and every head hiked 'round to see what was the matter.

A gray old duck in a high-crowned Stetson and flapping vest was coming up as fast as he could waddle. He had a beer-barrel girth and fence-posts for legs, but he covered ground all the same and pulled up wheezing like a wood-burner locomotive.

"Got the—wrong damn—man!" he panted, scowling at the sheriff. "What the hell—kinda business—is this? Somebody fixin' to settle a grudge? Happens, Pool, I'm on the Board of Commissioners; I'm goin' to look into this an' don't you ferget it!"

And his glaring regard of the sheriff proved they were not friends.

158

But Pool was not a man easily to be taken off balance. He said suavely: "If you can do anything with this crowd, Quenter, you're welcome. I've done my best—pleaded, begged and threatened. But nothing I could say would turn 'em. They've got the goods on this fella and are primed to hang him."

"If any primin's been done," snapped Quenter, "you're the bird that done it! This horseplay's gone far enough—turn that fellow loose!"

And he gave them a look that would have split a white-oak post.

The would-be lynchers shuffled their feet uneasily. But Concho cried: "Eet ees the hombre! We 'ave foun' the girl—she sayd thees Two-Gon Boyd ees the fella that—"

"Bah!" snarled Quenter contemptuously. "You boys goin' to take the word of a crazy Mex? What the hell kinda country is this where a white man's hung for a low *pelado's* word? By God, in Texas—"

"This ain't Texas," Pool interrupted curtly. "All the evidence points toward this skunk, Quenter! It ain't just about the girl—this here's the vinegarroon that snuffed Sheriff MacIllwraith's light! One of his gloves—"

"Never mind that—I don't care a damn if his *horse* was found by Angus' body! I'm tellin' you this guy Boyd ain't the man!"

They eyed each other wickedly.

"You got evidence to support that claim?" Pool asked him sneeringly.

"Best evidence a man could have," said Quenter. "You may remember I was in town two nights ago when Angus got his ticket. I saw the bird that bumped him—"

"You *saw* him?" Collins cried.

"Yeah—though I didn't realize it till just a little bit ago," said Quenter quietly. "I wasn't there when they found the body. But somethin' brought the man to my mind this afternoon an' I rode in to put the truth before you—not knowin' of course that you'd already picked you a victim."

"A victim, eh?" purred Pool. "Have a care, Quenter, how you sling your language 'round."

Quenter ignored him. He said to the others, "The guy you want is tall an' slim; not so tall as Boyd, though, an' slimmer. I can't tell you what his mug is like because I only glimpsed him as he went into Angus' office, an' I was across the street. But—"

"Don't sound like much of a alibi for Boyd," growled Collins nastily. "Anyway, my girl's words is good enough fer me! If Kate says Boyd is the—"

"But you don't know Kate even said so!" shouted Quenter. "You've only got this *pelado's* word that's what she said—"

"Yeah," Cross-Draw broke into the argument, "an' me an' Lovin' saw this crawfish snakin' her out of that abandoned line-camp on Boxed Heart range the other night!"

He whirled in the saddle to confront the paling Concho. The Mexican stepped back and put a hand to the saddle horn beneath the concerted gaze of all those staring eyes. "W'at I tell you ees the trut'," he muttered. "Thees man—"

"Boyd's right," cut in Quenter coldly. "I've talked to Loving myself. He tells the same story an'—"

"Who the hell is Loving?" Pool demanded.

"Albert Loving. He's a Britisher—or was one. More to the point, he's the man sent down here by the Cattlemen's Association in answer to Collins' wire." And he looked them over triumphantly.

160

"Collins, you're basing your suspicions of Boyd on the fact he left your spread unguarded the night of the fire. That he disappeared—ain't that so?... Well, Loving says him an' Boyd went over to have a look at Rey's place. He says there wasn't anyone home, which there wasn't because the Boxed Heart crowd was over to my place. Loving says further that, leaving Boxed Heart, him an' Boyd ran into this Mex—"

"Eet ees a lie—a gatham lie!" shouted Concho, whipping a hand down to his gun belt.

But Quenter was too quick for him. He grabbed the Mexican's wrist and twisted just as the gun came clear of leather. A quick jerk and the pistol dropped from the half-breed's hand.

Concho glared at him for a moment. Then, spluttering obscene Spanish curses, climbed into his saddle and whirling his bronc went larruping off.

"Hey! Don't let that whippoorwill get away from here!" cried Cross-Draw. But no one paid any attention. They were too wrapped up in the wrangle between Quenter and the sheriff, and Concho rode off unmolested.

"This Loving," Pool muttered. "Where is he?"

"I don't know. He was out to my spread this morning. Fact, he was there when I left. But this I *can* tell you," said Quenter. "Boyd never set that fire at Window-Sash—"

"The hell he didn't!" snapped Collins.

"He sure didn't. You remember I wasn't at the ranch all evening that night?" Quenter looked at Rey, and Rey nodded. Tobias Waters nodded, too. "I wondered where you went," he growled suspiciously. "Not goin' to tell us *you* set that fire now, are you?"

161

"'Course not. I went to town. Had to pass the Window-Sash—you know the trail. Goin' to town I saw something damn suspicious, though it didn't strike me that way at the time. I saw a fellow," he said, and paused, while the others hung breathlessly on his words. "By Tophet! It was the same damn bird I saw the other night goin' into MacIllwraith's office!"

Collins broke the startled silence roughly. "What the hell about this fella? D'you see him at the Window-Sash?"

"Yeah," said Quenter thoughtfully. "I saw him makin' toward your ranch house. Didn't think nothin' of it at the time, though your place was dark. Anyhow, when I came back—which couldn't have been over an hour later—the Window-Sash was blazin' like a bonfire."

"Well," remarked Rey. "I'd say this lets Boyd out. Him an' this Loving was at my place again that night—later. Don't seem likely he could have been over to my place twice, encountered the Mex at that line-camp, an' still set fire to Window-Sash all in one evenin'."

He looked at the sheriff. "Reckon we've grabbed the wrong fella at that."

"Turn 'im loose," Pool said curtly, and with a thin gleam of teeth went striding back toward his office.

.28.

Gracie Saddles Her Horse

"WELL," GRUNTED Cross-Draw when the rest had gone and he and Quenter were alone beneath the tree. "I reckon I owe you somethin' for gettin' me out of that jackpot. Ugh!" he muttered, running an exploratory finger 'round his neck above his collar. "Another couple seconds an' I'd sure been doin' that jig!"

"Yeah, it's lucky for you I got here when I did," said Quenter grimly. "I'm glad you appreciate the favor, too. I got somethin' you can do for me, which is why I been lyin' my head off to make 'em turn you loose—"

"WHAT!" gasped Cross-Draw, blinking. "Mean to say you think I *am* the bird back of this? That you think I *did* kill MacIllwraith an' run off with Collins' girl?"

"Well, gouge my spurs an' fan my saddle! You was loadin' that crowd, eh?"

"Not entirely. I *did* leave Loving at my ranch today," said Quenter dryly. "An' he did confirm your story about what you two were up to the night of the Window-Sash fire. But the rest I salted plenty. I didn't see no bird goin' into MacIllwraith's office and I didn't see anyone around Collins' spread."

Cross-Draw just looked at him. "May I never meet a more convincin' liar," he said piously.

163

"Brother, I sure get out from under my hat to your gall!"

Quenter grinned bleakly. "The results, I'm hopin', are going to justify the means. I want you to do something for me, Mister. My—"

"But why *me?*" demanded Cross-Draw suspiciously. "Why not some other jasper?"

"What I got in mind needs a cool head an' quick gun," murmured Quenter harshly. "May even come to a killin' if—"

"If that's Opportunity I hear knockin'," grunted Cross-Draw, "I'll tell you right now there's nobody home."

Quenter regarded him scowlingly. "You can't back out on me now! By God, you try to crawfish out of this an' I'll have that rope back 'round your neck inside two shakes of a live lamb's tail!"

Cross-Draw could see this Quenter was in earnest. Anyone who'd risk his neck snatching buzzard bait from the gallows, just about had to be in earnest!

"O.K.," he said with the best face he could put on the business. "What's the story?"

"You'll find it short," grunted Quenter. "An' unless I'm wide of the mark, you'll find this business right up your alley. I'm not askin' you to kill anybody," he went on with a quick look 'round the clearing. "But I'm not sure it won't come to that in the end. The set-up's this: I got a daughter who's engaged to marry Tobias Waters. I ain't too crazy about him personally, but his ol' man left him right smart of a ranch. Gracie—that's my daughter—likes him well enough, but she's kinda gallivanterous sometimes—comes from readin' too many of them damn magazines. Tam O'Reilly—the crazy Irish nitwit, is another in the same wagon; thinks he's

Casanova, or somebody. To cut the story short, he's been playin' 'round with Gracie, an' Tobias Waters is too good a bet to have it spoiled account of a loud-mouthed Irishman!"

Cross-Draw scowled. "Why not speak to Gracie—?"

"No use." Quenter snorted. "I've talked myself blue in the face! She keeps right on—she's bugs about the fella! If she tried meetin' him 'round the place here I might be able to do somethin' about it. But she sneaks off some place—"

"Why'n't you go after O'Reilly—?"

"Hell, that's what I rescued *you* for!" Quenter said impatiently. "I ain't no match for no shootin' fool like him—he'd wind my string up quicker'n the devil beatin' tanbark!"

"Tam?" Cross-Draw cried amazed. "Why he don't even pack a pistol half the time!"

"Mebbe not," admitted Quenter. "But did you ever see him use it? That kid shames lightnin' by comparison! An' with a .45-90 rifle—"

"A *what!*" demanded Cross-Draw. "Did I understand you to say a .45-90—?"

"Yeah. He's one of the few fellas 'round here that's got one; an' he sure knows how to make it talk. He—"

"Who else 'round here's got one of them guns?" broke in Cross-Draw, scowling.

"Well... three-four of the boys 'round here has 'em. Tobias Waters has one, Bill McCloud's got one, Ballard over at Boxed Heart's got one an'—Guess that's all. Now, look here: I want you t' put a bug in Tam O'Reilly's ear—sabe? I want you t' tell him to lay off my girl or you're goin' to work him over so his own mother wouldn't know 'im. I—"

"Hold on," growled Cross-Draw testily. "What give you the idee *I* got any control over him? Me an' him's been on the outs ever since I struck this golrammed country—"

"Sure!" said Quenter; "that's howcome me to give you the job. Don't you want to pay him back for that slick business at the cliff?"

"You heard about that, did you?"

"I hear about most of the things that come off 'round this range," grunted Quenter. "An' I'm free to say there's precious few of 'em I take a hankerin' to these days. The country's gone to the dawgs."

"You said it!" growled Cross-Draw most emphatically. "They oughta call this Haywire Range!" And he scowled out over the countryside like he was mad enough to bite a railroad spike. Then he jerked his head back 'round to Quenter. "What is it you want me t' do?"

"I want you to scare the livin' daylights out of that fool Tam!" snapped Quenter. "An' if he don't lay off Gracie pronto, I want you to give him a lickin' he'll remember to the grave. I—"

"What gives you the idee I'm able?" asked Cross-Draw curiously.

Quenter's grin was bleak. "I've heard about you before, Boyd. I know what you done in Texas—I know you're a guy that would jest as lief fight as eat. I've heard you never forget a injury—"

"You're golrammed right I don't!"

"O.K. Here's your chance to pay off Tam an' do me a favor at the same time—"

"All right! All right—don't *rush* me! There's a couple things I'd like to know. Mebbe you can tell me. This guy that's tryin' to grab the range—the guy behind that fire at Harp an' the one at Window-

166

Sash: is he a lone wolf or do you reckon he's got help like some of these birds seem to think?"

Quenter looked at him curiously. He seemed to be scanning something in his mind, and whatever it was it appeared to be giving him a deal of amusement. Then he looked at Boyd again and his glance was bright and hard. "Taking quite an interest in that fella, ain't you? What's *he* done to you?"

"*Done?* Ain't he responsible for most of the tough luck that's come my way since I got here? Ain't I damned near been hanged on account of him? Hell's bells, he's done plenty if you're askin' *me!*" Cross-Draw snarled, and swore in a fury. "But *I'll* fix him! You wait an' see! No whoppyjawed chipmunk can treat me the way I been treated, an' keep on livin' to brag about it!"

He shut his mouth up suddenly with a quick, hard look at Quenter. "You ain't answered my question."

"No. . . . I was thinkin' it was quite a coincidence, you an' me gettin' our sights lined on the same point, that way. I think the fella's a lone wolf. Albert—the range dick—tells me him an' Tam were away from the Harp that night it was raided. Apparently everybody just naturally assumed it was a bunch jumped O'Reilly's spread. But I'm not so sure; like you, I been wonderin' if mebbe it ain't all the work of one hombre. Same way at the Window-Sash. Same with Collins' daughter. One man could have done the whole business."

"Pool?"

"I dunno. He's got guts enough, all right. I can tell you this much: whoever it is, it ain't so much range that he's after as gold—"

"*Gold!*" gulped Cross-Draw, staring. "Did you say *gold?*"

"I sure did. Hadn't you got wise to it? You bein' a stranger I figured you'd spotted it first thing. Been years since anyone's hit a paystreak in this country—the idea's got around the Superstitions been washed up. Spanish Flats is practically deserted, Sleepy Cat here's gone to seed, Tortilla Flat's a ghost town—s'far as gold's concerned, this whole range looks about dried up an' ready to blow away."

He stared at Cross-Draw grimly. "Goes to show how dumb most folks can be. I got a notion there's better ore still under these hills than has ever been taken out. I got a notion gold's the reason Pool tried to scare you out. I—"

"D'you know where this gold is at?" demanded Cross-Draw, cutting to the heart of the matter.

"Sure." Quenter nodded. The glint of his eyes changed subtly. "I know where some of it's at, anyhow—the gold this range hog's after."

It was a strange place to drop the matter, but that was where Quenter left it. And Cross-Draw, meeting the cold bright stare of Quenter's gaze, felt no urge to reopen the subject.

"Where's Tam at now?" he asked.

"I don't know. Best way to find him, I'd say, would be to keep cases on my girl. Gracie starts gettin' fidgets if she don't see him every couple of days. My advice to you's to come out to the ranch and trail her when she goes for a ride."

CROSS-DRAW DID, but for a week Gracie never left the spread. He saw her on the second morning and was not surprised at Tam's interest. She was blond with a shape like DeMilo, and with none of the Greek dame's afflictions. But Cross-Draw kept out

168

of her way; being too worried with thoughts of Kate to get up much enthusiasm. He felt if he didn't find Collins' daughter pretty soon the bats would take over his belfry.

He had a couple more sessions with Quenter on the subject of Tam—the old boy had Tam on the brain. He spent all his time in his office, and from the two talks Cross-Draw had with him, appeared to be engaging his energies figuring out hotter and crazier purgatories for the last of the O'Reilly clan.

As he'd pointed out that day beneath the cottonwood in town, this chore was right up Cross-Draw's alley. Cross-Draw felt no compunctions about putting the fear of God in Tam. He owed that crazy Irishman a few for knocking him off that cliff.

But, mostly, Boyd took up his time with thoughts on other matters. Kate's whereabouts and peril were like to drive him mad. Again and again he racked his brain, trying to figure where the kidnaper could have cached her; and more and more he came to the conclusion that she was hid near at hand some place—in some spot too obvious for searching. Had she been taken to some out-of-the-way concealment, Collins by now would certainly have found her, for with his crew he must have raked the entire country 'round here.

A part of Cross-Draw's waking hours were given, however, to consideration of the sinister range-grabber behind this country's troubles. And the more he thought, the more firmly he became convinced that Quenter was the man.

Quenter's hand was on the country's pulse too close, in Cross-Draw's opinion. He knew too much about what was going on. True, the man had shared that knowledge with Boyd—but only up to a point. He'd said that gold was the thing behind the catclaw killer's greed, and he'd said he knew where that gold was—but he'd not confided its location, Cross-Draw noticed.

And that business of the .45-90 rifle! Tam had one, and Ballard, Chalmers Rey's foreman, had one; and Tobias Waters and Bill McCloud—they each had one, too. According to William Quenter.

But Quenter might have one himself—or he might be borrowing one of those others. Or even hiring one of the owners to do his long-range shooting.

Cross-Draw had about given up the idea of Zeneas Pool having been the man behind that attempted drygulching that had laid him out in the chaparral those twelve long, sore-shouldered days. That vision he'd had of Pool's sneering face he now put down to fancy—an hallucination conjured by that mocking laugh.

After all, he reasoned, a lot of guys might be able to laugh like Pool.

In Cross-Draw's opinion, Zeneas Pool's whole enmity was probably based on his fear of Cross-Draw's discovering the gold that was this country's secret. Pool knew about that gold and probably hoped to get it for himself. Or, maybe the gold—some of it, anyhow—was on Pool's land. If such were the case, Pool would be bound to see a claim-jumper in every stranger who came over the hump.

Yes, Pool, he thought, could be safely left outside his calculations.

Then one morning Gracie Quenter saddled up her horse.

29

Sleepy Cat—Express!

IT WAS the day before her marriage to Tobias Waters was scheduled to come off, so Cross-Draw was sure she was riding to a last-time rendezvous with Tam.

O.K. Here was where he'd put the fear in Tam's heart.

He gave her a twenty-minute start, then went hotfooting it to the corral. Inside three seconds he'd thrown his hull on a fast-stepping bay that would not be too conspicuous against a skyline. A mouse-colored dun would have been his choice, but there was nothing in Quenter's corrals but creams, bays and blacks. Two minutes later he was heading a dust streak out of the ranch with his nose on Gracie's trail.

But only to the crest of the first hogback.

Pulling his bronc down to an easy trot, Cross-Draw took up the pursuit. It was not the kind of chore he could ordinarily put his heart into, but thought of his grievances against that crazy Tam clapped spurs to his distaste and he stuck to the trail like a leech.

Mile after mile he followed; through catclaw and mesquite, up hill and down. Then in a great half-circle they headed back toward the ranch.

Humph! Kind of looked like maybe she wasn't out to meet Tam after all! If she was, she was sure going one long ride out of her way to do it—or was she, Cross-Draw wondered, just being cautious?

Had she seen him?

It was hardly a complacent thought for a man who prided himself on his tracking. Another thought struck him: Suppose she *had* seen him and was laying pipe to lose him?

He decided to close in a bit. Fellow could never tell with these skirts. They didn't work according to logic.

Yes, he'd better close in some; he would sure get hell from Quenter if he lost her!

She was down behind a distant ridge now. He had seen a dry wash cutting across the country over there a while back. Probably she was in it—maybe that was where Tam was waiting.

Now was his chance to cut down the distance between them and Cross-Draw took it, giving the bay both spurs.

For fifteen minutes they threw the sand hat-high. Then he saw her again and pulled his bronc down to a walk.

She was nearer, now. He had cut off two-three miles by striking across at an angle. There was no longer any doubt in his mind concerning the likelihood of her knowing she was followed. She knew, all right. She was cutting straight for town!

With a curse he put the bay to a lope. This Gracie was nobody's fool!

But what the hell was she heading towards town for? Surely Tam wouldn't meet her in Sleepy Cat—but wouldn't he? On more sober second thought, Cross-Draw decided Tam was just fool enough to do it. He'd probably take a malicious satisfaction in flaunting his conquest under Waters' nose!

Hell's Hinges! This was just the thing Quenter'd been trying to avoid!

Cross-Draw began using his quirt.

He was hitting the high places, taking the sand hills right in his stride, when a rifle slammed dust in his path.

It was a long way off; he couldn't even hear the reports. But dust spurted three times around his horse's hoofs, and at the fourth Cross-Draw pulled the bay up.

He sat there and cursed in a passion.

They'd out-foxed him. That long-legged Gracie dame had deliberately led him 'round to where Tam could take a crack at him—and it was not their fault that he hadn't got planted!

He took a hot-eyed squint around.

The terrain ahead lay pretty broken where a spur from the badlands reached out between himself and town. If he could make that maze of tumbled hills and arroyos he might be able to get to Sleepy Cat before them. He had no doubt now that town was their destination.

A wild thought struck him like a slap across the face.

Somehow Tam had persuaded her to run off with him and they were heading for town to get married!

A wild thought it was, and far from the truth, but Cross-Draw took off like a twister.

30

Cross-Draw Throws Up a Dust

BEYOND THE SPUR of the badlands was a little strip of Window-Sash range Cross-Draw must travel before swinging over toward town. He was going full tilt, but sawed sharp on the reins as the line-rider's shack hove in sight.

Tam—if it was Tam who had laid those shots across has path—was beating up the bush two-three hundred yards off to the right. Cross-Draw couldn't see him, but behind the intervening hogback, horse hoofs were raising a dust. Tam—or whoever it was—appeared to be aiming to intercept him at that little flat half a mile farther on.

On the off chance that another trap was in the cards, and it did not seem unlikely from the way that dust was rising, Cross-Draw swung the bay to the cabin. Jerking his .30-30 from the scabbard, he slipped from the saddle and, with a cold bright glance at the yonder dust, slid inside and pulled the horse in after him. It was a tight squeeze, but he made it.

Softly shutting the door, he stiffened to a muffled sound behind him. It was the kind of sound any horse would be likely to make, and whipping out both pistols, Cross-Draw spun with a sudden oath.

Then stood there gaping, bug-eyed at what he saw.

On a bunk against the farther wall a blanket-covered form showed lashed from head to ankles. Its back was toward Cross-Draw, but he didn't need any facial identity with that great crop of red hair showing. There was only one head in all this Superstitions country that packed such chestnut curls as that—Kate Eileen's!

And with a whoop he was beside her, clawing at her bonds.

At last he had her free, started chafing at her arms to get the blood to circulating. It must have been plain hell being lashed up here the way she had, but Kate never uttered a moan. She laughed when she saw who had rescued her, a low trill of sheer exuberance, and gazed adoringly up at him with all her soul lying bare in her eyes.

Cross-Draw gulped, "Gawd—*honey!*" and grabbed her into his arms, fiercely covering her face with his kisses.

But suddenly she pulled away, her eyes going big and scared. Cross-Draw heard it, too—not horse sound, but the stealthy tap of a boot. "Oh!" cried Kate with a tremulous gasp. "Quick, Bob! There's somebody coming!"

Cross-Draw gritted a curse. But he whipped out both pistols and went to the door. "I'll fix 'em," he whispered; "stay right where you are!"

Outside the bright nooning sun beat down like brass hammers, but gave no least thought to the heat. Somewhere about lurked that damned catclaw killer, and Cross-Draw was craving his blood.

He went twice round the line shack in a catfooting crouch, eyes raking fierce stabs at each bush, rock and shadow. And each time his bafflement grew. The placer of that stealthy step was nowhere to be seen, and the baked adobe underfoot showed not the faintest track.

Where the hell had the whippoorwill got to?

Cross-Draw circled the shack once more, both pistols ready and a prayer in his heart for some sign. It was uncanny! But the skulker was not in sight.

Then a sound from off yonder—the restless stamp of a hoof—drew Cross-Draw's narrowed gaze to the hogback. It seemed impossible for the fellow to have slipped over there. And yet he might have—something was over there, certainly!

Ducking low in a zigzagging crouch Cross-Draw sprinted forward, crested the ridge and peered down.

Nothing in sight, but the ground took a bend with a dry wash cutting off at a tangent. He could not see the dead creek's bed but he could hear the faint creak of saddle leather—the tiny tinkle of chains—and with an oath he went hotfooting forward.

Thirty yards it was to the cutbank's lip and Cross-Draw made it in a hurry. But even so, when he peered down to the dry wash's bed there was not a soul in sight. There was, however, another bend. Without wasting time for thought, Cross-Draw went skidding down the sandy slope and pounded up the dry creek bottom and slammed around the bend.

He came to a sudden stop. Six feet away from him and leading her bronc was Gracie—Quenter's daughter.

"What the hell you doin' here?" Cross-Draw snarled ungallantly.

She flashed a kind of surprised little smile and pointed to her bronc's right foot. "Got a stone in his frog and I can't get it out. Will you try your—"

But Cross-Draw was off with a curse.

At the line shack his worst fears were realized. The place was empty. Kate Eileen was gone.

He understood now where that scorpion had

hid—he'd been on the flat roof behind the parapet's masking. And soon as Cross-Draw had gone ramping off he'd jumped down and made off with Kate Collins.

Cross-Draw cursed with a passion.

It was bad enough to have Kate grabbed right under his very nose. But worse and more of it, they'd ridden off with Cross-Draw's bay bronc.

There was one chance though—and Cross-Draw took it. He dashed back over the hogback's crest, 'round the bends of the dry wash's floor and came panting up to Gracie.

"Quick, girl!" he rasped, "which way'd they go?"

She returned his impatient look blankly. "Who on earth are you talking about?"

"Kate Collins an' that fella who was with you!" he snapped harshly.

"But there was no one with me! I've been off on a ride all alone."

"I saw a guy quartein' across this gully not fifteen minutes back," he snarled. "He was aimin' to come up with you, an' if I ain't a cockeyed Chinaman, the hombre was Tam O'Reilly!"

"You're out of your head," she said curtly. "I've not seen Tam O'Reilly for a week—not since I broke off with him. If you saw somebody—"

"I saw him, all right!" snapped Cross-Draw. "What were you headin' for town for if you weren't running off with O'Reilly?"

Her brows shot up indignantly and she stared at him with scorn. "Did my father hire you to spy on me? Well, you're wasting your time. I haven't seen Tam and don't aim to. I'm marrying Tobias tomorrow—"

"I don't give a damn if you marry the devil! What I

want to know is where Kate Eileen has gone off to!" and the glare he put on her would have withered a leaf.

But it didn't disturb Gracie Quenter.

"I thought she'd been kidnaped—"

"I just got her free—"

"Then it's too bad you didn't have the wit to stay with her," she said sweetly, and made to swing up in her saddle.

Cross-Draw grabbed her roughly by an arm and shoved her away from the horse. "Excuse me," he sneered, and grabbed up the critter's right hoof. No stone cramped the frog; nothing else was the matter, and Cross-Draw's glance showed a cold, steel glitter.

"So you was lyin'!"

"I was not!" she flared. "I just got the stone out myself!"

"Real smart of you, ma'am," Cross-Draw drawled grimly. "You can wait at the cabin. I'll send a bronc back for you later—"

"What do you mean?—*Here!* What are you doing?"

"Read the papers tomorrow an' see," Cross-Draw answered, and put the girl's bronc to a gallop.

SHE WAS IN this, all right; he'd no doubts on that score. She's pulled him off neatly. But she was safe from his anger—he didn't fight women and children.

But just let him line his sights on that vinegarroon who'd been with her! Just *let* him! He'd lay the lug out cold!

He rode into town in a lather of fury.

But Pool wasn't there and no one could say where he'd gone to.

Cross-Draw left his borrowed horse at the livery

and rode north on the fastest range pony in town. He was beginning to see the light. The pieces were falling in place now. If he could locate Collins' riders—

But he couldn't. He spent half the afternoon hunting them, then in disgust cut a beeline for Quenter's.

Quenter met him on the porch. Cross-Draw cut short the fellow's questions. "Your Gracie's at Collins' south line camp. Anyway, that's where I left her this mornin'. She—"

"Left her! Didn't I tell you to keep her in sight? Didn't—"

"Never mind that! While I was following her I stumbled on Kate—Collins' daughter. They had her hid out at that line camp. But they've grabbed her again; an' purposely or not, your Gracie sure done her share in the business!"

Quenter scowled grimly but made no comment. After a moment he growled: "Was O'Reilly—?"

"Couldn't say. She was goin' to meet some guy, all right. They were cuttin' for town, ridin' a tangent. I figured they'd connect near that cabin an' larruped to get there before 'em. I did, an' found Kate—"

"Didn't you see the guy?"

"Not close enough to put a name to him."

"Where you off to now?" cried Quenter, grabbing his arm.

"I'm off to find Kate Collins." Cross-Draw turned in the saddle, giving Quenter a look of quick interest. "One thing you can do that may help—you can tell me on whose spreads this gold is that somebody's after." And he looked the man square in the eye.

Quenter met the look darkly. "Seems to me my daughter's safety—"

"If you're worried about it, take a bronc an' go

179

fetch 'er," snapped Cross-Draw. "I'm—"

"Our bargain was that you were—" began Quenter. But Cross-Draw cut him off with a curse.

"I'll take care of Tam! Where's that gold?"

"Flyin' V an' Window-Sash. But—"

But Cross-Draw was building a dust.

31

The Man With the .45-90

IT WAS CLEAR now the range-grabber was neither Collins nor Zeneas Pool. They'd plenty to do with gold on their ranches without trying to bite off some more. Collins, maybe, was unaware of the ore on his; but Zeneas Pool was a sharp one, and if he had gold then he knew it.

The killer was somebody else.

Not Quenter—not if Cross-Draw's conclusions were right.

He was recalling again Albert's words on the night Al had come to the Window-Sash—the night of the Window-Sash fire. Those words now showed up in a far different light, and Cross-Draw set out for the badlands.

The killer would have made for them surely this time. With Kate Eileen on his hands, and the old hideout discovered, he was bound to go digging for cover.

Cross-Draw was no longer concerned with the reasons back of Albert's hastily switched assurance as to who the range-hog was. First Albert had been bound the man was Pool; then equally certain he wasn't. Cross-Draw didn't give a damn whom Albert suspected; he was playing a hunch of his own.

A red sun was slanting down behind the Weaver's Needle, throwing mile-long shadows dark and blue across the range when Cross-Draw pulled up suddenly, arrested by the rattle of distant firing. The sound was drifting from the broken country southeast of his position, and with a muttered oath he slammed his horse in that direction.

But as the sound grew louder, resolving into the crash of battling rifles, he slowed its pace and finally stopped its progress altogether. For long moments he sat his saddle tensely, listening.

Then, with a hard, tight grin, he urged the animal in a wide half-circle that would bring him back of a low red butte that seemed to be the focus of the tumult.

It looked like somebody had gotten the killer trapped.

Cautiously he worked his way forward. It was no easy task, keeping in mind the danger of showing himself against a skyline. Not only had he to watch out that the sharpshooter atop yon butte didn't see him, but in this fading light it would be equally hazardous to be spotted by the crowd who'd run the range-hog to earth.

After half an hour of forward movement Cross-Draw abandoned his saddle and left his horse on grounded reins.

It seemed to him that the attackers were starting a circling movement intended to surround the man on the butte; that they intended taking no chances on the fellow slipping clear.

The truth of this theory was established suddenly.

Cross-Draw was inching tediously forward on his belly, carefully wriggling his way between clumps of prickly pear and catclaw, when with the hot breath pouring sharply between his flashing teeth a man rose up in his path with a triumphant, "Gotcher!"— and covered him with a pistol.

"You'll get hell, too," Cross-Draw muttered

direly, "Less'n you point that popgun some other way. Try usin' your brain-pan for somethin' besides a hatrack. Look—I'm headin' the same way you was, ain't I?"

"Does kinda look like it," muttered the other, scratching his head. He stood there, one hand still holding the now sagging pistol and the other reaching down for his dropped rifle, and was like that when a shot from the butte raked a perfect seem across the back of his leather vest. He jumped like a bee had bit him.

Cross-Draw whistled. "In this kinda light I'd call that shootin'. Easy five hundred yards, if it's a inch. 'F you hadn't moved just then, that slug woulda got you planted. Sounded like a high-powered rifle. Any idea who's workin' it?"

"Sure," growled the fellow, shaking an angry doubled fist toward the lip of the butte. "It's that golrammed, double-damned Concho what used to work for the Harp! I hope he—"

"Concho, eh?" mused Cross-Draw softly. "We been sort of forgettin' that hombre, I reckon. Anybody up there with him?"

"Can't say—there might be. Might be Collins' daughter's up there. We—"

"You better keep down out of sight or that Mex'll tag you yet," observed Cross-Draw. Then, as the fellow pulled his head down, "What outfit you with—who's this crowd that's fixin' to hang the greaser's hide out?"

"What's left of the Window-Sash. After that fire a lot of the boys pulled out—"

"Yeah. I guess so," muttered Cross-Draw, thinking swiftly. He squinted up at the butte. "Collins with you?" And, at the fellow's quick nod: "How come you're treein' Concho?"

"Bustard just put a window through Loving's skull!"

"*What?*" gasped Cross-Draw, shocked. "Mean to say Albert's dead?—Albert, the range dick? The guy the Association sent down? You *sure?*"

"Oughta be—we come onto him while the Mex was still buildin' his dust! He's dead all right an' that damn *pelado* killed 'im!"

"Then get out of my way," growled Cross-Draw, and shoved him aside. "I owe that chipmunk a few on my own for tryin' to get me strung up! Give 'im a broadside—let him have every slug in your gun. When he comes up, I'll drop him!"

The Window-Sash rider cut loose. You could tell pretty close from the spurts of rock dust just about where his smacking slugs landed.

Cross-Draw dropped to a knee, clapped rifle to shoulder and waited.

He didn't wait long. Almost instantly there was a tiny blur of movement along the butte's lip. Concho, making ready to get himself a man. He had the right idea but was somewhat slow. *"Geev eet to heem!"* breathed Cross-Draw, and, as a metallic gleam showed Concho's rifle coming up, he loosed three slugs like a flash of lightning.

Up on the butte Concho jerked to his feet like a marionette yanked by a wire. He hung there a second, starkly limned against the afterglow at his back. Then to the crash of rifles all around he went pitching forward, diving to the rocks below.

"C'mon!" growled Cross-Draw, and without waiting for an answer he went tearing an avalanche path through the clutching chaparral. Slipping, stumbling, cursing, they went clawing their way to the butte-top; other riders clambering after them.

But the place was empty. Concho had been alone.

"WELL," SNAPPED COLLINS, "what have you done with my daughter?" and bent his gun grimly on Cross-Draw.

"Don't be a bigger damn fool than you have to! I ain't got your daughter—if I *had*, I'd been hurryin' her across the border. Like I said, I'm goin' to marry her, an' livin' 'round you would be like takin' a vacation in hell!"

"You—you—*you*—!" Collins swelled up like a carbuncle. He was fit to be tied. Cross-Draw whipped a bit of pigging string from his belt and slapped it into the hand of a Window-Sash rider. "Watch out for that fella," he grunted. "He's mad—all same a hydrophoby skunk. Better tie him up before he bites someone." And with a jeering laugh he strode away, leaving Collins to choke in his spleen.

But when he reached his horse, Cross-Draw's face was tight and grim. He was badly worried. No telling *where* the range-hogging killer had taken Kate Eileen *this* time! It was hardly likely he had taken her back to that line camp; nor would he, Cross-Draw thought, dare to trust again the sanctuary of that abandoned shack on Boxed Heart range.

Yet if the killer was the man Cross-Draw thought he was, he'd not leave this range till he grabbed it or died.

Cross-Draw was pretty sure now in his own mind who the fellow was. But how to prove it? How to catch him? How to force the pot-shooting bustard into giving himself away?

"An' worse," growled Cross-Draw with an oath,

"how to fix it so Kate'll be safe from his vengeance in case we don't cut it an' the son of a so-an'-so wriggles clear!"

It was certainly quite a problem and he thought about it all the way to Quenter's. But when he stepped up on the porch and hammered the door with a pistol butt, his cheeks were bland and his eyes were bright with purpose.

Quenter opened the door himself, and his manner was not cordial.

"Always turnin' up like a bad penny, ain't you? What is it this time? Did you fix that triflin' Tam?"

"I will. I will," muttered Cross-Draw impatiently. "You got to give me a little time. I'll salt him down to the queen's taste an' put a lily in his hand. But first there's a little favor—"

"I've done you all the favors I'm a-goin' to," said Quenter harshly. "When you've scared that philanderin' Irishman out of the country, come 'round an' we'll talk about favors."

"You've got the cart before the horse," drawled Cross-Draw coldly. "After you've done the favor, I'll get 'round to fixin' O'Reilly. Right now I'm layin' pipe to grab off this range-jumping killer—this guy with the .45-90."

"What you want me to do?" Quenter asked, unfavorably considering this stranger he'd snatched from the gallows.

"Just this," answered Cross-Draw quietly. "Come over by the corral an' I'll tell you."

"What's the matter with tellin' me right here—"

"Over by the corral suits me better."

"All right," said Quenter grimly. "An' no monkey business or—" And he tapped the butt of his pistol suggestively.

Cross-Draw led the way, and when they reached

the corral's slatted outline, he picked a place in deep shadow. "Don't want this scheme to kick back," he said. "Here's what I want you to do. When we go back to the house we'll step inside to your office. All the time you keep up a running fire of questions like you can't believe what I'm tellin' you—"

"That won't be hard to do," said Quenter dryly.

"No—because I'm goin' to tell you there's gold on this spread, an' plenty of it—No, there ain't none here that I know of. But you got to play up to my lead."

"What's the big idea?" growled Quenter suspiciously. "You think one of my boys—?"

"No. It's Gracie we're puttin' on the show for. She told me this morning she ain't been meetin' Tam—ain't seen him for a week. But she's sure as hell meetin' *someone*; an' I'll bet a buck to a chunk of blue sky it's the killer!"

Quenter swore and reached for his gun.

Cross-Draw grabbed his wrist roughly. "None of that now! It's not *my* fault if your girl's like that—but since she is, we got to use her. You shoulda been more careful of her upbringin'. Now cut out the horseplay an' listen. She gets an earful of this bull about gold. She slips out an' hits for some place where she's pretty sure of gettin' hold of the guy we're after. We follow, an' when she makes contact we grab him."

Quenter cursed softly, but in the end he gave in. "But what about Collins' kid?" he objected. "Ain't you forgettin' about her? What if you have to kill this bustard? Even if you get him alive, he ain't like to be a fool enough—"

"I've thought about that. I think he's got Kate with him—"

"Hell!" snapped Quenter savagely. "That means

you think my daughter is hep to the whole damn business!"

"Sorry," Cross-Draw said, and nodded. "That's exactly what I think."

32

Satisfaction for All Concerned

THERE WAS a ring around the moon and something was due to happen. Cross-Draw knew it. They'd been cautiously following Gracie for an hour. It was becoming obvious that Cross-Draw's guess had been a good one. She was taking them to a rendezvous with the killer and was heading straight for town.

"I don't like it," Quenter muttered for the hundredth time.

Cross-Draw didn't like it much himself. He was playing a wild hunch; a long-odds game to get the killer, and Kate's life might well hang in the balance. But he'd racked his brain for hours and could see no other way.

Gracie was entering town now. They could dimly see her urging her horse behind a darkened row of Sleepy Cat's gaunt buildings. "By Gawd," swore Quenter, "I'll give her a lacin' she'll not forget in no damn hurry! Carryin' on like this! By Gawd—" And then he grabbed Cross-Draw's arm with a sudden worry. "What'll happen to her? Christ, this thing is goin' to implicate her in—"

"Not if we cut it right," said Cross-Draw darkly. "If we pull this off, you'll have nothing to worry from Kate or me—we're clearin' out of this country anyhow; goin' someplace we can rusticate in quiet. Far as the killer's concerned—" He looked at Quenter and made a clucking sound with his mouth. The rancher nodded grimly.

"You see," Cross-Draw explained, "Kate's word'll be enough to prove the bustard's guilt. No one'll need to know Gracie ever had any connection. . . . We better kick up these broncs a bit or we're goin' to lose her."

They pulled up at the edge of town beneath a cottonwood's clustered shadows, leaving their mounts on grounded reins, and catfooting stealthily forward in the trail of Gracie's wake.

"Right about here, wasn't it?" Quenter muttered.

"Yeah. Hotel, I think. See—that back door ain't quite shut. Musta been in too much of a hurry. Take it easy now; we don't want to muff this."

They slipped forward softly, keeping to the deepest shadows. They reached the door and stopped, crouching there tensely; listening. They heard no sound of footsteps, saw no faintest glow of light. But vaguely, as though muted by closed doors and distance, they caught the low excited mutter of voices.

"Too faint to make anything out—"

"No matter," said Cross-Draw grimly. "Follow my lead an' play it careful." He reached out a hand and the door swung back on soundless, well-oiled hinges. He drew one gun and with a final warning to Quenter, entered. Pistol in hand, and scowling, Quenter tiptoed after him.

Cross-Draw stopped. They stood before a door, but the mutter of voices, drifting out from beyond it, was not much plainer. Faint cracks of light, however, edged the doorframe, telling them they were right.

"A candle," Cross-Draw whispered. "Prob'ly got the windows hung with blankets. Now look—you take care of your Gracie. Leave the—"

"Wait! Who is he?" Quenter rasped hoarsely. "You—"

"Tam."

Cross-Draw could feel the man stiffen; could hear his quick breath of surprise. "But you said," Quenter snarled, "Gracie told you she hadn't—"

"Gracie lied," Boyd said curtly. "Come on!" He flung open the door.

IT WAS LIKE a scene cast in wax, and as brittle.

A man, flinging 'round, was reaching to scoop up a rifle.

By his side a girl screamed, and the man's eyes flamed hate. It was Tam; and he grabbed up his .45-90.

But Quenter's slug took him square in the chest and smashed him backward across a table that splintered beneath his weight.

Gracie jerked both hands to her hair and screeched.

Quenter was savagely slapping her face when Cross-Draw sprang to where Kate Eileen was gagged, lashed to a chair. And the Quenters were gone when he turned.

It took no more than a moment for his knife to sever the ropes that bound Kate; less to rip the foul gag from her mouth. Then she was in his arms, and what happened immediately thereafter took quite a bit of time.

But presently he held her off and looked her over bitterly. "Damn ory-eyed hound," he growled. "Wisht I'd killed the bustard myself! I sure aimed to—but Quenter beat me to it."

Cross-Draw had some right to feel sore. For what O'Reilly had done to keep Kate from being

191

recognized should she have been seen when he sneaked her into town was a first-class desecration. He had shorn her glorious chestnut curls and darkened her face like an Indian's.

But she was safe, and *"I love you anyhow!"* Cross-Draw declared, and that seemed to satisfy both of them.

RED-HOT WESTERN ACTION
BY JACK SLADE!

Rapid Fire. For a handful of gold, Garrity will take on any job—no matter how many corpses he has to leave behind. And when the lone triggerman rides into a dusty cowtown, the locals head for cover. They know there are a hundred ways to kill a man on the savage frontier, and Garrity has used them all.

___3488-3 $3.99 US/$4.99 CAN

Texas Renegade. Cursed by the hard-bitten desperadoes he hunts, Garrity always gets his man. And for a few dollars more, he promises to blast the shiftless vipers terrorizing a small Texas town to hell and beyond.

___3495-6 $3.99 US/$4.99 CAN